NATIVE ARCANA

C.J. CAUGHMAN

For Courtney

Contents

CHAPTER 1

OKLAHOMA CITY, OKLAHOMA

APRIL 19TH, 1995

A Ryder moving truck rolled the stoplight going down 5th Street. Uncle Royce was close enough to slam the bottom of his fist on the truck's side and curse the driver while holding Nita's hand with his other. The truck never stopped. It meandered through its turn and disappeared around a building. The vehicle prowled through the downtown area, making Nita anxious. Her seven-year-old imagination was nothing short of vivid, and she conjured the many malevolent intentions of that vehicle.

Her uncle gently tugged her arm, comforting and snapping her out of the daydream. The pair continued across the street, following the vehicle's direction towards a McDonald's a few blocks away. Nita's uncle promised he would take her earlier in the morning after her father dropped her off at his house.

"Don't tell your father about the big words I yelled at that driver, or else he won't let me take you anywhere ever again... he questions me enough," Uncle Royce said.

Nita wasn't sure what he meant, but she loved her uncle. It was always an event when he came around. That wasn't often, but she couldn't deny that she loved his company, and he was always nice to her. In fact, the only time she'd seen him angry was at that truck and its reckless driver. She knew his words were bad, but seeing as the driver could've hurt someone, they seemed appropriate.

"What do you mean, questions you?" Nita said.

"What's that?" he asked as he kept her close and double-checked for incoming vehicles.

"You said Daddy questions you."

Uncle Royce gripped her small shoulder with his calloused hand. "Well, Little Wolf, I've made many mistakes, and your dad's... caution is understandable."

She nodded, pretending she understood. Nita liked how her uncle didn't talk to her like a child like most adults. "Why do you call me *Little Wolf*?"

"Well, because we are of the Wolf Clan, going back many generations. Your mother not tell you anything about that?" he asked, whipping back his long, black hair.

She shook her head.

"*A-ni-go-te-ge-wiause*," he said in Cherokee. "We are the protectors and warriors. The War Chief is of the Wolf Clan, Nita. I'd say the name suits you perfectly. You're small, but fierce... tough... loyal. What all should be, but either can't be because they're not strong enough or good enough. In the end, not everyone can fend for themselves. People need help. It sounds like Nita, the Little Wolf, could accomplish whatever she wants."

She grabbed her uncle around his waist, squeezing him as tight as she could.

"You're getting strong, Little Wolf." Nita let go and flexed. He gripped her bicep and pulled away as if the mere act of touching her muscles hurt his hand. She smiled at his playfulness. "That's impressive. We're gonna have to call you Big Wolf before too long. What are you gonna feed those muscles today?"

"Chicken nuggets!" she yelled while hopping over each line in the sidewalk.

"Who could've seen that coming." He laughed. "Is that all kids eat today?"

"All kids I know do. It's all my friends' favorite food."

"Of course it is."

"What's so bad about chicken nuggets?"

He smirked, glancing down at her as they meandered toward the McDonald's. "Not a thing."

Her smile faded as she took in the tall, foreign buildings. If she had her preference, it would be the waves of lush hills and small stores of Eastern Oklahoma. The idea of exploring the lands her ancestors explored, ran, and settled occupied her mind for hours. Any of that disappearing brought her sadness. "I don't want to move here, Uncle."

"Why not? It's not so bad."

"But all my friends are at home."

Uncle Royce nodded his head. "Yeah, I get what you're saying. But it's not like you'd live downtown with the big buildings. You'd be closer to Norman, and your dad would be coaching the Sooners. Wouldn't that be great? Besides, it's good to get out of Tahlequah from time to time. The earth is rich, and it's good to get away and see what it offers. Regardless of what anyone says, all the lands are yours to adventure and claim for yourself. Don't let anyone tell you differently."

"Yes, sir." She recognized the change in his voice. There was a passion that took over towards the end of his message. "I don't even like football," she mumbled with her head down.

"Well, I'm sorry to say, Little Wolf, but you live in Oklahoma, and your dad's a football coach. You're gonna have to find some care somewhere. You may have to fake it till joy seeps in."

They approached a shadowy and bare alleyway, like one she'd seen in the movies where all wicked things happen. Nita stopped. A homeless man, barely maintaining consciousness with a lit cigarette between his fingers, sat on a flat piece of cardboard and leaned against the brick restaurant. The man's dirty appearance and ragged camo jacket scared her. His eyes opened, and his head turned. The nametag sewn into his camo jacket read: *MERCER*. Uncle Royce pulled her away and continued down the sidewalk before she could lock eyes with the man, and she was thankful.

"It's just an alley cat," Uncle Royce said. "Don't worry about him... It's the white men in the fancy suits you gotta worry about."

Again, she didn't know what her uncle meant.

"Your dad's got football in his blood," Royce continued. "It's second nature to him—almost instinctual. When you find something you're gifted at, you must take advantage of it. That's all your dad is doing. He's using his gift to make money for his family and do something he's passionate about."

She understood, finally. "But there's no Indians here, Uncle."

"There are. They're just white."

Up ahead, on the opposite side of the road, Nita clocked the Ryder moving truck that nearly struck them. It was parked in front of a massive building. The driver got out, shut the door, and crossed the road at a brisk pace. His head darted all around.

"Yeah, you see this!" Uncle Royce said while holding their clasped hands in the air. "Use them eyes, asshole!"

The man didn't reply. In fact, he turned away while keeping his pale scowl.

When she looked upon the man, her stomach churned, along with shortness of breath, and her hands became clammy. Nita's breathing stopped when his shadow trailing along the building altered its form. The human frame altered into a maniacal entity with serrated shoulders. She was reminded of the endless tales of shapeshifters by her great-grandmother, who claimed she had not only seen the monsters before but knew them closely. She died never telling anyone their identity.

"Jackass," her uncle muttered.

The man and his sinister shadow rounded the corner, but the feeling in her stomach remained.

"What's wrong, Little Wolf?"

Before the hyperventilating took over, her eyes shot back to the moving truck and to the sign in gold letters next to it reading: *ALFRED P. MURRAH FEDERAL BUILDING*

Then, the world bloomed white. She felt the firm embrace of her uncle as her feet lifted off the ground. The earth shook as if the end of days were upon them.

She didn't know how long it was after the blast that her sight came back to her, but dust and smoke clouded her vision when they did. The once proud and tall building was now destroyed. Chunks of it broke off and fell to the ground continuously. Sparks and fire flew out from all along its sundered frame.

Nita had no sense of place. There was a lone brick wall behind her, but nothing in front of her remained. The four-walled building was down to one. Scattered bricks, metal scraps, and wood lay splintered around her. Pain radiated through her shoulder where a piece of glass stuck out. But it was a pale comparison to her uncle who laid motionless on top of her with shrapnel littered across his back. His clothes were torn, and the flesh was blackened from the blast. She wiggled, grabbed him, and yelled his name to get him to respond, but nothing happened.

Her hearing slowly came back to her. She cried and screamed for help, but the sounds of car alarms, sirens, and nearby shrieks drowned her out.

"Uncle! Uncle Royce!" she cried as she couldn't move. She was too weak to lift him.

Another man emerged through the smoke, wearing familiar tattered camo. The homeless man checked her body. He went to move Uncle Royce, but she stopped him and hugged her uncle's body, not letting go.

The man gently took both of her wrists, put his face right above hers, and said, "Look at me. Look in my eyes."

Beyond his sun-battered, dirty skin were the bluest of eyes. Eyes that, at the moment, she trusted.

"Just look at me," he repeated.

With that, Nita let go, accepting the stranger's help in the aftermath of the explosion.

CHAPTER 2

TAHLEQUAH, OKLAHOMA
TWENTY-FIVE YEARS LATER

The porcelain coffee mug left a perfect ring around the xeroxed image of a corpse. The police report said the elderly woman was found in her home strangled and stabbed three times. Nita wiped whatever residue she could off the paper, but the damage had already been done as it seeped through the glossy copy, leaving slight moisture on the table beneath.

A shadow shrouded her in the low-lit diner. "I got it, Nita."

Jimmy, the owner of Jimmy's Diner for over forty years, had a damp rag ready. The wilted piece of scratchy fabric looked like it had been over his shoulder for the entire ride. He was the kind of man who would only close his diner if a tornado were directly overhead. For the holidays, he and his wife Mary would keep it up and running to serve breakfast for veterans and the homeless that made use of the nearby Hope House.

"Thanks, Jimmy," she replied. "How's Mary doing?"

"Oh, still as wild and free as the day I met her." Jimmy replied. "She's visiting the girls up in Tulsa for the weekend. They're gonna go to the Arts District downtown and look at the new exhibit they got."

Jimmy grabbed her mug and filled it to the brim. There were few visitors on weeknights like these, when the rain trickled and the surrounding glass windows fogged to zero visibility. Nita had the diner to herself, and that was how she liked it. She was not a fan of crowds and avoided occasions that drew large gatherings.

"What exhibit?"

Jimmy waved his hand around as the words came to him. "Oh, you know, some homage to Native women. They got paintings, sculptures, and such. Apparently, they're honoring this year's removal riders as well. You not hear about this?"

She didn't respond and decided on coffee.

The Remember the Removal Bike Ride was a local event where youthful Cherokee men and women followed in their ancestors' footsteps and made that grueling trip known as the Trail of Tears. It was a popular event around these parts.

Nita had slight disdain that it wasn't as well-known as it should be. It appeared that it was actively suppressed like the rest of her history, where the Trail of Tears was labeled in footnotes of modern history books as "voluntary" or a "migration west." But Nita knew, as well as any, that some history wasn't just read; it was passed down through word and blood, where the story and images conjured in the recipient's head were more accurate than the events of one's own life.

"You should go tomorrow," Jimmy said. Mary said that all former riders get free admission. You could even take your boy with you."

Nita smiled as wide as she was capable, which wasn't much. "He hates crowds more than I do, Jimmy. Besides, the last thing I want to be doing is looking at a bunch of paintings of women who look like me with greater achievements and accolades."

Jimmy couldn't help but laugh. "Very well. I disagree with you, but I understand." His eyes moved down to the picture, and like the stoic man he was, he didn't react much to the image of the brutalized corpse in the photo. "That doesn't look good."

Nita nodded and studied the deceased elderly woman again. Her once-white hair was stained red as her nightgown had been ripped to shreds. "I heard on the news that she'd been living in that house in Akins for thirty-five years, and her husband died a few years back."

Involuntarily, Nita cleared her throat and reached for her mug. The black coffee was bitter and still piping hot as she felt Jimmy's hand clench her shoulder. "I'm sorry," he said. "I wasn't tryin' to—"

"It's fine."

She knew his intentions were genuine. It was an innocent and awkward moment Jimmy would take back if he could. She pushed her wedding ring back down to a more comfortable position as it had crept up her finger.

Jimmy did his best to alter the subject; for which she was grateful. "Are you on your shift break?"

She took another gulp of coffee to keep her going into the night. Nita pulled her thick black hair into a ponytail with the hair tie wrapped around her wrist like an athlete's bracelet. "I'm off the clock."

She noticed Jimmy's judgment in his pause. "It's a weeknight. What's your boy at home do—"

"My parents are watching him."

Jimmy took that old rag and flicked it over to the other shoulder. "I ain't one to be giving advice in this sort of situation, but perhaps the boy needs a mother, especially at this time."

"You're right about the advice... and whether or not you should be giving it," Nita snapped. Jimmy took the slightest of steps backward. "This is the second woman above sixty-five to be murdered in the area in the last two weeks. I don't think it's a coincidence, unlike the rest. You've worked nearly every day for the past forty years. You of all people should understand the necessity of work ethic, especially when lives are at stake."

A forced smile crept across Jimmy's face. "You're right, Marshal." He pointed at the photograph. "These things are very important, and I wish you good luck. Should there be a bastard out there killin' these women, I hope you show 'em like we all know you can."

The neon blue and pink coming from the welcome sign out front melded into a purple shade on the right side of Jimmy's face. "I'll leave you with this, though, since I've been around for so long and have worked the whole time, as you mentioned. But even then, I never missed one of my girls' ball games."

CHAPTER 3

Mist fell as Nita left the diner. Her destination was her marshal-issued Ford Interceptor. She caught a whiff of herself as she climbed into the driver's seat and couldn't help but curl her lip and shake her head.

She basked in the glow of the neon lights for a moment as if it was some sort of multi-colored light therapy. Nita tossed her folder of crime scene and autopsy photos into the passenger seat. She looked in the rear-view mirror and wished her eyebrows were sharper.

Nita pondered Jimmy's words of wisdom on the drive. She didn't have a destination when she drove out of the parking lot. However, after contemplating what he was saying, she decided to head home and face the music. Which, at the moment, just so happened to be at her parents' house. She didn't feel right pawning her son off on her parents, especially since they were both in their mid-seventies.

The adage "the law doesn't apply to everyone" could not be more appropriate as Nita scrolled through her phone on the Tahlequah backroads. She spent more time scrolling through her emails for more information about the latest murder of the elderly Susan Deed than she did the road in front of her. The mist was persistent and did an adequate job of concealing a clear view. The windshield wipers screeched across the glass, only to be conquered by the wetness again.

Nita looked up from her phone just in time to see a small black mass race across the road. She swerved in time to miss it and maintain control. Unlike in most movies, there was no dramatic slide as the tires cried. No, just a turn to the left and a quick stop.

She rolled the passenger-side window down to see if the creature that caused this inconvenience was still there. In the distance, she heard the faint hooting of an owl that came in threes. She tensed. That was a bad omen.

What more could happen to me?

Just off the road, in the tall grass, was a small dog. However, as she squinted for a better glance, she knew it to be a coyote pup. She called it for reasons she didn't know. But, before her thoughts ventured on, a larger coyote barreled in and clamped down. The nocturnal predator sank its teeth into the pup's neck. There was no resistance. The coyote looked up and gave Nita a moment of attention before it took its familial prey into the cover of the trees.

She had seen worse in her line of duty. But all in all, witnessing the dark side of nature on a night like this left Nita unsettled.

————

Her parents' home hadn't grown with the times. Brittle wood paneling lined the walls. Grabbing it would cause it to break and turn to dust before hitting the floor. The sliding glass door was covered by yellow blinds that had been abused by years of cigarette smoke.

"There she is," her father said without looking away from the television. The seventy-inch LED screen was the house's only touch of the twenty-first century. He somehow managed to negotiate that the TV was necessary since his eyes weren't getting any better. The reality was that the old Indian wanted to watch all the Oklahoma Sooner games in all their crimson and cream, high-definition glory. "Honey look, they put your Championship Games on YouTube!"

"Stepping up to lead off for the Sooners is Nita Ross, one of the true Oklahomans on the roster out of Tahlequah. What an excellent season so far at the plate, leading the team in on-base percentage."

Her proud father watched as if he hadn't watched the game a hundred times before. "Here it comes…"

Nita watched her younger self step up to the plate in her baggy crimson and cream uniform and fire the first pitch of the game over the back wall.

"Hell yeah! That's outta here!"

"Robert!" Nita's mother yelled. "Aiden's in the other room."

With a beer, he threw his hands up in submission. "You're right, honey. I'm sorry." He was allowed to critique. He was no armchair quarterback or fan with baseless knowledge of sports. Her father had spent many years as the defensive line coach at the University of Oklahoma until he quit to spend more time with their family, especially when Nita became more active with sports in high school. He took the head coaching job at Sequoyah High School and retired shortly after Nita's career was over.

Nita smiled. "It's only the first inning, Dad, and you're already apologizing to Mom for something you said?"

He lowered his voice. "Listen, the key to a good marriage is to apologize sooner rather than later." Nita kissed his head as she walked behind his chair. "There's beer in the fridge if you want some."

"I may take you up on that."

Her mother was throwing paper plates into the trash can and boxing up the last few slices of pizza. "Got about two pieces left. You want any?" her mother asked.

"I'm fine, thanks. Aiden in his room?"

"Yep, he is. Go easy on him. He had a little outburst at the library earlier."

Nita rubbed her eyes. "What kind of outburst?"

"In short, they didn't have the book he wanted."

———

Aiden's head was down in the middle of the floor with a large piece of tabloid paper recreating the contents of an atlas on display in front of him. He didn't stop when she entered the room. His posture was that of Schroeder from *Charlie Brown* when he played the piano. She knelt next to him. At the tender age of eleven, there was no wasted movement in his wrist as he effortlessly drew the geographical information of a random European country.

He was a sweet boy, but he was Jackson's, not hers. When Jackson had been with her, the two of them were a complementary duo. However, motherhood evaded her. She'd seen the worst of humanity and couldn't live with herself if she contributed. She didn't feel equipped to deal with or help Aiden with his condition. She had a hard enough time taking care of herself, let alone a boy with autism. Now, he was higher functioning. His schoolwork proved satisfactory, but his communication skill kept him in a self-contained classroom separate from the general education students. Jackson fought hard to get him out of the self-contained class because he wanted Aiden to socialize with kids his age, but Aiden didn't care for that.

"What are you working on now?" she asked.

It took him a moment to reply. His undivided attention was on completing the blue line on the map labeled the *Siret River*.

"This is Romania."

"Romania," she reemphasized. "Home of Dracula."

His very name garnered an immediate reaction, which didn't happen often. It only occurred when something piqued his interest. "Who's Dracula?" he asked with his wide yet blank brown eyes.

"He's a vampire. I think even the first vampire. I don't know."

Aiden didn't miss a beat. "Daddy said vampires aren't real."

"They aren't."

"Then how could something that isn't real have a home in a place that *is* real?"

Nita rubbed her chin. She often found herself having to explain the nuance of things to him, and she didn't fancy herself good at it. "Well, the man that wrote the story about Dracula said that's where he lived."

His expressionless face didn't change. Nita could never tell if her son did or didn't comprehend her knowledge. Aiden returned to his work as if she wasn't even there. She planted her hand in the carpet and used it as a crutch to watch him for a while.

He stopped again. "Are you sure vampires aren't real?"

"I'm sure."

"Because they're monsters."

"Yes," was all she replied.

"So, a monster didn't kill Daddy?"

If Nita hadn't been used to off-the-wall questions like this, she might have been caught off guard. "No, a monster didn't kill Daddy." She put her hand on his back. His spine straightened, and his muscles tensed. "You understand that, right? I can't explain it, but Daddy... It was an accident."

Her eyes swelled.

Aiden returned to his map as if he were a good worker, and his break was over. She asked him again, but he was gone. The cities, roads, and rivers of Romania called to him.

CHAPTER 4

Nita pulled into the Cherokee Nation Marshal Service Office on South Bald Hill Road. She couldn't hide from her fellow marshals' probing gazes, including her longtime friend, Charlie Soap.

Marshal Evans turned with wide eyes and said something to Charlie. As Nita adjusted her belt getting out of the car, it was clear they were talking about her. Charlie held out his hand and kindly brushed Evans away. He cautiously approached Nita, which she eyed out of her marshal-issued peripherals.

"Nita," Charlie started. "You're workin'?"

"No, I just love putting my uniform on."

Charlie stumbled over his words. "I guess we just figured you were taking time."

"No."

———

The glass door shut behind her, and Nita marched towards the briefing room while adjusting her body armor as it rode up her armpits.

The door to Director Lowwater's office swung open. "Nita," he said softly. She kept walking to avoid this conversation. He cleared his throat, raising his volume, "Marshal Ross."

Her marital name of Philips never stuck. Her family had been around these parts for so long, it was hard for the populace to adjust to the name change. He held the door open. Like her father, Marshal Director Lowwater had that old Indian technique of saying a lot with very little. He shut the door behind her, and Nita sat before his proud, L-shaped oak desk that said, "I am the director." Behind was a list of tribal and service awards from a thirty-year career.

"You know what that number thirty-seven on your chest means, Nita?" Lowwater asked.

It was a trick question, but she obliged him anyway. "It's my nation number – my call sign."

"Good, that's known. It also means you're not the only marshal." Each Cherokee Marshal's call sign was equal to the number of marshals employed. She was thirty-seventh of the forty-one employed Cherokee Nation marshals.

"Yes, sir," she said.

"Now that we understand, you head home and get your family in order."

Nita leaned forward. "Director, Jackson's funeral is over. I'd like to get back to work."

"So you can distract yourself, I know." Lowwater reached into his desk and grabbed a lighter. He swiveled back in his chair, reached into his humidor, and lit a cigar. It was 9:35 in the morning. Nita wasn't about to call him on that. Nita could see the proud red and white Cherokee Nation Marshal Service sign from the director's office. At the bottom, in smaller print, it read: *Tobacco-Free Facility.* "Police chief in Sallisaw called me and asked if there was any reason one of my marshals was inquiring of one his detectives for information on a pair of murders in the county."

He stopped there. His morning cigar took priority. Lowwater looked out the window, watching marshals and tribal workers walk to their daily posts. It was as if the world melted away for a moment. He spun the brown stick back and forth in his mouth while keeping the flame of his custom lighter going.

Nita let him enjoy his morning ritual if that was what this was. "Two elderly women killed just a couple days apart from another in the near-same manner is not a coincidence to me, sir."

Lowwater exhaled a thick cloud of smoke. "No one is saying it is, Nita. But you aren't a detective. Let the guy in Sallisaw work it. God knows he needs something to do, and I'm sure he's capable."

She looked off and shook her head. Frustration mounted inside her, but she stifled it into silence.

"Listen," he said. "You're not even a week removed from burying your husband. Take time and grieve... as the white folks say."

Nita didn't respond. Proudly displayed to her left was a wood-framed photograph of Director Lowwater in front of the tribal court. It was dated October 4, 2000, and underneath read, *Swearing In.*

"I'm not gonna do that."

He smoked his cigar, leaned back in his chair as far as it would go and closed his eyes. "Yeah, I've been with a Cherokee woman for thirty years. I have two Cherokee daughters, and none of them listen to me. Why should you be any different?"

Nita cracked a smile, probably the first since receiving the news about Jackson.

"You make a deal with me then," Director Lowwater demanded as he spun to face her. "I don't want you patrolling. You can help the detective, track records, and contact CIs, but I don't want you involved in much day-to-day here. Got that? You've barely taken time since the Marble City incident, let alone... Jackson."

"I can manage."

"Like hell." He glared at her. "You're going to go see Dr. Whitekiller too."

She expressed her dismissal through a head shake and puffing. "I don't need to see Whitekiller."

Dr. Whitekiller administered the prior mandatory counseling sessions after Nita's shootout in Marble City. She was a good woman and good at her job, but Nita wasn't rushing to see her again, let alone have her pick around in her brain.

"Yes, you do," Lowwater argued. "Seeing her was good for you. With all that's happened, it's mandatory. Not for debate."

That was a better offer than she thought she would get. If Nita was honest, it was a compromise where she got what she desired. Nita made her way out without overstaying her welcome or meandering long enough for Lowwater to change his mind.

She reached for the fine brass handle just as Lowwater said, "Just because I let you walk over me doesn't give you the right to start busting my balls like three other women in my life that shall remain nameless."

Another smile came over her, and she left him with a "Yes, sir."

"Eh, one more thing before you go, Marshal."

"Yes?"

Lowwater removed his full-rimmed, prescription glass and rubbed his eyes. "The kid's funeral is tomorrow."

"What kid?"

Lowwater rolled his ashes into a tray he kept buried in his desk. "The, uh, the kid who hit Jackson."

Nita squinted. She wasn't sure why Lowwater would be telling her this information. "I didn't know that he had died."

"That's because it only happened about an hour ago. No brain activity. Parents pulled the plug."

"Which cemetery, Tahlequah or Caney?" she asked, knowing those were the two largest cemeteries in the area.

"Crittenden."

She took a step before halting again. "Off Baker Rd?"

"Yes."

CHAPTER 5

Crittenden Cemetery was not grand or well-kept by any stretch of the imagination. The rocks of the gravel road were losing their battle against the unrelenting weeds as they dissipated into an open field. The welcome sign was held upright by rusted poles and a chain-length fence that failed to envelop the entire property.

She idled in her father's 1999 GMC Sierra, which he labeled "a classic." It had been grim the past few days in Tahlequah. The sun barely crept out from behind the clouds. Nita related the weather to her husband's passing, telling herself it wasn't a coincidence.

Nita counted nine people huddled beneath a wilted tree as the minister said his final words. The windshield wipers went back and forth on the lowest setting as the mist obstructed Nita's view. Nita recognized the minister from one of the local Baptist churches. She couldn't recall the names of any of them, and she damn sure wouldn't be able to place his church's location. Nita grew up going to the Cherokee Baptist Church, as her father was an elder, but due to recent events, her faith wilted. She never denied the Creator's existence, only his relevance, and purpose. For now, the thought seeped into her mind that God had left this rock a long time ago. She did her best to push the blasphemous thoughts away like demons to be exorcised.

In his black suit and fat tie, the minister closed his pocket Bible and made his leave.

Memories of Jackson flooded her mind. So much so, that they drifted into intense daydreams that placed her in limbo. She could have been in another dimension for hours for all she was aware.

It wasn't until someone knocked on her window that she was jolted out of it

"Nita?" the minister said as he continued tapping the window.

"Yes?" she replied to make him stop. "How can I help you, Brother Barry?" Nita rolled the window just far enough that she wouldn't come across as rude for making him talk through glass.

Up close, she recognized him. Brother Barry had been one of the pastors at First Baptist of Tahlequah for many years. He often organized luncheons and potlucks for the marshal service and the police department. He was a well-respected member of the community and his family, the Cunninghams, had been in these parts for generations. Barry was the black sheep. He entered the ministry while his brother and sister continued the family business, that business being Cunningham Grocery. In Eastern Oklahoma, Cunningham Grocery stores served their purpose of providing food and necessities. However, no one in any of the counties that Cunningham Grocery operated would praise the store's quality or product.

"What are you doing here?" he asked.

"Attending the funeral."

"From your car?"

"For this particular funeral, I think it is the right circumstance to view it from this distance."

"I see." Barry covered his Bible with his jacket as the rain fell harder. "Well, I just wanted to let you know that my family and congregation have been praying for you and your family. It's a... It's a... yeah, I'm sorry."

It's not often a Baptist minister is speechless.

"Thank you for your prayers, Brother Barry," Nita said while putting her car in reverse. She took a final glance at the funeral. The uncomfortable reminiscence of the one she attended last week bubbled to the surface.

CHAPTER 6

Sallisaw, Oklahoma was similar to Tahlequah. It had a more small-town sensibility with less action. Along the rural roads were countless dilapidated church signs and billboards of congregations that no longer existed. Downtown still looked as if it had never moved on from the Depression era, where outlaws like Pretty Boy Floyd flourished as he was considered a folk hero in these parts instead of a criminal gangster. Hospitality was abundant, and everyone kept to themselves except on Friday nights when the Sallisaw Black Diamonds played under the gridiron lights.

However, there was a ribbon of white trash and methamphetamine that weaved itself through many communities of rural Oklahoma, and Sallisaw was no different. The proud town of Muldrow would be coming into town in a couple of days. The Black Diamonds would face off against the Bulldogs in the marquee rivalry. It was a game that brought townsfolk closer together. In Oklahoma, those who weren't religious found their faith in football despite having no pro teams in the state to follow.

Nita pulled into the driveway of Detective Martindale's house. She hadn't been to Sallisaw in a few years, and this was the first time she would be meeting the detective. A little girl was playing in the yard. Nita's educated guess placed her around ten years old. A middle-aged man walked out the front door of the model home and tried to find Nita's eye through the tinted windows as the girl dropped what she was doing and followed close behind. Nita got out of the car to greet him.

"Tom Martindale?" she asked.

"Ah, yes. You must be Marshal Ross?"

"Nita works fine."

The little girl never took her eyes off Nita as she wrapped her arms around Tom's waist. Nita averted her gaze, but the eyes staring up at her were unwavering.

Tom took notice. "Say hello, honey. Don't just stare. It's not polite."

"Sorry, Daddy," the girl replied. "Are you a police officer too?"

Nita wasn't in uniform. She kept it business casual today, wearing slacks and a navy-blue blouse.

Detective Martindale answered for her. "Honey, this right here is Marshal Ross. She's very important and here to help me with the case." He put his hands on his daughter's shoulders and gave them a slight squeeze. "Ain't that right, Marshal?"

"The second part of that sentence was correct." Nita extended her hand to the little girl, who continued to look up at her with star-filled eyes. "What's your name?"

"Emma."

"Nice to meet you, Emma."

"Run in and get cleaned up for dinner, sweetheart," Tom said, resting his hand on her back and guiding her in the direction of the house.

She followed her father's orders. The detective had to prompt his daughter to quit staring at Nita and continue inside.

Tom chuckled. "She's obsessed with you already."

"Why's that?"

"I got two older boys. It takes an arm and leg to get them to do anything other than play video games. Emma's my explorer and the one in the backyard playing cops and robbers. And since her brothers don't play with her, I'm happy to state that all the criminal activity in my life revolves around being her villain in whatever fantasy she conjures. You got any?"

"Kids?" She cleared her throat, "Yeah, a-a boy."

The conversation ended there as she followed Tom up the pair of porch steps and into his house. It had old bones, but it was apparent heavy renovations had taken place. It was humble and undersized for a family of five. The hallways were narrow, the tile floor was halfway ripped up, and the cabinets were being redone to replace the unfinished oak. A woman was mashing potatoes when Tom and Nita strolled in.

"Honey, this is Marshal Ross, the one I told you about." His wife patted her hands on her apron and wiped them clean. "Nita, this is my wife, Lauren."

They shook hands. Their southern hospitality was not lost on her. She felt more welcome in their fixer-upper home than in almost any other. The room smelled of seasoned meat and brown gravy. The aroma made her salivate.

"Nita, you mind Salisbury steak?" she asked, placing a wicker basket covered by a kitchen towel in the center of the table.

Bread.

"That sounds great to me. I hope you don't feel like you have to cook because I'm here."

"Well, if I'm being honest, it's one of my better dishes. I've had a long week, and I'm hungry. Either way, you're free to join." Lauren hardly looked up from her station. Her short brown hair was tied back, and fingernail polish was chipping away. She had a natural beauty to her. Nita's intuition said she was a former prom queen-turned-housewife.

She smiled when a picture on the wall showed a much younger Lauren and Tom dressed in a poofy purple dress and a baggy suit in front of a tacky 80s backdrop as they both wore plastic crowns on their heads.

———

After everyone's plates were cleaned, Nita offered to help with the clean-up. Lauren refused and said, "Go, go, get y'all's asses to work and quit stalling." A smile followed, and Nita couldn't help but give one.

Tom made use of the small garage. Stall mats were perfectly aligned on the right side of the garage, with gym equipment scattered across them. On the opposite was a small, stand-up toolbox filled with rusted tools with withered handles. Above that was a corkboard with headshots of the elderly victims. Nita looked upon those pictures, and her eyes narrowed.

Tom put his hands on his hips. "Both crimes took place approximately ten miles apart. The first in Sallisaw, the next in Brent." Tom opened a manila folder with all the details of the victims. "First woman was named Sandra Oly, and the second was named Mary Barlow."

"Those sound like elderly women to me."

Tom let out a quick puff of air through his nostrils, admiring her morbid comedy. "I've gathered that neither had any family in the area. The two of them didn't share any mutual friends or family. I found that odd for the towns being so close together and the populations being smaller."

"No family?" Nita asked. "No kids to look after them or anything."

"No, neither of them had kids."

"That could be something..."

Nita's eyes never left the corkboard. She stared into the eyes of the two white-haired women who were no longer amongst the living. She scanned the image hundreds of times and noticed that in Mary's picture, she wore a necklace with the initials *BS*.

"I don't suppose the initials on this necklace stand for 'bullshit'?"

He laughed again. "Yeah, I don't suppose they do."

Nita rubbed her eyes. "Now, Sandra was stabbed over a hundred times, but Mary, only three..."

"Correct," Tom replied. "Perhaps that's evidence that we're dealing with two different killers?"

"Maybe, or perhaps Sandra just pissed him off. They both had drugs in their system, right?"

"Correct, some strange combo of meth and LSD," Tom said while handing a pair of papers to Nita. "These are the final autopsy reports. Apparently, no matter how grotesque it may be, this guy was careful... I'm willing to take another look at the murder scenes if you're not pressed for time."

She scoffed and echoed, "Pressed for time," under her breath. Nita had the luxury of all the time in the world. "Let's do it."

"All right. I'll let Lauren know we're headed out."

"Yeah, make sure you get her permission," Nita said with a snicker.

"This is her domain, Nita. Everyone in her domain must abide."

CHAPTER 7

The day had come and gone, and the sun was beginning to set. Nothing compared to Oklahoma skies during the setting sun. The abstract colors from colossal brush strokes of violet, orange, blue, and red collided to form a sky painting not even Bob Ross could recreate.

The police radio in Tom's car uttered incoherent jargon that always needed repeating, a process Nita knew well. Officers checked in with the station and vice versa. A fender bender was in the casino parking lot, and a small fight morphed into an all-out brawl. It was enough of a scene to cause around fifteen squad cars to police the outbreak.

Mary Barlow's home was along a string of backroads consisting of heavy gravel and potholes the size of moon craters. Oklahoma suffered from an annual storm season in the months of April and May, where tornados descended to wreak havoc and decorate the earth with debris. Nita was reminded that some places didn't recover after such events as they drove past several mobile homes scattered about along the backroads.

"Don't worry. No one died," Tom said.

"Which one caused these?"

"Oh, these are from a few years back. Maybe 2017... I can't remember. Their new home is about three miles east now."

"They didn't move very far away, did they?"

"Nah, guess they figure tornados are like lightning, and they don't strike the same place twice." Tom took a sip of black coffee from his thermos that Lauren brewed. "I like to joke and say that God wanted them to move on from this place, and they responded by building just down the road, and God was like... *really?*"

Night fell over Sallisaw when the muffled and static radio sounded again. "Units, we got a Brick Morgan complaint. Says there's been a vehicle driving around, seemingly circling the neighborhood."

Nita involuntarily twitched her head. "What's a Brick Morgan complaint?"

Tom smiled and fiddled with the console to turn down the air conditioning. "Brick is a former Black Diamond star. He was all-state in football, baseball, and track. Now he's just an old man who complains about the other residents in his addition. We get about six or eight of these a year. He claims we're worthless, and we never do anything about whatever his complaints consist of. Are you all right with catching this one with me real fast?"

"You choose to spend your day off however you want, Detective. Don't worry, we get the good people of Cherokee Nation who think we're worthless too."

"I guess it's just the way of the world regarding people's perception of the law and those who enforce it." Tom grabbed the mic. "Dispatch, this is RC-1 along with Nation-37 responding to the call."

"Roger that, Detective," Dispatch responded.

Tom pressed down on the gas, and the view of the trees out the passenger window blurred as they whipped past.

"I find it hard to believe that anyone would think the 'Hero of Marble City' would be worthless. Plus, the–" He stopped.

"What?"

He cleared his throat. "No, I was just gonna mention the whole OKC thing too."

"Ah, yes, the OKC thing." Flashes of that wretched day appeared like scattered puzzle pieces tumbling around in her brain.

"Trouble seems to find you, doesn't it?"

"I don't know if I'd call it that."

"What would you call it then?"

"Evil."

Awkwardness took over.

About a minute of silence followed before she changed the conversation. "Is Brick his real name?"

"Actually, yes. Get this, his father was a bricklayer."

Nita scratched her brow. "Jesus Christ."

———

Brick Morgan lived in a rural neighborhood. Houses weren't right on top of each other. At least thirty yards of breathing room separated the homes, if not more. His house was not far from their victims'. As of now, this visit was only a minor inconvenience. Nita spotted a man on the front lawn with crossed arms and a shaky leg. Tom didn't have to confirm that the man in Wrangler jeans and a tucked flannel was Brick.

"Your response time is better than usual," he greeted the law officers.

"We provide premium service to repeat customers," Tom replied.

"Always a smartass, Tom. Hell, why they send the detective out here anyway? Sallisaw PD backed up?"

The detective seemed to have no interest in carrying on a conversation with the man. Tom kept it professional, but his patience for Mr. Morgan obviously wore thin at a rapid pace. "You could say that. So, what's the deal, Brick? You got a car coming by?"

Brick went full, dissatisfied citizen, rambling on about how cars didn't just drive by like that unless the people occupying them were up to no good. That rant evolved into a complaint about the policing problems he claimed Sallisaw had.

The conversation faded out of existence. Nita glanced over at the house across the street, a beautiful farmhouse with a modern edge. It had a wraparound porch and three picture windows exposing a dark living room. She scanned the yard as the resident took the trash can to the end of a long driveway. The man walked hunched over and at the slowest of paces. He paid no attention to the conflict and complaints of Brick Morgan as if he was used to it or too old to care. Nita's shoulders involuntarily shuddered as she glanced back to see a silhouette in the neighbor's picture window. The black mass was featureless, faced the street, and even though Nita couldn't make out any detail, she felt eyes upon her. In a quick flash, they glowed yellow.

Nita turned away. Tom and Brick were still bickering.

"All right, do you know what type of vehicle it was? Did you get any plate numbers?" Tom asked.

"You bet your ass I did."

A long pause followed.

"Are you gonna enlighten me on either of them?"

"I'm waiting on you to get your little detective notebook so you can write it down."

Tom's eyes twitched. He turned, cracked his neck, and walked back to the car to retrieve pen and paper, and under his breath, Nita heard him say, "Jesus Christ."

"Oh, sorry to inconvenience you! Brick just inconveniences everyone nowadays!" He waved his arms in the air in a far too dramatic fashion.

"Well, Brick, no one wants to help anyone who speaks in the third person. That's some high and mighty cult shit."

"So, everyone that speaks in third person is in a cult?" Brick asked.

"No. I'm not saying that. However, anyone who has led a cult has spoken in the third person."

Nita agreed.

The tapered municipal streetlights were sparse and spread apart, copying the homes in the rural edition. Everything outside the lamp poles' light boundaries was void and empty. Only the homes breathed life into the black abyss that was Oklahoma country. Civilization could cease to exist in these surrounding woods or breed endless possibilities; to Nita, those prospects were not hopeful.

"Where are we at in society today?" Brick continued assisting his words with his hands, waving them around with reckless abandoned. "The police don't help their citizens without piss-poor attitudes and a chip on their shoulders. Maybe we should adopt a more community-policing approach like they are in Tulsa to help the Black folks feel better."

"We already practice that here too, Brick," Tom said, rubbing his eyebrows. "And go and ask the Black folks how that's working out for them."

Nita felt guilt for enjoying the back and forth between the Sallisaw natives from differing sides of the track. In this case, the train tracks were quite literal. All that was missing was buttered popcorn.

"Southern hospitality? Neighborhoodly love?" Brick stated. "That shit's all gone too."

"Neighborhoodly love isn't a thing," Tom replied softly.

"Hell." Brick pointed through his house, signaling he was addressing something behind his home. "The head of the HOA and I are in dispute about pond access. It's mine by the way." Then, the farmhouse across the street felt the wrath of Brick's pointer finger. "I got this hermit asshole in front of me that lives by himself and waits to mow his yard till its waist-high. At least he takes his goddam garbage out. Only time I see his ass."

A detail caught Nita off-guard, and the hairs on the back of her neck stiffened. "He lives alone?"

Brick cocked his head. "Now you with the irrelevant questions. Yes, he's lived alone ever since he moved in a few years back."

"Does anyone come to visit him frequently? Anyone you've seen around recently?"

She noticed Tom narrow his eyes at her, wondering what she was getting at.

"No, like I said, old man Herb keeps to himself." Brick said. "I've only spoken to him a handful of times, and those conversations didn't last long. Wait, why the hell are we talking about him? Are you here to help me out or what?"

Nita turned her back on the pair and made a beeline toward the farmhouse.

"Marshal?" Tom asked, concerned.

"What's Herb's last name?" Nita asked.

Dumbfounded, Brick replied, "Burnham..."

She ascended the trio of concrete porch steps and saw nothing through the picture windows. All the lights in the interior were turned off. Nita hoped that wasn't for the purpose she feared. She hammer-fisted the door over and over.

"Mr. Burnham!" She waited and continued to knock. "Burnham!"

Without a reply, she decided to look once more through the window. Nita hoped her eyes were deceiving her when the bodily outline on the floor made its presence known.

"Mr. Burnham!" she roared louder.

The front door was locked. Nita removed her firearm and drove the bottom of her boot into the door, isolating her kicks to impact around the handle. It only took two push kicks with adrenaline coursing through her veins.

On the inside, Nita got confirmation, looking at the carnage of Herb Burnham's mutilated body—a man she witnessed taking out his trash minutes prior. She slammed the bottom of her fist into the wall and a portrait dropped and shattered on the floor. After the aggressive impulse, the image of a once happy family were now covered in jagged and sharp lines, overwhelming their existence.

Just then, the back door, which was out of view from the entrance, slammed shut. Nita peeked her head out front and yelled at Tom, "10-35! 10-35! Suspect went around back!"

Nita left Tom to go on the offensive—to do something that was in her blood, a task she missed: hunting.

"Marshal! Nita!" she heard Tom yell.

Nita didn't know the purpose behind his yells, but she didn't have time to converse. She followed the suspect's trail, roaring through the house with reckless abandon.

Into the wooded abyss behind Herb's home, she went. The only light came from her paracord bracelet that Jackson had gifted in her stocking last Christmas. Her late husband cultivated her love for gadgets. Yet, even in such moments, Nita felt his presence as if he was the light personified.

Low and guttural vibrations traveled down her spine. Nita followed the animalistic sound as it softened ahead of her. She felt eyes all around her as if she was the only one occupying these woods that didn't have dark vision. Whether the eyes were there at all, she did not know, but her heightened and proven senses seemed justified. As she continued, any sign of the fleeing suspect faded with each passing moment.

A dull light beamed low about fifty yards ahead of her to the right.

It had an orange glow and swayed from side to side. For a moment, it vanished before prevailing once again.

Tom's faint voice yelled her name. Nita wasn't waiting on him. She dashed straight at the dull light with her gun (SIG P365 X-Macro), ready to squeeze if needed.

The light she chased was an old, battery-powered lantern hanging from a dead dogwood's branch. Its dead limbs jaggedly spread out like a river delta. A collection of blood surrounded a chunk of human flesh beneath the light.

As she stepped forward, Nita was jerked back. The dark figure she once saw on the other side of the window looked her eye to eye as he ripped the gun out of her hand. The man stood a foot taller, had broad shoulders, and wore a feathered mask that shared the likeness of an owl. Nita gasped. The figure reared back with a bloody knife. Nita halted the thrust with both hands and drove her opposite elbow into the mask.

Her gun was barely visible at the end of the lantern's dull ray. She went for it, but strong hands grabbed her waist and threw her back about five feet. She had fought plenty of men before in her line of work and come out on top. Fellow marshal spec-ops members, drunks, martial artists, men on PCP, none of which were as strong as whatever thing this man claimed to be.

Nita reached down to her ankle before pressing for her gun once more. The man settled the crooked mask back on his head.

A little anticipation went a long way.

Her crawl escalated upward into a run. In that upward progression, the masked man swung his shin into Nita's torso. Nita rotated her body to catch the blow, expecting something of the sort. Then, she drove her boot knife into the meat of the owl man's calf.

The screech of pain was that of a man, not some machine or upright beast. Yes, he might be large, with immense strength, but still a man.

A man could be killed.

She pulled the blade towards her, embedded deep in his leg. Nita felt the warm blood spill onto her wrist and forearm on the slice. The assailant thrusted his knife at her again in retaliation. All she could do was let go and abandon the damage done by rolling underneath his leg. Now behind him, Nita repeated her door-breaching kick by firing her boot into his back. The towering individual proved sturdy. The blow only drove him a step forward, even with a wounded leg.

She lost her direction in the scuffle. Her head darted around, looking for the gun. Nita spotted it behind her and shuffled back, finally claiming it again. Having her blindside open to a killer was a position she wanted to end as she spun around, ready to fire.

Nothing.

The man in the owl mask was gone. At that time, she heard Tom calling her name and emerged through the forest void.

"He's here," Nita said. "It's him."

Tom didn't reply. Nita admired that he didn't question her, or the situation. "I called it in, Marshal."

Luckily, her detective companion had a flashlight with a snub nose .38 as they trekked deeper into the woods. Unfortunately, the comfort of added light did little to defeat the nerves the evil in the pitch black brought on. The low moans continued. A hooting owl called behind her. Nita whipped around and had her finger pulsing on the trigger, but nothing was there. Tom's eyes were white, and his face was paler than before.

"The fucking odds," he said. "You were right... evil finds you."

Nita kept her elbows bent and her sights up high. Out of the corner of her eye, she clocked Tom mirroring her movements.

A stick cracked ahead of them, and they froze. Then, a burst to her right.

Tom's gun went off simultaneously with the masked man's thrust. Nita didn't have a shot until Tom's body dropped to the ground while he held his neck. Sprays of blood escaped through his fingers and the embedded blade. He couldn't even cry out in pain.

Nita's first shot found her target, but it only slowed her attacker by a little, if at all. His massive palm enveloped her hands together as his offhand grasped her around the neck and drove her back against a tree.

She tried to rip her hands free from his grip, but his strength prevailed. Nita glanced into the manufactured, amber eyes of the mask. Its intricacies were unlike anything she had seen, not to be confused with a cheap masquerade mask one would wear to a Halloween party and discard after. No, this thing looked as if it was part of the wearer. It wrapped around the man's head, including his ears. The beak curled down low, and the feathered ears looked like horns. Her grandmother believed all owls were shapeshifters with sinister purposes. Nita didn't know if she believed in that, but she did know owls were lethal hunters. She flashed back to that poor coyote on the side of the road, hearing its yelp clear in her mind once more.

He hoisted her off the ground, and her shirt ripped against the tree bark, scraping her back. Then, his massive fist began striking her in the head. She was able to use her shoulder to partially block some of them, but plenty still got through. Her ears rang, her head pounded, and the world wobbled.

Nita brought her knees up to her chest in a haze, followed by her hips to gain separation. The fact that she wasn't going to out-strength this individual was obvious. She had to be innovative. Her feet walked up his body until they found a solid purchase on his chest. Her legs straightened in a swift and violent motion.

She achieved separation, but Nita couldn't catch herself in time on the descent and smashed hard against the tree's base. The masked man was on her again, but she was quick enough to fire four shots that travelled up her attacker's body. The last of them found his head. Blood and feathers flew off the side of his skull.

The remaining shots in her magazine didn't find him. A shoddy life raft in the open ocean during a tsunami had more stability.

She reloaded the extra mag she kept in her EDC tac holster. She chambered the round and brought her pistol up.

Nothing.

He was gone.

She kept her defense up in the groggy state. All she wanted to do now was catch her breath, which proved difficult.

Reality settled in, and she wanted nothing to do with it. Her fellow officer's color faded as he was no longer breathing, lying in the blood that only expanded around him.

Chapter 8

"I assure you, faith and goodness have vanished from these lands. Everywhere, from your elected officials, neighbors down the block, and your own flesh and blood flap their lips and whisper lies. These lies they attempt to utter as truths. Do you know how many false prophets there have been? I would guess a great number, but perhaps it's not significant enough. All of these fools have abandoned God, including you. I have a way of seeing people. Call it a gift. Call it a blessing. It matters not. As I look upon your unfocused visage, I know your genuine desire. You don't wish to be an ambassador for God. You don't wish to lead a flock into the light. You may have convinced yourself at one point in time that those prospects were true. You practiced what you truly wanted. You told yourself it was for the greater good, the Lord's good and His glory."

The room was dark. His hands were bound to the chair beneath him by chains, and he didn't know why.

"The fact remains that you care little for the Lord's glory. You merely want it for yourself. You see a few more chairs brought out during worship each week. You must put in more frequent orders of communion wafers and grape juice. You feel the weight of the offering buckets increase ever so slightly, and a smile drifts across your face. All of this is for His glory? No. No, it isn't. I know you've reasoned with yourself upon the countless hours of wrestling with the contemplation. After so long, though, you've convinced yourself that the increase in the number weekly is due to you. In the end, you're the one on stage, speaking your word. All these people aren't here for him. They're here for you. That feeling used to bother you. Now, you can't get enough of it.

"I see you have a new campus opening in the fall. Good for you. Not to mention the fact that this new location is in one of the wealthier parts of the state, so up goes the weight of those offerings. We used to live in a world where looking outward was commonplace and looking inward was frowned upon. Now, that's all people do. Everything is in reverse, even the cameras. Perhaps you began your journey to godhood with good intentions but strayed far from that path. Haven't you?"

Pastor Rick Folk was finally allowed a reply after his captor ripped the tape away from his mouth. Luckily, he had shaved in the morning, or else any residing facial hair would have followed. But his skin still throbbed.

The man berating him with questions of mostly rhetorical nature remained in shadow. He didn't show his face, but his voice was distinct. The man wasn't from around these parts.

Rick gathered himself as best he could but begged all the same. "Please, let me go. I don't know what I've done to have wronged you, but I am deeply sorry."

"I've been telling you everything you've done wrong. Weren't you listening?"

"Please, let me go," Rick pleaded as snot formed on his upper lip, mixing with the sweat that poured from his forehead. The space was dark. Regardless of the situation, the heat would have caused him to sweat no matter what.

"Why?"

The reply should have been obvious, but still, he fumbled, "I-I have a family. I'm a father—"

"Most everyone has family, Rick. If you're looking for reasoning out of a special circumstance, don't give common reasoning to be free of it."

"P-Please."

"Who are your favorite children?" the man in the shadow asked. "Which children do you prioritize?"

Rick exhaled a defeated scoff. The words fell out of his mouth as his head drooped. "What... I don't understand."

"Do you prefer your biological children or the children of the flock who sing your praise?"

The pastor didn't respond.

The silence built.

"Or do you prefer the women you bring to your hotel room when you guest preach at various locations across the country?"

More silence.

"How many people were in attendance, you'd say, that Sunday in Whichita a few months back? Three... four thousand?"

"Five," Rick whispered.

"I was certain you would know the number but unaware of whether you would reveal it to me. I'm more conscientious of my sense of myself doing the right thing. I bet it was also tough to deny all those pretty young gals in the front rows holding their hands up in worship to you while you owned that stage in your skinny jeans and lensless glasses."

Rick began to weep. His cries were not uncontrollable to the point where he was a well of tears, but enough to take his breath away.

"You're so corruptible. How you achieved such heights is quite frankly frightening. The idea that someone would put you and I in the same class is infuriating."

"W-who *are* you?" he stammered.

"I'm who you should be."

"I don't know what that means."

"It matters not," the man said. "I need you to do something for me. In return, it might just so happen to help you. Perhaps you will even find some freedom in it."

Reluctantly, Rick asked the man what he wanted from him. His mind conjured up all sorts of harsh and brutal scenarios this man could have in store for him. Nothing, however, could have prepared him for what was to come.

"Confess," the man stated.

"Confess?" Rick repeated.

A red light blinked ahead of him. Then, from behind him, a flash illuminated the room. Rick found himself sitting alone in the middle of a condensed sound stage. It was no larger than a storage room, but its purpose seemed broad. Everything behind the camera remained in shadow as the light above shined straight down on the top of his head.

"All right, Pastor Folk, I want you to look into the camera and confess to what you have done. Do not leave out any details. Any. Details. If you do so happen to skimp on the particulars or stray away from what you are supposed to be doing, you will regret it."

"P-Please... I can't."

"You will."

"I can redeem myself."

"Redemption is not up to you."

"Listen, this will ruin my life. I will lose everything. My wife, my kids, my home. You can't expect me to do this willingly."

He saw the man's teeth first as they peered through the dark. The rest of him stepped out from the shadow, revealing his whole self. The man was average. The image Rick had in his mind was much more sinister. If he saw him amongst the Mass at church, he would merely be a face in the crowd.

The man stepped to the side of him and unchained him from his restraints. Rick wanted to dash for the door but was too afraid. He remained petrified in his chair.

"This is why you must do what I'm asking. So far off the path, you've strayed. If you weren't here with me at this moment, imagine how far this would go? You might not have ever stopped. You should know the truth that men in service to God can't lose everything. So, let us begin. I will help you along the way. You're in Ezell's hands, and I am in God's. Redemption will find you."

Ezell stepped back into the obscurity of the dark. He looked at the small monitor before resting his elbow on the top of the camera in a casual manner.

"Let us begin. First, you will repeat after me. Then, you tell the camera who you are and what you have done." Ezell cleared his throat, initiating the sequence of words Rick was gearing to utter: "*Hello, my name is Pastor Rick Folk, and I have abandoned God...*"

CHAPTER 9

"Pastor Rick Folk of Calvary Crossing Church is still missing. This disturbing video of him confessing his 'sins' to his congregation went viral shortly after he was reported missing. At this time, there are no leads on Pastor Folk's whereabouts. The family and members of the church are deeply caught off guard by the alarming video, its pastor's admission, vanishing, and the timing for this upcoming Sunday to mark the tenth anniversary of Calvary Crossing."

The subtle vibration of the hospital bed as the door shut snapped Nita back to consciousness. She attempted to focus on the room, the newscast, and its message. Unfortunately, the sunlight reflected off the white walls, making the room unbearably bright. Soreness overwhelmed her as she shifted ever so slightly in her bed. A single gulp felt like she was swallowing shards of glass. Nita growled involuntarily at the uncomfortable inconvenience.

Bruises littered her body in places she didn't even know had been impacted by the confrontation. The clock on the wall said it was almost twelve, and the IV in her arm made her antsy. She fumbled with the foreign wires and tubes flowing to and from her body, pulling them off in a manner unaware of repercussions.

The door cracked open, and in a monotoned command, she heard, "Hey, hey, knock that shit off."

Nita froze.

Director Lowwater walked through the hospital room door. "You're gonna pull something out you shouldn't." He casually sipped on his coffee from a foam cup he must have gotten from the hospital kitchen or God knew where.

"Does my family know—"

"They know. They've been here all morning," Lowwater said. "They went to go get something to eat. I told 'em I'd watch you. Didn't think you would be awake, though. Now I actually have to talk to you."

He dragged over one of the chairs, leaning against the wall beside the bed. Lowwater was sarcastic and dry in his everyday life, and the gravity of the situation that had come to pass didn't seem to change that.

A long silence filled the room alongside the steam from Lowwater's coffee.

"Did y'all get him?" Nita asked.

"No."

Nita rolled her neck around to loosen it up a little and took acceptance of the outcome. "You didn't bring me one?" she asked, looking at his coffee.

Lowwater blew on it once more to cool it down. "Normally, I would tell you to get your ass up and get your own, but since you can't... Yeah, I guess I did bring you one." He gave her the foam cup, which warmed her palms and eased her body. "Yeah, he messed you up pretty good."

Nita stared straight ahead in a daze, replaying yesterday's events in her mind. That fucking owl mask appeared with each blink. "I shot him. His blood is all over the place."

"They're still testing the site, but it looked pretty clean, Nita. You sure you made contact?"

"I'm positive."

"If there is, they'll find it."

She took a sip. The coffee warmed her sore throat as it ran down her body.

"Now, it's officially time to take that sabbatical we discussed,"

Lowwater said. "Relax. Drive to Galveston, Branson, goddam Cocoa Beach for all I care. Just *do* something."

The door creaked open, and another big Native man walked in. Her father was followed by her mother. She held Aiden's hand as he carried folded paper tucked behind his arm.

"Who let you in here, Randal?" her father asked

"Oh, you know, when they give you the title of Director, they let you just walk in anywhere in this county," Lowwater replied. He stood to shake her father's hand, hug her mother, and pat Aiden on the head. "I'll get out of your hair." He pointed to the cup of coffee in Nita's hand. "You owe me one of those," he said before turning his back to the room.

"Let's get lunch soon," her father said.

"I'd like that," Lowwater nodded.

All growing up, Nita heard stories of how the pair of them ran around town together. The two had been buddies since elementary school and played sports together year-round. Their bond was solidified in high school when they played on opposite ends of the defensive line for Sequoyah High School. They both went on to play for Northeastern State University, the local Division II school in town. However, while her father stuck with football, Lowwater pursued baseball.

The door shut, and her parents gave her delicate hugs. Nita embraced them as firmly as her body would let her. Emotion began to climb out of her, but she swallowed it and dealt with the pain. Her mother ushered Aiden in front of her and essentially had to tell him to hug Nita. His facial expression never changed from its default position. However, with his elbows tucked into his side, he leaned over and hugged his stepmother. Nita patted him on the back a couple of times before he rose up, keeping herself reserved.

"I finished my map," he said.

"Did you?" Nita asked.

Aiden unfolded it after removing it from his back pocket. How he got the thick paper in such a tight fold was beyond her. He spread it across her sore body, knowing little about her pain and discomfort.

"Aiden, maybe we should hold off on that, buddy. Your mom's been—"

Nita cut her father off. "It's all right."

Aiden's map was on full display as she held it in her hands from end to end. The intricacies never ceased to amaze Nita. The details of the landmass her eleven-year-old stepson could capture on the page were brilliant and improved every time. He always illustrated the lakes, rivers, and roads; however, he had graduated into a full-on, physical map, showing elevation and even a distance key.

"Very good," she said. Their relationship before Jackson was stable, but she never graduated as a primary parental figure. Everything she offered had been channeled through Jackson; that was how she liked it and believed it should work. She loved him. However, that was not her problem. Her issue was committing to offering the specific kind of love a boy like Aiden needed.

CHAPTER 10

Blake Edwards was a cowboy through and through. His family had owned Thorpe Ranch going on six generations. The official name came later from his grandfather. He had a deep friendship and admiration for Jim Thorpe, whose legend sweeps across the entire state. Nowadays, he spent most of his time at the Tahlequah Stockyard shooting the shit with buddies while his hands tended to the land. Their work was cut out with thirty thousand acres to oversee, but Blake had the right men, most of which consisted of Marine buddies. One thing he knew about Marines: they get the job done.

Everyone around him sported plaid or Carhart somehow, and no matter the weather, blue jeans and boots were required. Dogs wandering around were expected, but to compare his German Shephard, Nova, to an ordinary mutt would be insulting. She was a gift from his ex-wife, but his disdain for her didn't carry over to Nova. He treated her like a family member, and since he was no longer married, he could devote much of his time to her needs and training—something his ex would find ironic.

Blake would pick an aisle seat and watch his fellow ranchers and farmers bid on cattle and equipment while Nova sat perched on the concrete steps beside him. Little kids would come along and pet her, which Blake advised against, but most of the time, these kids came out of nowhere. Yes, Nova was as well-trained a dog as any, but the potential danger was still there when sneaking up on a dog of that caliber. They were not far removed from their wolf ancestors.

————

It was a hot Oklahoma day with the rare absence of wind sweeping down the plains, as the musical suggested. Blake walked the yard as a beautiful 333GCompact Track Loader with an auger, cutter, and hydraulic hammer attachments was being auctioned. He was tempted to place a bid, but he had two older models at the ranch with all the same capabilities. He clenched his jaw and forced himself to look the other way.

The Edwards name carried a modicum of sway and celebrity. So, Blake did his fair share of greeting every passerby that made eye contact and shook his hand. Most were low-earning farmers and ranchers, but there were a few contemporaries. Blake's father was the social butterfly, and years of redneck networking had already been established before it merged into his son's. Blake didn't ask to be the sole inheritor of fortune, but he accepted it because he believed that to deny such a thing in a world where people were barely scraping by would make him an asshole. He often told himself to be confident and not project any sadness or anxiety. *People won't care, and they shouldn't.* For he was the boy that was born into cowboy luxury.

"You takin' a bid on the loader, Blake?" local rancher Jim Hocking asked. His farm was near Cookson, and it fed into the game refuge. Ole Jim was also sitting on a fortune, with a thousand cattle roaming his fields.

"No, I'm not in the market for an upgrade, Jim. I gotta check with my sister when I make a big purchase," he joked. His sister Olivia lived in the Dakotas, operating the oil side of the business that Blake wanted no part of.

Just then, the gavel slammed. "Sold!"

"Guess neither of us is," Jim said.

They both looked to the purchaser. Blake squinted. The man wore a long sleeve button-up, plain as ever to be stitched, choking his new school tattoo that countered his alabaster skin to jarring effect. His expression and overall manner appeared confident yet out of place. He slicked back his pomade-infused hair and began exchanging the money. He used cash out of an envelope, which was expected, but Blake rarely saw an envelope bulging.

"You seen him around here before, Jim?"

Jim sloshed around a heavy portion of tobacco-ridden saliva in his mouth before spitting it into the dirt. "Nah. Don't look like he belongs here, if you know what I'm saying. I don't see an ounce of the country in him."

"It's not like this place is exclusive for ranchers and farmers."

"It ain't?"

Blake smiled but let his silence speak his disagreement. "I'll see you around, Jim."

"Take care."

―――

Blake rolled the window down so she could take in the breeze on the drive home while he scratched Nova's ears. Gravel crunched nearby, halting his exit. Nova's head vibrated as she growled. He gave her a few pats on the top of the head.

Always alert. Always ready. Semper Fi.

The new owner of the 333G Compact Track Loader stood behind him with a cunning grin. "Mr. Edwards, we haven't been introduced. It's nice to finally meet you," the man said.

Blake shook, although his guard was still up due to Nova's trepidation. "I'm fine with Blake. Helps me ride out my youth for a little longer."

"I understand. I'm Amos Dyer."

That name caught Blake by surprise. "Any relation to Steven Dyer?"

Amos nodded and put both hands and a ledger behind his back.

"Yes, he's my grandfather. I'm in the beginning stages of picking up his mantle. He's getting old now, and I'm the only one in my family willing to do so. Also helps with changes in scenery and land prices. You know, shit like that."

Blake missed the last half of what Amos said because he was distracted by the tattoo climbing up his neck. Several jagged lines poked out underneath Amos' collar and nearly touched his jawline. They looked to be dead branches on a tree. On the opposite side of his neck were the words *Semper Fi*, the motto Blake knew all too well for the Marines.

"It's good you stepped up then. You have any plans for the new track loader?"

Amos rolled up his sleeves then ran his hand over his slick hair. "Tearing down the old barn and building a new one. I was shocked to see it still standing. It was breaking off into pieces when I was a boy."

"How long has it been since you were here last?"

He looked off and squinted, thinking hard on the exact date. "Roughly ten years, I'd say. Afghanistan and California were my homes prior to this one."

"I'm more familiar with Afghanistan than I am with California. Still, I wouldn't call the former *home*."

"I heard you served. What years were you there?"

"I was everywhere over there from 2005 through 2013."

Amos paused. "Some shit years. I might've caught you on the tail end of your deployment."

Blake didn't reply as he clocked Amos's holstered Baretta M9 bulging through his shirt.

"I just wanted to introduce myself quickly before I get to work," Amos said. "Pleasure meeting my neighbor and fellow Marine."

"Likewise."

Blake stood his ground for a while. He socialized with his fellow farmers and ranchers while keeping his eye on Amos loading up that new tractor.

———

The gas cap clicked shut. Blake's refueling routine was strict: fill the
truck up, roll the windows down for Nova, get a large bottle of water,
teriyaki beef jerky (shareable size), and some portable trail mix. He rued
the day he offered jerky to Nova, not thinking it would lead to her
obsession.

On his walk back to the truck, the melting pot of cowboys, white
trash, and Indians combined to fuel up and go on about their seemingly
miserable lives. A rare occasion would arise when Blake would get a
hate-filled glare. If one came from money around here, respect was
much harder to come by, as it appeared with the naked eye that the
masses were scraping by.

"Get the fuck in the car, Jenn!" he heard behind him a few tanks
over.

Blake peeled the seal off the jerky and threw one to Nova, perfectly
postured in the passenger seat. Further yelling between the couple
continued, and Blake decided to give it a look. Others did as well, but
they continued about their day all the same. A pair of meth-looking
white folks fighting in a gas station parking was ordinary. One had better
odds of seeing that in a day than finding a quarter on the ground.

The man held the girl, Jenn, by the wrist and forced her into the car.
She fought it, but not too hard.

"I'm gonna tell you one more time: get in the fucking car!" he
shouted.

"Hey, there's kids walking around here." Blake said. "Can't be
talking like that. Y'all settle this somewhere else."

Turning his head, the man let go of Jenn's wrist. He kept his gaze,
and Blake didn't shy away. The pair didn't look familiar but appeared
around the same age—early thirties, but surely their organs were going
on sixty.

The man began taking off his thin, weathered jacket. "The fuck did
you say to me, cowboy?" he asked, revealing a wife beater underneath.

Blake chuckled to himself. "You dressed for the occasion?"

White trash threw his jacket to his girlfriend for her to catch, and
she did so, but awkwardly. "What's that?" he asked, only getting more
heated.

"It's okay. I wouldn't expect you to understand irony. Listen, just get back in the car and drive off."

"No, if you're so hell and bent on getting in my business—"

"Hell-bent," Blake corrected.

"Then, I think I'll stick around to work it out."

People began to slow and turn their attention on the two of them. A pair of older cowboys, Randy Lowe and Clint Johnson, leaned against their truck to watch the show. Their tobacco-stained teeth poked out from under their mustaches.

The man walked towards him.

"Son, I wouldn't come any closer," Blake warned, standing his ground with his six protected by his truck.

"Don't *son*, me, bitch! I ain't your *son*, Blake. You were only a year ahead of me."

"I would still be a year ahead of you, then. So I don't think anything has changed."

"In school, damn it! I remember you, walking around like the whole fucking place was yours and everyone suckin' you off."

"You and I recall high school very differently. I'd remember the sucking off... probably would've enjoyed my time more."

"You don't even know who I am, do you?"

Blake looked him up and down. "Nope."

"Eric Honeycutt... Sound familiar?" he asked, taking another step forward.

"Can't say it is. You're getting closer." Blake replied, still unmoving.

"I guess it would've been hard to spot me on your high horse looking down on everyone back then."

Blake rubbed his tear ducts and leaned in, lowering his voice. "Or perhaps it was obvious from the outset how insignificant and irrelevant you would be. You see, Eric, in this world, we all can shed that initial perception others may have of us. You know, to prove we aren't white fucking trash losers. However, it appears you did little to nothing to do so."

He cocked his fist and swung, but Blake got there first. Nova's growl evolved into a bark that would frighten a Navy SEAL.

As Eric's nose broke from a single punch, blood flew through the air. Blake caught Eric's shirt strap. "You're all right. Come on, get up. You're embarrassing yourself."

"You broke my fucking nose!" Eric cried, cupping his face.

Blake dragged him across the concrete, slick with grease and gasoline. Eric's beer belly bulged from under the wife beater, looking like a chunky toddler. He slammed him against Eric's driver's side door.

"Repeat after me," Blake said.

"Fuck you," Eric spewed through his hands.

Blake grabbed the back of Eric's head and used his other hand to press fifthly palms farther into his nose. Eric helplessly squirmed around as Blake had his head in a vice.

"*I'm sorry I angered your dog.*"

"I'm sorry I angered your dog," Eric repeated.

People watched on.

Blake lowered his voice. "*I'm sorry for hating myself so much that I tried to blame you.*"

"I'm sorry for hating myself so much that I tried to blame you."

For any onlooker, it probably looked like Eric was crying and Blake was consoling him. Not quite.

"*I am worthless, and I must change.*"

"I am worthless, and I must change."

Blake patted him on the back. At that time, a Tahlequah squad car pulled into the gas station and blocked Eric's car.

"I'm glad we understand each other."

The door to the police car opened. The cop was young and fresh-faced. Blake knew a lot of Tahlequah PD, but this appeared to be a new recruit. "Is there a problem here?" he asked.

Blake could tell this guy was ex-military just by how he carried himself. Army, he guessed, perhaps even Ranger.

Another pulled himself from the passenger side. His massive gut impeded his movement. "He's all right, Jack," the hefty officer said. "Everything good here, Mr. Edwards?"

"Everything's good, Bill."

Eric collected himself and rose to his feet. His hands fell to his sides, revealing his bloody face. And much to Blake's surprise, Eric said, "We're all good."

All parties went back to their vehicles. Blake took a few deep breaths. It had been a while since he'd been in a confrontation with anyone. The juices of adrenaline began to flow through his body, but he was able to slow them down. Compared to what he engaged in overseas, a tank-top-wearing wife-beater was nothing to stress over.

Nova rested her head in his lap. She lived up to her registered support dog status. He petted her from her head down her back. His pocket vibrated, followed by the urgent message from his best friend.

———

Blake swung down from atop his horse before he'd even stopped. Nova trailed in the distance and barreled across the pasture at full speed. Four of his cowboys and best friends stood around a tree, still and unmoving. His Marine buddies who needed jobs after service came to work for him here on the promise that Blake wouldn't ride them too hard.

Blake squinted and lowered his head on his approach. The elm stood by itself around twenty yards from the tree line. He and his four Marines had seen a lot overseas. In Afghanistan and Iraq, they witnessed violence, brutality, and hatred aimed directly at them. Yet, while all those were present before them, an added sense of pure evil prevailed. The fact that this grotesque act was orchestrated on his land angered Blake with every fiber of his being. Nova sat close to him, her body leaning against Blake's leg as she looked upon the horror.

A young woman's body was nailed to the trunk of the tree with railroad spikes. The blood in her hair was dry and stained as it dangled in front of her eyes like dark icicles. Her body was littered with stab wounds. Her once-green, floral-patterned dress was black and brown with spatters of crimson. Her hands had smears of a dark, chalky substance. Perhaps charcoal.

Blake walked in between his guys, their eyes fixed forward. Staked to the ground with a long piece of rebar was one of his best friends, Wyatt. His pale body signaled he had been dead for hours. His hands were cupped and held together by wire as his chin rested on the thin metal stake embedded at a downward angle through his chest. In his hands were his gouged eyes. He was placed in a manner that appeared he was watching the unknown woman on the tree. Stab wounds also covered his body. However, his knuckles were bruised and exposing bone.

"You put up a fight, brother," Blake whispered. "I know you did."

"Who the fuck would do something like this?" Cody asked.

Parker looked away, shaking his head in the process.

Wyatt had no one. All the remaining family was currently gathered around his desecrated body.

Blake dropped down, sitting like a frog with his forearms on his knees. Flashes of Ramadi came to him. 2006 was a year that would never leave him. In that desert wasteland, these lush green hills flowing with cattle and wind came to him in the darkest moments. It wasn't until he turned his back on this place that he missed it so much. It had to reconcile and come to terms with the guilt. But, he realized, it wasn't the land he needed to abandon—it was his father.

The place was more than solace. Especially when he could still feel the dirt and sand hitting his face from nearby bombs in the markets. There, violence was always cooking in the pot, but in Ramadi, it bubbled over. Every man here fought against al Qaeda insurgents; since then, he hadn't seen anything as evil as what was in front of him. His place of solace had been infiltrated, and nothing angered him more.

"What do you want us to do, Blake?" his longest and dearest friend Little J asked.

He had to think fast, or at least he put that pressure on himself. "First thing, we all discovered this together. Let's make sure we all have our story straight in case they suspect one of us in this," Blake said. He didn't have to clarify anything else. "Floyd, go ahead and call this in."

Floyd was born in Akins, a town close by, and he did what Blake asked with his phone already at his ear.

"Let's go ahead and back up while we wait." Blake insisted. "Don't want to be any closer to this anymore."

They settled under the shade of the collection of trees.

Parker returned to the group, and Floyd followed. "A crime like this is gonna draw a lot more attention. More agencies are gonna be sniffing around... OSBI, FBI, Marshals, local. Possible media shitstorm too. Best be prepared for that," Floyd said.

Little J stepped close to Blake, petting Nova along the way. "So, again, what are we gonna do about this?" he asked. Like the rest, they kept their anger inward, but it bubbled to the surface.

"We're waiting for the police." Blake said. "They'll do their investigating, and then we'll start ours. And we'll burn these hills to the ground to find out who did this if we have to."

CHAPTER 11

Charlie panicked. He realized that flowers were probably not the right message. He kept his head low, carrying the bouquet. Perhaps his intel was flawed, but apparently flowers were a good gift for someone when they were in the hospital. His research came from a brief Google search and a conversation with his grandmother, but he failed to factor in the apparent reasons to avoid such a thing that rushed to his mind on the walk to the hospital entrance.

This is a woman whose husband just died. What the fuck am I doing? Should've gone with Grandma's frybread.

There was little action at the Cherokee Nation W.W. Hastings Hospital in the middle of the day. A handful of nurses passed, and none paid Charlie any mind. The front desk was vacant, with no sign of anyone returning to their post. Charlie decided to use this as an opportunity. He placed the vase of flowers on top of the desk and walked away like they weren't his.

The long, white corridors were blinding in the noonday sun. Charlie began to believe the design was to help awaken groggy nurses on long shifts as the light peppered his sensitive eyes.

"Sir?" he heard behind him.

Shit.

He turned to see that the once empty and unoccupied desk was now up and running via a gray-haired nurse with enormous forearms. She seemed a no-nonsense type of caregiver.

"Are these your flowers?" she asked, peering over her glasses.

"No, they aren't."

"They aren't yours because you didn't buy them, or they aren't yours because you changed your mind?"

Charlie gave her an involuntary, quick grin. "The latter."

Without skipping a beat, she said, "I'll give 'em to a sick kid or something."

"Thank you."

———

Nita's father was well versed in the art of intimidation. Hell, Nita inherited the gift. His large frame and stone face did most of the work on their own. Robert "Big Rob" Ross walked hand in hand with Nita's stepson down the hall in Charlie's direction.

Robert's scowl turned into a smile. "Marshal Soap, how the hell are ya?" he said, covering Aiden's ears a tad too late.

"I still heard you, Pa," Aiden said.

They shook hands, and Charlie relaxed his shoulders. "I'm doing good, Mr. Ross. How are you?"

"Charlie, it's been a long time since high school... Robert is just fine."

For the past ten years, Charlie had fought, chased, and imprisoned "bad guys," but the former football all-star and father of his ex-girlfriend still made him nervous. "Very well, Robert. It's good to see you. How's she doing?"

"Ah, she's good. Ready to get outta here, though. She's too tough for her own good. She's tougher than half the sons of bitches I played ball with." But, again, he was late covering Aiden's ears.

"I heard that too, Pa."

"Listen," Charlie said, scratching his brow with his thumb. I wanted to apologize that none of us were with her when this happened."

"You don't have to apologize. Nita's been through a lot these past

few months... in her life. But I think you'll agree when I say she can
handle herself."

Charlie nodded. "Yes... yes, she can."

"Well, head on in there. I'm sure she'll be glad to see you."

He opened the door into her room, and there she sat, and to
Charlie, even though she was battered and bruised, she was beautiful.
She carried the bandages as well as a person could. He did his best not to
have those thoughts. His hands moved awkwardly for a moment before
settling in his pockets. Without the flowers, he didn't know what to do
with them.

The room was silent for a moment as they locked eyes.

"You certainly eased back into things," Charlie joked.

She laughed. "Yeah, I wanted to take it slow."

"Wish I could've been there," Charlie said. His eyes darted off, for it
came out of his mouth awkwardly.

"No, you really wouldn't have."

Charlie accepted that.

Nita looked his uniform up and down before facing forward once
again. "You on duty today, Nation 33?"

"Yep, I'm on my extended lunch break."

"What makes it extended?" Nita asked.

"The fact that all the criminals are hiding because of you."

"Ah, they're scared of the Cherokee Bitch?"

"Something like that." Charlie laughed and took a step closer. "Life
was a lot easier when all we had to worry about was getting scholarships
for ball, wasn't it?"

"It was," she said. "Although, it was still a little more stressful for me
because I had to worry about scholarships in three different sports..."

Charlie chuckled. "Oh, you're gonna rub that in my face now?"

Nita simply shrugged. The room fell to a hush. The pair of them sat
in silence. The soft sounds of the television acted as white noise at the
moment, for Charlie paid no attention to what was being said.

"Listen, I never... I never got to say I'm sorry for your loss—"

Nita cut him off. "Charlie, it's okay. Thank you."

He scratched his five o'clock shadow. "And this is a horrible segue, but I wanted to let you know that Detective Martindale didn't make it."

Nita appeared to go blank. Her gaze was locked on the blank wall ahead of her. Charlie gripped the hospital bed rails. "Nita?" he said softly.

"You're right. That *was* a terrible segue," she said.

"Again, I'm sorry." He went to leave. "Grandma offered to whip up some frybread if you want it."

Nita smiled. "I'm disappointed you didn't already have it with you."

Shit.

The vibration in the center of his vest halted his progress out the door. He removed his phone from the center pouch to view the emergency notification.

"What is it?" she asked.

His head dropped, he scratched his brow, and his tan skin went white. "Uhm, something... something's happened."

CHAPTER 12

Nita ignored Charlie's plea for her to stay behind. She checked the wraps around her body to make sure it was tight. Her deep cuts irritated the back of the car seat, even with the bandages. Nita pulled down Charlie's passenger seat mirror to get a better look at her neck. She had her mother go and retrieve one of her collared shirts to conceal the bruises.

They took Highway 51 through Hulbert. "Did it happen in Hulbert?" Nita asked.

Charlie hesitated. "No."

"Where?"

"Thorpe Ranch. Lowwater's gonna shit a brick when he sees you. Then, hit me over the head with it."

Nita stared off for a moment. "Blake's?"

"Yes... that asshole. If his daddy was still alive, I would bet my life that old fuck did it."

The anger was present in his entire body. His hand gripped the steering wheel tightly, and occasionally, Nita would see him shake his head out of the corner of her eye.

"You still harboring some resentment?"

Charlie scoffed. "It's deeper than resentment. You know this. Blake being an arrogant asshole just amplifies it."

She didn't reply, allowing him to wallow in the grudge that went back when wagons rolled over these plains.

Charlie cleared his throat. "When's the last time you saw him?"

"Been a few months. I see him around town. His daughter and Aiden are the same age."

The idea of being around two of her exes so soon after her husband's death seemed like a cruel joke. She had no desire to be around anyone, let alone them. Those two men represented different stages of her life that she was happy to be rid of, as if they were practiced in a three-step process that ended with Jackson.

She loved him. She missed him. She drifted.

Flashes of gunfire blinded her vision.

She emerged from the house. Spent rounds and shell casings littered the front porch. Brass clanked beneath her feet as her boots landed on top of them. Her Watchman LE rifle was slung across her back at rest. The butt of her Benelli M4 was pressed into her shoulder. Every magazine she had was empty. Every shell had been fired, including her Sig. If the fight continued, knives and jiujitsu would be the next course. That wouldn't be necessary. Everyone in the house behind her was dead. All of them. She left no doubts.

In a haze, she walked back to the vehicle in the yard, nearly stumbling with each step. No bullets hit her, but she checked multiple times. Blood caked her skin and dried, forming a body scab to be peeled away.

Two police officers were dead in the grass of the front lawn. Their eyes were wide open, and they followed Nita wherever she went like one of those optical illusions. Blood seeped from their wounds and sank into the earth. Another officer was down by the car. However, his wound was fresh, and blood flowed from his neck like a spout. She rushed to him, dropped her shotgun, knelt, and applied pressure to the wound. Nita added another layer of blood to her arms.

She was too late. Detective Martindale already lost too much blood and died in the grass with the others.

The smell of smoke caught her attention. She looked back at the poor excuse of a house-turned-meth-lab now in flames. Crashes of glass breaking followed throughout the house, and those bursts spread the fires. It wasn't long until the entire house was engulfed.

She watched.

Burn.

A shadowy figure stood in the window. Flames rose behind it and waved. The figure showed no distress, almost welcoming it.

"Nita," someone called out from the car, taking her attention away from the house. She went to the passenger side window and saw her husband in the driver's seat. He wore a blue-eyed smile with dimples forming deep creases on his cheeks. "Come on, babe. Let's go home."

She loved him.

Nita climbed into the passenger's seat, leaving the violent scene behind her. Jackson drove away on the gravel road, kicking up rocks and dust behind them. She watched intently through the rear view.

"Nita," he called as he drove, but she didn't respond.

She continued to stare.

"Nita," he repeated. "How's Aiden?"

As she turned to face him, blinding headlights emerged from behind him, getting brighter. He never took notice and continued to talk, but his words were muted. Nita yelled at the oncoming vehicle racing towards them.

A jolt went through her body, shocking her awake.

"Hey, you all right? You dozed off for a second," Charlie said, carrying on with their conversation from when Nita was still conscious. "They're claiming this murder happened last night."

"And?" Nita replied.

"Well, it could've been your guy..."

"I-I suppose."

———

A long line of wind-battered caution tape held the media at bay. Fort Gibson and Hulbert PD managed the crowd as Nita and Charlie were allowed passage. Then, a helicopter roared overhead and blew the grass and dirt of Thorpe Ranch skyward. Many times, Nita had passed under the T welcoming them onto the property. A weird sense of déjà vu overwhelmed her. It had been years, but not much, if anything, had changed in that time.

It took another twenty minutes to arrive upon the fleet of black law enforcement vehicles. A splash of yellow surprised them both.

"OSBI... FBI..." Charlie said.

"Looks like it."

CHAPTER 13

The flash from the cameras burst ahead. A veil of men stood on the edges of the crime that had since passed by hours, as if stepping into a ten-foot radius would bring damnation on their souls.

Nita scanned the tree line in front of them all. The massive wall of green and brown stretched to the end of both horizons. The longer she looked, the more her senses ran amuck. The leaves deteriorated, and the limbs of the trees curled and formed spiked edges. Distant howls followed by violent thrashing followed from beyond the shadows in the sea of trees.

She turned away.

"Yep, I thought you'd be here," she heard Director Lowwater say.

She didn't reply.

"Just can't keep you away, can I?" he asked.

"Are you going to make me leave?"

Lowwater removed his hat and rubbed the back of his hair, still trying to get used to his ponytail no longer attached to his skull. "You're as qualified to work this as anybody."

Nita nodded.

They stepped past the FBI, who shot them a glance, not one of judgment but of superiority. As she walked up on the scene, pressure in her head built. All she heard was dissonant echo, like being underwater. Charlie stayed behind her and walked along the edge of the caution tape, surveying the crime scene from a distance for now.

She'd known Wyatt for as long as she had known Blake. Nita struggled to even look at him in this state. Wyatt was the one who would saddle her horse and prepare everything for her when she wanted to come ride on the ranch while Blake was on active duty.

She didn't recognize the girl at all. Her dress was old, as if it were Laura Ingalls' hanging. She didn't have any shoes on, and her feet had turned purple. Her stiff hair formed sharp points like sewing needles. Charcoal covered parts of her body: the neck, wrists, and ankles. Its chalky form flaked away with each gust of wind.

The forensic operations specialist paid them no attention as she was hard at work examining the bodies and taking notes. The photographer did the same, capturing everything from every angle.

Nita noticed a line of grass leading from the forest pressed against the ground. "Drag marks."

"Yep," the investigator said with all her energy focused on inspecting Wyatt's body. "He was dragged from the forest. I'm sure she was too. What's interesting, though, is that the murders happened right here. The stab wounds and the amount of blood isolated in this area say as much. If he were stabbed in the forest and then dragged, there would obviously be a streak of blood along the drag lines."

Nita was no crime scene investigator, but the examiner seemed good at her job.

"You the one they're talking about?" the examiner asked.

Nita scanned the lawmen of varying agencies side-eying her. "I guess so."

The woman smiled but didn't extend her hand for a shake with the latex gloves. "You think this could be your man?"

"I would've thought I took him out of commission for a while, but I'm doubting many things right now."

She nodded and continued her work. "I'm Cindy. Don't mess up my crime scene, Marshal," she snickered.

Nita admired her. "You think the woman was killed here too?"

"No, she's been dead a lot longer than him. I can tell that just by looking at her." Cindy caught her fellow investigator extending the border of the crime scene. "Max, we're done with securing the crime scene. Make a pass at the bodies, tell me what you see, and mark anything of interest."

"Yes, ma'am," he said. He couldn't have been any older than twenty-three.

"He's fresh out of university," Cindy informed Nita. "Bottom of the class, but his uncle is the Executive Assistant Director of Human Resources. He meets the qualifications only by the whisker of his nut hair."

Nita's eyes widened as they looked at each other with their peripherals. Cindy didn't seem to care or acknowledge their reaction and moved along.

The FBI, OSBI (Oklahoma Bureau of Investigation), and other authorities were all talking with one another and discussing how to deconstruct the scene. A few were on the phone talking with God knows who. A collection of cowboy hats caught her attention through a pair of SUVs.

Little J spoke to an agent who was taking notes while holding an audio recorder between his forearm and bicep. Blake locked eyes with her from afar and tipped his hat to her.

"You mind if I take a look?" Nita asked Cindy.

Cindy raised the caution tape for her. "I'd love it."

Nita ducked under. Up close, dead bodies didn't look real. It took a moment for the mind to wrap around the fact that a person was deceased, and their lifeless body wasn't some Hollywood creation.

The world went dark. Shadows crept in from beyond the yellow tape, consuming everything in sight. Only Nita and the two, no longer amongst the living, remained in twilight. In this state, Nita had to remind herself that she could still be seen by everyone else, not experiencing what she was going through. Nita's will to keep it cool in a place such as this took strength. Her behavior was that of a high-functioning drunk, making her best sober impression. Every day consisted of keeping the shadows at bay. She feared allowing them in would bring forth consequences. Yet, in the shadow, she could see its intentions, motive, and darkest desires.

She went to Wyatt first. His eyes were back in his head as he looked upon the woman smiling bright and dancing beneath the branches of the tree. She never met his gaze but continued to sway. Her dress brushed across the top of the grass as she spun in a gentle circle. Faint yellow beams shot from his eyes like headlights.

Then, the dancing stopped. The woman's body language changed. Her knees trembled as she looked in all directions. The shadow enveloped her, swirling around her like a tornado. It slammed her against the tree, and her screams were drowned out by the static howl of the dark.

Nita looked back at Wyatt. His eyes were ripped from his head, and his screams fell on deaf ears. Then the yellow beam grew brighter... brighter... and brighter. She looked away and brought her hand up to block the light as it hurt her eyes. The shadows retreated. It appeared they were being conquered by the overwhelming illumination.

She closed her eyes.

When she opened them, the light, shadows, or any form of the supernatural was no longer present.

Nita returned to the world of the now amongst her fellow colleagues and contemporaries, who continued about their business with not an inkling of what she had just gone through. "He wasn't supposed to see this," she said.

"What?" Cindy asked.

"Got a boot print!" they heard from the woods.

————

About seventy yards in, they found another forensic investigator marking the location of the print.

"Jesus," Charlie said.

The flash of the camera went off as the investigator replied, "I know right?" He took a small tape measure from his pocket. "Size sixteen."

The dense woods became crowded after the discovery. Every agency flooded the area circling the print location. Director Lowwater emerged from the crowd and settled at the front as his status demanded. "Looks like all the Thunder players are persons of interest," Lowwater said.

"Well, they didn't make the playoffs, which isn't a shock to anyone. So, they won't have that as an alibi," Charlie joked to the amusement of the grim crowd. He turned to Nita. "You think your owl guy could match?"

The woods, that were once quiet, began to bend and thrash with wind that grew more intense. A few of the hats of the FBI agents flew off into the dense foliage.

"Wouldn't shock me," Nita said.

They travelled deeper into the woods to see if they could find the origins of the man's trek. Rushing water flowed ahead of them. It was subtle but moving all the same. A new set of tracks began as the grass wilted away, and mud overwhelmed the surrounding area due to the ever-changing water level.

"Same size boot," Agent Teller of OSBI said. Nita had only exchanged pleasantries with him prior. He had been working in Tahlequah for a couple years now, but he had moved here from Utah. Apparently, he went by a few nicknames that weren't too flattering, and most likely not approved by him: "Wonder Bread" and "Powder."

A total of five prints emerged from the creek.

"You all have creek monsters down here in Oklahoma?" Agent Teller asked.

"Not any that wear work boots," Lowwater replied.

Charlie caught on first. "He floated down with a boat."

The water had risen enough to conceal the proof of landing.

"How much of this creek is on the ranch?" Teller asked.

"Most of it. Feeds into the lake."

Nita's vision stretched away while looking up the creek. The overhanging trees curled, looking to swallow the creek whole.

"How many miles to the lake?" the agent asked.

"Three miles. Maybe a little more," Nita responded.

"So, we need to find a launch point for a small boat."

"There's more than two hundred miles of shoreline with the surrounding lakes, rivers, and creeks. And there's no shortage of boats."

Agent Teller seemed up to the challenge as he finished jotting down something in his notebook then tucked it into his jacket pocket. His glossy shoes were caked in mud. "How many marshals can you spare, Director?"

"How many you need?" Lowwater replied,

"Only a handful. I know you're limited, but I'd like to restrict local PD's immersion to avoid media leaks and egos. Perhaps the marshals and OSBI carry more of the load."

"That's fine. I'll give the manpower you need."

Agent Teller locked eyes with Nita. "I wouldn't mind having the Marble City Gunslinger."

All the surrounding heads turned to her. She nodded, submitting her service. Nita made her way back out of the woods to escape attention.

"As far as nicknames go, Marble City Gunslinger is pretty badass," Charlie said. "Probably better than Deer Lady."

"I'm not seductive enough to be Deer Lady."

Her work wasn't finished. Nita didn't know how to feel about that. Fatigue and exhaustion were becoming enemies on their own. But part of her—most of her was looking forward to the challenge. Another puzzle to solve, another chance to put blinders on in the pursuit of one goal.

CHAPTER 14

Nita brushed her hand along the caution tape. Examiner Cindy continued to train Max on proper protocol like it was another day at the office. The tone of voice said he was tired of answering her process questions, and he wanted to attempt the work on his own. However, his superior desired perfection.

"Hello, Nita," Blake greeted. His smile made many women in Eastern Oklahoma weak in the knees. He was charming, no doubt, but she adapted to it long ago.

"Blake," she said.

It was evident that he didn't know where to begin the conversation.

Something brushed past her leg from behind. Then, a furry, black and tan mass sat in front of her, desiring to be petted. Nita couldn't resist and obliged. "Who's this?"

"That's Nova. She's usually very untrusting of strangers."

"Maybe her instincts are more acute than you think." Nita scratched her behind the ears.

"Maybe you're right."

Nita stood. "I'm sorry about Wyatt."

Blake looked down. "Me too."

He'd always been known as a stoic person, even as a kid. Blake was difficult to rattle or shake. His default position was an apathetic charmer. But that was not the man in front of her now. Maybe he had softened over the years. Perhaps his daughter broke through that emotional barricade, exposing it to all.

He kept the elephant in the room. He didn't offer any condolences or anything of the kind for Jackson's passing. Perhaps he didn't want to bring it up for her sake.

"You talk to the investigators?" Nita asked.

"All of 'em."

"You have no idea who could've done this?"

"None at all. I hear you had a tussle with a possible suspect."

She nodded, and stretched, working out the soreness in her back. "Seems you're informed. Have you been reading the paper?"

"No one reads the paper anymore, Nita. I've been following along with everyone else on Facebook, of course. That's how I keep up with things going on nowadays."

She spotted his graying hair poking out from beneath his hat. "Are you showing signs of age, white boy?" She puckered her lips towards his temples. "Plus, you're on Facebook? Is it all downhill from here?"

Blake nodded and gazed out over his green pasture with pockets of trees scattered about in the rolling landscape. "Well, maybe I'm finally old." That must have been painful to admit, but he concealed it well. His eyes failed to meet hers. Instead, he stared at the ground as if watching his grass grow—until he finally gave in. "Listen, I'm sorry to hear about Jackson. He was a good man."

"He was a great man," she said through gritted teeth. "I'll never let him be demoted to anything beneath that."

"That's fair enough."

"Sorry to hear about you and Tara."

Blake seemed caught off guard, as his head shot back. "For someone that's not on Facebook, you sure know a lot."

"You're the richest man in the county. Hell, the waitress at Katfish Kitchen knew about your divorce before Tara had her bags packed and the papers signed."

"Georgina? That bitch," he said jokingly before the heaviness of his current situation returned to him.

Footfalls through the thick grass sounded behind her as Charlie
made his way back from the car. "I'm going to drive farther up the creek
to see if there's anything of merit."

"I'll come along," Nita said.

Blake and Charlie made eye contact as the latter passed by.

"Soap," Blake greeted him.

"Fuck off," Charlie said.

And the pleasantries ended as quickly as they began.

"Nita," Blake said, taking a long pause, looking out over his pasture
before leering into her soul. He removed his hat and ran his fingers
through his long hair. "I'm gonna kill whoever did this."

She didn't say anything. Nita allowed him to have that moment of
declaration; it seemed like the right thing to do. Through her eyes, the
world would spin more efficiently if a bit of frontier justice were allowed
from time to time. She'd seen the courts hold men on trial for years,
getting fat on taxpayer money with more freedoms than they deserved.
The price for one bullet was cheaper than death row.

"Are you sure there isn't any more information you can give me to
help?" she asked, shrugging her shoulders.

"No," Blake said.

They held each other's gaze. Nita's confidence in him dissipated.

CHAPTER 15

The media frenzy was unlike anything Nita had experienced in her career. America's fascination with serial killers reared its ugly head. All surrounding police precincts were hounded by reporters attempting to get a quick soundbite for their station. The hierarchy of media outlets ranged from bigwigs like FOX, ABC, and NBC. Plus, any idiot with a true crime podcast within a three-hundred-mile radius. All local law enforcement buildings were blanketed by reporters at all hours of the day. Parking was a nightmare, and navigation through a sea of reporters even worse.

Nita had the overwhelming urge to stomp, snap, and chuck every phone and recorder that was pressed up to her face. Violence and death sold; she knew that much. But being within arm's length of the ones who profit off those things made her fists clench.

"Do you have any suspects?"

"Why has crime seemed to have a rapid rise in the area?"

"Is this a serial killer case?"

"Evidence—you found any?"

"How should the community be taking precautions?"

She did her best not to even process their questions. The answer to them was terrifying, and the media, or anyone who followed along, would hate it. The truth was, they had nothing. No leads. No evidence. Just a big boot print, and an unknown person of interest.

The poor girl that had been hanging from the tree had been raped both vaginally and anally, but no DNA was found. To find this guy would take some old-fashioned police work and a little bit of luck. Nita was up for the challenge, but she saw the look in those reporters' eyes and the pale faces of the people around town. They wanted answers, and they were going to get them.

———

Any store that sold a gun was wiped clean and in need of a restock. Ammo's value surpassed gold. Nearly anything that could be used as a weapon that could be purchased at the local hardware store was bought and sold. Nita figured that reaction was suitable for everyone. Perhaps it would take a citizen with a shotgun to blow this person away while trying to sneak into his house.

Nita burst through the glass doors of the station, and the sounds of questions of reporters at her back scattered. Charlie stood by the coffee pot, rubbing his eyes watching the bitter liquid spill into his mug. Without making eye contact, he offered it to Nita, and she accepted.

"Thank you. You sure you don't want it first?"

"I'm already working on my third, so you can take priority on that one."

She sipped. The warmth flowing through her body brought her instant comfort, even with a partially burnt tongue.

"Mercer still got you drinking that veteran coffee?" Charlie asked. Greg Mercer was her tactical shooting coach, and the question reminded her of the mountain of missed calls she had from him. It had been weeks since she'd seen him. She couldn't recall any time seeing him after Jackson's funeral, but then again, her mind had been a muddy and bloody haze. She owed him so much. His shooting insight and tactical knowledge gave her all the skill in the world to survive several gun-involved conflicts, including the shootout in Marble City, where she would've surely died without him in her life. Before that, he had been a random drifter on the streets, begging for change. He got what a good man deserved after the events of that unforgettable day when he shielded Nita's eyes, protected her from falling debris, and pulled her from the rubble. The veteran got his second chance.

"You all right?" Charlie asked, as his question was left unanswered.

"Black Rifle Coffee? Yeah, Mercer got Dad hooked on one of their darker roasts. Blackbeard's Delight, I believe it is."

The final drip dropped into Charlie's mug, and he blew on his coffee for a long time before taking a drink. He kept it close to his face to take in the pleasant aroma. "Too bitter for my taste. Although, I do find it ironic that there's a coffee blend named after a pirate and your dad has to get it. So, I'm assuming he's still into pirates? Which reminds me, what Native is into pirates?"

She took another sip, further warming her insides. "We like a good dark roast," she followed up to his initial comment. "And from his 'research,' there were apparently many historical accounts of Native pirates. They were free as pirates, along with slaves escaping indenture."

"Okay, I guess I understand. Kinda badass."

"Well, you can assist him in constructing his model ship then."

Nita yawned, put the palm of her hand on her lower back, and twisted back on both sides. A sequence of clicks and pops traveled up her spine. She exhaled in relief.

"That was a good one," Charlie said, admiring the back crack with an amused grin. "Press conference in an hour. DNA came back on the girl. Colette Graber... Amish girl from Choteau."

"Choteau? How did she end up in all of this?" Nita asked.

Choteau was in Cherokee Nation. However, it was around an hour away from Thorpe Ranch.

Charlie seemed to know that question was rhetorical and didn't reply.

"What's the plan?"

"When are you gonna be ready to go?" Charlie asked.

"I'm ready now," she said.

"Best get going. We don't want anyone out there finding the girl's name. Better take advantage of our head start."

CHAPTER 16

Buggy and horse tracks led the way to a humble farm with a barn, silo, and an extensive clothesline. Detectives from the Choteau Police Department and a pair of OSBI agents joined them. All those famous movies and television shows about one or two detectives solving a case of this size or even bigger, she found out, was total horseshit.

It was quiet here. Even though this Amish home wasn't but a couple miles from town, it had the appearance of a place lightyears away from civilization, and perhaps from generations past.

Detectives greeted them. All were fresh faces. They approached them on the gravel driveway. Their polished dress shoes were caked in gray dust. A harsh gust of Oklahoma wind blew their ties over their shoulders.

"Thanks for getting here quickly in the morning like this. I'm Detective Foster. This is my partner Detective Coates."

"Nice to meet you. I'm Marshal Ross. This is Marshal Soap." Nita stopped as the FBI agents approached. "And I don't know these two."

The agents seemed used to the protocol and introduced themselves without much thought. Agent Ramirez. Agent Graham.

"Who do we want asking questions?" Detective Coates asked.

"It might be best if Marshal Ross does," Agent Ramirez said.

Nita was surprised by that, but she didn't ask why.

"I agree," Charlie said.

It was probably because she was the only woman.

———

The somber atmosphere hit her like a ball-peen hammer. The smell was unique, but familiar, like her grandparents' house when she was a little girl. A mixture of wood and moth balls overwhelmed her nostrils. The house was compact, and every shade of brown presented itself. A wood-burning stove was planted in the middle of the living room. The cast iron was well-oiled and had yet to rust.

Three bonnet-headed girls sat on the sofa while the mother consoled them. The father sat alone in the kitchen drinking dark alcohol she assumed was whiskey. He paid no attention to his daughters, including his two youngest boys, one of them being a crying infant.

"Are you a policewoman?" the boy who opened the door asked.

"No, I'm a marshal," she said.

"What's that mean?"

Her presence piqued the girls' interest. Their red and wet faces looked up from their handkerchiefs to catch a glimpse of her. They didn't seem to expect a Native woman to walk into their living room and start asking questions, or any woman, for that matter.

"It means I'm a Cherokee that can go to great lengths to hunt evil people."

As soon as the words left her lips, she knew that it was maybe too heavy for a child's ears, or any of the family members, for that matter. She cleared her throat in an attempt to somehow change the subject or move along to the topic at hand.

But the boy persisted. "Like the evil man who killed Colette?"

"You're the woman from the paper," the mother realized.

People still read the paper. Well, at least the Amish do.

For a split second, the prospect of being Amish and living the simple life seemed oddly attractive. Living off the lands and focusing on herself and the family was what she loved about her culture. But those simplicities took more work to come by, especially when those she chose to spend her life with had been taken.

"Marble City," the mother continued. "Before that, you were a survivor of the bombing in Ok–"

"Yes, ma'am," Nita interrupted in a selfish attempt to not relive such events. "I'll just say that things in the media get exaggerated. Do you mind if I ask you and your family some questions about Colette? I understand if you don't feel—"

"Yes, of course," Mrs. Graber said. Her pace quickened, and she ordered the girls to watch after their baby brother. "Dwight, get Marshal Ross some tea, please," she instructed the other boy.

The bonnet-headed girls on the couch stared at Nita with wide-eyed interest as she made her way over to the kitchen table.

"Mr. Graber," Nita said. "Thank you for letting me into your home."

"Call me Caleb. My wife is LeAnn." His white collared shirt had yellow stains around the neck from dried sweat, greasy hair matted down on his head as his wicker hat rested on the table.

"Don't worry, I'm not going to stay long." Nita was used to asking questions from victims and witnesses, but she never had to do it on this big a scale. Murder cases were often left to county detectives and OSBI. This would be considered a special circumstance by Nita's interpretation. "So, I'll go ahead and get right into it. Where was Colette supposed to be that night? What was she supposed to be doing?"

"She was supposed to be working at the store," LeAnn said. The Amish mother poured Nita a glass of sweet tea into a mason jar, and took a seat at the kitchen table.

Sweet tea was her vice. It flowed through her veins as much as her blood did. These folks had been good to her up to this point, and after taking a sip, she wasn't going to ruin that by insulting Mrs. Graber's tea.

Could be more sweet.

"What store would that be?" Nita asked.

Mr. Graber took a large gulp of whiskey. "The bakery up the road."

"Okay, and she didn't go into work. Is that what you're saying?"

"Yes."

"Could you think of anywhere else she might have been?"

"Colette was good. She did what she was told and did everything with a good attitude and respect."

"I understand," Nita replied. She clocked one of the girls still staring at her. The curious girl averted her gaze. "The Cheese House? That bakery, I'm assuming?"

"Yes, ma'am. It's just over two miles down our street."

"I see... and would she walk to work?"

"I used to give her a ride, but like LeAnn said, she was so responsible we would let her walk. She said she liked it."

Nita nodded and glanced out the kitchen window to see the green tractor sitting there, knowing that was the Grabers' sweet ride. "Do y'all get many visitors or people that drive down this road often? There didn't appear to be much traffic."

"No, hardly anyone other than the Milners, who live at the very end. It's a dead-end road," Caleb said, tapping his wedding ring on the glass.

"Okay, did she have any friends from school or work that might know more?"

"She hadn't been to school since eighth grade. So, Colette was really on her own... Not many kids in the community were the same age."

"That being the Amish community?"

"Yes, ma'am," LeAnn said.

Nita tapped her pen twice on the table. Any more would be excessive. "Do either of you know a Wyatt Leonard?"

The Grabers looked at one another with confused glances and shook their heads.

LeAnn's head tilted as she looked off. "Is that the man that was found with my daughter?"

Nita hesitated. "Yes."

Caleb took another drink of whiskey. "No. We don't know him."

"Did she happen to have a boyfriend or anyone she was interested in?"

LeAnn looked around the room at her family, "Not that I'm a—"

"No," Caleb finished.

A pair of bonnets bobbed to one another out of the corner of Nita's eye. She leaned forward. "Is there anything more you can tell me about her? Anything at all?"

It appeared he wanted to ask something, but he couldn't bring himself. He never took his eyes of the glass as he spun it in place. There was no life in his eyes. Everything beyond that glass didn't exist to him now.

"Why was she covered in charcoal?" Caleb asked.

"We're not quite sure at the moment."

He slammed his hand on the table. "What the hell do you know! Nothing! My daughter is dead!" His chin and lower lip quivered, and he succumbed to the emotions. He began to weep, tucking his head into the pit of his elbow.

Nita kept her unshakable gaze on Mr. Graber. His anger was justified.

"You don't know me, Mr. Graber, but I promise I will give this investigation everything I have. You may not have hope in me or in any law enforcement, but trust me when I say I know what you're going through." Nita took another sip of tea so she did not appear rude or ungrateful. The chair scooted out from beneath her on her rise. "Thank you for the tea, LeAnn. If you don't mind, I'd like to talk to one of your girls in private."

LeAnn's head shot backwards with a hint of confusion.

Caleb retreated to the bedroom. The day was over for him.

"Which one of my girls, Marshal?" LeAnn asked.

Nita clenched her face and forced a smile. She pointed at the blonde girl with meerkat eyes who had been staring at her for the entire time she was there.

"That's Hannah," LeAnn said.

"Hannah, can we talk outside for a moment?"

The girl wiped her runny nose. She awaited her mother's permission.

"Go with Marshal Ross, dear," LeAnn commanded.

Nita led Hannah outside and wrapped her arm around the girl. She glanced at Charlie. He stroked his chin a single time before his hand rested on his gun belt. She took in the nature and the sunshine. Such a beautiful day that could not be appreciated. Nita liked stormy days, cozying up with a blanket, a cup of coffee, and a binge marathon. Being amongst nature was inherited in her blood, and she enjoyed its variety.

Her late husband, not so much. He wanted to take advantage of every sunny day, for as the day was bright, so was he.

"Hannah, do you believe God can stop evil people?" Nita asked. She hoped this wasn't too heavy or complex for the girl to answer.

Her big eyes trembled. "Yes."

"How do you think he stops them?"

Hannah hesitated. "I don't know. He just does."

"Believing in God is an act of faith. For him to believe in us is an act of faith." The faintest squint. Nita could tell she was losing the girl. "He trusts that the good people can stop the bad ones. Now, if we're going to stop these bad people, I'm going to need your help. Do you understand?"

The girl's nerves remained.

Nita glanced back at the house, and Mr. Graber ducked out of view from the other side of the window. "Is there anything you know about your sister that your parents might not have known?"

Hannah peeked back into the window. A moment passed before she waved Nita's ear down to hear. "Colette had a boyfriend. She would sneak out and meet with him."

"How often was this going on? How many times do you think she snuck out to meet with him?"

"I-I don't know." Hannah began to quiver "I think the first time she did it was around the Fourth of July. I can't remember if it was before or after."

Nita patted her on the back. "Good. You're doing great. Did you know his name, Hannah? Did your sister ever mention it?"

"One night, when she thought me and my sisters were asleep, she started praying." Her eyes darted around some more. "She prayed that her and Travis could be together forever."

"Travis... Did you ever hear her say his last name?"

Hannah scratched her blonde hair. It was thin, with red blemishes across her scalp. "Travis... Travis... Fields! Travis Fields was his name."

CHAPTER 17

Blake lied to Nita and the rest of the law enforcement agencies. Lying to Nita was difficult—the rest, not so much. He rubbed the hard piece of plastic he found stamped in the mud near the creek. One side was smoothed and curved while the other was jagged and sharp. The connection came to him instantly, knowing it was the broken end of a paddle. It had a distinct logo of a largemouth bass jumping from the water and the letters *BPM* beneath it.

"You think it's the right decision not to tell anybody?" Little J asked.

"The authorities now know that there was a small boat involved. Probably a canoe, kayak, johnboat. They'll be doing the same thing we're doing." Blake ran his thumb along the jagged edges where the fracture took place.

"I hear ya. But, hell, it's only a chip off a paddle?"

Blake climbed into the truck, and Little J followed on the passenger side.

"You know who Rodney Alcala is?" Blake asked.

"I don't watch TV," Little J responded, as if that had anything to do with what Blake was asking.

"He's confirmed for killing eight women, but it's believed he could be responsible for the death of over a hundred... You might consider him Bundy-esque." Blake started the engine, and they drove away from Thorpe Ranch. "He was killing for over a decade in the sixties and seventies. You know what happened to him?"

Little J shook his head.

"He's still alive today. Been on death row since 1980. Three meals a day, getting to read, work out, and keep on living. I don't know about you, but that shit makes me sick to my stomach, brother. Anyone who kills a friend of ours—a brother, especially in the manner that he was— isn't gonna live that long. Cause I'm gonna take it from them."

The justification seemed to sit well with Little J. "I hear ya," he responded.

———

The sun was falling as Blake and Little J pulled into Bass Point Marina (BPM). Construction blanketed the parking lot, making it claustrophobic and appear inoperable. The concrete was poured, but stacks of wood toppled over one another.

A bell rang above the door to announce their entrance. Blake wanted to keep a low profile, so luckily, the ring didn't garner attention of any curious eyes. The marina office was empty. It wasn't a well-run establishment by any stretch of the imagination. A nomination from the better business awards didn't seem to be coming their way.

The canoes and kayaks were tilted in their rows along the walls both inside and outside. A large cardboard box held a collection of paddles of varying colors and sizes. Everything in the fishing aisle was in the wrong section and most of the prices were either on the ground or nonexistent. The total purchase price on the receipt was a surprise every time.

A light flickered in the back of the marina as Blake heard, "We're just about to close up shop, fellas."

An old, bald head bobbed up and down through the aisle before Larry Cooter rounded the corner. He was the owner and operator, and he matched the aesthetic of his store. His hands were filthy, with blackened fingernails and dark spots of God knew what across his face and neck.

Larry's eyes widened. "Well shit, M-Mr. Edwards. How the hell are ya?" he said, now fiddling around with his pockets and stammering over his words.

"I'm good, Larry. How are you?"

Blake sent a quick prayer up, hoping the shop owner wouldn't offer to shake hands with those bait and tackle shit smears across his palms.

But he did.

Larry extended his hand for a shake. "Like a pig in slop."

"No shit," Blake said. They shook hands, and Blake twisted his torso away to look at the marina, all in an attempt to conceal himself wiping his hand across his jeans. Little J took this as a golden opportunity to duck off to the side and survey the merchandise. Which was smart because he avoided the handshake. "Hey, I got a quick question for you. Do you happen to keep inventory? I found a piece of a paddle on my land and was wondering if you had anything go missing recently."

Larry took a half-step back. "I'm sorry. I make sure to tell my renters not to venture into any creeks beyond the lake for safety and trespassing purposes."

"No, no, no, it's fine, Larry." Blake waved his hands to settle him down. "I was just trying to return something for you. There's no issue here."

Larry had doubt all across his face. "See, the thing is, I haven't been taking much inventory. I'm gettin' my new shop built out back, and I'm gettin' all new equipment... so I ain't been valuing my stuff as much. I mean, you've seen it. It's shit, anyway. Ain't much money to be made off it."

"I understand," Blake lied. *That's shit business.* "You remember anyone that's rented in the past couple of days?"

"Ah, well, my boy's been running the store. He'd know, but he ain't here now."

"Could you maybe give him a call for me and ask?"

Larry squinted. "Everything okay here, Blake? This have anything to do with that vile shit that happened on your ranch?"

"I'm just trying to return something of value to whoever floated my creek."

The old man wasn't fully convinced, but Blake didn't need him to be, only a little bit. "Oh, Mr. Edwards, I sincerely apologize. If you want, I can have that entry point roped off—"

"No, no, it's fine. I promise, I'm not here to complain, Larry. Just looking to return some valuables like a good Oklahoman."

Larry gave a wide-eyed head nod and scooted off in the corner behind a horrible excuse for a check-out counter. "I'll call my boy."

Blake turned to Little J, who was scanning the other aisles. "My dad really did a number on the people around here."

"What you mean?" Little J asked.

"He's been dead a while now, and some folks around here still think I wield the same iron fist that he did."

"You don't?"

Blake's head shifted back. "Am I really that bad?" he asked sincerely. Little J scrunched his face and scratched his neck. He took too long. "J—"

"I'm just fuckin' with you, man." His best friend slapped him on the shoulder. "Nah, but I think power jacks up your sense of humor. You're a dud sometimes. Gotta loosen up a little, get laid. Is your belt too tight, or need new jeans, perhaps—"

"All right, shit, I get it," Blake said with the hint of a laugh contrasting Little J's uncontrollable snicker. "You act like I have prospects to even get laid."

"Yeah, women are kinda over the whole handsome, multimillionaire, cowboy, landowner thing."

Blake shook his head, feeling J's sarcasm seep deep beneath his skin. His only defense was to play along. "You think I'm handsome?"

"Shut the f—"

Larry returned and ended the verbal repartee there. "My boy said no one has done any renting the past couple of days."

"Is that normal for the summer?" Little J asked, "People not renting?"

"Eh, not during the week."

Blake exhaled. "Okay... thanks for your help, Larry. You need anything, just let me know."

Glee washed over old man Cooter's face. Blake did his best to erase any lingering fear his father might have instilled in the man.

———

"That was a dead end," Little J said as the door shut behind them.

"It probably wouldn't be if they ran their business properly," Blake said.

Blake made his way to the water's edge. From here, he could see the small opening across the water that led to the creek flowing through his land. It was a dark area where the trees hung low over the water. The grass along the bank in this area was either flattened or nonexistent. "This must be where a lot of renters launch from.

"No one would go down that creek voluntarily. Especially if it looks like that," Blake said. He pressed his boot into the soft bank of the lake. Water emerged from the Earth and began to rise around his boot. Before his foot was covered and got wet, he stepped away.

"A sick bastard like the one who killed Wyatt might," Little J, while skipping a flat stone across the lake.

"Ah, you may be right about that."

Around the other side of the marina store, a pile of canoes and kayaks were sloppily arranged together. Blake didn't have confidence in their abilities as sufficient floating devices. Then, his eye caught the glimpse of an object dangling from the roof of the store. It was a camera aimed at them. It was old and didn't appear to rotate from its spot. "Now... what are the odds that camera works?"

Little J looked at the camera, then back to Blake, and he scoffed.

CHAPTER 18

Nita struggled to look upon Colette. The chill in the room didn't help matters. A rigor shook her body and never ceased like aftershock. Charlie kept his hands on his hips. He had also seen far fewer dead bodies than her, and his anger showed through his restlessness. Colette maintained a tragic beauty even in the aftermath of such brutality.

"No prints on her at all," Dr Rowan said in a matter-of-fact way. "Evidence of vaginal and anal intercourse. Loss of blood seemed to be the cause of death."

"Any semen?" Agent Teller asked, as if it was just another day for OSBI.

"No, none. I didn't wash this charcoal off yet because I was waiting on you guys and the other investigators to get a closer look at it. The boyfriend still unaccounted for?" Dr. Rowan asked.

Charlie rubbed the back of his head. His palm made a scratching sound as it ran along his short fade against the grain. "Choteau PD went to his house, and he wasn't there. The parents say they haven't seen him since that night. They appeared to be worried sick and are completely shocked by his absence. Let alone the potential of the crime."

"Is he enrolled in school?" Nita asked.

"Yes, he's going into his senior year. His reputation and grades are average. Nothing negative stood out. He's an agriculture kid, so it seems that's where his focus lies. We got a warrant to search the house and the rest of their small farm—nothing out of the ordinary, other than pornography on one of his old phones."

"That's not out of the ordinary?" Nita asked.

"Not for a teenage boy," Charlie snorted.

"Oh yeah, Charlie?"

"Well, it's easy with the internet, Nita."

"Back in the day, you had to work for a porno mag," Agent Teller said.

"Gentlemen," the coroner interrupted. "I forgot to mention that we found meth in her system."

"Meth?" said Teller.

"Correct, meth and LSD. The same combo was in Wyatt Leonard's system."

That tipped Nita's prior knowledge of the two elderly women, Sandra Oly and Mary Barlow, who had the same concoction in their system when they were killed.

"Still, we have a God-fearing Amish girl who had no prior instances of delinquency, beloved in her community, apple of her parents' eye... definitely not the meth type," Teller said, stroking his goatee.

"The boyfriend could tell us a lot," Charlie reiterated.

"Regardless," Dr. Rowan continued, "Whoever did this used a glove. I'm unsure of any significance or reasoning for it. I did some web searches and couldn't find anything significant."

Wandering eyes told Nita no one else in the room had such knowledge.

Her palm rested on the cold slab elevating this once beautiful and innocent girl. The urge to hold her hand wouldn't escape her, but she refrained.

"Well, I always have a smoke after, so I'm not going to stop today," Rowan said. "Although, given the circumstances, I might have a few. I'll be outside if any of y'all need me."

Colette's body had a bluish hue that broke Nita's heart. A girl so innocent and bright didn't deserve to have her glow taken away. Nita vowed to continue the search until justice could be found.

As if a concussion grenade rolled into the morgue, a flash occurred. The migraine began subtle and aggressively skyrocketed to an unbearable thumping in her forehead as if a parasite was fighting to get out.

Undead life found Colette once more as she screamed. Agonizing and hellish screams. The charcoal turned into shackles that held her in place. They were thick, rusty chains confining her to the slab. Shadows emerged beneath her and started consuming her body. Tears ran down her face as she cried out to God for help. The metal clamp around her neck, choked her, turning her face purple, and her eyes were bloodshot.

Nita let go. She had to. The air in her lungs had been yanked out of her. Her forearms on the slab held her upright as her legs went numb.

Charlie ran to her side. "Nita! Nita, are you all right?"

She leaned on him to stabilize herself.

Unsettled, Nita went to the sink, grabbed one of the rags on the counter, and ran it under the water. With a shaky voice, Nita said, "We have to clean... the charcoal."

In a feverish fit, she scrubbed Colette's wrist so hard that she feared it might peel away after the skin went purple. Charlie and Teller stood idly by—until Charlie followed in her footsteps and began washing Colette's opposite wrist.

Then, Agent Teller made his way around the slab, still appearing skeptical. He moderated them for a while, passing his judgment. Nita focused on the task at hand. The charcoal smeared across her forearms, and they turned red from the rabid scrubbing. She went for a dry towel to wipe away what remained, but it was already waiting for her. Agent Teller retrieved them and made his way behind Nita to wash Colette's ankles.

They put her faith in whatever phenomenon remained left unseen on their end. For that, she was grateful, but her attention now was on making sure Colette could cross over into the afterlife that awaited her.

CHAPTER 19

"You think it's the boyfriend?" Little J asked with one hand on the steering wheel and the other on his coffee.

"Who the hell knows? Doesn't look good for him, though. He's a big kid, could match the boot print. And those two were scootin' out in that canoe together," Blake replied, eyes on the screen. The quality of the security footage from Bass Point Marina was horrendous. It was black and white, grainy, and out of focus. However, knowing the two in the video was the Amish girl and her boyfriend was unmistakable. The time matched, the dress matched, and their canoe started in the direction of Blake's land. Many questions remained, huge ones at that: *Who did this? How was Wyatt even involved? Where's the boyfriend? Where's the canoe?*

As a Marine, Blake was prepared to go to any depth imaginable to find answers and adapt to any scenario that was presented itself. Nobody operated alone. He had his brothers to watch his back, but they were down one. All of them would have to deal with the weight of losing their brother under their watch. They would share this collective guilt, but none more than Blake. He was the one who brought them all to Oklahoma to work on a ranch. His motives were pure by giving them an opportunity to make a good living doing far less than any other ranch of this size. Never in his wildest dreams did he think it would be the ruin of them.

Perhaps that's what this place is to be for all of us. Perhaps that's what I deserve. Perhaps it's what my bloodline deserves.

They were only on the highway for a couple of minutes until they pulled off towards home. Blake was tired, and by the sight of Little J's head bobbing forward and jolting back up, so was he. Little J at least had the advantage of caffeine.

———

The call of prayer sounded. Bullets fired through the wall in the upstairs room where his platoon held firm. Dust irritated his eyes coming off the aftermath of the oncoming fire.

Blake stepped back from the window, tripping over a crack in the foundation. The trip saved his life as another round crashed through the wall where his head would have been. As he scooted back, the bullets followed him. Debris in the form of clay and wood scattered overhead as dust filled the room in the heart of Ramadi.

Wyatt poked his M16A4 out another window that had yet to receive fire. From there, he popped off shot after shot, reducing the enemy fire with each trigger squeeze.

Blake shot up, ready to assist. Another bullet whistled into the room. Warm liquid smeared his vision. He wiped it away with his sleeve and saw Wyatt's lifeless form on the floor with a quarter of his head shot off. Bone chips found their way under Blake's shirt, irritating his flesh. He froze.

Machine fire from the opposite window riddled Floyd. He was pushed off balance and fell through the open window. His body slammed on the dirt road outside, and the insurgents continued to fire on his body to make sure the filthy American stayed the way they preferred: dead.

Cody took a bullet in the collarbone that dropped him to one knee, but he kept firing out the window. Little J burst through the room to assist in the fight. His smile faded when atop the adjacent building, a pair of RPGs flew towards them.

· · ·

Blake snapped awake. Both of his fists were clenched as he exhaled a battle cry.

Little J remained unfazed, as if he had seen or experienced the same thing many times before. "How often those happening?" he asked, casually sipping his coffee, and continuing to drive.

Blake didn't respond. The answer was too painful for him to admit. He fought against the notion of post-traumatic stress disorder. He believed to be above those labels. A Marine could adapt to these feelings and emotions embedded into the soul and overcome them, but that had yet to manifest. His fight ended years ago. Things were good, but the dreams and flashes of war persisted.

"I'm glad I'm not the only one," Little J said, whether his words were honest or not. "Is it the same dream goin' on this long?"

Blake took a moment to gather himself. "The details change, but the location stays the same."

"Ramadi?"

"Ramadi."

"Well, brother, if it makes you feel any better, don't forget we owned that bitch."

It was the most jarhead response Blake had heard in a while, but it was comforting. He agreed. The response of the American military during the events of that battle were awe-inspiring. Nearly every branch had been there to lean on one another for support and accomplish the mission.

"So, you wanna tell the guys to go out looking for the boyfriend?" Little J asked during Blake's patriotic reminiscence.

"Nah, best let them sleep. We'll pick it up tomorrow. Besides, we still got a ranch to run."

"I hear ya."

Blake turned up the music Little J had playing through his phone. Something modern that pissed Blake off to no end. "Changin' that shit," he said.

"Why? It's country."

"Sure as shit ain't," Blake said while pounding the Next button over and over until something of merit came over the speakers. "Give me some Stapleton or Combs if it's gonna be modern. Rest of 'em suck ass."

"Here we go," Little J said, as if he'd heard this rant hundreds of times.

"Bunch of sparkly jean-wearing, perfume scented boys, panderin' to people who actually work in the elements."

"What, you gotta work on a ranch to be a country star?"

Blake's energy was coming back to him as he was getting worked up, and Little J seemed to notice. His best friends shit-eating grin remained while he sipped his drink. "I'm not saying that. I'm just saying that there's a genuine nature to art that must be met."

"Genuine nature? Shit, look at you. You've been working on your master's with all that money and free time?"

"I don't know what's more insulting, you thinking I'm a dumb cowboy-Marine like you or insinuating I don't work."

They both shared a laugh. Giving each other a hard time was the charm of their relationship, and it had been that way for many years. Blake recognized early on he needed people like Little J to keep him in check. He'd been wealthy his whole life, and most people came into his life wanting it.

"All I'm saying is," Blake continued, "you can tell when an artist is being real or not. When they are real, that breeds originality, cause it's their own. When it's not real or original, it'll sound a lot like someone else."

Little J contemplated. He was probably working on some type of devil's advocate angle, and Blake was ready. "People like what they like, man. I mean, there's a reason it's popular."

Blake placed his hat on his knee. The Oklahoma he knew all too well whipped by his window at a rapid pace. "Sure, it's popular now. But as time passes, it'll be so derivative of every other song hitting the country quotas that the waters will be too dirty of all the same shit, no one will be able to tell who's who or what's what."

"Quotas?"

"You know, how every contemporary song talks about a backroad, a pickup truck, a light beer, blue jeans, and the goddamn rodeo they never attended."

Little J nodded. "I can't argue that one."

"One point for me then."

"However–"

"Jesus Christ."

"We are currently on a backroad, in a pickup, wearing jeans, on our way to get beers."

"Shit... point for you then."

Little J eventually stopped on a track that they could both agree on. They looked at one another, knowing it was Wyatt's favorite song. He would play it over the speakers at the house all the time when they'd all stay up drinking— "Loud and Heavy" by Cody Jinks.

———

The hushpuppies the size of baseballs were perfectly breaded, fried, and seasoned. The crunch of the initial bite was satisfying alone. The flavor of the moist interior was a bonus. A lot of eyes attempting to be concealed looked Blake's way. The military taught him situational awareness, but he didn't have to serve almost half his life to recognize the wandering eyes in the local catfish spot. Their intent was always a mystery.

Was it fear, admiration, or a sense of violence knowing what had taken place on my land in regard to the recent crimes or the ones of the past allegedly involving my family?

"Nita seemed good," Little J said with a mouth full of catfish.

"Yeah, she's strong. Tougher than most men I know."

"Seems that way. Hell of a couple months she's had. Jackson dies, she's gotta look after his kid, gets up close and personal with a fuckin' psycho in a mask. She needs a break, man. Been dealt a shit hand."

"She's been fighting uphill her whole life." Blake could tell Little J dissected his words. "We'll do our part to lighten the load."

Blake sipped on some of the sweetest of sweet tea in the county. A part of him couldn't help but ponder how Nita dealt with her trauma. She appeared unfazed by the world and its vendetta against her, but that couldn't be true. Part of him wondered if he just wasn't as strong.

The waitress, Annabelle Horton, whom Blake and Little J went to high school with, filled his glass.

"Annie, go ahead and put everyone on my bill until nine." Blake said.

"Sure thing, Blake."

"Thank you."

He'd paid for all the restaurant patrons several times before, so it wasn't new to Annie. With the recent dark deeds, he figured the gesture would be good karma.

Another coin in the karma jar. A jar his father, grandfather, and so on, never filled. He had no steadfast belief in the idea of karma, but he didn't deny its existence. Each penny, each gift, each good deed was a stone of rebellion cast against his father, his memory, and the Edwards' history of unethical activity.

The sun blasted through the front door as it opened, blinding everyone dining. A group of male natives strolled through, looking to enjoy the finest catfish along with the cowboys. It was a group of Cherokee Marshals, including Director Lowwater. As they were escorted to their seats, Blake and Charlie made eye contact. The Cherokee rival's stoic demeanor and scowl was unmatched, even for a bearded Marine. He never had anything against Charlie. In fact, Blake always liked him, but he couldn't deny that Charlie's hatred towards him and his family was justified. If things went down as the rumors told it, Blake's family was on the wrong side of history. He was certain that the last thing Charlie wanted after being on Blake's property all day was to dine near him.

"That ain't going anywhere, is it?" Little J said, adding more sugar to his tea and stirring it around with his straw.

Blake sighed. "Guess not."

A long and lanky mass blocked the view of the restaurant to Blake's right—a man in a tailored suit beyond formal for Katfish Kitchen. His hair was so black from coloring that his scalp had leftover residue. It looked more like he used spray paint to keep his youth rather than the proper channels.

"Mr. Edwards," the man said. "It's a pleasure to finally meet you.

You're a hard man to track down. I've been trying to reach you via call and email. My name is Alexander Bloom."

Bloom extended his hand, which Blake did not oblige to shake. Bloom's extended hand returned to his side awkwardly. "I represent a client that is interested in buying a piece of your land or all of it if the price is right. I'm aware your father passed away this past year, and the word is that you don't share the same attachment for the land or the ranching business as he did."

"I don't answer calls from numbers I don't recognize," Blake said.

"I see. However, I find that could be difficult when interested parties are inquiring about potential business ventures for a well-established man such as yourself."

"I'm doing all right. I'm involved in as many business ventures as I want to be at the moment. I'm not interested in new ones. You could check back later if you'd like, but you might not like the answer then either." The man in the suit remained, clearly not grasping the sarcasm, or perhaps ignoring it all entirely.

"Why not free yourself up a bit and retire early? Hell, with the money we're talking, you most definitely could. The land has little value anyway. We all know the real valuable land is being managed by your sister up north in the Dakotas."

Little J laughed and continued eating. He'd heard this conversation near a hundred times before. Blake glared at the man from under his cowboy hat and then to Little J. He left the lawyer on deaf ears and crunched down on a hush puppy.

"Mr. Edwards, I can—"

"I can retire whenever the hell I want," Blake said plainly. "Who's your client?"

"They would like to remain confidential at this time."

"Is that an option? If so, so would I." Blake's glare forced Alexander to take a half-step back.

But the lawyer remained. "Mr. Edwards—"

"I've told you no. I don't know where you're from, but you failed to have the awareness that I am having dinner with my best friend. You're a stranger. You don't get to interrupt. I suggest you have a seat and enjoy your free meal."

Not long after, Annie returned with a to-go to load up on hushpuppies. Mr. Bloom sat in the opposite corner, observing Blake the whole way.

However, the Cherokee eyes that stared him down a few tables over from Charlie Soap leered much harsher. He didn't tip his cap or offer a wink. A free meal wasn't going to make up for the past.

CHAPTER 20

Teller had one hand on the wheel and the other hanging out the window with cigarette smoke trailing behind them through Choteau. "Spent my childhood in Tahlequah, but I moved to Coweta in high school to follow my AAU coach who got hired on as their head coach," Charlie said.

Teller had collaborated with the Cherokee Marshals on a handful of occasions. Like most law enforcement divisions, their reputation differed from person to person. Some believed they were essential, and a good step in the right direction for tribal sovereignty. Others would say they were as worthless as any other law enforcement agency. Perhaps there was truth in both stances, but Teller didn't care. After a long career working with law enforcement on the local, state, and federal level, he'd seen every type of officer and/or agent. In a way to simplify his life after a pair of failed marriages, he decided discipline and efficiency was the key to success on the job. Those that didn't have that, he did his best to avoid. Through his veteran, investigative lens, Nita and Charlie fit his description as efficient workers, and ideal for cross-deputization.

Teller asked a follow-up since Nita was currently tracking down a CI: "So, the thing that happened in the morgue, you seemed to have an indication about what was taking place. What was that?"

Charlie hesitated. "I don't think it's my place to speak on it. If she trusts you enough, she'll let you know. Fair warning, she's not very trusting. But, for the record, she's not fucking crazy. Trust me. If I'm being honest, I think she might be the only one who sees the world clearly."

He nodded, observing Marshal Soap the entire way as he continued to drive. He couldn't turn off his analytical mind. Charlie's deep admiration for her gave him the impression that he still had feelings for Nita so many years later. If what he said was true about her, Teller could see why that was the case.

———

Travis Fields played basketball for Choteau High School. With summer coming to a close, Charlie ushered Teller and a few other federal agents to the gymnasium, where Travis should be practicing if he was accounted for.

"Superintendent said they've been having off-season workouts. That normal?" Teller asked with an uneducated knowledge of high school sports. Charlie cocked his head a little. "I was a military brat. I couldn't play sports 'cause we moved around too much."

"I'm not saying anything. No judgment here," Charlie lied. "Yes, summer workouts are normal for high school and junior high."

"Choteau known for their basketball?"

"It's high school ball. One year they're contenders, the next, they're not."

———

The group of law enforcement officers turned the heads of the handful of high schoolers and the pair of coaches wearing plain gray shirts with wildcat logos.

The bald coach twirled his whistle upon his cautious approach towards law enforcement. "Y'all enforcing those OSSAA rules seriously? Now?"

Charlie was sure that comment went right over Teller's head, as it was against the rules to conduct official practice in the summertime. Charlie scanned the boys. At the moment, none stood out. They all shared the same bewildered face, with a hint of fear in all of them.

"Coach..." Teller probed.

"Coach Taylor."

"We're going to talk to your team," Teller continued.

"This about the girl?" Coach Taylor asked.

"It is."

A sense of recognition washed over the longtime coach's face. His finger came up and pointed at Charlie, not in a rude way, simply his body reacting to the gears turning in his head. "Coweta? '04? Soap?"

"Yes, sir," Charlie said. "Good memory."

"Well, it's hard to forget the Indian that dropped forty-three points on our ass."

Charlie smiled, attempting to decipher the subtle racism, but he let it slide. He had clocked the young man he wanted to talk to since they walked into the gym. An everyday white kid with a horrendous haircut. Acne like chicken pox assaulted his forehead, and he looked like a Kobra Kai captain from *Karate Kid*. The only thing lacking was the confidence. The boy's eyes trembled under Charlie's gaze. Keeping up the intimidation could prove useful, so the marshal kept his stare fixed on him.

"Is it legal to talk with my boys here? Don't y'all need a warrant for that sort of thing?" he asked, twirling his whistle faster.

"We're just asking questions, sir."

"It won't be long. I can assure you of that, Coach," Charlie said.

"Very well."

Coach Taylor turned around and addressed the team, informing them of what was going on. The kids weren't idiots. Their eyes didn't widen or faces pale upon hearing the information. A couple of boys carried on a conversation while leaning against the wall and sitting atop basketballs. The kid Charlie was after tried to avoid eye contact, but he knew Charlie was coming to him.

He approached slowly. He let the boy linger on his thoughts as he nervously spun the ball in his hand.

Charlie deepened his voice for effect. "You seem like you might have something you'd like to get off your chest, son."

"Nah, I don't," he said.

"Listen, we can do this here, or you can come down to a place where we'll stick you in a room for a few hours—because it's obvious you know something. What's your name?"

"Will," he admitted, surrendering to the questions.

"Okay, Will. Were you friends with Travis Fields?"

The kid took a towel a wiped the sweat from his forehead. "I mean, yeah. Not like best friends or anything, but yeah."

"When was the last time you talked to him?"

"Not long ago. I... I think before everything happened?"

"Before the murders, you mean? Is that what you're referring to, Will?"

"Yes, sir."

Teller and a few of the other agents and officers questioned the rest of the boys. Coach Taylor stood idle but rocked back in forth in a nervous manner.

"All right," Charlie said, rubbing the back of his head that he feared would go bald if kept that habbit. "Let me ask you this, do you think Travis would be capable of doing anything like that to the girl or someone else?"

"No, sir. Not at all." There was conviction in the kid's voice that made Charlie believe him. It was a pleasant sentiment, but it didn't bring any more answers.

"You have any idea where he may be staying?"

"No, sir."

Charlie wanted to shake his head but resisted the urge. "Well, thank you for your time. I'm gonna see what else your coach may know." He turned, finally taking in the smell and atmosphere of the gym. It'd been a while since Charlie was in a gym. Last time he played was a couple years ago for the Cherokee National Holiday 3-on-3 tournament.

"Wait," Will said from behind him. Charlie faced him, and regret washed over the pale baller's face. "Travis told me about Colette."

And he stopped there.

"Yes... and?" the young man side-eyed his teammates and coaches that weren't paying them any mind.

Will lowered his voice. "There was some shack or barn or something on someone's land he was gonna take her to after church."

"Why's that?"

He fumbled over his words, as if he'd said too much. "I-I believe they were going there to..."

"Have sex?" Charlie finished.

Will nodded.

A long, drawn-out exhale escaped through Charlie's nostrils. "Was it going to be their first time?" Charlie asked Will.

"Sir?"

"Were they both virgins, Will?"

Will wiggled in his seated position. His nervous ticks grew with each passing second as he began rubbing his arm. "I believe so, sir. Guys around here tend to brag about which girls they'd been with. Travis never did. Even to me."

"They don't just do that around here, Will. Guys do that everywhere. Believe me." Charlie cleared his throat and flipped to the next page in his notebook. "You said something about all this going down after church. What church was this? Did she attend with him or vice-versa?"

"Uhm, well, sir... once upon a time he went to my church, Choteau Church of Christ. But he ain't gone with me or been there at all in months, and he wasn't there that night, or at least I didn't see him. I don't think he went to her church either."

"Why do you say that?"

"Well, she's Amish, so I don't think they attend a church. They do a service in their house or barn or some shit. Oh, pardon my language, sir."

Charlie nodded, assuring the kid all was well.

"From what he told me," Will said. "Colette's parents didn't know anything about him because they wouldn't have wanted her dating him."

"So him attending a church service at her house would be unlikely."

Will nodded.

Charlie finished jotting down a few notes in his pocket-sized notebook. "I appreciate you talking with me, Will. Good luck this year with school and ball."

Will rose to his feet and started away. "Oh, I won't see the court this year. Maybe not even smell it."

Charlie couldn't help but laugh and shake his head.

They spent another half hour or so questioning all the other boys on the team, seeing if they could garner any more useful information. Charlie even went around to each of them, whether FBI was interviewing them, OSBI, or Choteau detectives, about the church. All had no idea of what church it could've been or its location.

Teller eventually found his way back to Charlie. "Both of these kids are from here, and yet this crime happens forty miles away in another town."

"Do we follow up on the church lead?" Charlie asked. "There's no evidence they even attended church that night either way."

Teller scratched his bare chin. "How many churches are there, you think, in this town, in Tahlequah, and in between?"

"Well, this is the Bible Belt, so... thousands." It was a slight exaggeration, to be sure, but one that spoke a semblance of truth.

CHAPTER 21

"This is our vision. An endless barrage of undeniable outreach. Sons and daughters, bear witness now."

A few amens sounded all around. Ezell Sunderland owned the pulpit like he had stood there many years, dispersing his doctrine as wisdom of the greater good for a better world.

"O, how I see the sea of nonbelievers. They still have not acknowledged our call, our message, our ultimatum for this world."

Beneath the tin roof, surrounded by cinderblock walls, his flock hung on his every word, as if he was the direct line to God.

"This Temple—our vision—will not be denied."

Ezell scanned the room. His head moved like a preying snake. There was not one person amongst the roughly hundred strong whose gaze he did not meet. "Do we have any new visionaries this evening?" he asked, knowing the answer before posing the question.

The congregation looked around. They wouldn't be labeled as a particularly diverse group of people. There wasn't a college degree amongst them, let alone a GED. Ezell believed in words without a shadow of a doubt. He knew his teachings to be true. But what he knew more was the ability to gather lost, directionless, wandering individuals to claim as his.

Through the crowd of shaky individuals, he spotted a younger man, maybe early thirties. He wore a yellowed button-up that was wrinkled and had sweat stains around the collar that failed to conceal a neck tattoo. Amongst the faces of the crowd, this man's head seemed fuzzy or out of focus. It was the same way he saw all his followers at one point in time. This moment was crucial. It was an opportunity to right a wrong. To bring a vagabond into his home. To add clarity to the unfocused addition to his flock.

Ezell approached him, as his hand had yet to raise. "What's your name, young man?"

"I ain't so young anymore."

"Oh, yes, you are. You could be new today. Brand new. That would make you a fresh-faced, young visionary."

The man didn't appear convinced.

Ezell repeated his question.

"Eric Honeycutt."

"And why are you here, my son?"

Eric's eyes darted down. He scratched his neck and witnessed the people staring back at him in silence.

"They were once you," Ezell said, resting his hands on Eric's shoulders. "Lost lambs looking for their flock." He held out his hands. "Sons and daughters, have you found your flock?"

In unison, the flock spoke: "Hail, eyes of the Temple."

Ezell couldn't help but smile. "Let me see your hands," he instructed Eric.

As Eric reluctantly offered his trembling hands that were riddled with needle marks, Sunderland grasped them, and a surge of energy went through his body that was equivalent to an electric shock. Ezell hid the sensation well.

He closed his eyes for a moment. The room was as silent as the grave when he stood. The sensation washed over him, and then he started in with purpose. "You are not worthless."

"Wha—"

"You don't have to change for anyone. If there was any conflict in your soul that says you must change, don't listen to it. I say, come as you are. Indulge in who you are and your desires. Look around you, my son.

These people don't want you to become something you're not. Do you, visionaries?"

"No, Father," they all said as one.

"We are what God made us. He looks upon us with gladness if we live for him no matter what... should we believe, that is. Let's not forget that, flock. How often does the world encourage your commitment to the Lord? Nearly every second of every day. The devil, or whatever dark dealings of the earth have cleverly disguised themselves. Let me assure all of us here that the devil has worked its way into all of us. He takes the form of corporation. He takes the form of politicians. He takes the form of the church. All of these organizations shove their agendas down your throat, put machines in your hand to distract you and look upon one another to blame and persecute! All the while you're trespassing against your neighbor, they continue their circle of unchecked debauchery, pedophilia, and excess. They—the devil wants to strip you of all your power, using tragedy to propel their motives. Each dead schoolboy and girl is simply a pawn for them to set up a greater move that pushes them closer to victory."

Amongst his flock, in the middle of the aisle, he leaned back against the pew. All the eyes in front of him and behind him were upon him. He loved it. "The government wants to steal your guns. Big businesses and even the church want your money, no matter the cost. We cannot succumb to their desires. We will push back against these wicked things! Amen!"

"Amen! Hail!" said the flock.

He relaxed. His enthusiasm fell away for now. "We will fight back. We will do what we must to protect what is ours. Our freedom, our faith, our kinship."

Ezell leaned over the pew where a pair of bald gentlemen sat staring up at him. They were more than happy to move to make way for their leader's calling. They parted like they were the Red Sea, and Ezell was Moses.

"It's failure and lack of opportunity that defines your life, doesn't it?" he asked.

Eric's gaze darted about like someone could save him from the spotlight. "I-I don't know."

"Are you where you want to be?"

"N-No."

"Your life has been a boulevard of endless red lights, hasn't it? You can't do this because authorities or higher-ups say you can't." Then, he addressed everyone. "My life will not be defined by the ones locking the shackles to my feet. We were given this world by God, yet man made it their own. I ask you, my children, who destroyed the world? Satan?"

Ezell laughed as if posing that as the possible answer to the question was insulting. "Well, I have news for you all. Satan has been more active in our world than even God." He paused for a long time, closed his eyes, and held out his arms. "People have failed to realize that the real devil amongst us is mankind itself. Man committed genocide. Man waged war. Man created the atomic bomb. Man created the internet, the phone—not to bring us together, but to divide. They are merely conduits to destroy us without a trigger. Sons and daughters, our freedoms will not be dictated by the evil creations of the world. Our duty is to cast aside these things, destroy them if we must, but never, absolutely *never* give in to them."

A round of applause followed. Even Eric clapped.

Ezell took notice. Mr. Honeycutt's form was still hazy but beginning to focus. He turned his attention back to the individual. Honeycutt jolted back for a moment when Ezell reached for his neck, but stopped when he opened his palm, pinched the top button that was clamping Eric's collar to his neck, and released it. He pushed the lost man's collar, revealing an encircled, capital A—the common symbol for anarchism.

His commanding voice lowered to a hush. "You're in the right place, my son. Today, you wander no longer. You are fatherless no longer."

"How did you kn—"

"Acceptance has found you this day. Do not turn away from it. The freedoms of this world is yours for the taking, and this family you now have amongst us is here to lead you through it all."

Eric Honeycutt began to cry.

"Flock, tend to your brother."

With that, the pews emptied out, and the congregation surrounded

Eric, huddling around him like an experienced football team of a hundred players on the field.

Ezell gazed upon his work, and a sense of euphoria came over him, like an injection of heroin. His eyes shifted to Amos, who stood in the corner of the room that led back to the office. His right-hand man, who was responsible for the construction of this practical place of worship, shook his head with eyes down, and his heel tapping on the newly laid floors.

Ezell went to him. "Why the concern?" he asked.

Amos' head nodded backwards, ushering them both to speak more privately. A corridor leading into Ezell's office had a communion table yet to be set up. Beyond that, a pair of waiting chairs sat outside the office door. They both took a seat in the rotating leather. Ezell never altered his demeanor. He was always unflinching. The way of his life was set.

"Edwards is still fighting us hard on selling. He's stubborn like his old man, and the Edwards name is too connected with the land for Blake to be the one to give it up. We're going to have to look elsewhere."

He interlocked his fingers, rested them on his sternum, and leaned back in his chair, "Convince him."

"But I just—"

"I heard what you said. I don't care. Everyone in this world has a price. Make him realize that there is no value to him holding the land. Eventually, someone down the line of succession will piss it all away. Make him realize."

His right-hand man nodded. It was Amos' job to interpret that in whatever manner he saw fit. However, that manner had to align with whatever Ezell desired, or else. Ezell knew that was a lot to put on somebody, but he knew Amos could handle it. He was the soldier amongst them.

CHAPTER 22

Meet the Teacher Day arrived out of the blue with poor timing during such a high-profile case. Aiden walked beside Nita as she observed his reaction to the new school out of her peripherals. For a split second she reached out to hold his hand, but he pulled it away as he played with the beat-up lockers. His tiny fingers spun the lock clockwise over and over.

"Aiden. This way," she said.

He followed. The boy's eyes took in everything: every sign of encouragement, every clock on the wall, the intercom system, and the small rectangular windows on the classroom doors, attempting to get a snippet of intel lurking on the other side. He stopped when he stumbled upon the evacuation plans in case of a fire or more commonly around here, a tornado. It would be considered a dull year without at least one tornado touching down in the middle of the day. A laminated piece of green construction paper listed all the room numbers, teachers, and all the exits or shelter locations.

Parents and students walked the narrow hallway back and forth while Aiden stood stagnant in the middle, his gaze fixed on the evacuation plans. Nita guided him, lightly pushing his back forward and out of the way of oncoming traffic. Her hand fell away, and so did his fascination with the map on the wall.

"In case of a fire, exit three, north side of the building. In case of a tornado, into the boy's bathroom," he said.

"Now you know. Let's go meet Ms. Kaitlyn."

His self-contained classroom was tucked away behind a pair of water fountains that had been there for decades. They looked to be the same ones Nita drank from when she attended this school in fourth grade. With the emergence of rust around the spout, she began to believe that was true.

Nita opened the door for Aiden, and he walked into the classroom. The room was bright, like stepping into a safer and alternative space that contrasted with the rest of the school. Nita had a good feeling. Painted handprints of varying sizes and colors bordered the single window. The ABCs and a number line ran along the top of the wall just under the ceiling. In the far corner, there was a reading nook with small furniture resting atop a shag carpet.

A chair creaked in the opposite corner. A young woman rose. She didn't look native, more European, but in Oklahoma, it was hard to tell sometimes. "Well, hello! Who do we have here?" she said, approaching Aiden first, giving him top priority as she should. "Let me guess... you're Aiden Philips?"

"Yes."

She didn't appear to be far removed from school. "I'm Ms. Kaitlyn. I'm going to be your teacher this year. It's very nice to meet you!"

Her enthusiasm was appreciated and appropriate for the job she had. Her reputation was overwhelmingly positive. Her smile never left her face, even with Aiden's blank gaze staring back at her.

"What do you like to do, Aiden?"

He shrugged his shoulders, and his gaze went to the floor. "I don't know."

"Are you sure? You just like to sit around and do nothing? That doesn't sound like too much fun."

"He likes maps," Nita said.

Rightfully so, Kaitlyn made eye contact with Nita for the first time. "Is that right?" she asked Aiden while kneeling in front of him. "And what maps do you like?"

"All."

"That's really cool! Would you like to draw a map of the school for me in class? I get lost here all the time, and I could use a map to help me find my way." It was a valiant attempt at motivation.

"Yes." Aiden's subdued enthusiasm made its presence known. Nita could sense his eagerness towards the potential project. "It will probably look like the Mission Intermediate Grade Center Evacuation Plans posted on the walls of every classroom and at the front of the building. If you are getting lost, those can help you until mine is done."

She had broken through his thick, defensive shell in record time—a shell Nita had yet to fully penetrate. Every time she looked at Aiden, she loved him. However, that love seemed to only go so far. She saw all of Jackson in him, with the dusting of another. That other was not her.

"He saw those on the way in," Nita said. "He was *transfixed*, I guess is the word."

"I would say so." Kaitlyn placed her hand on Aiden's back. "Would you like to go play in the nook for a little bit, or go look around? I think there are several books with maps in them—the big books."

Aiden didn't reply but went regardless.

"Aiden," Kaitlyn stopped him. "Don't leave me hanging. We have to answer others when they ask questions."

He caught on. "Yes."

Kaitlyn approached Nita and introduced herself once again. "Are you Mom?" she asked.

"No," Nita said, but attempted to correct herself and scratched her brow. "Well, stepmom."

"I see. That makes sense as your last name for his IEP is different from his enrollment form. Would you like me to have any of that changed for you one way or the other?"

"Philips is still correct, but I've been going by Ross around here for thirty-plus years, so it's probably easier that way."

Kaitlyn jotted a quick note. "I see... Well, I can promise that Aiden is going to have a great year in here. As of now, he's only got four other classmates and two paraprofessionals with him, so he will get plenty of attention."

"Yeah..." Nita nodded, rubbed the back of her neck and stretched her back, "I've heard good things."

"Good. Good."

There was a pause between them. Aiden continued to metaphorically dip his toe in the water around the nook. He hovered over a beanbag chair, lacking the commitment to plop down.

"Do you have any questions for me, or concerns?" Kaitlyn asked. "I read his file, so I'm aware of what's happened with his father, and I wanted to offer my deepest condolences for your—"

"No, I don't have any questions or concerns." Nita surveyed the room once again. "Thank you though. This seems like a great place for him."

"I promise it will be."

———

More parents arrived down the hallway as the general education students took their turn meeting teachers for the year. They piled out of the gymnasium upon the conclusion of a school-wide address regarding the recent crimes.

As Nita followed Aiden out of the self-contained room, a cowboy hat prevailed through the crowd farther down the hallway. Blake Edwards approached while holding his daughter Lyla's hand. His ex-wife Tara walked on the opposite side. The two of them kept it cordial after the divorce, which seemed mature for the sake of their daughter. When they were married, any time Nita ran into Tara around town, the blonde bombshell would act as if Nita didn't exist or avert her gaze. But now that the separation papers had been filed, Tara was the first to greet her.

"Hello, Nita," Tara said reaching out with arms wide up and hugged her with a firm embrace that Nita didn't know how to interpret or respond. She patted Tara on the back with a single palm, as her arms were pinned down from the squeeze. "How have you been? I'm sure you're exhausted."

Nita pressed against her hips to gain separation, and nodded.

"How's the case going?" Blake asked.

Tara smacked him on the chest. Old habits die hard. "Blake, I doubt she wants to talk about that, especially here."

"The case is going... but I have no information to offer you at this time, Mr. Edwards," Nita said in as cordial a tone she could manage.

A shit-eating grin formed on Tara's face. "Yeah, cowboy."

Blake smiled and shook his head, as cool as a rich cowboy could be.

"Hi, Aiden," Layla said. She was a sweet, blonde girl. She sported pigtails, kindness, and confidence.

Nita nudged Aiden for a reply.

"Hi," he said.

"Are you excited for school this year?" Lyla asked.

Neither Blake nor Tara were known for being sweet people. Polite, maybe. Well-mannered, perhaps, but never sweet. Not like their daughter.

"Yeah."

"I won't get to see you in any of my classes, but I'll come see you at the swings during recess," she said with her dress swaying.

Aiden's love for the playground swings trailed closely behind his love of maps. He'd been known to swing for the entire duration of recess since Pre-K. "You'll swing next to me?"

"Well, yeah."

Aiden's repeated nods said that he liked the prospect of that.

The sound of sexual noises and high-pitched moaning sounded. Every head of every parent turned as two boys walking by themselves with no parents around them laughed with no repentance. One wore a ball cap and mullet poking out in the back, believing he was the king of this place. Nita hated that of all the things to die off in the 80s, only to return was the damn mullet. The other kid was skinny with reader glasses. He was merely a follower of the mullet's allure.

"Whose damn kid is that?" Tara asked with a sour expression.

"I'm guessin' it's either Clint Grady or Bill Bacone's kid. I saw the two of them cuttin' up and sharing a cig in the parking lot." Blake covered Lyla's ears. "All of them need their asses kicked."

The boys walked further down the hall, and the parents continued whispering amongst themselves, very much carrying on a similar conversation to the one the three of them were having.

CHAPTER 23

Blake had a love-hate relationship with events like this. Even something as casual and insignificant as Meet the Teacher Day brought plenty of undesirable people with undesirable conversations his way. The enjoyment came from spending time with his daughter and watching her grow into a beautiful and kind girl while running into people he went to high school with to reminisce about the old days. Ronald Wayne was the first guy he saw walking into the building with his son who was in Lyla's homeroom class. Their junior year, he and Ronald hopped on the eastbound Union Pacific train and didn't get off until they hit Fort Smith.

The problem with seeing people from high school... was seeing people from high school. Every nostalgia-filled conversation usually ended with a plea for money or sob story of classmates he barely remembered or liked.

He invited the pity of poor farmers and ranchers, both of which would address him like a lord of old. Men no longer called him by his name. No, it was *Mr. Edwards*. No matter how often he corrected them, desperately encouraging them to call him Blake, his formal status remained.

Lyla's history teacher, Mr. Schofeld, introduced himself to the flock of parents and children. He had excellent classroom command and a slideshow presentation going over his life and credibility. His only negative quality was his admiration for the Sooners, but he wasn't going to hold that against the man. It was "Go Pokes" on Thorpe Ranch.

His phone rang. Luke Comb's "Beer Never Broke My Heart" sounded. He attempted to silence it as it was less than appropriate for school, let alone the fifth-graders. The fact that his ex-wife sat next to him was the icing on the cake. Although a couple of parents sung the rest of the chorus after the panicked mute, Tara gave him a red-faced death stare.

"I have to take this," he mouthed.

Blake enjoyed the quiet of the hallway. The teachers were on rotation, each briefly introducing the classroom and what was in store for the year. Each teacher got five minutes before the rotations, so Blake didn't have much time before things got loud again.

"What is it, J?" he asked.

"You gotta get to the ranch. Southwest at the old barn." The tone in his voice was ominous, a tone not relative to Little J.

Blake hung up the phone, well aware his best friend meant urgent business, whatever it might be. He peeked back through the rectangular window and waited for Tara to look back. When she did, he nudged his head and pointed away, telling her he had to leave. She gave him the hand that coincided with an attitude he knew all too well. It was as much permission he was going to get from her. He was going to pay for that later.

He did his best mall walk out the door. Blake was so concentrated on Little J's phone call that he didn't even take in his surroundings.

"Cutting out early?" Nita said, sitting on a bench beneath the flagpole near the entryway.

Blake stopped in his tracks, and glanced around, and was disapointed that his Marine observation skills failed him. "Ah, you know, duty calls, as they say."

"It's a shame you don't have some of your best friends that you trust with your life workin' it."

"Sometimes you gotta do things yourself. You of all people should understand that."

Nita nodded. "Sure." The small boy behind her played in the school garden, letting a caterpillar crawl across his hand. "Aiden, come here," she said. Her stepson never took his attention away from the insect as he balanced it on his hand the entire way. "Say hello, Aiden."

"Hello," he said.

"How are you, Aiden?" Blake asked.

"Fine." Aiden finally glanced upward at Blake, and his eyes widened. "Your hat is huge!"

Blake tilted it down. "You like it?"

Aiden shook his head. "No."

Nita scratched the side of her head. "Aiden, be nice. Don't say—"

"It's all right. The boy's just being honest." Blake removed his hat, slicked back his greasy hair, and placed it back on. "I like people who are honest with me. I've gotten to the point where it's hard to tell the difference between the genuine ones and those holding the knife in my back."

He could tell Nita contemplated his every word. That was what she did. That was what she was good at. "Everything smooth for Wyatt's funeral?"

Blake tucked his hands into his Carhart vest and checked the bottom of his boots for dirt or gum. "As funerals go, it was smooth enough. He didn't have a lot of family, so we had it at the ranch. Few of his kin came by, but his home was with us."

"Good," she said. Nita began walking back to her car, ushering Aiden along the way, but keeping him at arm's length. "You have a good day, cowboy."

"I'll have Lyla keep an eye on him," he promised. He didn't avert his eyes as she walked away, and he looked her up and down. He took a moment to notice that he was blatantly checking her out in the open. He faked a cough and looked off to the side, but his eyes returned to her, as he was lost in the moment, forgetting about the task at hand.

Nita never replied or looked back. She was good at saying things without words, leaving people, especially men, wanting more. Blake was no exception.

———

The southwest barn was far off and hadn't been used by him or his father in probably thirty years. The trek to get there went through a series of wooded hills that one could easily get lost in for weeks. The terrain was unforgiving. It would be impossible to tell in many areas what lay beneath the fresh fallen leaves and thick foliage. Cars and trucks would be useless and could only make it so far, and that wouldn't be far enough. ATVs could work, but that wasn't a cowboy's way.

Blake didn't ride as much as he used to, but he had to get on horseback any chance the opportunity would arise so he could stay sane. He pushed his stallion hard up and down the steep inclines and declines of the wooded hills.

Four horses were tied down outside the ramshackle barn. The roof was covered in dead leaves, and there was a fissure ripping the heart of the building. Little J crept out from the shadows beneath the tilted awning. Blake pulled the reins and dismounted his horse. The two of them didn't say a word to one another. Blake simply followed him inside.

Nova greeted Blake by walking alongside him as soon as he entered the dark barn. His ranch hands all wore work gloves and bandanas over their faces. Floyd was the only one with a drawn pistol, casually resting on his crotch with his finger tapping on the trigger guard.

A teenage boy in the center of the barn was on his knees with a feed bag over his head. He wore a ripped flannel with blue jeans and tattered boots. A circle of moisture formed around the front of the bag where his mouth would be, telling Blake their detainee was afraid. That ring of moisture was most likely snot or spittle from a mouth breather.

Blake stepped in front of the kid. "How long have you been here?"

The baghead darted around. "I'm so sorry. Please, just let me go!"

"Let me tell you how this is gonna go. You tell me everything that happened to the best of your abilities without leaving out any of the details, and I let you go. Now, you don't do that, you never leave this barn ever again. Understand?"

The boy began to weep under the burlap bag.

"Let's start over with an easy question. What's your name?"

The boy was fighting through sniffles, the way Blake wanted him. "Travis," he said.

"Travis what?"

"Travis Fields."

Blake's eyes went around to his guys. They all knew who the boy was—the alleged boyfriend of the Amish girl, Colette. The last person to see her before she was butchered.

"A lot of people are looking for you, Travis." A piece of old and rotted lumber fell from the dilapidated ceiling and slammed on to the floor. Travis jumped and the tears returned. "The US Marshals, Cherokee Marshals, FBI, OSBI, police... cowboys. Why is that?"

"I didn't kill her. I promise. I promise."

"Then why are you hiding out in a place like this? How have you even been here for so long?" In the corner of the barn amongst rotten wood were grocery bags of empty cans, chips, and water bottles. "Have you been stealing from Chock's Grocery at the bottom of the hill?" If that was the truth, Blake would be impressed. From this point, it would probably be three or so miles on foot to Chock's Grocery.

Travis shook his head before Blake finished talking. "No, I haven't stolen or killed anyone! I promise! I didn't know what to do 'cause they'll think I did it. I-I-I'm fucking scared!"

Blake squatted in place with the tip of his nose not far away from the burlap sack dangling in front of him. "The girl that was strung up was your girlfriend or something?"

"Colette." Saying her name caused the boy's voice to break. "Yes, she was my girlfriend."

Blake rotated to all his guys, who took in the revelations. "Do you know who I am?"

"No, sir."

"You being a hundred percent honest with me?"

The bag quivered. "Yes, sir."

Blake grunted. "Here's what's gonna happen. You're gonna start telling me every detail of what happened, starting with how you found this place and eventually getting to the point where a poor girl and one of our best friends was murdered and put on display like some fucked up Halloween attraction. Because if you don't, Travis, I'll kill you right here."

Travis nodded in agreeance.

"Do you believe I would do such a thing?" Blake asked.

"Yes, sir."

"Get to talking then."

Travis tightened his shoulders. Surely, he felt the weight of five efficient war fighters pressing down on him. "I go fishing at the lake a lot and ended up following the creek down through here a few months back. I found this barn and thought it would be a good place to bring Colette. We planned on losing our... uh..."

"Virginity. Keep going."

"Ever heard of a motel?" Floyd asked.

Travis' head beneath the bag popped up. "I don't have no money."

Floyd just shook his head and didn't acknowledge the excuse. Military, especially Marines, weren't fans of excuses regardless of the circumstances. Floyd was a man who once risked AWOL status to hook up with a married Afghani woman.

"Keep going," Blake demanded.

"Well, we floated down the creek, and we eventually made it here. But when the time came for the both of us, she didn't end up wanting to do it."

"Have sex, you mean?"

"Yes, sir."

"Was she scared?" Blake asked. And the posing of that question garnered more sniffling and tears from Travis. Blake narrowed his eyes. "Did you force yourself on her, Travis?"

"It wasn't until she pushed me off that I knew I was wrong. I apologized over and over."

"What happened after that?"

"She left."

"What do you mean, left? Where did she go?"

"She ran into the woods. By the time I got my pants back on and went after her, I couldn't tell where she had gone." The boy took a few deep breaths.

In that time, Blake glanced to all his guys as they were split as to whether Travis killed the girl. Cody and Parker were giving a thumbs down, while Little J and Floyd were thumbs up all the way.

"You've been here the whole time?" Blake asked.

"After hours of looking for her in the dark, I-I-I finally heard something... something far off. Then, the sounds of her screaming... Those will be in my head forever. I've never heard anything as terrifying. By the time I got to her she was... She was..."

"Strung up?"

"Yes." The tears flowed harsher, and his words were barely escaping his mouth.

"There was another man that was killed with her. Did you see him as well?"

"Y-yes, sir. But I only saw him after everything had already happened as well."

Blake finally stood. "All right, Travis. You've done well, but now is the time you tell me honestly. Do you know the man that did this? Or did you get a good look at the one who did?"

Travis went to speak, but he stopped himself, letting out a weird moan before going silent and crying more.

Blake put a heavy hand on Travis' shoulder, pressing down hard enough to make his presence known. "You know, Travis, one of the men in this room, who shall remain nameless, tortured al Qaeda agents in Iraq. Now, mostly that was because we needed information regarding potential threats against our country and the men who served it, but the reason he was so good at getting information out of these people was because he fucking liked it. I don't know if seeing the enemy suffer brought him overwhelming delight, but I know it brought some."

Travis held out his hands for mercy or a plea to wait. "No, please, please, please. I—I—don't know what I saw. I don't know what it was."

It didn't appear he was being dishonest. He was simply frightened.

"He was... He was Death," Travis said.

"And what does this version of death look like?"

After a long pause where Travis remained still, almost petrified, he said, "He walked, but he was not human. His head was an animal."

"What kind of animal?"

"Some kind of bird."

CHAPTER 24

Ezell bathed in the creek for over an hour. He was naked, but that didn't stop fellow congregation members from joining him. Just eyeballing it, he'd gather around thirty people joining him. A wicker basket was overflowing with crudely shaped bars of soap on the creek bank. Fall was beginning to descend upon them, so Ezell took advantage of the hot day before the weather change took place.

"I would like to thank all who could join me for this midday cleansing," he said, washing his upper body with a bar of soap. "I know many of our fellow visionaries couldn't attend due to work obligations, which is perfectly okay."

All the attendants who joined him were no longer lumps of unmolded clay. No. To Ezell, these people were proud works of art, sculpted into the most desirable piece of craft imaginable—followers.

"Father Ezell," Hillary Tolliver said timidly, "may I ask why we are doing this?"

"Cause we all stink, of course." Everyone recognized and ate up his humor. He had them in his hand, and he knew it. "In all seriousness, Hillary, I believe to inherit the Earth, we have to embrace it. Everything is given to us, and it's not to our benefit. We no longer acquire our own meat. It's given to us in horrible and inhumane ways. Even the water of our beautiful world comes out of a metal pipe or in a plastic bottle. So, I'd like to apologize in advance, if not everyone is comfortable with this, but I felt it necessary. For when we are the ones given passage into God's kingdom, it will be because of our willingness to do things his way. Let us not forget the Son of God himself as well as his followers, were baptized in the river. So, whenever you think perhaps the water is too dirty to cleanse you, just remember that the water of the river was clean enough to wash away the sins of Christ himself."

A few scattered "Amens" sounded all around him.

Ezell began to make the rounds. He talked with everybody, asking about their past, cracking jokes, and praying with the ones who desired either guidance or further indoctrination. It was also an excellent time to look upon the women as they bathed half-naked. Hillary Tolliver was bustier than he initially thought she was going to be. She made minimal attempts to show off her features, always wearing sweaters or vests of dull colors.

Jenn Foster was a little younger. She had never been anything but white trash, but perhaps she was more beneath the spaghetti strap tank top. Ezell waded to her in the thigh-high creek and grasped her hands. "Thank you so much for being here, Jenn. God certainly has a plan for you."

"Thank you," she replied as she covered herself due to the wet tank top leaving little to the imagination.

Ezell held onto her wrists momentarily, doing his best not to squeeze too hard. "Look at me."

She did, staring right into his soul.

"Don't you dare be ashamed," were his parting words as he rubbed her back and was onto the next.

The Nichols trio all bathed together in the creek. Sam, Sally, and Susan. Sam and Sally were an overweight couple who were victims of the fast-food-and-no-exercise culture that ran rampant in Oklahoma, especially in this area. In fact, when making his pilgrimage here and hearing all the rumors of the fat people in middle America, he thought his entire congregation would be plus-sized followers.

He spoke with both parents. He thanked them for coming, asking about their jobs, and seeing how they liked the new pergola they added to their home. Both of them appeared shocked that he remembered nearly everything about them. That was what Ezell did, though. Being a good leader wasn't simply knowing the mission. It was more about understanding the people he'd lead on this expedition.

His attention went to their daughter Susan. "Look at this one, maturing right before our very eyes," he said as he brushed her hair behind her ear and grasped the back of her skull. He kissed the top of her forehead and admired her developing body. "Are you going to enroll in our academy when we get it up and running?" he asked as if she was the one who had the say in the matter and not her parents.

Susan looked at her mother and father and smiled. "I hope so!"

"Me too," he said, stroking her cheek with his thumb. He eventually released her and waded back through the creek to where he had bathed prior. "My fellow visionaries, as we partake in the old way of doing things, shedding ourselves of some modern convenience for the time being, I'd like to offer up a challenge if you're willing: no phones."

CHAPTER 25

OSBI informed Nita they took Travis Fields into custody. He had been hiding out at Thorpe Ranch in an old barn. The location wasn't far from the scene of the crime. Nita didn't know what to believe. She had difficulty believing such a young man, no matter how big, could have been the one she crossed paths with. Logic would say that Travis Fields was the most likely culprit. *Perhaps if I got a good look or spent a moment with him, I could know...*

A black cowboy hat angled away from her as Blake leaned against the wall with his arms crossed. "Marshal," he said.

She skipped the pleasantries and cowboy charm. "What happened? This where you ran off to?"

"Good to see you too."

Agent Teller and Director Lowwater conversed at the end of the hallway. She walked to the window, ushering Blake to follow. "I thought you were cutting out of Meet the Teacher early because you just couldn't take it anymore, but now I know that's not true. One of your boys found him there and told you to come running."

"They did good giving you that badge."

She didn't know whether to take that as a compliment or not. It was hard to tell with Blake. Ask anyone. It always was. "What did he say?"

"What do you mean?"

"Blake," she said.

His face softened as they stared into each other's eyes. Perhaps he was thinking the same thing she was, but she wasn't going to press it.

"He's gonna tell you all the same shit he told me, even if he does lawyer up. I'll be happy to relay everything, don't you worry."

She inched closer and lowered her voice, "You questioned him? What the hell were you thinking?"

"Is it against the law to ask questions to people trespassing on my land?" Blake shrugged his shoulders. "Hell, anyone would understand my reasoning for doing so, and no one is even gonna know I talked to Travis unless he says something. I doubt he'll be prompted to do so anyway."

"I get it, but maybe leave the police work to us."

"I police my land. Everyone else is assisting."

"You know who you sound like?" Nita asked, insinuating that the apple didn't fall far from the tree.

"Easy, ice queen."

Nita smiled, "Wow, you've lived here a long time and still have no idea, white boy."

He nodded, glanced around the room, at the wandering eyes finding them. He inched even closer. "There's more to it, but perhaps we should continue to discuss this elsewhere."

————

The back corner of Jimmy's Diner was always open for a wide array of conversations, no matter which side of the law they fit on. "Bird? A bird mask?" she asked in a hush, leaning over a cup of hot coffee. "Are you certain that's what he said?"

"That's what he said." Blake poured in a double shot of cream and sugar into his own mug. "And if you just so happened to believe he's not being honest or shellshocked to the point of seeing things, he ain't..."

"What makes you say that?" Nita asked.

"Because I scared the shit out of him."

"Did you torture him?"

"Shit, you jumped to that quick? Am I that bad?" he said, pulling away from the scalding coffee and scrunching his face.

She gave him the Native glare.

"To answer your question, no, we didn't torture him." Blake took a sip and winced from the heat. "I only *threatened* to torture him."

Nita gave him that. "Regardless, it doesn't look good for Travis Fields, especially since he's eighteen. Even if he didn't do it, he's gonna have a hard time convincing anyone he didn't have anything to do with it. Teller is gonna administer a polygraph."

Blake leaned over the steam rising from his cup. "The public is gonna annihilate this kid with no help from the media. However, you can't convince me that this kid committed any crime. He may know something, but he's not the one who did this."

Nita's eyes narrowed. "What makes you so certain?"

"He may have been able to kill that girl, but not Wyatt. His pride was too great for a kid like that to kill him. Plus, he was a tough son of a bitch. Not to mention the giant-sized boot prints we found. They don't match up with Travis'. We checked. The kid's big, but not quite."

Nita soaked it all in like a willow after rain. She contorted her back to stretch it out. The soreness and pain of the interaction with the man in the owl mask still afflicted her muscles.

"You good? I got some pain meds in the truck. Let me go get 'em for you." He started to leave.

"No, no, it's fine."

She wanted them. Her instincts told her that Blake would have the good stuff. The type of stuff that was the subject of an Eminem track.

Blake leaned back and cleared his throat. He took a long look around the diner as he admired Jimmy scrambling eggs in bacon grease. "I get what you're saying, though—bout evil or—monsters." He took his hat off, revealing a greasy and nappy head. Blake and his trademark wavy hair began to show signs of humanity as his male-pattern baldness took shape, but still in its infancy. "We were on a spec-ops mission in the city of Kunduz. Our task was to rescue any local police or midwives targeted by Taliban forces. It was simple: find anyone still alive and get them out." From the beginning stages of recounting the story, Nita could see Blake's eyes glaze over. "There were reports of militia all over the place, so we had to keep quiet in the aftermath of a couple airstrikes we fired down their throats. As we approached the hospital, there must've been ten or so bodies of women dragged out into the streets that were raped and killed. Their bodies were still deteriorating from the acid."

Nita slid the rest of her coffee to the side.

"I heard grunting from an alleyway not thirty feet away. When I rounded that corner, I saw a happy group of insurgents having their way with a midwife as a bucket of acid was tilted over sideways, eating away at the remains of what used to be her head. After we sent a hailstorm of bullets in their direction, only one of their little group was still squirming around. I walked up to him, pulled him close, looked into his eyes, and you know what I saw?"

Nita left the rhetorical question in the air.

"Not a goddam thing." Blake glanced around the diner, removed a mini-whiskey bottle from his vest pocket, and poured it into his coffee. He rubbed his temples. "I saw a man who was living but showed no signs of life. That day, I knew damn well monsters were among us. They must be killed."

Blake put his hat back on and wore the brim low.

"You save anyone?" she asked. "The midwives or the police?"

"Not my unit."

Nita nodded.

"Would've been a better story if I had."

"I reckon it would have been."

"Timing is something I've always seemed to struggle with in this life. Seems I've either been too early or too late for things that matter. Maybe one day I'll get it right." He went blank, becoming lost in the neon sign on the other side of the glass. The lights of the electric bulbs flickered as did his presence in the moment.

She couldn't resist. "Don't get your hopes up."

Blake laughed as he snapped to attention. He finally committed to standing. "There it is. I'll go pay Jimmy. Unless the ball-bustin' is on you?"

"I'll let you take this one, money bags. You need to call Olivia and let her know you're buying something?"

"You're a laugh a minute, aren't ya? By the way, I promised Tara I would pick Lyla up from school every day. If you ever need me to get Aiden, just let me know."

Nita smiled. "Thank you. I'm sure that occasion will come up eventually, but I'd have to warn you, he's not too trusting."

As Blake walked away, fiddling with his billfold, he said, "Must take after his stepmom. You sure about the pain meds?"

"I'm sure. Thank you, though."

"All right," he said. When he toed the threshold of being out of earshot, he turned, eyeing her. "Make no mistake, we may not have saved the midwives, but we avenged them."

CHAPTER 26

The walking carried on like an endless river of slow current. His scalp pained him for days after being dragged from his home alongside his family. In the dark, they had been removed, and in the dark, they stayed for eight hundred miles. When he attempted to look back at his home, he was turned around and told there was nothing there for him. Not anymore.

The ones that weren't packed into caravans made the Walk. Slow movers were beaten to death to lighten the load, noncompliers were shot to avoid judgment, others fell ill to assist in the genocide, and a number of the rest wished they had been one of the formers. With his head down, he heard bodies drop all around him. All he was allowed to do was step past his brother, uncle, aunt, and cousin. For if he was to look back, he was told his fate would be no different.

The repetitive humming woke her. Agent Teller was calling. Dreams of the Removal came to her nightly. Each brought a different perspective of someone forced on that horrible trip to these lands, as if she were the lightning rod for all their sorrow and pain. Ever since the bike ride, her connection with those forced upon the trail was strengthened, as if she had built a straight line of communication with them. However, she didn't know why. Perhaps it had to do with her sensitivity. Perhaps not.

She remembered what Dr. Whitekiller discussed about her ancestors and their people's relationship with trauma. "Seventy percent of adults have experienced at least one traumatic event in their life. Twenty percent of those have experienced some form of PTSD as a result. With everything you've been through, showing signs of struggle is okay. Perhaps a lot of your strength comes from the fact that you're Native. Now, I'm not saying because we are Native that we are excluded from experiencing trauma. Quite the opposite, really."

Whitekiller had stopped, collected her thoughts, and continued, "Trauma is woven into our DNA through genocide, ethnocide... I could go on, but I certainly don't need to lecture you. The connection I am trying to make is perhaps you're more equipped to deal with the trauma in your life because it flows through your veins. The vast majority of people would crumble or struggle greatly, given all you've gone through, but here you sit, a shining example of strength. You should be proud of that. But don't be so prideful that you forget to focus on yourself from time to time and your mental health."

Nita had doubts, but she hoped those words were true.

She answered her cell phone. "Hello?"

"Nita, sorry to wake you if that's the case, but I was just calling to let you know I'm administering the polygraph later today." Teller said.

She rubbed her heavy eyes. "Yeah... Yeah... I'll be over shortly."

"Good deal."

As she rose, her back and shoulders cracked to life. She exhaled a relief that was ultimately unsatisfying because the pain remained. She sat upright on the bed in the room she grew up in. Paintings and pictures of horses still littered the walls, as well as a portrait of her and Jackson on their wedding day. That day seemed more like a dream than the ones currently occupying her sleep.

The vibration of the phone rumbled atop the nightstand once more. She grabbed it and answered without looking. It was still early, and no one else other than work called her at this time. "Yeah, Charlie?"

"Nita? This is Brother Barry. I'm really sorry to bother you at this hour."

"Oh... it's fine, Barry," she replied, even if she didn't mean it. She was awake but by no means prepared for the day. She was not a morning person, for the morning only brought her soreness and a longing to return to sleep. However, with her reoccurring dreams, she wasn't rushing to go back. She was prepared to be quite rude over the phone if this call was about some fundraiser. Not because she hated the thought, but shut-eye was hard to come by these days.

"I'll just cut right to it then," he said, lowering his voice. "I got a girl here from NSU dealing with some stuff, and I was wondering if it wasn't too much to ask if you could come down here and talk to her? Just for a little while?"

Northeastern State University. One of Oklahoma's Division II schools, her alma mater, and where Jackson had worked as an English professor.

She held the phone away from her face for a moment and wiped her face, as if she were washing away the urge to deny his request. "She in trouble, Barry?"

"Well, no, but I feel like she could benefit from some counsel from someone as respectable as yourself. At the very least, give her some words of wisdom and someone to admire."

"Barry, I don't know if you're aware, but there's been a lot happening these past couple weeks. I don't have much time for giving sage advice or even the ability."

Barry's silence spoke volumes. She could tell he didn't know how to proceed.

"This girl Native, Barry?"

"Yes, she is."

Ah.

"Listen," he continued, "she's been a part of the congregation for a while now and has been struggling with some... addiction issues."

Then, guilt came to her.

———

Nita met Barry outside his office, which was hidden deep within the bowels of the large and modern church. The scale of this church was nothing like anything she attended as a girl. Growing up, her congregation was fewer than seventy members, and many, if not all, the sermons were spoken in Cherokee. Then, as she grew up, the number of members stayed stagnant, as was the comprehension of the Cherokee language. Time passed, and English crept into the sermon to avoid alienating growth with each passing year. That continued until the native language was pushed out almost entirely, aside from a few hymns. Cherokee speakers became rare or nonexistent. Knowledge of their way was cast aside and pushed away to make room for the new.

As she rounded the corner, there was a Native girl with black hair traveling all the way down her spine. She raised her head, and Nita blinked excessively to rid the belief she was staring into a mirror of fifteen years ago. As she approached, the lights dimmed, and shadows curled around the girl's legs and arms from behind the chair. This was one of those times when Nita had to remind herself that no one around her saw the same things. Vile things surrounded this girl's soul.

"Nita, this is Mariah Paddock," Barry said awkwardly.

Both nodded to one another and wore the same forced smile. She couldn't speak for the girl, but it appeared neither of them wanted to be here.

She waited. Barry finally took the hint. "Well, I'll go ahead and leave y'all to it. If you need me, I'll be in the office."

And Barry made his exit.

"You know, when he said he was going to call someone, I expected him to get some white woman." Mariah didn't expand on that train of thought.

Nita squatted down into Barry's office chair. She noticed the chair was extended to its highest point. She grabbed the adjuster, pulled it, and lowered herself to be at eye level with Mariah.

"Comfortable?" Mariah asked sarcastically.

"Got nothing to do with comfort. I'm just farther away from God than Brother Barry. So, best not pretend I am."

Mariah nodded her head. "Are you here to give me some sage advice to help me with why I'm so fucked up?"

"I'm not one to be giving advice. I got problems of my own."

The girl scoffed. "Then why are you here?"

"Bother Barry told me he had a girl that was struggling with addiction and wanted my help. But if I'm being honest, I'm only here to confirm or deny whether you're worth my time."

Mariah was taken aback. "What do you mean?"

"What are you addicted to?"

Mariah tucked her forearms into her body and leaned forward. She scratched the outside of her sleeves. Nita didn't know if she was doing that because her arm genuinely itched or perhaps it was some involuntary signal for help. Nita didn't consider herself a psychologist, but she was observant. A little bit of unexplainable sensitivity to the supernatural went a long way.

"How long have you been cutting?" Nita asked.

"H-how did you know—"

"Again, how long?"

"I don't know, a few months, maybe."

"What kicked it off?"

Mariah cocked her head to the side as if she didn't understand the question. "I-I don't know." She wiped her face. Mariah's eyes were so dark they could be considered black.

Nita arched her back. The soreness from her encounter with the Owl Killer still pained her. *I'm horrible at this shit. She needs proper help from Whitekiller or, hell, Jackson.* "What the hell am I doing here?" she whispered to herself. A crucifix hung on the wall, and the harrowing visage of white Jesus stared upon her. She wanted to roll her eyes, but perhaps this was a sign of accepting her role as someone capable of guidance.

"My uncle's funeral," Mariah said.

"Excuse me?"

"When all this started. I think it was around then."

"You two close?"

Mariah shook her head. "No, not so much. When I was younger, we were. He would stay at our house. Sometimes we'd go get some Indian tacos, or he'd take me out for ice cream."

Nita didn't know what to do with that information. Advising with her circumstances seemed counterintuitive. She was good at patrolling, researching, and shooting, not life guidance. She breathed. "You know, I have vivid dreams. They got worse after my husband died. I have the same dream every night. Every goddam night." Her eyes flashed to Jesus after blaspheming, and she apologized. "No matter how they start, or whatever ones fill my subconscious, they all lead back to the same one each night. Jackson and I driving down a backroad... They're horrible."

"Were you in the car too?"

"No, I wasn't. Sometimes I wish I was. It would save me a lot of questions and pain that threads its way into my daily life." The girl went silent. She rubbed her arms and picked at her nails, nearly peeling them from the skin. Nita feared that perhaps she had come on too strong. She made a poor attempt at changing the subject. "What are you studying? Barry tells me you're at NSU."

"I know who you are. You're the marshal that was in that meth shootout in Marble City. They underestimate the situation or something? My cousin said that house was locked and loaded?"

"There's more to it, but *underestimate* is as good a word as any."

"So, what? You show up and shoot them all?"

"Let's get back to y—"

"I have dreams, too," Mariah interrupted.

Nita sat there, waiting at full attention.

"I'm in my bed, wearing a nightgown, which I haven't worn in who knows how long. I realize I can't move, and an antlered beast rises past my feet at the end of the bed. It moves like a man, but its head is like a deer or something."

"Like a mask?"

"It could be, I suppose, but its eyes glow like a candle or something."

Nita rubbed the back of her neck. "What happens next?"

Mariah went to talk but stopped herself as if she didn't want to say. "Whatever it is begins to crawl over the top of me on all fours and lick my neck. Then it begins to remove my clothes, but I'm eventually able to wake myself up by that point."

"Did these dreams start happening around the time you started cutting yourself?'

Mariah lost herself in contemplation. "Yeah, I'd say that's probably around the same time now."

Nita watched her closely. The wheels in the young woman's head spun on and on. "How did your uncle die?"

"H-he had a heart attack."

"You said he would stay at your house when you were younger?"

"Yeah, a lot."

"Mariah, you may not even know the answer to this question, but were you sexually abused by your uncle?"

Mariah's face went white, and she stumbled out of her chair and dived for the trashcan tucked underneath the receptionist's desk. She made it just in time not to stain the church carpet with chunky, beige puke.

————

They cleaned the carpet in relative silence. Nita evaded notice from Brother Barry even after wandering the halls, utilizing her sleuthing skills to maintain the whereabouts of the janitorial closet.

Mariah gathered herself as her color returned. Nita comforted her to the best of her capabilities. She rubbed the girl's back for a few seconds. They shared a similar status of staring, their eyes wide open but taking nothing in. Nita could have cried as her mind drifted to Jackson, but she didn't. She remained firm, not succumbing.

"I remember the first time he did it," Mariah began. "He bought me all my favorite candy and a beautiful toy horse because at that time, I was obsessed with them. Then, he asked if we wanted to become closer to each other—closer than anyone. I was stupid enough to say yes."

The proud young Native girl began to weep. Her shoulders curled into her body as her head drooped low. She wanted to melt away, and Nita knew this all too well.

"Make no mistake, you were not stupid." Nita said. "Naive, perhaps, like we all were at that age, but not stupid. Don't you ever believe that any part of this is on you. It's on him. Many people walk through life without experiencing evil. They think it isn't there just because it's not tangible in front of their face. Or, even worse, they know it exists, and they either do nothing or let someone else worry about it all." Nita clasped her own hands and held them as if she was praying. She dropped her head, but she sent no prayers upward to heaven. Then, she shot up quick. "You had a brush with evil, Mariah. You survived it. Perhaps it will affect you for the rest of your days. No one with the knowledge I have would fault you for spiraling down a path without much light at the end. But, if you emerge from the place and breathe that fresh air, you'll prove something. Not only to yourself, but to others as well."

After a pair of sniffles, Mariah wiped a bit of snot leaking from her red nose like a faucet. "Prove what?"

"That you won."

Chapter 27

Nita typed *Dustin Paddock* into the criminal database. The mugshot of a Caucasian man emerged on the screen, wearing a pair of black eyes. Several aggravated assaults and a couple DUIs, but nothing to the extent of child molestation or sexual assault had ever been reported. He was Mariah's uncle on her mother's side. Her father was half-blood Cherokee, and her mother was Scottish-Irish from Missouri. Dustin served eight months in prison but was released early for good behavior.

As Nita thought it was a dead end, she continued down the page that provided additional information, and it read, *Former member of Bohemia Society*. That information was bolded and underlined in blue, providing a database hyperlink.

Bohemia Society was nothing more than a private community in Adair County that flourished in the 80s to mid-90s. Their mission was to promote white supremacy and anarchy, seeking absolute freedom from society and the government. A notable member was none other than Timothy McVeigh, whom she knew well. His image had been burned into her brain since that horrible day in 1995.

Nita could see the appeal of liberation from the government, as she believed most Natives would share the sentiment, but extremism, not so much.

Upon further research, she discovered that Bohemia Society disbanded after an OSBI and FBI raid on their compound confirmed their suspicions of pedophilia and satanic worship.

CHAPTER 28

Father Ezell pressed hard for the completion of a multitude of projects that were in development. His assurance of the greater good was what pushed them every day. Upon seeing the vision clear, Mick Logue had recently quit his job as a construction manager. The world had grown so foul, allowing such atrocities, the most horrendous being freedom in the absence of God. Father Ezell made sure to focus on those persecuting from on high, in positions of power.

Regardless of the mission, Father wanted to maintain the most crucial element of Temple's Vision: establishing a culture. A culture was hard to destroy. A culture could withstand pitfalls and aggressors. Culture was what victims of a larger society could effectively resist.

Mick impressed himself. The gate and surrounding wall of the compound were no small feat in terms of construction. None of it—the chapel, schoolhouse, main house, and a multitude of storage buildings —would have been possible had he not had an effective shorthand with his guys that had followed his lead and became visionaries themselves.

Pride flowed through him, being useful and essential to Father's vision. Father told him that none of this would have been possible without him. Mick had never received a level of gratitude and validation from any set of parents. As a child, he bounced around from foster home to foster home, but those were merely buildings.

Amongst his fellow visionaries, he soon found what the difference between a house and a home should be.

Chapter 29

At the OSBI office in Tahlequah, Agent Teller wrapped two expandable tubes around Travis Field's upper and lower torso to monitor chest expansion and contractions. Then, he Velcroed two electrical monitors on the boy's fingers. He was eighteen, but "boy" didn't seem appropriate to describe the big guy. However, during this process of getting friendly with Travis, Teller noted his immaturity. Travis had unchecked expectations and delusions of grandeur, which could sometimes be a sign of alarm. However, Travis' delusions were more boyish. He discussed moving to Alaska to run his own crab-fishing boat with his backup option as Hawaii. He would provide fishing tours for travelers and live on his boat there.

Teller wanted to keep his friendly nature with him, so he never called out the logical concerns that a bright-eyed teen might consider with those pair of "dreams."

The final element of the polygraph was for Teller to slide a pad underneath Travis that monitored the slightest muscle contractions. Essentially, if Travis or anyone else sitting on this thing attempted to lie with their asshole winking, the pad would catch it.

Teller recently finished training in a twelve-week course for his certification to administer polygraphs across the state. He gave Travis a yellow legal pad and told him to write down any number between one and ten. This was a process for the pre-test in order to get the subject to intentionally lie and record the reading.

"Regarding the number you wrote on the paper," Teller began, "did you write the number one?"

"No," Travis answered, tapping his heel into the floor over and over. The new set of clothes he wore was a plain, sleeveless shirt, cargo pants, and flip-flops.

"Did you write the number two?"

"No."

The process continued until they went through every number. Luckily, Travis understood the assignment, which was a relief.

I don't believe it would take much to push the limitations of this boy's mental capacity.

Travis wrote the number five but lied and said he wrote the number seven. The knowledge of his lie spiked on the reading and showed that he was untruthful. Since he was confirmed as a terrible liar, Teller was ready to run the official test.

———

Nita was hanging outside Teller's office at the Northeast Investigative Regional Branch, one of nine offices across the state.

"Waiting for the results?" he asked in reference to the polygraph.

"No, I just like dispersing my ray of sunshine across the county for even distribution," she said sarcastically.

Aware of all the tragedy that had befallen her, he took her playful banter as a positive. Many people would have crumbled under the weight of their trials, and she didn't. He respected that.

"Well, I've been in dark rooms all day, so I appreciate the vitamin D. Come on in," he said, ushering her into his office. The last time he spoke to her was during her episode in the morgue with Colette's body. He remained skeptical of her. Sometimes the men and women enforcing the law should not be in any position of power or influence. By no means did he question her manipulation of power, but her mental state did concern him. A number of events, some very recent, could all be a nasty recipe for post-traumatic stress.

But the more he questioned her, the more guilty he felt. He had been in his fair share of shootouts, seen horrific things, and experienced loss. His trepidation faded away the more time he spent around her. He respected her consuming every aspect of the job as a coping mechanism. It wasn't lost on him that he would have done the same. In the same vein, she seemed quiet, unassuming, and not looking for any attention. She didn't fit the type to desire attention by way of some supernatural ability or psychic gimmick.

"Have a seat," he said.

His office was bare. Teller considered himself a minimalist, or at least that was what he told people. In reality, he was lazy. He didn't want to decorate his office with pictures, awards, and little trinkets to make it a second home for himself. There was one picture of him and his daughter from when they went fishing nearly five years ago. Back then, they used to go fishing quite often, but as Taylor had gotten older, she'd been busier, and quality time with her old dad wasn't a priority.

"That's a big cat," Nita said as she turned the frame back around on his desk. Taylor was clutching the catfish with both fists under its mouth, and the rest of its body was almost as long as his girl's.

"Ah, yes, thank you. She was proud of that one."

"She should be."

"Yeah." Teller cleared his throat. "That was a good day. We haven't gone back since then. You go fishing with your boy at all?"

It was a simple question, but he was caught off guard by the contemplation and self-reflection in the time it took for Nita to reply. He was kicking himself. He hated asking, given her circumstances. He didn't think the question was insensitive, but he'd been wrong before.

"No, I haven't."

"Well, better do it now before junior gets going. I've lost out to softball, friends, junior high boys, and stepdad."

Nita's interest seemed to pique. "How's the softball coming along?"

"Good, she's pitching right now, but she wants to go back to first base. She's got a glove on her. Not much goes by."

"Very nice." The hint of enthusiasm was the first she had shown since her arrival.

Teller fell into the ugly statistic of divorced law enforcer, something he wasn't proud of. It was difficult for him to prioritize family after working homicide for so many years. When every other day was a matter of life and death for all the people he encountered over the years, an average family man was something that escaped him.

His office was barebones consisting of white walls, a modern desk, a chair that didn't roll, and a whiteboard with dried-out markers.

"I'm going for a minimalist vibe," he said pre-emptively.

"I can see that."

"I hear you were a phenom back in the day. I hear you still have the record for RBIs as well as the assist record for basketball. That's incredible. Did you all ever win state?"

"Yeah, in softball and basketball."

Teller smiled and shook his head. "I'm jealous. We were always runner up or close."

They sat there in silence as Teller reminisced about the days of old, remembering them more fondly than what they actually were.

"Anyway... as you know, like all polygraphs, this won't be admissible by the courts. However, there's a couple things here that are interesting. Even though he was nervous, once we got into the test, he only flagged on two questions. Everything else appeared truthful."

She nodded and lowered her brow. "Which ones flagged?"

Teller shuffled through his manila folder and found the paper he was searching for. "The two questions he answered that jumped off the screen were: One, were you responsible for the death of Colette Graber? Two, are you currently withholding any information regarding information on this case?"

Nita's instincts were quick, and they were on the same page. "So, he could feel responsible for her death without killing Colette and Wyatt. He knows more than he's letting on?"

"Possibly, but we've already put him through a couple rounds of questioning. It's looking like he's going to lawyer up too. However, I say we get back in there, ask about that church, and see what's going on there."

———

They walked through the bland hallways into the bowels of the building that sunlight didn't touch. Teller informed the office that he would read Travis the poly results and follow up along with Nita. She was grateful for his willingness to allow her involvement in the investigation as he ushered her along into Interrogation, where they were keeping Travis.

"All right, Travis," Teller said, dropping the folder onto the table from up high. I got your results back from the test. But before we get into all that... how you doing? Can I get you some water or a cereal bar, anything like that?"

She stayed by the door, observing Teller keep up the friendly rapport with the kid to keep him comfortable. However, Travis was naturally nervous. His cheeks were red, and his eyes were puffy. His emotions had appeared to be on a high ever since they took him in, perhaps even longer than that if he was innocent.

"Travis, this is my friend, Marshal Ross." Nita leaned against the back wall. "She may have some questions for you, but I assure you, she's here to help."

Travis' shaky eyes struggled to look upon her. "Y-you the Marble City marshal?"

She took a moment to reply, thinking how best to proceed. "I'm a marshal, and I've been to Marble City. That's the only connection there is."

Teller garnered Travis' attention away. "How do you think the test went for you, Travis?"

"Fine. I-I didn't lie."

Nita uncrossed her arms and placed her hands in her pockets.

"I don't think you did. However, there were a couple questions I'm going to need you to elaborate on if you can. That sound good?"

"Yes."

"Good." Teller flipped through some of his notes. "Why Thorpe Ranch, Travis? Of all the places to get away for the evening, why did it have to be a place an hour away, in the middle of the woods? Hell, you took a canoe to get there."

Travis sniffled. "I heard a rumor that there were possible riches on the land."

"Did either of you know who owned the land?" Nita chimed in, getting her feet into the interrogation waters.

"We both did. I was worried about it, knowing how much wealth the Edwards family had, as well as some of the history I'd heard. My dad used to tell me stories about some of the dark deeds that the Edwards family had done. But I wanted to go because..." Travis scratched his flaky scalp while stressfully thinking. "I heard Pretty Boy Floyd threw a sack full of stolen coins down a well a long time ago that was never found."

Nita kept still, not revealing that she had any prior knowledge of any dark deeds. However, Travis was not wrong. The history of Blake's family was steeped in the blood of their own making. However, she managed to jot down a note of the well on Blake's land to ask about later. Pretty Boy Floyd was a famous Depression Era outlaw. His life of crime and violence struck a chord with the people around here as he hid from the law in the Cookson Hills. Tales of his generosity to locals garnered him acclaim in the area. Nita struggled with idolizing such a man.

"Travis, you also wanted to take Colette to church somewhere." Teller paused, took his pen, and clicked it a couple of times. "Why?"

The boy's eyes watered. "I just... I just wanted to make her feel comfortable with me. I wanted more than anything for her to like me."

"What was the church called?"

Travis dropped his head into the pit of his elbow on the table. His voice was muffled, but still audible. "I-I don't know. It was off the beaten path... Temple something... We left as soon as it was over."

"How did you find out about it?"

"Some of the guys at work were talking about it—"

"At the car dealership? Snyder's Used Auto?"

"Yes. They talked about how great the preacher... pastor... father? Whichever name he went by, they liked him."

"Is there anyone at the church that may have followed you and Colette to Thorpe Ranch?" she asked.

"I-I don't think so. Maybe, but I don't know." With that, Travis used his sleeve to wipe his snotty nose and return his position.

Nita was reserved. The odds weren't in his favor. It was still likely that he either did or had something to do with Colette and Wyatt's murder.

"You heard a scream that night after Colette fled from you, but you're not sure if it was her?" Nita asked.

Teller glanced at her, keeping most of his attention on Travis. No doubt he was questioning how she obtained that information since that wasn't something the two of them had discussed.

Travis's whiny tone ceased for a moment. He seemed as sure as ever. "It wasn't her. There was no way it was her."

"You wouldn't believe the sounds people make when they're terrified. Do you think it was from the killer? Was it low-pitched or—"

"It started low. It was a vibration you could feel in your bones, then it went high... like the squeal of a dying animal."

"What kind of animal?" Teller asked.

"I don't know."

"You've got to try and help us, Travis, so you can help yourself. What kind of animal?"

A cold blast of air shot down through the back of Nita's shirt. Her spine stiffened, and goosebumps poked up across her body. A bloodcurdling screech impacted her ears. Her eardrums trembled, and she feared them rupturing. Her palm slammed against the wall. With gritted teeth, her sealed eyes opened to see Teller and Travis with curious gazes.

"Marshal?"

She gathered herself, all the while cursing her sensitivities. She pulled her phone from her pocket and began searching through YouTube. The deafening shockwave was familiar. Perhaps it was the Native in her that propelled her instincts of nature forward. She began playing with the sounds of feral hogs. They were becoming more of a problem throughout the state, with increasing numbers in nearly every county. There were current efforts to deal with them within Cherokee Nation due to the negative environmental impacts of these animals because that was mainly disease-related. The primal, animalistic screams were loud in the confined echo chamber of this interrogation room.

Travis' eyes widened. He looked like a veteran experiencing trauma that scared the soul.

He nodded, though he was still in an wide-eyed, shuttering state. "That's it. That's the sound."

CHAPTER 30

Vision Elementary began its first day of classes. Former schoolteacher Annabelle Rollins taught ten kids throughout the day. Their parents saw the proper way of the world—Ezell's way. Temple Vision's way. The ten students' ages varied, so Mrs. Rollins spent most of her workday teaching through individualized instruction.

Their small school resembled something from *Little House on the Prairie*. Short steps led to a small porch with a white railing. A bell tower was placed at the top and rang at the end of each hour throughout the day. The chime sounded throughout the whole compound and signaled meal and service times.

Mrs. Rollin's student at this hour was the daughter of Sam and Sally Nichols, Susan. She was twelve years old and had the most adorable flower gowns. Working with her was Annabelle's favorite part of the day. For Language Arts, today's task was understanding forms of figurative language. While metaphors and allusions were still advanced for her age range, Mrs. Rollins decided to focus on teaching similes and personification.

They sat at a desk in the corner of the room beneath a new and glossy whiteboard. "Okay, so personification is one of our figures of speech, and it's used when the writer gives human characteristics to something that is not human, like an idea or a thing. For example, if I said that the stars danced in the night sky, I am personifying them because they don't actually dance. Does that make sense?"

"Yes, Mrs. Rollins," Susan replied.

They continued through a few more examples before Annabelle made her try to come up with a couple on her own and incorporate them into paragraphs. Though Susan was young, her comprehension and writing skills were a few grade levels above her standing. Annabelle didn't have to completely break down every minute detail of the assignment.

In less than three minutes, she had several examples of personification that she came up with on her own, using proper punctuation and sentence structure.

"Great," Rollins said. "Let's look at your first one. Go ahead and read it aloud."

"The Bible speaks to us."

Annabelle smiled. "It absolutely does. Great job, Susan. How about another one?"

A voice from behind their backs spoke his example of personification: "The bell calls us to service. Quite frankly, that bell yells rather loudly."

Mrs. Rollins turned and responded, "It certainly does, Father."

Despite his busy schedule, Ezell gracing them with his presence brought her great happiness. Growing up with an alcoholic and abusive father, she never thought she would find a patriarch so inspiring. She had given up on men for the most part. They had abused her like her father, both physically and emotionally. They had judged her for circumstances beyond her control. Growing up poor wasn't her decision. Not having the right clothes wasn't her decision. Not knowing how to behave normally in a social setting at school wasn't easy when things at home weren't even close to steady.

What Father was building here was something that she never had: a true family. Their family had fellowship, a mission, and one that would lead them and see it all through. There wasn't a doubt in her mind that Father could accomplish anything. *His will be done for the greater good.* The world had become a corrupt and vile place filled with demons, those who had twisted the word of God to their benefit and gain. Father's mission was to eradicate the blasphemers while establishing their beacon to heaven.

He walked closely behind their backs, even closer to Suzie as he stopped. He leaned over her, wrapped his arms around her tightly, and placed his palms on the table. He then kissed the top of her head. Suzie slightly retreated but smiled all the same.

"How's she doing, Mrs. Rollins?"

"She's doing fantastic, Father. She's one of my brightest, as you know."

"Oh, this I know," he said with a wink. Ezell placed his hands on Suzie's upper arms and rubbed them both. "Her parents should be very proud."

He backed away for a moment and shifted all his attention to Annabelle. "Could I borrow Susan for a while? I need her help at the chapel."

"Of course, Father. Whatever you desire."

CHAPTER 31

Nita, Charlie, and Teller discussed how to proceed with their new information over fajitas and tacos brought in from El Molcajete, or Elmo's, as everyone referred to it, and one of Nita's favorites. But like most things as of late, her enjoyment was ripped from her.

"I had the researchers narrow in on possibilities of where this church could be. Teller said. "This is the list I got back." Teller slid a list of around thirty churches in the area that could fit the bill.

Nita scanned through them while gorging herself on chips and queso. "Shit, thirty?"

"Trust me, they narrowed it down," Teller assured him.

The case began to weigh on them. Through Nita's eyes, it was evident as she scanned her fellow law officers eating silently, not exchanging pleasantries or glances.

She went for another chip but stopped. "You think our suspect could have followed Travis and Colette from the church?"

"Could be our only logical conclusion as of now." Teller was particular and extreme about the specifics. She believed he had some semblance of OCD the more time she spent around him as she also took notice of his unused silver aligned in proper order next to his plate and his sleeves tightly rolled up halfway up his forearms. He was anal about this, but at least he still had a sense of humor.

All the phones on the table vibrated at once. The emergency response notification went off. At first, she assumed it was an Amber Alert, but upon further investigation, the notification stated that fire and police were being sent to First Baptist Church of Tahlequah. Then, flashing lights lit the night sky to a blinding effect as fire trucks rocketed down Highway 62.

Everyone dropped the Mexican food in their foiled containers and raced out the door.

———

"I was just here yesterday. I was just fucking here," Nita ran her fingers through her hair and squeezed and pulled.

Charlie didn't reply. There was nothing he could say. He just continued to drive.

Up ahead, she could see the orangish glow from the fire growing in the distance. The same church she met with Mariah in. Nita hadn't followed up with her and felt horrible for not doing so. All she could do now was hope she wasn't in there. She remembered the two of them exchanging cell numbers. Nita hurriedly fumbled her phone out of her pocket and made the call. It rang... one... two...three... four... voicemail.

"God... dammit," she whispered.

The youth building was engulfed in flames, separate from the worship center.

"Fuck me, it's Wednesday night," Charlie seemed to realize. Most all youth activities in the church occurred on this night. A chill raced down Nita's spine.

They both exited the vehicle about fifty yards from the fire burning so hot they could feel the heat. The flames traveled high into the night sky while the firemen did their best to fight the rage.

Nita ran to one of the policemen standing by, trying to keep hysterical parents at bay. "Did any get out?" she asked.

The policeman, whom she had never met, wore a face that spoke his answer. It was not the one she nor anyone else wanted.

An explosion amongst the flames sent the families into a frenzy. Cries sounded all around her. She was a girl once more, clutching the hands of her late Uncle Royce in OKC so many years ago. She grew nauseous. She could only rub her eyes, clench her jaw, and push those memories away.

She stared back at that fire, watching the flames and black smoke curl out of the building like a cruel, malevolent, elemental creature. Through one of the windows, a black mass returned. Like all the others, its form was human but featureless, aside from a white smile of crooked teeth. She hated being familiar with such entities.

She turned away to see a fireman stumbling away from the building. He ripped off his breathing apparatus when he returned to his men, revealing a sweaty face with his hair sticking to his forehead. Nita got close.

He breathed heavily. "The doors were fucking chained shut!"

There was nothing they could do but stand and watch the fire overwhelm the youth center. The building was a refurbished used car-selling business before it went under. The adjacent church purchased the property, and they took the bones of commerce and flipped them into a sanctuary of youthful praise and worship. Old car garages were turned into an indoor skate park with half-pipes and rails to drive in more "alternative" youths, and the main office area was the worship center and kitchen. As the flames blazed from the windows of the metal doors, Nita fretted at the hellish images of the interior.

CHAPTER 32

Twenty-two souls died in the fire. The memorials were arranged, and the whole town participated in some manner. Authorities were at a loss on how to proceed, given the recent murders still weighed heavy on locals' minds. However, the weight of so many high school and junior high kids dead was unparalleled. The random chain of violence had all law enforcement officials spinning their heads. The agencies involved labeled it as arson and, of course, murder.

Nita walked the scene of the crime. The former youth building was nothing more than a series of a blackened array of wood and brick. Three of the four walls remained but wilted and ceased to exist towards the rooftop.

Agent Teller stared at the carnage with a blank face for far too long. His hands rested on his hips, pushing his jacket behind him. She went to stand by him, not saying a word, merely basking in the eerie silence.

Twenty-one kids along with their youth minister. Twenty-two innocent and good souls were no longer with them.

Nita hoped God had mercy on them and allowed them all passage through whatever barrier resided on the other side.

"What the fuck is happening here, Nita?" Teller muttered, flabbergasted.

"I wish I knew."

"Those murders were one thing... This is a monster all its own."

"It's all random. I think it thrives most when it is."

"What thrives most?"

Teller's head finally turned to face her as she looked off to the woods at the back of the youth center.

"Evil," she said.

A long pause followed.

"When the Amish girl was lying on the slab, and you examined her, something clicked for you, and you started washing the charcoal off her like her soul depended on it. Why?"

"You helped wash it off too. Why were you so ready to do so?"

Teller adjusted his shirt sleeves by unbuttoning them at the wrists. "I've been asking myself that. I'm not entirely sure. Maybe it was the concern on your face or that Soap assisted so quickly like he knew what was happening."

Nita nodded.

"I'm in the dark here. Perhaps you could shed a little light or humor me."

She gauged her response carefully. She'd never told anyone outside her family and close friends about her abilities. Distrust ran deep in her veins, and for good reason. "It's difficult to explain, I assure you. I've researched this and traveled to many places to talk to many different types of people to discover what I have. I have it on good authority a medicine man is roaming around that knows somethin', but that's neither here nor there. I guess I could be classified as a clairvoyant, even though it pains me to say shit like that."

"Why?"

"Because I don't fucking want to see anything else that isn't there. I just want to see the world through the same eyes as everyone else."

Teller didn't appear judgmental or in doubt. "So, what exactly do you see? Sprits or something?"

"What do I see?" she repeated to herself. "When I finally figure that out, I'll let you know."

They shared the silence. There was a comfort to it, and the tension in Nita's shoulders eased.

"Agent Teller!" came from behind the smoldering building. A crime scene photographer was peeking out from around the corner on the east side. "Over here!"

They followed as he retreated around the youth center. The two jogged but were left hanging as the photographer was nowhere in sight.

"Here!" they heard from further east.

They pushed through a dense patch of unkempt forest to see the photographer kneeling over and snapping several pictures of tools on the ground.

The first was a wrench, followed by a hacksaw ten feet away. Nita was reminded of the horrible crime scene on Thorpe Ranch. Her mind flashed to Wyatt's and Colette's bodies on display. The person responsible used rebar, wire, and railroad spikes—all tools and items an everyday citizen wouldn't utilize on a regular basis. It would be foolish to assume many people in this state would have at least a few of these items in their house, barn, or shed. However, they couldn't shy away from the wealth of tools from both crime scenes.

She continued forward. Silver caught her eye. A few broken links of a short chain were buried amongst the grass. Rust gathered on the links. However, another substance covered them—black powder identical to the charcoal that covered Colette.

"And up ahead, we have rear tire tracks," the photographer said.

Nita and Teller followed the photographer's lead. Sure enough, the clear-eyed photographer was correct.

"Jeremy, is it?" Teller asked.

"Yes, sir."

"Well done."

"What are the odds they're related?" she asked.

"Pretty damn good, I say."

CHAPTER 33

Blake stared at his black ceiling. The longer he lay there, the more details emerged. The clock on his bedside table read 2:24 a.m. He found great comfort in his king-sized bed by himself, but a part of him still desired to pull a woman he loved closer to him. If it were merely a desire for sex, he figured that wouldn't be such a difficult task to accomplish. However, since he was a father with mounting responsibilities, he didn't want his moniker of "Most Eligible Bachelor in Oklahoma" to come to fruition. His daughter only stayed here on the weekends. Hence, the idea of women filtering in and out of the house wasn't anything he hadn't done before, but that empty feeling always remained once they left him. His past reputation around the area was of a "Cowboy Womanizer" or "Cowboy Casanova." They were terms he wasn't openly fond of and felt embarrassed by. The last thing he wanted was for those nicknames to reach his daughter's or ex-wife's ears. Although, with how Tara treated him as of late, she was well aware.

He was finally at that point of drifting away when Nova's deep bark thundered outside. It took a moment to discern whether it was the sound of his subconscious or reality. It wasn't uncommon for her to bark in the middle of the night; all sorts of critters could set the German Shepherd off.

The barking continued.

Raising himself from the bed proved difficult. He groaned on his ascension and went through the dark in his large house and onto the front porch. Blake squinted. Nova was at the end of his line of sight along the fence.

"Nova! Knock it off!" he yelled.

She stopped, but her gaze stayed forward, into that black abyss. He'd never seen her behave in such a manner. It took several times calling her name before she turned back around.

The wind whistled across the darkness. Blake tried to fight the instincts that told him something was out there. He attempted to suppress that thought like a child would when believing something was under the bed, but he couldn't shake the feeling.

Little J exited from one of the guest bedrooms where he resided. "Everything all right, brother?"

Blake responded by retrieving the loaded Henry Model .30-30 Lever-Action Rifle from the coat closet. The firearm had been in his family for generations and had seen a pair of refurbishments over the years. It was an item that preceded the home itself. His father always told him the rifle "built their home as well as any other tool." He never questioned the meaning behind those words, but he suspected them of being cursed.

In the closet, he grabbed a pair of boots to go with his boxers and plain sleeping shirt.

"Wait for me," Little J said, ready to go wherever or whenever Blake needed.

While he could retrieve his dog back to him, Blake was still competing with the dark for her attention. From time to time, she would growl and show her canines.

A high-pitched shriek sounded straight ahead. Blake carried himself as unshakable, but the frequency of that sound sent a volt through his ear and tased him all the way down the spine. There was no way to discern the noise or where it came from. It was as if it was inhuman, as much as Blake hated to admit such a thing could be that way.

He sprinted forward, with no regard or thought at all. A piece of his inner thigh caught the top of the wooden fence. He cursed out loud, knowing he was most likely bleeding at this point, but hoped it wouldn't require stitches.

The night converged all around him. He commanded Nova to stay behind, and like the well-trained dog she was, she obeyed. Little J yelled for Blake to wait, but he was already committed, full speed ahead.

He couldn't even make a guess as to how long he sprinted. He readied his rifle. He stopped in the field about four hundred yards away from the crime scene of Wyatt and that poor girl.

He locked onto three figures at a distance. They wore all black with the tree line behind them. Their white goat or sheep masks almost glowed with the moonlight. He didn't hesitate as he lined up a shot at the one in the center. His first instincts told him these were the ones responsible for Wyatt's death.

The trio stood there like scarecrows, unflinching and unmoving.

His father once told him, "Anyone who disturbs our home in any way, we put them down. I've bled for this. I don't care about the cost or the stakes. Anyone who trespasses against us will die quickly."

Blake was eleven when his father provided him with that doctrine.

He aimed the rifle, placing his front sight center mass on that son of a bitch in the middle. His finger rested on the trigger, but he released. Out of the void of the wooded tree line, more white masks emerged. They appeared like stars in the night sky. The longer he looked, the more he made their presence known.

Blake froze, unaware if he had drifted off to sleep this night.

The wind carried their whispers of an incomprehensible language like they were tongues of a snake-handling church. The growls and deep dogs' barks followed as five quick-moving shadows burst toward him. These black masses were accompanied by a strange series of white stripes traveling from their skull to their hindquarters.

He fired four shots and killed two of the large breeds. The remaining ones descended upon him in an almost supernatural fashion. He couldn't tell if they were Rottweilers, pit bulls, or a hybrid of the two, but the first one that got to him hit his legs so hard it knocked him completely off his feet. The other latched onto his forearm and dragged him like a ragdoll God knew how far. Maintaining his grip on the rifle, he put the end of the barrel on the beast's forehead. Before he could pull the trigger, another dog bit into the meat of his tricep.

A loud bang echoed across the pasture. That coincided with one of the attacking dogs bursting into pieces on top of him. Blood sprayed into his eyes.

Another shadow emerged from the corner of his eyes as Nova sank her teeth deep into the neck of the other dog on his arm. She latched down on it, and that dog squirmed and fought like hell, but she wasn't letting go.

He took his loose-fitting boot and drove it into the head of the dog on his leg. It released, giving him enough time to grab his rifle and end that hound's life with a shot to the head.

Little J ran up to him with his rifle in hand. It was a risky shot he took, to be sure, but Blake wasn't about to complain. All it would have taken was one clamp down on his neck, and the cowboy life of Blake Edwards would be finished.

Nova finished off the last of the dogs.

In the commotion, Blake forgot about the masked individuals of the tree line. His leg and arms were in pain as well as sore. The morning would be unpleasant. He readied his rifle again and aimed forward, but no one could be seen. The masked people vanished or ceased to exist. A silence fell over his land.

"What was it? What was it? Whose fucking dogs?" Little J asked.

Blake didn't answer. He kept his finger on the trigger, ready for anyone wearing a white mask to creep its head out of those woods to meet their end.

CHAPTER 34

Ezell sat in a chair on stage. This time he was in front of the pulpit. He used a handkerchief to wipe his brow as he stared into the cardboard box at his feet. His flock waited patiently for him to begin the Sunday sermon. The contents of the box remained unknown to the congregation. He felt their curiosity grow with each passing silent second. They had gone two weeks without phones, and their faith in him and his words had only grown. He saw it in their faces. He saw it in their eyes. He felt it in their aura. They were made clear.

He reached down, gripped the scaly serpent, and raised it from the box. Its body stiffened to a degree, showing its discomfort with the manhandling. A deadly strike from the rattlesnake could occur as the bottom half of the creature curled around Ezell's forearm.

There was an audible gasp from his congregation, which had doubled in attendance since the preceding Sunday. Their faith in him remained, but fear was present amongst them. That was by design, for the motive of his sermon today was to relocate their fears.

The serpent's rattle shook its way into the nerves of all in the chapel.

No one spoke up or questioned him verbally. Their faith would be rewarded, but they would have to wait.

"Many thoughts rushed into your heads. I know this. Those thoughts might consist of trepidation in me or my approach to offering God's Word this day. Before a judgment can be established, let me do my best to help you curb those instincts." The snake never stopped moving in his grasp. "Many 'preachers' that reside in the south believe this an efficient method of establishing faith in the Lord. Their whole reasoning for doing something as foolish as this comes from the gospel of Mark. Mark 16:15-18 states: 'Go into all the world and proclaim the gospel to the creation. Whoever believes and is baptized will be saved, but whoever does not believe will be condemned. And these signs will accompany those who believe: in my name, they will cast out demons; they will speak in new tongues; they will pick up serpents with their hands; and if they drink any deadly poison; it will not hurt them; they will lay their hands on the sick, and they will recover.'"

His visionaries' faithful and wide-eyed looks remained curious but were still not on the verge of faltering.

"A large portion of their doctrine stems from a minor allusion in a bite-sized passage. The reality is that the act of doing something like this should not be done." Ezell gently rested the snake back into the box, letting it leave his hand on its own power. He shook his arms since becoming free of the serpent's wrap and joked, "I'm glad that's over."

The tense emotions in the room faded, and his visionaries relaxed. The finely-molded faces looking back at him mainly consisted of plaid-wearing white folks that could be considered not aesthetically pleasing. There was also a thread of obesity that filtered through the congregation, as it did through the whole state of Oklahoma. None of that bothered him. As long as they basked in his light, they were welcome.

"We must be wary of those who misinterpret the Word. It's a difficult thing to see for certain. Oh, that is for certain," he repeated glancing up to the roof. "This world was built by those who have twisted the Word of God and used it for their advantage. These interpretations can be as insignificant as the snake wielders or as grand as those 'world leaders' in their pale buildings, insisting on war because the enemy is an abomination. All the while, there is no enemy at all, only a resource to be cultivated amongst them."

The congregation flocked to most of his words, but he could tell when they drifted away. His confidence in himself was high. He could always get them back and make them commit, even if their core beliefs fought against his ways.

Ezell pointed to the box where the snake slithered around atop the cardboard. "Let's return to the devil in the box, shall we? Again, the passage in Mark reads: 'They will cast out demons; they will speak in new tongues; they will pick up serpents with their hands; and if they drink any deadly poison; it will not hurt them; they will lay their hands on the sick, and they will recover.'"

He held out his hands and shrugged. His visionaries waited patiently for him to proceed.

Ezell pointed to Herb Elmore, a roofer with a weathered face and hands. He was considered an original visionary. At the ripe age of sixty-two, Herb believed in Ezell with all his heart. He sat three rows back in an aisle seat. His occupation was not kind to his skin, but a strong frame of a man remained. He wore a pistol at his hip, which was welcomed by Ezell, and many of his followers appreciated that about him.

"Herb, can I ask you a question?"

"Yes, Father. Of course," Mr. Elmore submitted.

"You've been a God-fearing man your whole life, correct?"

"Yes, Father. Although, I'd say I was still lost until you came around, Father."

A collective "Amen" sounded throughout the chapel. Even fresh visionaries nodded their heads. Then, their blurred form began to focus.

"I appreciate that, Herb. I appreciate that from all of you." Ezell smiled, but he calmed the room back down to accept his teachings. "Herb, you said your mother took you to church when you were a boy?"

"Yes, Father."

"And when she grew ill, did no one come to lay hands on her and heal her?"

Herb was at a loss. His eyes darted around.

Ezell slammed his finger into the gospel. "But it says right here that if anyone who is saved and believes can heal those who are sick!" He followed with a slew of rhetorical questions. "Was Herb's mother some exception to the rule? Was she unable to accept healing? Were there no true believers that could aid Herb's mother?"

The room fell silent.

"No... that's not the case," Ezell said softly. "You cannot heal those who are healthy in the Lord. Had Herb's mother not been a believer, perhaps healing would have been a requirement to save her soul, but it wasn't, visionaries! What I'm trying to get across here is simple: be wary of lesser people interpreting the words of those far more intelligent than they are!"

He again slammed his finger into the Bible as the head nods continued. "Sure, we will cast out demons, but not those in a classical sense. The demons are the thoughts that lead us astray from God and this Temple we call home! The new tongues we speak in are not some mythical languages! No! The new tongues are *us*, the flock doing whatever it takes to adapt to those outside our native language to give the gift of our beautiful destiny!

"I don't know about you all, but I don't intend on drinking poison or cyanide. The poison is not literal! The poison represents our faltering faith that can sway like a cheap wind chime, but with grace, we remain! And no, we don't just pick up damned snakes. The devil himself represents the serpent, and we are to control him because, with God, we can. However, our duty is not to tempt the Lord or the devil. For that would be the act of a fool!"

More sweat dripped down the side of his face. He wiped it away, adjusted his suit jacket, the only one amongst the congregation, and settled. "Ultimately, what I'm trying to get across, what I hope *is* coming across, is that we must be wary of those who misinterpret the Word. Those that do will eventually come for us, claiming that we are in the wrong. They will cast us aside and make us out to be the devil in their story. What's the greater sin: those who manipulate the word of God? Or those who reject it entirely?"

CHAPTER 35

A break finally arrived.

A hit came back on the fingerprints on the tools left behind at the burned-down church. They belonged to a man named James Arnold from the town of Jay. The database showed that he was sixty-two and owned Arnold's Construction as an independent contractor. The company had been out of business for over a year, but that didn't stop the pursuit of the OSBI or the Cherokee Marshals.

Nita tightened her bulletproof vest as Charlie drove, tailing Agent Teller and the OSBI the whole way.

"What's his first name?" Charlie asked.

"James—James Arnold," she said, assuming that was who Charlie was asking about.

Ahead, the OSBI and local PD pulled off the road and parked outside an old house not far off the main highway.

Nita and Charlie shot out of their seats. The first thing she noticed was the absence of a pickup truck in the driveway. All that remained was a 2002 Buick LeSabre, as plain as a pair of Walmart khakis.

Having secured a warrant for the house, the Cherokee Marshals' tactical team burst onto the scene in the beige military surplus vehicle as it barreled down the dirt and gravel road with seemingly unshakable momentum. It came to a screeching halt, and the tactical unit erupted from the drop-down back door. The breacher had a battering ram with support at his back. The operation gave Nita flashes of remembrance as she was once a part of this unit.

Every law enforcement officer had their guns drawn. Seeing there was no need, Nita kept her hands on her hips and watched the tactical unit take control of the situation. She had faith in her Native brothers and sisters.

The home was a shoddy mess. The wood beams holding up the awning on the front porch were rotting away. The windows were fogged beyond repair, and a tarp, held in place by cinderblocks, covered a hole in the roof.

The large blast of the battering ram slamming through the front door could've been heard from a mile off. The tac team rushed through the door, screaming, "Get down!" repeatedly.

Mr. Arnold was in the building. Perhaps a knock at the door would have sufficed, but when it came to murdered kids, caution was no longer a rule of engagement.

The team carried what looked to be the man in question from the worn-down home. Arnold kicked and screamed his innocence. Even at this distance, Nita could see the man's reddish sores and dry skin on his neck and face.

"What are the meth odds?" Charlie asked rhetorically.

As the commotion around the house wound down and Mr. Arnold was secured in the car, Nita and Charlie approached the house with Agent Teller leading the search party. A few distant neighbors were sitting on their front porches drinking coffee, watching the event like a Saturday morning episode of *COPS*.

"What's your initial thoughts?" Nita asked, tucking her shirt into her pants and stretching her back that still pained her.

"I'm not ruling him out. He's definitely coming down off of something at the moment, though. We're going to take him to the hospital and get an IV in him, so he's ready for questioning. I'd like you to be present for that, Marshal."

There was no hesitation. "Absolutely."
"Coming down off something, you say? Meth?" Charlie asked.
"Looks like it."

CHAPTER 36

Nita met Agent Teller at the hospital a few days later. It appeared Mr. Arnold's meth withdrawals were no joke and were in no condition to be questioned. He remained in a private wing in Hastings Hospital.

Teller overlooked the railing on the second floor when Nita walked through the sliding glass doors. Native memorabilia filled the space behind thick glass, beautifully displayed on every wall and beam.

She flashed her badge to the receptionist at the desk and was greeted with a smile and a, "Go right on ahead, Marshal Ross."

"Thank you."

"Marc," she said with a smirk as he met her at the top of the stairs.

"Are we on a first-name basis now?"

"We've had enough conversations. I think it's finally appropriate."

Nita understood more than anybody the seriousness of his job and what they were trying to accomplish. It was a task that didn't offer a lot of levity, but the more that remained present, the easier it was to cope.

She followed him, and he looked back and said, "This place is something."

"You've never been in here? You don't have an Indian card?"

"Nope."

"Really? Even the white folks around here have Indian cards."

"I'm originally from Utah, remember?"

"That's right. That's like the Great White Capital, is it not?"

Teller bobbed his head. "Eh, you're not wrong."

They made for Arnold's room.

"How many wives you rockin'?" Nita asked.

He laughed. "I saw that one coming."

———

James Arnold lay handcuffed to an angled hospital bed. The meth-using suspect declared his innocence as soon as they walked through the door, even in a weakened state. "I didn't kill those kids! I swear! I didn't burn down shit! I build shit. I don't burn or break it down."

"I'll tell you what you're going to do. You're going to calm down and wait for me to ask the questions," Teller demanded.

"Yes, sir," Mr. Arnold replied, defeated.

Teller cleared his throat. "We found tools and tracks from a work truck that appears to be under your name found near the youth center that burned down. Can you explain why that would be?"

"No, my work truck was stolen over a month ago."

"Why didn't you report that to the local authorities?"

"I did!"

"No report was ever filed."

"I don't know what to tell you. I spoke to the officer, and he said he'd do it."

Teller stood there a moment and side-eyed Nita. A stolen vehicle was not something an officer would let slip through the cracks, no matter how worthless the person.

"What was the name of the officer?" Teller asked.

"Hell, if I remember something like that!"

"Well, it could get your truck back and also help lead to your eventual innocence in the involvement of the murder of twenty-two people."

Mr. Arnold scratched his mustache, followed by the top of his head as if he needed the verbal slap in the face that Agent Teller gave him.

Nita rubbed her arms in the small hospital room as the air conditioner kicked on.

"Could you at least supply us with your whereabouts for that night as a possible alibi?" Nita pleaded.

"No, I can't."

"Why's that?" Teller asked.

"Well, special agent man. If you must know, I had my business license revoked two months ago, and my truck got stolen not long after that. With few options and not a lot of money, I decided to spend it on something that would help ease the pain."

Teller was at a loss for the moment.

"Mr. Arnold?" Nita chimed in. "Do you have anyone that you've been at odds with recently? Maybe a former employee?"

"Welp, you see, not paying my employees got me into hot water in the first place with the legalese people."

"So, do you believe a former employee could have stolen your truck as some form of revenge?"

"That's not likely," he said.

"And why's that?" Teller asked.

"He's currently in jail."

"For what?"

Arnold's eyes roved over them with a matching crooked smile like they were idiots. "Meth," he confirmed in a very matter-of-fact manner.

Teller exhaled under his breath and let out a not-so-subtle "Jesus Christ."

"Is there anything else you can give us?" Nita asked. "We believe the person driving your truck last night burned the youth center and all those innocent ones inside. We need something. Are there any jobs you may have done where someone was unsatisfied? Any sketchy people in your neighborhood that you had your eyes on?"

"Yeah," Teller assisted. "Any of your most recent jobs go bad?"

Mr. Arnold thought about it, but a connection clicked sooner than Nita expected. "I mean, I did get fired from my final job before my truck got stolen."

"Did you? Did it not end well?"

"Nothing too bad. He just said he wouldn't be needin' my service no more. Guess he wasn't thrilled with the work I had completed."

"And who was this?"

Arnold squinted and looked off. "Oh, I believe the fella's last name was Dyer."

CHAPTER 37

School proved difficult for Blake growing up. He had all the tools to succeed, but one thing persisted above all: laziness. He understood the concepts and teachings well enough; however, his interest needed to be more. Sitting at a desk all day was an issue from kindergarten to his senior year. He preferred sports and agriculture as opposed to his traditional classroom settings. It wasn't until his sophomore English teacher Mrs. Gable gave him a vital piece of advice that he longed overlooked as his father's apathy maintained. She told him simply, "You're here. Might as well apply yourself." The words were honest, unpretentious, and cliché, but they worked.

That year, he remembered they read Homer's *The Iliad*. The quote that always stuck out to him from the epic poem was arguably the most famous one, or at least what Mrs. Gable told him: "We men are wretched things." He fought hard against the urge to associate such a harsh quote with the men of his family, but he could never shake comparing them every time he read or heard those ancient words.

Still, Mrs. Gable's advice powered through, and he applied them to his life to resist being a wretched man. When he decided to join the military, he wanted to apply himself for the greater good. To represent something more than himself and serve his fellow men and women in uniform, forming a bond more powerful than anything.

However, wretchedness always crept through.

Blake tended to his damaged flesh from the dog bites on his arm and legs. The morning brought unwelcomed soreness. Nova was aware of his ailments and gently brushed up against his thigh, doing her best not to inflict any more pain like a good, instinctual dog would.

All the boys were present. Little J led the way into the master bedroom. Blake leaned forward, the tips of his long hair tickling his eyebrows and temples, but he did nothing. He took in a few deep breaths as he looked at the boots of all his men. Cody's stuck out more than the rest. The cowhide was beginning to retreat from the heavy-duty leather.

"We gotta get you some new boots, Cody," Blake said.

No one spoke. There was an intensity in the room that, indeed, everyone had picked up on by now. His bedroom could house everyone comfortably, perhaps twice the size of an average living room. A family portrait of his father as a young boy beneath his grandpa hung above a fireplace. His father's favorite subject was preserving what his family had built. The words he passed down were like a creed intended to burn a hole into Blake's head.

"Boys, I wanted to start by apologizing to you all," Blake said before raising his head. "My father branded my mind with the idea that what we had was something special, something that was fought and killed over a hundred years ago. It was also something almost lost or taken countless times, and one day it would be mine to defend. I always thought he was a fucking idiot because this wasn't the Wild West anymore. One night, my father was on a drunken bender when I came home from college. Who knows when he started? From the looks of the place, he had been at it for a while. He ranted on and on about how this land was cursed. He yelled it at the top of his lungs and begged the demons to leave him be."

Blake stopped. He stared off thinking of nothing and taking nothing in. Little J brought him back, "Blake?" he asked.

"Sorry... My first thought when I saw him stumbling around the living room with a bottle of Jack was how pathetic he was. He'd rather curse and blame the demons rather than fight against them. I can't help but think about my subconscious motivations in bringing you all here as these repressed thoughts dominate my brain. I knew I had an opportunity to help you financially, and I had peace of mind knowing y'all'd be well-off because of it. At the very least, I was potentially saving my brothers from peddling or begging beneath an overpass."

Blake nodded to all his brothers standing at attention like good soldiers. Behind the wall were the war medals his grandfather received during World War II. Above them, eleven dog tags were displayed to be held in higher regard. Blake took solace knowing that his brothers were still alive after the fighting ceased and that they all made it out together. However, that wasn't the case anymore with the loss of Wyatt.

Fuckin' Ramadi.

"But a part knew that my dad's warning could somehow become valid one day. Most of the time, I thought he and my grandfather were just paranoid old bastards who grew up in a different time. Call it the Wild West... or... fuckin' whatever... I don't know. I guess the ulterior motive I had to bring you all here was to help me keep the wolves at bay."

He never wanted to be this. He never wanted to be his father or his grandfather. Once, he had dreams of playing pro ball. Play linebacker for the Pokes in Stillwater. He'd even flip sides and join the Sooners if Nita's dad had stayed on staff. All it took was a pair of ACL tears to derail those aspirations. The next best option to join the military was to avoid his father for a while, which drove a wedge between them until his father's dying day.

"Some wolves revealed themselves to me last night, and if you all would forgive me, I'd like to cash in the solid I've done for y'all. I don't know who those people were last night. I believe they had something to do with Wyatt. Maybe even more than that, or perhaps my head is so foggy and fucked up right now that I don't even know, but it's time to start digging a little deeper. People are gonna get hurt because of it. I'm not forcing you all to participate in what happens next, but—"

Parker cut Blake off. The long sleeves of his plaid shirt were rolled up his muscled arms. "You don't gotta worry about cashing anything in, brother. We're ready to hurt people."

Chapter 38

Nita and other law enforcement ascended onto the Dyer residence. The FBI also came along to follow this lead. The sizeable modern home was surrounded by hundreds of acres. She had grown up in this area, but this patch of land was new to her. She would be embarrassed to admit how long it took to realize that the location backed up to Thorpe Ranch. Blake's house was only a couple miles away.

Teller looked at his phone. "They identified everyone who died in the fire."

He didn't look back. However, he offered his phone for Nita to look at as she sat behind him in the car. She accepted his offering and scrolled through the lengthy list, praying. She stopped mid-prayer as the name *Mariah Paddock* appeared towards the bottom.

She handed the phone back to him. *I will find out. I will find out who did this, so help me, God.*

There were work trucks of all varieties. Massive renovations were taking place as mounds of dirt were piled in the field behind the house. A concrete truck laid the foundation for a long driveway leading from the house to the forest. Sheets of metal siding were stacked beside one another in endless rows.

"Jesus," Teller said.

The crew consisted of men with neck tattoos and countless cigarettes. The badges seemed to draw the eyes of all the laborers, but these eyes were not ones of surprise—no, contempt.

"Is the residence's owner here?" Teller asked one of the workers.

The man took a long beat in his faded white shirt and jeans, not a hard hat or vest in sight. He spat to the side and pointed to the woods. At the same time, the sound of an ATV came from that same direction. It was probably two hundred yards away, and that four-wheeler was on them not long after the initial sighting.

With that, a man with two tattoo sleeves offered them a much warmer greeting. "How can I help you all?" he asked, stepping off his vehicle.

"Are you Amos Dyer?" Teller asked.

"I am. Everything all right?"

"Mr. Dyer, we had some questions regarding a former contractor of yours."

Amos looked around as he rubbed his bald head. "Okay?"

"A gentleman named James Arnold said he did some work for you not long ago."

"Uh, yes. Yes, that's true. He good?"

Nita had a hard time discerning Amos's tone of voice. His concern bordered on genuine and apathetic. Perhaps he was baiting for more information. As far as instinct went, nothing stood out to her.

"His truck was stolen not long ago," Teller said. "We're just trying to see the whereabouts."

Amos surveyed the field of law enforcement officers of different agencies. "This much effort for a stolen vehicle?" Amos asked with a cocked eyebrow.

"Important ones, yes," Agent Teller clapped back.

To that, Amos nodded. The eyes of the workers were still upon them all. Their work for the time being had either slowed or ceased entirely. "Fair enough."

"We have reason to believe it may be important to another investigation."

"May I ask why you fired him?" Nita interjected.

"Well, I'm old school." Amos said. "So, when you show up to work late to a job high or drunk and then proceed to do that job poorly, it's time to let them go."

A high-pitched tone rattled in Nita's ear. It was almost painful, and she tried not to react. It was like an amplified dog whistle squealing directly into her ears. In the direction of the woods, where Amos had just come from, she saw a man wearing muted clothes and a boater hat that looked too trendy for the area. She'd lived here all her life, and she'd never seen anyone wear one of those. Not even the hippies from the college.

The ringing continued. She adjusted her jaw and pulled down on her earlobe. The eyes of all the men surrounding her found her, and she did her best to play it off like nothing was wrong.

"What are you building here?" she asked.

Amos took a moment to answer. It appeared he took notice of Nita's hum in the drum. "New barn, chapel, guest house, chicken coop. I could go on and on."

"Chapel?" Teller asked. "To serve what purpose?"

"The purpose of serving, Agent. We all meet our standards of practicing our religions differently." Amos wore an all-black shirt with work jeans. The slithering tongue of a snake tattoo crept up his neck. He was pale, with slicked black hair. He didn't look the part of a DIYer, but Nita had seen stranger things around here. "I got a friend of mine who preaches the good gospel. He wanted to start something special, so I thought I'd help him. As far as the other stuff goes..." Amos pulled a pack of Marlboros from his back pocket, slapped them against his thigh, and lit up. "Shit, just splurging' and spending money to make money, you know what I mean?"

"Sure," Teller responded.

Amos' modern home didn't match the aesthetics of the neighboring farmhouses that occupied most of eastern Oklahoma. The house had windows and a balcony that traveled along the entire back side. A large hole was being dug for what looked to be an underground pool.

"If I gather correctly, you have no idea of the vehicle's whereabouts in question?"

Amos monitored the work being done in the surrounding area, growing less interested in the conversation at hand. "You would gather correctly." He finished off the first cigarette, flicked it into the dirt, and lit another one. "Listen, I'll help you in any way I can. If you need me to locate some paperwork or anything like that, I can try, but I know jack shit about the truck's location."

The ringing intensified, forcing Nita to close her right eye. She tugged on her earlobe and opened her jaw as wide as possible. Before a worried Teller asked how she was doing, another line of question came from another.

"Everything all right, Amos?" the man in the boater hat asked as he approached.

It stopped altogether at the posing of his concern. Nita monitored workers, upwards of thirty, watching this man very closely. Amos stayed behind and seemed surprised at this man's presence.

"I think everything's fine," he replied, looking Nita up and down. She cleared her throat and didn't make eye contact.

"Amos, perhaps the marshal could use a glass of water."

The order came off strange, considering that this was Amos' land.

"No, I'm fine," Nita said, holding out her hand with her palm facing out.

"And who are you?" Teller asked the man.

His head turned, but slowly, as if it was delayed. "Ezell Sunderland. I'm an old friend of Amos here. Pleased to meet you."

"I see," Teller said, "and what is it you do around here? You don't look too much like a construction worker."

Ezell laughed and laughed. It didn't bother him that no one else shared the humor, not even his "old friend" Amos. No, Amos' lips closed now that Ezell was amongst them. Nita caught him looking over his shoulder and fiddling with his sleeves.

"No, I'm not much for manual labor. I'm afraid the last time I used a hammer, I about hit my thumb so hard I thought I'd lose it. To answer your question, I am currently preaching to the congregation here. We aren't a large church, far from large, but we are proud, and hopefully, we will get more along the way. But for now, I am thankful for Amos providing me a platform to do what I love. That's for sure. I get carried away with the potential sometimes."

Teller nodded and asked, "Will you let us know if you see or hear anything regarding that truck?"

"Will do," Amos replied.

Ezell removed his hat. "Oh, are you all investigating that tragedy at the church?" He bowed his head to send up a quick prayer.

"We aren't at liberty to discuss," Teller said. "But I'm sure you can put two and two together."

Ezell's eyes never stopped. He was an observant fellow. He reminded Nita of one of those chameleons or geckos with big eyes. Those reptilian senses fixated on the lawmen present. "It's interesting the FBI and Cherokee Marshals cooperation," Ezell said.

Nita put her hands behind her back and raised her chin. "It's not uncommon."

Nita let him continue as she noticed Teller's raised brow.

"What an ever-changing world we occupy. At one point, the government, let's call them the FBI, was able to kidnap your people without cause and enroll them in a school to be Anglicized. You know, to exorcise the demons that were the Native Americans. How long does it take for an institution of such genocidal tendencies to grow beyond those atrocities?"

Ezell wore a sly grin as he exchanged looks with everyone on the receiving end of his glances. All the while, Amos stood there uncomfortably, clenching his jaw. Nita's eyes darted to each of them, and she nodded. Construction on whatever was being built on the land remained at a halt while they were all out in the open.

"What was the motto again..." he said, searching for an answer. "Oh, yes, 'Kill the Indian, Save the Man.'" Nita nodded, knowing that was, in fact, the proper mission statement of many of the Native boarding schools across North America. "I do hope for everyone's sake around here that a more prominent form of sovereignty of the Native nations can take shape. The last thing we all want is history to repeat itself."

"Where did you say you were from, Ezell?" she asked.

"I'm from many places. I was born in the Great White North, but I had my spiritual awakening in eastern Europe."

That said nothing.

Teller took the initiative. "Thank you all for your time. We will let you get back to it."

Amos fired up the ATV again.

"You all, please come back if you have any more questions. You are also formally invited to join us on Sundays if you so choose."

CHAPTER 39

VISION JOURNAL

BY: DALTON BRANSUM

Perhaps Father Ezell is the son of God. He keeps instructing us that he isn't, but there's denial in his voice. The glint in his eye tells us he believes there is something to his ways. Perhaps he is divine. Perhaps he is the son of the Almighty. His warnings of the fall of man have been realized so far. He's told us about the wolves in sheep's clothes who present themselves as holy men and act on their desires... That pastor out of Kansas who spewed his doctrine and lived by none of it.

Father Ezell has shown us the way of the light. We must reject the world at large. The world is sinful and spins in a direction away from all that is God. Father shows us his course correction and gives us who desire a pure life of service. The truth is with him. Wherever the Father goes, the truth follows.

He instructs on how to live our best life. He hasn't missed it so far. He informs us about what is good and what is bad for us. Things as little as the taste of sugar being rooted in evil in its correlation to the mass production of obesity.

Sure, he has rules we are to follow from time to time. However, those rules are only mandatory for the desired freedom he wants for us. He assures us that everything we need in this world is already amongst us and is ripe for the picking. No man-made government or societal construct should be able to dictate our ways or his teachings. For if that is the case, we must rebel against such rules of the world in order to live free on our own.

Perhaps he is the son of God...

CHAPTER 40

The bell chimed above the glass door as Blake and his guys entered the last of the few party supply stores in town. Their mission so far had proved fruitless, and Blake's frustration grew. He wanted answers. He wanted them now.

The men broke off, each going down a different store aisle. They flanked the counter like the clerk was their target. The only escape was the backroom, but for now, they didn't want to spook anyone too soon.

Only one worker was on the floor, for the shop itself wasn't significant. It was shoved in an unflattering corner of a strip mall next to a thrift store and a Dollar Tree. The worker was young, perhaps still in high school or college, but didn't strike Blake as a popular type. Dandruff was sprinkled atop both of his shoulders, for today, the black company shirt didn't conceal the scalp snow.

"How can I help you?" the employee asked. His nametag read: *Lucas*. The young man's shy demeanor told Blake he wouldn't have addressed them if it wasn't part of his job.

Blake took the lead. "Oh, just browsin'."

Parker stalked the aisles with a scowl on his face. He wasn't the most subtle of cowboys, but then again, all this was relatively new to him. He had been a former gangbanger in Tulsa before turning to the Marines for a new life after one of his boys was shot and killed in front of him. Beneath his clothes, he was covered in tattoos of a life of crime, violence, and history he wished to leave behind. His permanent ink remained a cruel reminder to him, but his thanks for Blake's opportunity never left.

The shelves displayed a variety of costumes, masks, and entertainment paraphernalia of plastic weapons and jewelry from all sorts of famous franchises.

"A-are you browsing for a certain occasion? I-I can help," Lucas asked, removing his headphones that now dangled on his chest.

"Well, maybe you can. You have any masks that are...expressionless... kinda like a hard-shell Michael Myers mask?"

Lucas nodded. Blake had to force himself to look away from the specs of white falling from his greasy hair. "Yeah, we may have something that fits that, uh... mmm..."

"Description?" Blake said, finding the right word for him.

"Yes, that's it. Thank you."

"No problem, Lucas. Can you point me in the right direction?"

"Uh, yes, sure thing, sir."

Blake followed while the rest of the guys hung back. Floyd stepped back outside to take a smoke and watch the door. Lucas showed Blake the back wall that displayed hundreds of isolated masks.

"So, this is our creatively named 'mask wall.' These are obviously just headpieces that don't have a link to any other costumes or pop culture... uh..."

"Property. I gotcha."

"Yeah, yeah, just regular, unlicensed masks." Lucas said. "Uh... I-I'll leave y'all to look around."

Blake's eyes were already moving up and down and side to side all along the wall. Most of them he was able to disregard in search of the one. A couple caught his eye at first, but either had too much expression or had additional pieces of fabric.

Cody's shadow crossed his peripheral. Blake nodded. Something from the row behind him caught his eye first. Something unrelated to any of the masks. Near the floor, a fully stocked display of stereotypical

Native costumes were on sale. A white guy with a tomahawk and a headdress smiled on the cover.

"Aye, Lucas?" he called.

The young clerk returned. "Yes, sir?"

Blake lightly kicked the display with his boot. "I'd consider finding a new home for that. That don't fly 'round here."

Lucas nodded as if he understood.

"I'll go ahead and purchase what you have in stock, but don't bother putting another order in for them."

Blake clocked a glaring, empty display rack at Lucas' back amongst an entire collection of surrounding masks. Lucas took notice of his focus and moved out of the way as Blake brushed his shoulder. The price tag read: *Generic Mask #13.*

It piqued his interest that these masks were the only empty ones in this aisle. For a moment, his faith grew. "Well, Lucas, I'm not seeing the one I'm looking for. However, it could be this one. Do you mind pulling up a picture of the ones that were here?"

Lucas' nervous energy at the unsolicited cowboys entering his store, which had been fading, began to return. "Yes. Yes, sir." He jittered back to the desk.

The boys followed. Blake got Parker up close with him. As a combat engineer and a cyber warfare specialist, he knew his way around a computer. He scored the highest on the ASVAB and could choose whatever MOS (Military Operational Specialty) he wanted. Parker was long and lanky. In the corps, everyone called him Tiki because he was as skinny as a tiki torch.

Lucas was intimidated. It was evident by the constant glancing out of the corner of his eye. Parker flanked the desk to establish a good position on the computer monitor.

Lucas' hands fluttered above the keyboard, too shaky to commit.

"I just want to check and see if you have any more in stock," Blake said, leaning in closer, looming his shadow over the young man.

"Yeah, of course," Lucas replied nervously. His fingers began moving. It wasn't long until Lucas confirmed, "Y-yes, they are out of stock."

None of the cowboys were convinced by his delivery and lack of eye contact. Parker took it upon himself to engage. His long-limbed frame meandered behind the counter, casting a shadow over the young clerk.

"You mind if I take a look?" Parker asked.

Lucas moved to the side, and Little J replaced Parker's position at the end of the counter. Parker's technical precision with the keyboard was beyond Blake. It didn't take long for his fellow Marine to find something interesting.

"Lucas here wasn't lying. However, he wasn't telling the whole truth," Parker said as Lucas hung his head. "Yes, they are out of stock but also listed as stolen. There's a new order of them that should be in by Thursday."

"Which day were they stolen?"

Parker glanced back at the monitor. "The eighteenth."

Blake blew air from his nostrils and laughed. That was the day of the assault on his land. He turned to look at the cameras that looked down the aisles. "Do the cameras work, Lucas?"

Lucas shook his head, but Parker checked anyway. Again, Parker didn't take long to check Lucas' bluff. "Got the camera video uploaded here, Blake."

He stared emotionlessly at Lucas until they eventually made eye contact, which was the last thing the boy wanted.

"Are you lying because you're scared or hiding something?" Blake asked.

Parker clicked away on the keyboard.

Blake stepped closer. Lucas leaned back like he could smell Blake's morning coffee. "You've been nervous ever since we stepped into this shithole. You know something, don't you?"

"Blake," Parker said sternly while spinning the monitor.

Grainy footage from the security cameras on the eighteenth at 9:37 p.m. saw Lucas grabbing a chest full of the masks in question and making his way to the back room.

Cody was perched by the front door. After hearing the back and forth at the counter, he flipped the sign on the front door to "Closed."

Lucas took a half step back, rotated his hips, and burst towards the backroom. But Blake grabbed his shirt collar and yanked him back. He pulled him in close, holding Lucas inches from his face.

"What were you doing with those masks? Were you there that night?"

"No! I swear! Please, let me go."

Blake nodded to Parker. His fellow Marine emptied Lucas' pockets, removing only his phone and key and placing them on the counter. Then Blake addressed Floyd, who was waiting to pounce. "Go check his vehicle and the back room."

Floyd dropped his jovial demeanor. It was time for work. Floyd was a MOS 0211, which meant he served in counterintelligence. Before walking into the back room, he told Lucas, "If I'm going to discover anything else that would put you in a precarious situation, I would suggest speaking now."

One could not simply lie to Floyd. He'd witnessed Floyd sniff out varying levels of bullshit like competing scents. His awareness of how the world and its people operated was second to none. As much time as he spent in the field as a spy, he spent more time writing highly detailed reports that required more mental strength than perhaps SERE training.

Parker continued with his expertise as Floyd escaped into the back. Parker held the phone up to Lucas' face to unlock it. "Hm," Parker said. "The latest model. No offense, Lucas, but I'm curious how you could afford this. Business isn't exactly booming in this boutique you're running."

Ten minutes passed. Parker scrolled through Lucas' new phone. Floyd returned, carrying a bike helmet with a Smith & Wesson – M&P 9 Shield M2.0. The cheap handgun had a green laser attachment. Floyd also carried a prospect biker cut of the Skull Draggers Motorcycle Club.

"This is your last chance, Lucas," Blake said. "Tell me something honest. I'll know if it's not."

Lucas surveyed the situation as his eyes frantically darted to all the Marines bearing down on him. Then, he dropped his head, and through sniffles he admitted, "My uncle wanted them."

"Who's your uncle, and why did he want the masks?"

The boy hesitated some more, wanting more than anything to speak. He'd probably rather cut his tongue off. "Travis Dell. He's VP for the Skull Draggers MC. He said it would place me in a good position to move up and lose the prospect patch. But I promise I didn't know what they were for. I'm just a prospect. They don't tell me shit!"

Blake's jacket vibrated against his chest. He reached in and pulled out his phone that read: *Mission Intermediate Grade Center*. He gave the nod to his guys to take over.

"Hello?" he greeted.

"Blake? This is Chrissie at Mission."

"Aye, Chrissie, everything all right?" Blake had known Chrissie for a long time. The sweet Italian woman found her way to Oklahoma. Blake and her son Joey used to run around with each other and get into trouble. She'd been the receptionist at Mission for nearly two decades. Lyla was a well-behaved girl with good grades and never rubbed teachers the wrong way, but call from the school usually meant something had happened.

"Well, Lyla had a little incident at school today. First off, she's okay. However, Ms. Pierce would like you to come down and talk with her at your earliest convenience."

Somehow, an ambiguous call from an elementary school had more weight and surprise to him than bikers attacking him on his own land.

"Yeah… sure. I'll be right there."

CHAPTER 41

Parking directly in front of the breezeway was prohibited at the grade center, but when it was in the middle of a school day, Blake figured he'd get a pass. The buzzer ahead of him sounded, and he swung the glass door open. Kids of all grades walked in single-file lines in the opposite direction, some louder than others. The school bell rang three times as Blake hustled to the office. He weaved through stragglers that were scolded for being a moment too late to class. Chrissie offered him a sincere welcome as Lyla ran out the door crying and into a firm grasp around his waist.

He pushed her away and got down to her level. "Are you all right?"

She nodded, indicating she was, but the tears remained. She was a strong young girl. At that moment, he was as proud of her as ever. The clapping of heels marched behind him. He had beat Tara to school. They exchanged looks before she embraced Lyla and asked the same question.

He took notice of Nita's boy, Aiden, sitting in the office by himself. Chrissie offered him a juice box while he stared off into the unknown. His shirt appeared damp and was unnaturally darker in color.

Principal Pierce waved the two of them into her office There was no question that Blake and Tara were taking this meeting together.

"Lyla, why don't you sit next to Aiden while your parents meet with Ms. Pierce?" Chrissie said.

The two of them were handed library books to pass the time.

Tara led the way into the office, and Blake followed close behind. Ms. Pierce's office was the standard array of inspirational quotes littering the walls, pictures of students from the past and present, and a couple holes in the drywall, perhaps from angry students or maybe even parents.

"Please take a seat," she asked. "I really appreciate both of you coming in. Most of our separated parents aren't so cordial."

"I'd imagine," Blake said.

"Well, we're willing to do what it takes to help Lyla succeed," Tara added.

"Good. Good, that's how it should be." The principal read through a couple of papers, then stacked them, patted them, and cleared her throat. "Well, anyway, there's no easy way to say this, but there was an incident of bullying today directed at Lyla and another student, but we are here to talk about Lyla so... At recess, a boy pulled Lyla's pants down, taking everything down with them, while another boy slapped her... backside."

"Are you fucking kidding me!" Blake bolted to his feet.

Tara whispered his name fleetingly to get him to mind his language. "They're in fifth grade. Is this a new trend, challenge, or some stupid social media thing?"

"Well, pantsing, as you know, has been around awhile, but the slapping is new," Ms. Pierce replied.

"I'd like to talk to the parents," Tara said while Blake fumed.

"I can't give you that information, Tara. You know that."

"Did the same thing happen to the other student? You said there were two incidents today. Were they both done by the same kid?" Blake pried, lurching forward and gripping the edge of the desk.

Ms. Pierce rubbed her eyes. "Yes, they were done by the same kid. Earlier today, while Aiden Philips was in the bathroom stall, a certain boy turned off the lights, repeatedly banged on the stall to frighten the boy, and then poured water over the door to get him wet."

"What kind of monster is this kid?" Tara asked, slapping her hands on the armrests now.

"You kinda have an idea now," Pierce said, glancing out the office window to look at Aiden. "The boy keeps to himself and doesn't harm a fly, and this is what he gets."

"I thought Nita's boy was in... what ya call it... isolated class or whatever." Blake asked.

"Self-contained, yes, he is. The self-contained class shares lunch and recess with the entire fifth grade."

"Have you contacted Nita?" Tara asked.

"Uh, yes, we have, but she is working an hour away and won't be here for a while."

"Blake," Tara said, "call Nita and tell her to stay put and you'll take Aiden back to your house."

He was at a loss for words for a moment. He scrunched his face, believing the logic to be sound, but coming from Tara, it seemed off.

His ex-wife lowered her voice. "She just lost her husband. Everything around here has been visions of hell as of late. She doesn't need to be worrying about this right now."

"You would need to get Nita's permission to take Aiden home." Ms. Pierce said.

Blake remained a bit taken aback by the insistence of his ex-wife to take the boy with him. "I'll call her," he said.

He stepped outside for a moment, and the phone rang.

"Hey," Nita said softly, and he remembered to breathe properly.

"Are you on your way to the school?" he asked.

"Yeah, how did you know?"

"Listen, don't worry about coming here, okay? Just keep doing what you're doing. God knows you're doin' the Lord's work. Let me take Aiden back to the ranch for a while with me and Lyla. That way you don't have to come all the way back here."

There was a pause. "Are you sure about this? He's not exactly your average kid coming over for a play date."

"Yeah, I get that. I get that," he repeated. "Still, I'm willing to do so. They tell you what happened to your boy?"

"They did. Fucking animals."

"I hear ya. Don't use that language in front of the principal. That's a no-no, apparently."

Nita let out a humorous scoff. "Everyone knows that but you."

"I'm sure you're right."

"So, is Tara gonna be all right with you taking Aiden back to your house?"

"Well, I suppose so. It was her idea."

"Wow," Nita said nonchalantly, "that's surprising."

"Yeah, she'll shock ya from time to time."

"Oh ya? You havin' second thoughts on your baby mama?"

"Well, my first thought was, *Fuck*, and my second thought was, *No*. So, I guess you could say I'm havin' second thoughts."

"Better make sure Ms. Pierce isn't in earshot, sailor."

He smiled and shook his head. "Better make sure you don't call Marines 'sailors' anymore."

"All right, I'll make sure to watch that." There was a long silence between them. "Hey, thanks for doing this."

"Don't mention it."

———

Blake gathered both Lyla and Aiden and helped them into the truck. Tara gave their daughter a kiss on the forehead before heading back to the hospital for work. He watched her walk back to her car. In the span of a few seconds, he thought of all the good times spent together, and how much better it would be to raise a child with the parents under one roof, but those feelings were for another day.

He climbed into the truck. "Alrighty, kiddos, you ready to head out?"

The loud engine of a dusty pickup turned into the school. The driver wore an old Arkansas Razorback ballcap that was probably the same age as the truck.

Blake knew the man well. A local, tobacco-ridden man by the name of Clint Grady. The Gradys had been around these parts for generations. But, by some act of the devil, they kept shitting out underachieving and borderline inbred offspring.

Seeing him here at this moment just proved his suspicions. "Lyla, did the Grady boy do that to you and Aiden?" Blake asked, watching Clint make his way into the school, presumably to pick up his now-suspended son.

Lyla nodded.

"Okay."

———

Aiden didn't say much the entire ride back. Lyla did most of the talking, pointing at things along the way and explaining their whole backstory while he just listened. He didn't seem to mind or be bothered by it. Although, the boy's eyes widened crossing underneath the Thorpe Ranch sign. His nose was pressed against the glass for the entire ride. Blake made a mental note to clean the smear marks later.

In pursuing the man who killed one of his best friends, he never thought about the daily life that would get in the way. Once upon a time, he could go out with his boys and get anything they needed done. That was what they did when they were kids. That was what they did in the military. However, that was no longer the case, at least for him.

Aiden stepped out of the truck and didn't take his eyes off the expansive landscape before him.

"What you think, bud?" Blake asked, but a reply or an acknowledgment never came.

Lyla took Aiden by the hand and ushered him inside. "Come on," she said. "We can play Mario Kart!"

They both barreled through the door, and he followed. Ahead, he saw Lyla get jerked back as Aiden stopped dead in his tracks in the entryway.

"What is it?" Blake asked with a raised brow.

All of the boy's attention was locked onto a physical map of Thorpe Ranch, with all its peaks and valleys, rivers and creeks, as well as trees and boundary lines.

"He loves maps," Lyla said.

"Is that right?" Blake asked, glancing into his office to all the potential supplies Aiden could utilize.

For the first time, with all the failed attempts in Blake's wake, Aiden finally acknowledged him. "Can I draw?"

"Yeah—yeah, of course."

"Can I draw that?" he asked, pointing to the map.

Blake laughed and repeated, "Of course you can, bud. Lyla, can you get Aiden some... What kind of paper you want?"

"Big paper," he said.

Blake laughed again. "Big paper, all right. Lyla, can you get Aiden some paper? I think I have some sixteen-by-twenty-three in the office closet somewhere."

"Yes, Daddy," she said.

"Colors," Aiden said softly.

Blake shook his head with a smile. "And some colored pencils too."

CHAPTER 42

Nita had to drag Aiden away from Nova. The boy couldn't get enough of the herding dog. He scratched her behind the ears, under the chin, and hugged her like she was going into active duty. He squeezed her neck so tight Nita had to tell him to take it easy. "Be delicate with dogs, Aiden. No matter how big they are."

He gave Nova one last pat on the head before making his way into the back seat of Nita's car parked beside Blake's truck.

"You see a dog in your future, Marshal?" Blake asked with that trademark grin. Depending on the person, one would either want to smack it off or kiss it.

Nita wasn't at liberty to divulge which one she preferred. "We had a dog once growing up. He was a good mutt, but he liked to wander a little too much. One day he was just gone."

"Well, they have fences nowadays."

"Where's Lyla at?" she asked, shucking his smartass comment.

Blake petted Nova's back in the passenger seat while Nita rubbed her neck. She could tell Blake kept her nice and pampered even though she was a working dog. Her fur was soft and smelled of shampoo. However, that powerful hint of wet dog couldn't be masked. She wore a fresh and untattered bandana around her neck that traveled down her back, and her claws were clipped.

"I dropped her off at her mom's on the way over. My time was up." The proud cowboy shifted in his seat. He checked the mirrors of his truck. All of them. "Listen, I was wanting to ask you about local gangs in the area... biker clubs, more specifically."

Her hand stopped scratching Nova's ear. "Why's that?"

Blake glanced around once again. The observant Marine in him never left. "A couple weeks ago, people attacked me on my land. They were wearing masks. Surely that means something, given what you experienced with the owl man and what Travis Fields saw."

She didn't know where to begin. "Why would bikers attack you? It doesn't make sense."

Blake gripped the steering wheel and cranked his hand down on the lever. "It could be something as old as time. The acquisition of my family's land has been at the forefront of my existence. So many have come and gone, using a variety of different tactics to claim it for whatever desire they have. At this point, I'm numb to it all."

"Forget me. Why didn't you report it to local PD?"

The sun began to set in front of them, and Blake stared directly into the orange fireball in the sky through his front windshield. "Nita, I respect officers more than anyone, but I don't see where their services could help me much."

Nita didn't reply.

"I don't want these people arrested. They'd be gettin' off easy." His eyes darkened below his hat. "You think that's unfair?"

"This world is unfair. I disagree with your reasoning, but perhaps you're not wrong." Her hands gently pulled away from Nova and went to her hips. "Not much gang activity in this area. There are small pockets of it, but not a lot. As far as criminal bikers go, you have your bigwigs recognized nationwide and the more local ones like the Skull Draggers and Devil's Riders MC. Homicide, gun, and drug running wouldn't be anything unusual. For lack of a better word, the Devil's Riders have remained idle or stagnant as far as growth. However, their rival Skull Draggers have surged in membership and output."

Blake's eyes shot off to the side at the mention of the two motorcycle clubs.

"But I'm having a hard time making the connection between biker clubs and gangs attacking you on your land."

"You know what's funny? I had some answers in front of my face for a while, but I never put two and two together. Not until now." He appeared to ponder memories of old, but didn't appear fond of them as he shook them away as quickly as they arrived. "My father had some run-ins with the Devil's Riders' president. Now, I don't know shit for details on all that, but it was prevalent enough to leave an impact. If I'm not mistaken, the vice president and I were in the same class. But I think he dropped out a few months before graduation. Must've caught wind he wasn't gonna be eligible to make that walk."

"So, the people that attacked you were a part of the Devil's Riders?"

"Not according to my... CI."

"CI? Criminal informant? Careful, Blake, you sound like a lawman."

The cowboy rolled his eyes. "No, they weren't from that MC. I was told they were Skull Draggers."

"Would the informant you're talking about be lying? Trying to get you looking in the wrong direction?"

"Not according to our intel, which appears reliable."

"'Cause you scared or borderline tortured your CI into giving information?"

"That's confidential, Nita."

His smartass remark landed as well as the rest. "Jesus Christ, Blake. As much as you want it to be, it's not the fucking Wild West. You can't take the law into your own hands."

His steely demeanor said, *Watch me.*

CHAPTER 43

Ezell's office was bare. He didn't take the time to decorate it with religious iconography. Only a map of the developing grounds hung behind him. The blueprints to his kingdom. The letter T intersected with the letter V were painted on the opposite wall, and a pristine taxidermized fox looked down on the office from up high. He liked to stare at it and ask it questions about its life that were never answered. One time, Amos walked in on him inquiring about the fox's run-ins with predators. Ezell thought that Amos must've considered him a madman. And just as Ezell spoke, "You're not the most cunning of foxes. If you were, you wouldn't be here," Amos padded his arrival with a knock.

"Mr. Dyer," he said formally.

Ezell gathered, by Amos' pale complexion, something was amiss. His right-hand man turned his head to the door and nodded, signaling someone to enter. In walked Gil Burke, a fellow visionary and hometown lifer. Gil was all neck as it stuck out of his plaid collared shirt by what looked to be a whole foot. He slicked back his thin and greasy hair and cupped his hands in front of him before placing them on his chest.

"Mr. Burke, is everything all right?" Ezell asked.

Gil looked to Amos for permission to speak. "Tell him what you told me," Amos said.

Still, the plumber, born and raised in Tahlequah, appeared so nervous to the point of shaking. He rubbed his arms like he was caught out in the middle of a blizzard.

"I-I'm the one," he said softly.

Ezell barely heard him at all. "Excuse me? You're the one for what?"

"I b-" He hesitated. "I burned the youth center." Gil couldn't make it through the whole sentence without breaking down. His bottom lip quivered as he inhaled, trying to catch his breath.

Ezell grew cold, his anger quick yet controlled. "Stop crying."

Gil sniffled a few more times, wiping away the snot and tears.

"Now, repeat what you said."

"I said, I burned the youth center."

"Okay. Now, tell me what you did."

"Excuse me?"

Ezell blew through his nose and fought off the urge to roll his eyes. "What happened as a result of you burning down the youth center?"

"You haven't heard?" Gil asked. "It's been all over the news–"

"I'm asking you to tell me. I don't get around to viewing the news much. So much information with no time to digest it." Ezell ushered Gil to the chairs sitting in front of his desk. "Besides, those who believe themselves informed are often led astray. I'll take the latter if I choose between misinformed and uninformed."

Gil dropped his head, peeking to Amos out of the corner of his eye, as if he'd help him in this matter. "I did it for our vision... to see it all through. To destroy blasphemers. But the kids... some of the kids died. I still... I still hear their screams."

Ezell took a step closer. "And these screams that you hear, what's it like? Are they deafening, overwhelming, or something else entirely?"

Gil never left his shelled space. His eyes remained glued to the ground as he said, "It's a... it's loud. If I close my eyes and calm down for a moment, I can hear like it's happening right now."

Ezell grasped his shoulders, then lifted Gil's sweaty face to look him in the eyes. "And how many times have you returned to the youth center since you performed the act?"

Gil seemed confused by the question, but answered accordingly, "Twice."

A presence of shame existed, but Ezell knew it false.

Ezell saw Gil in the clearest way imaginable. It was as if Gil's skin glowed. The open pores littered his face. Finally, Ezell released him. "I'm not here to judge you, Gil, or tell you that you've done wrong. Now, society and the people of this community may have a different response, but who are they to throw stones?"

Tears ran down Gil's cheeks. Emotionless tears.

"I know why you came to me," Ezell said, offering him a tissue from his desk. "I'm so proud that you did. I can't imagine the fear you must have had. I understand. As I said, I'm not here for judgment. That's for lesser men who believe themselves righteous with the Lord but will be the first to abandon their post once their faith is tested... like the ones in the church."

Gil cocked his head.

"That's right. You did this world a service doing what you did. Our mission is to not only know God but cast out those who blaspheme against him. 2 Thessalonians 1:8: 'In flaming fire, vengeance will be inflicted on those who do not know God and on those who do not obey the gospel of our Lord Jesus.' You've done the Lord's work, my son."

"Thank you, Father."

Ezell rubbed his back. "Now, how we should proceed. I don't want you going back there for a while, understand?"

Gil nodded.

"The last thing we need is for ruin to come to this place."

"Of course."

Ezell rubbed his back some more, brought Gil in close, and kissed him on the top of the head. His sweaty, greasy head. Ezell fought the urge to wipe his mouth. "I know what it's like to have urges. A lot of people do, but they don't act on them. They'd rather sit back and let the world happen to them. Not you. I understand the desire to set things ablaze. Truly, I do. Everyone has a place here... and believe me, there are fellow visionaries that have such desires, same as you."

Gil's eyes widened. Not of shock, but of pleasure. As if the thought of this being a haven for himself and others like him brought him a semblance of anticipation.

"There is a rite of passage."

"Rite of passage?"

Ezell ran the back of his hand across Gil's chin. "Yes. A way to test your faith. Do something for our temple, and you will see the way I do, and your fellow visionaries do."

"What can I do?"

"All I require from you is a letter confessing your sin to me so that we can proceed with a ritual of cleansing. Can you do that for me, Gil?"

———

Low, sputtering engines roared along the gravel in the distance. Ezell emerged from his office to greet Amos waiting for him outside as the Skull Draggers MC approached with a cloud of dust in their wake.

"What's the plan for Gil?" Amos asked.

Ezell kept his gaze forward. "I believe we have an opportunity to capitalize on a situation if it's executed properly."

"Father?" Amos asked with a cocked brow.

"Is Clarence around?"

"I believe he's hog-hunting around the southwest stand."

"When he gets back, bring him to me immediately."

Amos squinted and nodded in an unsure manner.

Ezell took notice. "Have I led you astray so far, son?"

"No, Father. I'll do what you ask."

"Good."

Around a dozen bikes came to the end of the long stretch of gravel into the heart of the Temple's Vision compound. A cloud of smoke followed them. Their president, Gray Erickson, led the way. He had volatile tendencies to most everyone outside of his motorcycle club family, aside from Ezell.

Gray's unfocused visage seemed impenetrable when they first crossed paths in Nebraska. That day, Erickson and his men rode with heat after a successful exchange between an Irish-organized crime syndicate near Chicago. The success vaulted them into a position of lucrative cash flow, but the workload had just begun. Before their first successful encounter, they would have only a handful of gun runs a month. Now, it was a weekly occurrence. Running arms wasn't easy, and it wasn't for the faint of heart. In this racket, people who didn't toe the line had to be dealt with in a subtle manner.

Those extremes didn't sway Ezell from participation. Instead, he offered Erickson another business venture, one that would utilize their talents and improve upon their situation with their higher-ups in Chicago. All the world cared about was money. If he could convince his followers that money was the root of all evil, hatred would be easy to cultivate in their hearts to enact dark deeds to those who benefited from excess.

Breaking into the methamphetamine business proved much more manageable than Ezell anticipated. The most challenging step was finding a group worthy and trustworthy enough to maintain the product and not blow themselves to kingdom come. But on the sixth day of his search, Ezell found such a man, a local cook by the street name Eon. They met only once, and that was enough. Eon's product quickly became more desirable, marketable, and profitable than the gun trade.

Ezell fretted about the bikers' ability to keep their wits about them by not getting caught on their runs or flaunting their increased flux in spending money. He liked to keep them close, for they were impressionable people for the most part. Every once in a while, a former amateur scholar amongst them tested Ezell's abilities, but they were conquered all the same.

The thundering engines idled in front of him as the dust settled, ready for the day they poured the asphalt. Erickson and his men's motors puttered out as they dropped their kickstands. Gray didn't show his admiration willingly, but he appeared impressed by the progress of the compound. "It's all coming together," he said. That was the limit of his complimenting capabilities.

His VP was Craig "Peck" Wood. Only those in the club called him Peck, but more often than not, they called him "Pecker" regardless of rank superiority. It only stood because the name didn't bother Pecker like it would his prez. No matter, Ezell kept it professional by calling him Mr. Wood.

"Pleasure to see you all again," Ezell said with open arms, welcoming his steel horse riders. "I must admit, I was surprised by the urgency of the call. I do hope that everything is all quiet along the western front."

Peck spoke first. His mediator personality lent itself nicely for the role he had to play amongst his peers. "We didn't mean to stir you up or anything like that. We just needed to discuss some things about a new shipping lane."

Ezell nodded and fiddled with his crucifix cufflinks. "You wish to take on a new client?"

"Perhaps," Erickson said. "They want a large shipment upfront, and if that transaction goes well, they seemed promising for continued business."

"You hear that, Amos? It looks like we're going to get to extend our kitchens."

"They're more interested in guns than drugs for the time being."

"Well, if they need guns in large quantity on an initial order, it leads me to speculate some desperation on their end. What was their desired timeline?" Ezell asked.

"Less than a week. Six days," Pecker answered.

"Desperation it is." Ezell pondered, his eyes scanning all of the high-resolution faces before him. "What types of guns?"

Pecker removed a slip of paper from his back pocket that shared space with his chain wallet and handed it to Amos. Ezell's right-hand man unfolded it and inspected the demands.

They all waited as the arms expert reviewed the slip.

"We should have everything they're looking for in the armory aside from one," Amos said. "We don't have a Milkor M32A1. I think I can get my hands on one, but with that time frame, a grenade launcher is going to be dicey."

"Very well," Ezell said. He focused his attention on the bikers. "If that's the case, I want you to counter our new business partners and let them know we will be charging an express fee. It shouldn't deter them from the deal if they are desperate enough. If it does, so be it."

Erickson and Pecker didn't have to think about it long before their agreeance was made aware with a nod to each other and back to Ezell.

CHAPTER 44

Ezell Sunderland didn't register in any database the OSBI or the FBI had available. That was cause for concern. If that was the case, he was using an assumed name. Nita didn't trust anyone, let alone someone who wouldn't use their name.

"Should we press more into Sunderland?" Nita asked from the passenger seat.

"Yes. However, if we don't find anything out on this arson and the murders, the chain of command will wring my neck for pursuing anything else," Teller replied.

She understood.

"You're the one with the sixth sense. Did you not get a read on that guy or the operation they had going?

Nita laughed. She watched the world she'd grown up in her entire life pass by through the window. "You're assuming that I understand how it works. All I can do is interpret what I'm given and hope I'm on the right track."

Teller fiddled with the air conditioning and adjusted his mirror. Then, he cleared his throat. "Well, something happened. I saw you react to something."

Nita nodded. "Yeah, I don't know. It makes it even harder to know what it means when it's a new sensation like that."

"Does it only happen around bad events or when something... I don't know... wrong is taking place?"

"No," she said as a smile followed. "You would think that, but no. I've had plenty of those happenings take place in the happiest moments of my life as well. Which, unfortunately, are a lot fewer in number."

Teller put both hands on the wheel and pulled himself up in his seat. He left them there like he was a student driver and Nita was a strict instructor. "If you don't mind me asking, do you care to share the difference between the two sensations? Or perhaps a time when you were sensitive to something good rather than bad?"

She was doing everything in her power to reach into her brain and find an occurrence of positive sensitivity revealing itself, but for lack of anything showing up, she decided to tell the only one she could remember—one that she hoped would never leave her. "Right after college, a friend invited me to some graduation party by one of my classmates I barely knew. I'm not much for parties or talking to anyone I don't know, especially where I would be surrounded by a sea of white girls so pale they were blinding."

Teller chuckled. "I know that sea well."

"I was going to try and do everything in my power not to attend. However, I knew the girl that was having the party would never let me live it down if I didn't go."

"Sounds like a white chick," he said sarcastically but at the same time completely serious.

"So, I ended up putting on some nice clothes and dragged myself to that house, wanting to pull off, turn around, and go home the entire time. I about did when I pulled up to the largest house I'd ever seen and saw a fleet of cars in the street and a flock of people migrating to that mansion." She stopped and kept her gaze on the outside world beyond the car. "But I stopped. I felt warm. My nerves about socializing and being in a new place fell away. I parked, got out of the car, and the sunlight was so blinding, as if I was in a whiteout. As it faded away, I saw him standing there."

"Who's that?"

"Jackson," she said. "He asked me if I wanted to walk with him to the door because he didn't know anyone there either, and he saw I was alone."

"Smooth move on his part—seeing you were alone and taking his shot."

"It was smooth," Nita agreed. "So, I awarded him for it, and we walked to the door together, and the rest was history. He knew what he was doing."

To herself, quietly in her thoughts, she repeated his poem:

Into the void, I travel
A vast thicket of engulfing black
Keep the pace, I say
Keep the pace

CHAPTER 45

"This is a moment that must not be taken lightly, brothers and sisters. We must recognize that this is the Lord's will, and it must be done." Ezell's closest followers of unbreakable loyalty gathered around him. The false prophet splayed out at his feet. "A spiritual war is taking place, children. One that has been so for thousands of years. In the end, there can be only one victor. I have chosen my side, and I pray you will all join me."

The clearing in the middle of the woods they called home ebbed and flowed with the dark winds howling through them. Their faces, including the bound preacher beneath him, were lit by torchlight.

Ezell leaned down and removed his captive's cloth gag that pulled the corners of his mouth back towards his ears. Tears mixed into the drool pouring out of his mouth.

"Pastor Franks." Ezell said. "It's time to confess here today."

"Please, I swear I've done nothing wrong." The spit flying out of his mouth was a mixture of tears, snot, and saliva.

"I'm sorry, Mr. Franks, but that is incorrect." Calling him by his title of Pastor no longer sat well with Ezell, and it didn't feel right passing his lips. "You turned to idol and earthly worship. The Lord has fallen to the bottom of your priority list, hasn't he? Your gospels revolve around personal wealth and gain in the absence of God."

Pastor Franks did not deny the claim. His crying resumed, and so did his pleading.

The fellow visionaries' disgust was welcomed. Ezell's appreciation for recognizing the blasphemy awoke his soul. One of his most loyal, Clarence Len Fletcher, stomped behind the broken pastor. Ezell nodded to him before addressing Mr. Franks once more. "You will see God today. Plead with him."

Clarence's massive paw reached around Franks' face, engulfing it all. One bulging eye looked through his fingers as he yanked their captive's head backward. Clarence pierced his neck with a thick syringe and pumped his system with a stew of backwoods meth and LSD.

Franks clenched his neck after Clarence released him. The drugs would act fast. Ezell completely shifted his attention to the ones observing the ritual. "Sons and daughters, this sinner is about to meet God."

He led the charge, placing the elongated goat mask on his face. They followed, placing masks of their own making onto their faces.

Mr. Franks' cries slowed and stopped altogether. His eyes glazed over, and his skin went pale but glistened in the torchlight. His drug-induced eyes widened upon staring at the bipedal goat casting his judgment down. "No! No! No! Please! God, please!"

"Welcome," Ezell said.

His haunting demeanor convinced the former pastor his judgment had been declared.

Hell.

"Sons and daughters, let's welcome another sinner into our domain."

Ezell's flock stalked their kill with matching blades, homing in on him like piranhas with fleshy prey.

The visions of hell overwhelmed Mr. Frank's senses. His voice broke from the screams. His body locked up. There was no fight from him as Ezell and his visionaries took him from this world.

CHAPTER 46

"Mr. Edwards," the stranger in the suit said, ambushing Blake in the Southern Agriculture parking lot with a sack of dog food draped over his shoulder.

Blake stood strong. His posture halted the man's progress toward him. The suited man's shoulder was tucked away, giving the appearance that something was stowed away yet ready to be accessed at any moment. A gun, a knife, a fist, no one, including Blake, would know until it happened what would be revealed.

"May I speak with you for a moment?"

"That depends on what this is about." Blake replied, standing strong at an angle, ready to fire whatever he needed with his dominant hand.

"I've been trying to reach you for my client interested in purchasing your property."

Blake turned, giving nothing away as far as his emotions to the prospect of selling what was his.

The agent in the skinny suit followed him, and his stature shrank with each step taken in Blake's shadow. "I work for Alliance Tech out of California, and they are prepared to offer you well over the asking price for your place."

"I didn't ask for any price. It's not for sale."

"You don't seem to understand, sir. Building a campus here would do nothing but boost the economy around these parts tenfold. We're talking about nearly a thousand new and fresh job opportunities."

"And what kind've jobs are those?"

"Well, Mr. Edwards, we are a software company specializing in digital networking, software, wireless, and security. Pretty much anything that can make your daily tech experiences sing can be improved by our services."

"Do they really need to be improved if they're already singing?"

"Mr. Edwards—"

Blake stopped and faced his pursuer, and the tech man backpedaled. "And no one calls me Mr. Edwards that isn't trying to sell me something. I used to think of it as others just being respectful. Granted, that is how folks around here do it. However, when people like you do it... you're perhaps the hundredth at this point. When you people do it, it's nothing more than an added sprinkle for your sales pitch."

"With all due respect, Mr. Edwards, I believe it's the best course to take in these situations."

A slow and contemplative exhale escaped through his nostrils. "What's the minimum requirement for a starting position at your company?"

The agent stopped and cocked his head. "A bachelor's degree in the desired field of study and a credible recommendation letter."

"And how many people around here do you think can attain a job like that at your company?"

"Mr. Edwards, this campus will attract people from across the area beyond state lines. Believe me, I see what you're getting at. You're worried that this big liberal company will come in and step on the cultural throat of the agricultural community around here. I do see merit in your concerns, but I assure you, our hundreds of hourly positions will have many academic and experience-based requirements."

Blake had heard enough and strode away again. He involuntarily shook his head as he wrestled with the argument. Maybe the agent was speaking facts when discussing the potential boost in the economy... maybe. Blake wasn't sure, however, and that made it worse.

"We are prepared to offer you twenty million dollars," the agent said and then repeated the number. "That's including you maintaining mineral rights."

Ain't no minerals of importance here.

A rusty and faded blue pickup truck puttered away in the parking lot. A slew of conservative vinyl stickers crudely touted the driver's political affiliation. Clint Grady's truck.

Blake caught a glimpse of the familiar mullet sported by Clint's boy. The very same that humiliated his daughter. Blake seethed from the encounter with the lawyer, but seeing Clint and his boy was far more aggravating.

"Mr. Edwards?" the tech lawyer said.

He didn't answer. Blake tossed the dog food into the back of his truck and peeled out of that parking lot.

———

Blake drove through the trailer park on the edge of town with his lights off. His phone resting in the cupholder lit the interior of the truck. The vibrations shook the center console. His ex-wife's name flashed on the screen. Now wasn't the time.

He continued to monitor from a safe distance. The single-family home's fence flirted with the trailer park boundaries. Branches and vines grew between the openings in the metal, even though lawn-keeping equipment littered the yard. Two teenage boys carried a six-pack in the middle of the road. Given their destination, he let them enjoy their underage drinking. Lord knew he did in his day. They made their way to a deck haphazardly nailed together off the back door of one of the many mobile homes across the street. They kept to themselves and were, at this point, over a hundred yards away. A dim streetlight in the middle of the park lit their frames.

His attention returned to the Grady house. The boy finally emerged from the house out the side door. Blake had yet to learn the little bastard's name and wanted to keep it that way.

His phone lit and vibrated once again. Only this time, it was Little J. His tinted windows shrouded him inside the truck, but he didn't want to risk anything. He answered, put the phone on speaker, and rested it on his lap. "Yeah, J."

"Aye, man, I'll make it quick. Floyd said he found something connecting the Skull Draggers' gun runs to several addresses in the area. Apparently, their cyber security defenses weren't top tier."

"Imagine that. I'll—uh, I'll take a look at them here in a bit."

"You good? Where you at?"

Blake thought of a quick lie. "I'm just about to order a late-night burger and fries in the drive-thru. I'll see you soon."

Blake didn't give Little J time to reply as he hung up the phone. A few moments later, Clint Grady exited from the same side door his son did moments ago. Clint walked to a ramshackle shed in their backyard that housed a minibike. They both held wrenches and proceeded to work on the bike. The father-son bonding moment would have been revered in any other circumstance with different people. Still, it only added to the anger boiling in Blake's insides. The boy didn't seem to be punished. They giggled while Clint tossed his beer on the ground outside the shed and cracked open another one. With each laugh, Blake breathed in and out through his nostrils and cracked his knuckles.

He reached in the center console and grabbed a thick, dark fabric. He pulled it over his head. Two eye holes offered him plenty of visibility in the ski mask. He went to adjust it in the rearview mirror but couldn't bring himself to do so. He went into the street, checking for eyes and passing cars that were not found. The world fell silent. A slight hint of adrenaline felt in another land not long ago returned. He tried his best to suppress it, like the nerves before a first date, but he couldn't shake it.

Concealment was key. His truck was different. And his clothes were all black with no logos in sight. There was a chill in the night air, but his rising heart rate and added layers canceled it. The beer drinkers in the trailer park sat in lawn chairs facing the other direction. Clint and his boy continued to cut it up in the shed. However, many years of tactical experience told him to avoid engaging head-on. Flanking would suffice.

Blake had to march through the nearby woods that backed into Clint's house to get behind the shed. The lights of his destination kept it in view. However, the trek in front of his eyes proved more difficult. He steered clear of crunching, early fallen leaves, thorns, and bulging roots.

He managed to achieve cover, and he wasted no time emerging from the woods and making his way to the shed. To his advantage, the chain-link fence was relatively short, and one of the top bars was bent so far that all Blake needed was a high step to get over.

He heard their voices converse for the first time, and the world's noise returned to him. Still, the backyard was dark. He remained in shadow on the side of the shed. A swinging bulb in the shed shot a light beam into the yard. Blake interpreted it as a welcome. Although, he questioned that logic. The time for second-guessing his actions never occurred.

Blake swung around into the shed, grabbed the back of Clint's neck, and thrust him into the workbench. He was clearly discombobulated from the massive blow as he wobbled around. His nose crushed on impact, and he leaked blood all over his crusty flannel shirt.

The boy was petrified as he shook in place. Soon, a fresh stain darkened his blue jeans.

Blake threw Clint's head into the workbench again, and again, and again. The inbreeding asshole's legs couldn't bring him to stand as consciousness left him a couple blows prior.

His son's agape mouth let out a soft cry, but Blake silenced it into nothing. The hand that sent his father into another dimension grasped the twelve-year-old around the neck. He squeezed, feeling the adolescent muscles contract.

"You know how many people I've killed, boy?" Blake said in a hoarse growl. "I can't even count that high. You know how many of them were good fathers and good sons? I don't show mercy to people like you or your daddy. You like to bully kids with disabilities? You like to bully little girls?"

The Grady kid shook his head side to side in a rapid motion.

"Don't you fucking lie to me, boy!" Blake punched him in the stomach and slammed his boot heel to his father's chest. The kid folded and coughed, but Blake righted and slammed him against the shed wall. Blind fury took over. "I'll be fucking watching you, boy. Here at your house, at school, when you go driving this thing around the backroads, I'll be watching. I'll end you if you ever lay another hand on anyone again. I'll take the handlebars to that little minibike you got there and shove them so far up your father's ass that every time you throttle, his asshole will throb and bleed. And if that don't work, we'll see how you like it. Do you understand how serious I am?" Blake asked as tears ran down his knuckles and onto the boy's collarbone.

He nodded in agreeance and sniffled away. "I-I-I'm s-so, so sorry."

Blake tossed him to the floor like a shirt he had changed his mind about wearing and escaped into the night, leaving the Grady residence better than he found it.

———

He drove down backroads that shifted from pavement to gravel, to dirt, and back again. They were as mapped out to him as the veins protruding and flowing across his forearms. The ski mask resting in the empty passenger seat taunted. He couldn't bring himself to look at it. The radio didn't play, and the air conditioning wasn't running despite Blake burning up in his adrenaline-soaked layers. Only the vibrations of the truck kept him sane.

"The fuck am I doing?" he asked himself before taking a deep breath and slamming his fist into the steering wheel repeatedly. With each blow, the reverb of the shaky steering wheel seemed to make the entire truck stutter. The bottom of his fist pulsated. Bruising developed rather quickly as he drove farther into the night.

His whole life, long-term goals evaded him, especially since his mother passed. There were aspirations, sure, but nothing he looked to as a singular and hyper-focused motivation. Playing Division I at the collegiate level was taken from him via injury. He stumbled ass-backward into the Marines to avoid home, and kids were never on his radar.

The one thing he attempted to avoid at all costs seemed inescapable. And as he sped through the backroads, the certainty of becoming his father washed over him. Growing up, everyone informed Blake how lucky he was to an exhaustive level. They didn't know. Money brought him no joy. There wasn't even money to be spent for himself until he returned from downrange. His father was as frugal with his finances as his love. The prospect of playing football in Stillwater got interest from his father, but nothing more. All the blood that flowed through his veins and to his heart was replaced with oil. The capacity to care about others and create valuable relationships didn't exist.

Expansion. Revenue. Competition.

Blake never believed the rumors about his family's land growing up. His father and grandfather always shot down any inquiries he made about it as a boy. Now, as an adult, it was true. All of it. There wasn't a doubt in his mind. The generational curse of greed appeared to be his family's strongest genetic trait. Rumors of a curse being placed upon the land that his family stole from the Indians over a century ago were undeniable. In fact, the only positive relationship he ever built in this county with a Native was Nita. He remembered how those who knew the origins of Thorpe Ranch cast their judgment over her.

It was a harsh reality to live in. One of the many things Blake had, as opposed to his father, was the ability to see himself through the eyes of others. Perhaps his father could, but he never had the desire. They were all right in this contemplation and the events of his life leading to this. They were all right. He might have assumed a role closer to the latter if the world consisted of good and bad people.

His engine roared. Despite regret and disappointment in himself, he wasn't finished. More had to be done, and there was no doubt in his mind that these thoughts would only amplify.

CHAPTER 47

EASTERN INDIAN TERRITORY
1889

Terrance Soap and his family called a ragged patch of land home. Harsh winds howled one evening and ragefully swept them here. In this place, those eastern winds carried the cries of the massacred in their wake. It remained a harsh reminder in the land of windy plains, where the wails of agony were a daily obstacle to overcome among their mounting companions.

In order to survive, the white man's way must be embraced. Cherokee culture was allowed so long as it stayed irrelevant and didn't prevail. The graves of his mother and father and his wife's mother and father were dug in the garden behind the cabin amongst the sunflowers. Their fathers did not survive the removal, and their mothers didn't last long afterward.

The only outcome Terrance demanded was one of success. How he envisioned that was providing his family with a life of happiness despite the world's desire to rip it from him and others like him.

On this midyear day, another wind carried across the plains, bringing a familiar but new chill. Five riders confidently emerged down the hill and in no rush on horseback. Terrance told his wife and children to get inside their home as a caution. The sun was directly above their head. The riders approached with coy smiles and high chins.

They wore beards aside from one, whose facial hair resided only on his upper lip. "You speak English?" the beardless man asked.

"Yes," Terrance replied.

"Good."

Silence built between them. The men admired the land, looking upon it fondly.

"You stay here?" the leader asked.

"This is my land. Yes."

The man laughed and looked to all his companions before setting his sights back on the unhorsed Indian before him. Sternly, the man said, "No, this is not your land."

"Then what exactly is mine? Everything I had was taken. Everything I was given I never asked for. Now you're telling me it's not mine either?"

The man with the mustache smiled. "What's your name?"

"Terrance Soap."

"Terrance Soap," the man repeated condescendingly. "Seems appropriate, I suppose. Mr. Soap, my name is Rick Edwards. Do you know why I'm here?"

"Are you a courier?"

"Courier? Fancy word for an Indian. I'm ashamed to admit that I hardly know what that word means. Perhaps another word for *messenger*?"

Terrance nodded.

The men's eyes moved across his land in a way that felt like an invasion of privacy. The feeling didn't sit well in his gut, based upon the trauma of recent events now embedded deep and permanently in his blood.

"This a nice patch of land you got here. Look over there," the mustached man said, as his pointer finger aimed towards the garden and the mule tied to an oak stump. "Even got you farming. If you could call it that. You have a vision for this place?"

"Vision? No, only a wish."

"What might that be?"

He felt the breeze against his face. If he could shake it away, he would. "For the wind to stop taunting me."

The Edwards man chuckled. "Well, you're in the wrong place for that."

"I'm aware. And here I stand."

"Here's my vision: a thousand head of cattle roaming these hills, the biggest cabin in the state right there, and a nice big rocking chair to sway back and forth as I watch the sunrise from the east and set in the west."

"That's a beautiful vision, then. Sounds like a simple life for you and your family. I hope you attain it, but keep a close eye on your desires, sir. You never know who might come along to destroy your simple existence."

The horses rocked side to side. Edwards patted his Appaloosa. "I'm going to ask you to leave," he said sternly. The playful cadence and his voice left all at once.

"This is our home. This land we were given to live in. I have papers that say it's mine."

Edwards removed a stack of papers from his saddle bag and waved them around. "And I have a half-dozen more that say it's mine. So, get your family together, gather your belongings, and settle farther west elsewhere."

Terrence dropped his head. "That's so effortless, isn't it? To settle somewhere else. When does it end? When does the taking for your people end?"

Rick settled on those words as if the winds now brought him whispers. "When I get what I want. When I get what I deserve."

Terrance laughed. "It won't end there for you."

Rick did not respond kindly and removed his repeating rifle, in all its polished glory, from the holster. "Mr. Soap, get off my land."

"If you do this, be wary of the unfortunate fate you'll place your family in for generations to come."

"You gonna place some Indian curse on me?"

"No. I won't do anything. Any curse that follows will be your doing."

Mr. Edwards side-eyed his men. "Any of y'all feel any curse or 'unfortunate fate' wash over you?"

They all shook their head with no care or concern.

"Very well." Rick continued admiring Terrance's home. He exhaled as if he did not want to continue to the next step. "Last chance," he said.

Terrance did not break his gaze or move in the slightest.

"Is your family inside?"

Still, Terrance remained unmoving and now unresponsive. Rick nodded his head to his men, and they dismounted. "I'll give you one last chance. If you leave now, I'll have my men help you settle somewhere else to the southwest."

The talking was done.

"Very well." Rick whipped his Henry repeating rifle to his shoulder, and an echoing clap sounded across the plains.

Terrance dropped to his back, and his bicep pulsated, blood leaking through his fingers as he attempted to apply pressure. His wife and sons ran out of the house, calling for him, but they were subdued by Edward's men.

The heavy steps of Rick's horse shook the ground beneath him. "You chose this. This may seem bad, but you know how much worse this could have been. Perhaps you should be thankful for your wife's sake that me and my men aren't savages."

They shoved his wife and kids down to him, and she clutched him, doing her best not to touch his wound. His boys reacted the same. Terrance tried to clutch them all at once under one arm but failed. Blood poured out of him like a rushing river when his grip came free.

Then, a flash of light sparked out of the corner of his eye. The light grew as the men ignited his home, and slowly, the fire grew, burning all his belongings and forcing him and his family to start over again. A cycle he worried would never end. A reality he feared would not stop with him but would carry on for generations.

CHAPTER 48

"All the local arsonists, which wasn't much, were checked and followed up on," Charlie informed Nita and Teller. "We got nothing. They either had strong alibis that night or were still in prison for another crime they committed."

He had a little notebook, like one a detective would use. It made sense because Charlie always mentioned that the only other job he'd take in law enforcement was homicide. However, Nita always thought he was too clean-cut. Most detectives weren't also simultaneously metrosexuals. With his weekly hair appointment, his tight fade always remained.

"You mind if I look at the lists of arsonists and fire incidents?" Nita asked.

"By all means. Knock yourself out."

———

It was tough researching local fires over the past fifteen years. Pages and pages of case files and incident reports scrolled up the computer page— all of which led to dead ends. The mundane aspect of scanning near-endless digital documents was something she needed to improve. It was moments like these where Nita wished she read more frequently. Reading was a hobby that was lost on her. She didn't like it as a kid, nor as an adult. Every time she cracked open the pages, she drifted away and woke up from a nap shortly after.

Something eventually caught her fatiguing eyes. An incident report from around 2002 stated a man named George Wilkerson called the fire department for a field fire started on his land. He claimed the field fire was done deliberately in his original statement, but he later retracted it, saying it was accidental by way of an improperly disposed cigarette. After that, there was no further investigation into the matter.

"You think it's interesting he retracted his original statement?" Nita asked both Charlie and Teller.

Teller leaned in, reached into his coat pocket, and removed a pair of readers. He cleaned the lenses with a cloth and placed them over his eyes.

Charlie smirked. "Glasses look good on you, Marc."

"Have we officially bonded to the point of shit-talking each other? Have I been here too long?" Teller asked.

Nita doubled down. "I don't know. I think Charlie is being genuine. The glasses are a nice touch, old man."

"Well, if I'm old, that's because this place made me that way. I was young when I arrived." Teller laughed.

"Welcome to our world," Nita stated in a serious and ominous tone.

An awkwardness built, even though that wasn't her intention.

Teller cleared his throat and attempted to brush past it. "It's not uncommon to retract statements in a situation like that, I would think. This guy still around?"

"Looks like it."

"Perhaps we should pay him a visit then."

"Skoden."

————

Nita made her way to the car but was stopped by the commanding yet slow drawl of Director Lowwater. He sipped his morning coffee and walked into his office without saying anything. Her job was to interpret his silence and follow behind him.

"Shut it behind you," he said.

She did. "Everything all right?" she asked.

"You're not exactly taking it easy, are you? I told you that you were not to be part of the day-to-day here."

"Aren't we past that, Randall? We're months into this case now."

"We are. In that time frame of a couple months, how much of that was spent with your son or your family at all? I talked to your father the other night."

"Oh yeah, and what did he have to say? That he's worried about me?" Nita said, irritated.

Lowwater relaxed his shoulders and a long exhale followed. "He's a father. He'll always be worried about you."

"And why's he talking to you about me but not directly to me?"

"He says he tries, but you don't answer and barely come home anymore."

Nita didn't have a retort for that. She shook her head and clenched down.

"Your mother and father are great parents. They care about you, as I do." She wanted nothing more than to be far away from this conversation, but he continued, "You're consuming yourself with work so you can avoid that boy. Perhaps you're buying yourself time until you figure out how to proceed. Listen, I get it, it's hard. Especially a child with his condition. However, no matter the circumstance, children all need the same thing... love."

"I understand... but I feel like we're close for this, and I believe I'm—"

"You're what? Needed?" Lowwater interrupted.

Nita flared her nostrils. "Don't start spinning my words and telling me who needs who."

"Apparently, I don't have to because you already know."

Silence.

"Nita, go home. They can handle whatever it is without you for a little while."

"And what if I can't do that?"

"Then, I'll have to suspend you."

That threw the chair backwards. "You can't suspend me!"

"Absolutely, I can. So, don't let it get to that point."

The chair scooted halfway across the room as she stood. She went to tear into Lowwater, but he interrupted her once again.

"It was Aiden's birthday yesterday."

That fact hit her like buckshot to the chest. She closed her eyes, taking in the realization of how much she had messed up. Worse, her pride wouldn't allow her to acknowledge fully that she was wrong.

She didn't want to look at him. Sensory blindness and deafness took hold. She grabbed her badge clipped to her chest, removed it, and tossed it on Lowwater's desk. It rattled back and forth as she marched out.

CHAPTER 49

Much to the displeasure of his men, Blake made them stay behind. While he assured them they were along for the ride in the pursuit of cowboy justice, now wasn't the time. He did little to nothing to blend in with the surroundings, sporting a denim shirt tucked into his wranglers. Walking into the sea of black leather and steel horses gave him a hint of trepidation as the bikers encased him on all sides, like a stone thrown into dark and deep water. The multitude of looks he received ranged from curiosity to disgust and indifference. A few of the bikers never took their eyes off him, all of whom wore the matching cut with red devils straddling a motorcycle as patches. Some of the higher-ups wore specific patches specifying their rank amongst the club.

Nevertheless, a few tightly crop-topped ladies with upper arm tattoos hit on him. They referred to him as "cowboy," and he was bombarded with innuendoes. One asked if he wanted to take them for a ride, while another wondered if they could hold on for eight seconds. The best he could do was tip his cap and judge their lack of creativity and whorish nature only in the confines of his own mind. The last thing he wanted to do in a hazy biker bar was draw unnecessary hostility.

As he took a seat at the bar, he didn't have to seek out anyone specific. They found him. A shorter man puffed out his chest on approach. The patch above his heart read: *Sgt at Arms*. "Can I help you find your way out of here?" he said. His voice was lower, and his mustache thick.

"You wouldn't happen to be Dan, would you?"

The sergeant got defensive quick. Two members backed him up out of nowhere. "Depends on who's asking, and what for?"

"Listen, I'm not here to cause any trouble. Believe me," Blake said, speaking both honestly and dishonestly at the same time.

"Well, you better get to talking then, cowboy."

Blake took a breath. "I need to talk with your VP."

"Our VP doesn't take walk-ins."

"Walk-ins," Blake repeated and chuckled. Dan didn't find it amusing. "Go on and tell him it's bout the Skull Draggers."

"What about the Skull Draggers?"

"Maybe you can also lead by telling him Blake Edwards is here to speak with him. That might be all you have to say. But, by all means, if that don't work, feel free to mention the Skull Draggers."

Dan never took his eyes away from Blake. Instead, he leaned off to the side and cocked his head back. One of his fellow members took that as a sign. All Blake could do was grip the barstool and wait until the prospect returned with either the VP or a loaded gun.

It didn't take long, but the awkwardness was not lost on him. Blake offered Dan and his unshaken gaze a drink.

"You trying to fuck me later or something?" the biker asked.

"I hope the offer won't lead to such things."

"Hmm."

A whistle shot through the noisy crowd like a bullet from one of the many guns tucked into the faded bikers' jeans. The whistler and messenger called Blake and the couple of bikers around him into the back room. Everyone in the bar went back to their revelry as it appeared such occurrences like this were regular. Blake was led to believe the bar was Devil-owned but not quite Devil-ran.

At the end of a narrow hallway was a beaded curtain making its best impression as a doorway to hell. The reddish hue coming off the lights beyond it made Blake question his existence. Also, being in this place dulled his senses due to the contact high. Now, he began to worry if he'd see the Devil himself sitting atop a stack of gold coins once he peeled those dangling beads away.

The VP sure wasn't the Devil. Not even close. He was met with a blond-haired, goateed individual wearing the whitest biker smile known to man. Based on the general consensus of the room, he didn't know such a smile existed. He was welcomed with a leathery hug and firm embrace. "Blake Edwards, how ya' been, you cowboy son of a bitch? How long's it been, fifteen... twenty years?"

Blake reacted in kind. "I think so. I think graduation day was the last we crossed paths. You look good, Jack."

Jack smiled again. "It's the veneers, isn't it?"

"It might be." Blake tugged on the plaid button down beneath his cut. "You still holdin' on to the country lifestyle?"

"My lifestyle might be wilder west than yours, old friend."

"I don't doubt that."

Silence built. Blake's eyes darted around. He waited.

It didn't take long to realize that Blake couldn't have this conversation alone. Dan flanked him well, and the prospects flanked Dan.

"Boys, why don't you give us a minute?" Jack asked. "I get the sense that my old pal here wants a private conversation."

"You sure, Jack?" Dan objected.

"I'm sure."

Jack proceeded to take a seat on the end of the leather couch. He took a drag of a cigarette smoldering in the ashtray on the coffee table that also sported a few stacks of hundred-dollar bills and a couple firearms, a sawed-off shotgun, and a pair of Glock 19s.

"So, to what do I owe the pleasure of speaking with one of the richest men this side of the river?"

"Depends on the river, I suppose."

"I suppose you're right. You look good, Blake." Jack said, offering the cigarette to Blake, but he waved it away. "Nice to see you're not getting fat on us."

"Back at ya. Glad all those countless hours of tearing up the streets haven't taken a toll on your health."

Jack paused. "Well, it ain't never been the riding that diminishes the health. It's everything else. Shit, the only peace I get is on the road. Perhaps you feel the same on the back of your trusty steed."

"You're not wrong."

Jack took another drag. The smoke escaped his nose like a diffuser and slithered past his glassy eyes. He waited for Blake to speak.

"I wanted to ask you a favor." Blake said, clearing his throat. "But I would never ask you for anything without offering something in return."

Jack's demeanor didn't shift much, but there was a subtle nod. Blake would've missed it if he hadn't examined his body language so intensely. "Carry on, then."

"I need information. I know you're currently at war with the Skull Draggers MC. It turns out we may have a mutual enemy."

"What do you mean?"

"A few weeks ago, a group of people wearing masks attacked me on my land. After a little investigation, my only potential suspects are the SD."

"Hmm. So, what kind of information do you need? There's no guarantee that I can get you anything. This war, even as you call it, has not been kind to us." The confidence and friendliness Jack showed earlier didn't disappear but faded for now. He finished off his cigarette only to light up another.

"Perhaps a list of people on the receiving end of their drug runs."

"So, you're thinking that someone put those motherfuckers up to it to keep their hands clean?"

"I believe so."

Another drag. "What you're asking me, Blake, isn't exactly light work."

"I know."

"I need assurances that it actually is SD. Are you sure it's them?"

"They sent the dogs after me, if that means anything."

"Pits?"

Blake planted his boot on the coffee table and pulled up his pant leg, revealing the healing bite mark below his calf.

"That's a yes," Jack said.

Blake covered himself. "They're the only club involved in dog-fighting, am I right?"

"Around here they are. That's how I know we're the good guys in this little war. At least we don't hurt dogs. That's fucking inhumane shit."

"I agree."

"What do you intend to offer us in return to get you what you want? If it's even possible."

"A lawyer," Blake said.

"A lawyer?" Jack scoffed. He didn't seem pleased with the answer.

"I know your president and a couple of your other guys are awaiting a parole hearing in the next few months." Blake stated. "You're short on men and getting your guys out of jail is imperative to your club's success in this conflict with the SD. Guaranteed, my guy can release your men and be back on those bikes quickly."

Jack fiddled with another cigarette in his opposite hand. "And who will foot the bill for this superstar lawyer?"

"I will."

"You sure you're good for it? I know Blake Edwards ain't hurting for money, but I guess you could say I'm a little cautious in harsh times such as these."

"Times have been harsh since the beginning, Jack. But perhaps this partnership can benefit both of us."

Jack's straight and hardened face finally smiled once again as he reached his hand across the coffee table. "You got a deal, cowboy." Their handshake was firm, and Blake trusted its merit. Jack stood. "You know your father came in here once upon a time when my dad was president and came to him with a mutually beneficial offer. He also asked him to keep it 'under wraps and under the table.'"

"Was there an 'or else?' on the end of that bargain?"

Jack smirked. "From what I was told, there was, but not one that was spoken."

Blake became numb. He clenched his fist and felt the urge to smash the neon beer sign next to him as its glow grew hotter and more irritating with each passing second since Jack informed him of prior dealings.

"I guess it's true what they say about sons and fathers. No matter how hard we may try at times, we always end up like them in some sorta way."

Blake kept his gaze forward as he made way for the exit. "You make sure to let me know any information you find. I'll be sure to set you up with that lawyer."

CHAPTER 50

Her Sig recoiled in her palm as the magazine ran empty. Nita returned it to her primary holster as she sidestepped a barrel and unholstered her backup Glock 19 Gen5. The fifth paper target was the recipient of her next three rounds.

Two to the chest. One to the head.

She sprinted through two beat-to-shit trucks acting as additional obstacles. Two more targets stood down range, and Nita repeated her shots. Two to the chest. One to the head. The pop of the gun grew more satisfying with each shot.

It had been months since her last run. After the events of Marble City, where her training paid off, she buried herself in work that geared her away from practice. She felt like an athlete spending years training for an Olympic event, only to succeed and struggle to find meaning after medaling gold at the podium.

The hobby led to accomplishments, including wins as Civilian State Pistol Champion and Oklahoma Law Enforcement Pistol Champ. She placed in other firearms outside pistols, including shotgun and rifle, but never won those competitions. Those losses bothered her as a born-and-bred competitor, but she did not practice with those firearms as much.

Another target was parallel to one of the trucks Nita was braced against. The shot task was to fire through the open vehicle windows. She squatted upward, keeping a solid base, drove her hands forward from her chest, and fired the remaining contents of her magazine. She had to take a half-step back from the window to avoid her arms extending into the vehicle's interior. Doing that would impede mobility should she have to make a quick pivot or turn in a real-life situation.

She holstered her secondary pistol.

A shotgun rested on the tailgate by design. She grabbed the Benelli M3, checked its status, and confirmed it was loaded. *One in the camber. Five in the tube.*

There was a fifty-yard sprint to the tree line. However, six clay pigeons were tossed into the air behind barricades sporting the Mercer Tactical logo. She shattered four into non-existence, but the one she missed low stung.

She began to sweat. Her breath was labored. Her shooting glasses were filthy, and that pissed her off more than anything. At first, it was a subtle irritant. Now, she wanted to slam them into the dirt, stomp on them, then fire a slug into them.

She resisted that urge.

The next section of the course was in a wooded area similar to a cross-country track. She turned the shotgun on its side as it rested upon her shoulder. Her offhand went to the 12-guage quad loader and grabbed two shells simultaneously, holding them like a trivia palm buzzer.

Strong side shoulder – weak side turnover.

Those words she still repeated in her head simply out of constant repetition and habit, but make no mistake, everything she did with a firearm was so embedded in her veins that it was instinctual.

Soreness in her shoulder would return, no doubt. But she enjoyed the gun's recoil as she ebbed and flowed with its kick. When all the shells spat out the side, and all the remaining targets were dealt with, a crate resting atop a hay bale concealed an M4. She replaced her shotgun with that firearm, strapping the assault rifle over her shoulder. Typically, a shooter would start with the larger guns and work their way down, but she made this up as she went.

Once the smoke and weapons were clear, Nita made for the course's starting position, around a hundred yards away. A man waited for her in the driver's seat of a side-by-side. White hair flowed out from under his hat and laid on the collar of a green Army jacket he hadn't taken off since the Gulf War.

On approach, he asked, "Hey, how you doin', kiddo? Long time since you've shown people how to do it around here."

"Too long."

Greg Mercer stepped out from his ATV, favoring his left side due to a knee brace strapped tightly over his jeans. That didn't stop him from giving her a bear hug that could squeeze the life out of someone. "I've missed you, kiddo," he said. He left plenty of condolences and offerings of prayer unsaid, and she preferred it that way.

After his heroism, Greg became a hero in the community and was offered jobs across the state, but her father helped him the most. After accepting the job at the University of Oklahoma, her father went directly to their administration and inquired about avenues to help Greg and other homeless veterans in the state. Since Greg was one-eighth Cherokee on his mother's side, Nita's father went to the Cherokee Nation Office of Veteran Affairs and asked them about steps to help him. Two months after the bombing, the University of Oklahoma and Cherokee Nation offered Greg ten thousand dollars to help kickstart his business, which soon became Mercer Tactical.

She placed her forearms on the heavy wooden table and started the process of reloading her magazines.

"How were your runs?" Greg asked. "Leonard told me you were down here, so I was hoping I'd catch one of them."

"Eh, if I'm being honest, they were better than I thought they'd be. I'll take that."

"Yeah, only you are surprised by that. I'd take you cold over others with months of consistent practice."

"You're just saying that cause Robbie and Justin underperformed last month." She winked.

"No, I'm saying that 'cause you have half the damn awards in the damn display case at the damn front office."

"Damn right."

They smiled.

"You gonna go one more time for me?" Greg said with his palms laying flat on the table.

"Sure, I'll load up and go again."

"Hell am I doin'? Let me help." Greg started loading another magazine for her, grabbing bullets from a large plastic bowl in the center of the table. "I'm not gonna start playin' into that notion of chivalry being dead."

"You're one of the good ones, Greg."

Silence built.

"You off today?"

Nita shook her head. "I'll be off for a while."

"They got you on a sabbatical or somethin'?"

"Something like that"

"That mean you still gettin' paid?" Greg asked, thumbing round after round into her magazines for her.

She cocked her head. "I guess I should've worked out all the details."

"It makes sense. You got a lot goin' on, kiddo."

"I've been told. It's hard for me to function when I'm..."

"Grounded?" he said with a chuckle.

She stayed reserved, only focusing on the task of reloading.

"Listen, you don't get into all your troubles here. This is the place to clear yourself of all that."

"Do you agree that I should step away for a bit?"

Greg finished loading up two magazines faster than her doing a single one. "Hard for me to say, really. There are no one's instincts I trust more than yours. Whether we were on patrol or in a foxhole, I'd be behind any choice you made. Because, at least for you, it seems to work out when you shoot first and ask questions later."

CHAPTER 51

Nita never tired of the ambiance of Jimmy's Diner. A handful of the noises that eased her mind were the porcelain clanking, tickets tearing, spatulas tapping on the grill, and the old cash register that dinged every time it opened. She sat at her corner booth, alone for the time being. Her black coffee steamed under her nose as she remained in a sort of trance. Her impromptu meeting with Lowwater was unexpected. She thoroughly disagreed with the result but accepted it anyway. After all the events in her life, rather traumatizing or not, the lack of control was something that she struggled with beyond all else.

"Anything else I can get you, darlin'?" the comforting voice of Jimmy asked.

"I'm fine, Jimmy. Thank you. I'm just waiting."

"All right. Holler if you need anything." Off he went, back to work in his yellowed apron.

Movement to her right was easy to spot as the sunlight blared through the open door. Her mother and father walked to her booth with Aiden between them. They smiled, obviously happy to see her. Even Aiden smiled back, though it was subtle. She stood to greet them, giving them full hugs in silence. Aiden eased in slowly and grasped his hands halfway around her waist. He kept his elbows tucked in and didn't commit fully to the embrace, nor did she. In response, she patted and rubbed the back of his head with one hand before sitting again.

"How are you?" her father asked.

She sighed, "Tired, Dad."

"We can understand that." He glanced at Aiden beside her.

She didn't say sorry. However, she hoped they picked up on her guilt.

They all sat in the booth. Aiden was next to her. Luckily Jimmy brought a kid's menu and a trio of worn-down crayons.

"Any progress at work?" her father asked.

"Some."

"I apologize for telling Randall about everything. I wasn't trying to get you—"

Her mother moved to a different topic, one that wouldn't be any easier to discuss for Nita. "Have you talked with Jackson's sister?"

"Heather? No, not since the funeral. Why? What brought that up?"

"She mailed you and Aiden a letter. It's at the house waiting for you. I'm sorry, I should've brought it."

"Well, I got time now, so I'll come by after we're done here." Nita was at a loss, both at Heather reaching out and her method. She scrunched her face at the idea of someone mailing letters nowadays.

Both her parents smiled, and she couldn't help but match theirs. Her mother shifted her attention to Aiden. "Honey," she said to him, "you wanna show what you made for Momma?"

An uneasiness found Nita at the casual usage of the word 'Momma.' Especially regarding Aiden. She never once instructed him to call her that, and she didn't know when that evolution would take place.

He perked up. He fumbled with his jacket, attempting to pull something out of his inside pocket, but whatever it was seemed stuck. With Aiden's autism, frustration grew rapidly. An outburst would soon occur if it wasn't resolved.

Her mother placed one hand on his shoulder and the other on the bottom of his jacket near the zipper so the jacket would stop fighting him. A thick piece of folded paper emerged. Aiden feverishly splayed it on the table and subtly inched closer to Nita. The right arm she used to hold his shoulder rested behind his back.

He proudly displayed a highly detailed map that seemed to take up half the table. Nita couldn't help but snicker at the intricate cartography display before her. "Thorpe Ranch," she said as she read it at the top of the page.

"Blake told us he worked on that for hours. Even said he tried to get Aiden to eat something, but he worked right through dinner," her mom said.

"You did all of this at one time?" She had a hard time believing such a thing. It was a comprehensive aerial view of thousands of acres, including the river, the creeks that flowed from it, the fence line, and so much more she discovered the longer she looked. Hell, it even had a compass rose and locations of deer stands throughout the property.

Aiden nodded his head.

"We had to take him back a couple of times to make sure he had an opportunity to finish," her mother said delicately.

"Is that right? A couple of times back to Blake's ranch?" she said, eyeing her mother and father. There wasn't anger in her glare but judgment. However, it wasn't lost on her that she had no moral high ground to stand on.

She admired the map once again, and she was impressed. A sense of melancholy and regret came over her. Her active role in avoiding Aiden caused her great shame.

"I think it's incredible, Aiden," she murmured.

"Thank you," he replied, admiring his work while refusing eye contact.

"So, how's Miss Kaitlyn's—"

"Excuse me?" a feminine voice said, cutting her off.

She turned her head. Immediately, she was agitated. However, upon looking at the woman attempting to make conversation, she unclenched her jaw. Her parents' eyes widened, and their mouths dropped slightly agape.

Joan Martin stood like a beggar with thinning hair and withered clothes. Her son's death had aged her harshly. While she and Nita shared the loss that evening, Nita felt Joan wore her wear. She hadn't changed for the better, even since the last time she saw her from afar at the funeral at Crittenden Cemetery.

———

The two of them sat at another booth at the opposite end of the diner. Nita's parents were still in the eye line and never took their gaze away from her. Aiden seemed to care less as he colored his grease-spotted coloring sheet.

"I'm sorry to take up your time. I just saw you over there and..." The woman trailed off for a moment, not knowing how to proceed with the conversation. "My son and I came to this diner every Saturday morning. I saw it as a way to bond with him as mother and son should. Or at least, that's what I was led to believe. But truth be told, I don't know if he enjoyed coming here much. Perhaps I dragged him here. He would probably have preferred staying at home and practicing on his keyboard... or anything else."

Nita sat, her hands in her lap, nodding at the woman across from her, letting her get these memories out of her head.

"I'm Joan," the woman said.

"I know."

It appeared Joan was doing her best to avoid the silence during every break of conversation. "I just wanted to tell you I'm beyond sorry about what happened to your husband. I don't know if that is strange for you to hear coming from me, but I felt that I needed to tell you that."

Nita nodded.

"That night... I know you probably won't believe me. You might think these are justifications and excuses from a grieving mother, but my son was a good kid. A very good kid. The drugs in his system that night... That was... a shock, and quite frankly, I still have a hard time believing it. I'm not coming to seek your forgiveness or anything, I promise. Bobby was a shy kid who didn't put himself out there very much and had many anxieties. He even took medication to control it... I just... I just know he couldn't get his hands on those drugs."

"You'd be surprised how resourceful high schoolers are nowadays."

Joan cried but kept her emotions in check in order to get her point across. "Bobby only wore what I got him. Bobby called or texted me every hour he was gone from the house. We were close, as I said before. However, all that changed about three weeks before that evening." Joan cupped her coffee with two hands and took a sip. "Those check-ins no longer happened. He would get home late, leave for school early, and I hardly saw him. I wasn't too worried about him because his GPA never wavered, not even a little bit. He didn't seem to miss any of his obligations with band or anything. If I'm being honest, I thought he had met a girl, and he didn't want to tell me. I almost convinced myself that was the case. I doubt everything now, though."

Joan reached into her pocket. "This was on him when he died. I didn't get it for him, nor do I have the slightest idea where it came from. I checked the initials on it," the late mother said.

She extended a leather bracelet across the table. Nita took the band that locked on the wrist with a single button. It was thin but engraved on the outside. It read: *The world is yours* – F.E.S.

"I checked with every girl at his school that may have had matching initials, but nothing came of it." Joan said.

Nita ran her finger over the smooth leather. "Did you check any of the boys' initials?" Nita asked.

Joan's softened features hardened. Her thin lips perked slightly, and her posture stiffened. "Bobby wasn't a..." Her head dropped.

"Homosexual?"

Nita nodded once again and gave the bracelet back to Joan.

"I don't know if I want that," Joan said.

"Regardless of its meaning, it's still something to remember your son by," Nita said as she stood. "I wish I had more of my husband."

Joan looked away.

Nita's intentions weren't to make her feel guilty, but that didn't seem to matter. Her phone vibrated in her pocket. "Excuse me, I have to take this."

"Perhaps we'll see each other around."

Nita gave her one last emotionless glance before turning away. She made her way outside. "Yeah, Marc?"

"Hey, Nita. Sorry to bother you. I know Randall wants you to take it easy, but we struck out with George Wilkerson."

She should have remembered the first half of his message. "What do you mean, struck out?"

"Well, that old bastard didn't feel like talking to any law enforcement on any level. It seems his distrust runs deep. If he won't talk to us, we'll drop it?"

She dropped the phone to her waist and looked in frustration at the hazy sky. A bird caught her eye and perched itself on the roof corner of one of the college dormitories. She froze at the sight of the pristine and sacred bald eagle. The bird was the master of the sky and should be revered with near angelic respect. In her culture, it was believed that the eagle should never have to walk on the earth. Instead, it should keep its interest in the air, nor should it concern itself with what lay beneath it. No harm nor ill intention should go toward the eagle, and Nita respected her ancestors' traditions and sentiments.

She was transfixed by its smooth, white head and lush feathers. It stared into the horizon like it was posing for a patriotic calendar. Until its head turned sharply and violently, its eagle eyes now leered at her from its perch. Then, those large wings flapped as the god-like bird took to the sky.

As she brought the phone back to her ear, a pair of good ole cowboys tipped their hats in greeting and walked into the diner. A strange sensation washed over her, but she could comprehend it.

"Elsewhere," she whispered to herself. Then, through the phone she said, "Maybe we can get someone else to speak to the old farmer for us."

CHAPTER 52

"Fuck Blake Edwards," Charlie stated passionately through the phone.

"Blake knows George Wilkerson." Nita said on the other end of the call. "He might be one of the few men that could get that information out of the old bastard. Blake said he's known Wilkerson for as long as he can remember, and he's willing to help us."

"You talked to that fucker already?"

"Yes, you should go with him and make sure everything checks out. If they give you a lead, you can follow up on it immediately."

Charlie gripped the phone. For a moment, he contemplated squeezing hard enough to snap it into pieces.

"Come on, Charlie, this could be a good opportunity. You know it."

"I absolutely do not know this." He exhaled, slammed the gas nozzle back into the pump, and screwed the cap onto the tank. "Fuck it," he said.

A mother covered her daughter's ears as they emerged on the opposite side of the pump and were heading into the gas station.

He gave an apologetic wave. "Sorry, ma'am."

"What's that?" Nita asked on the other line.

"Nothing," he said. "Tell that cowboy bitch I'm coming."

"I'll be sure to use kinder words."

He shook his head. Before entering his vehicle, a trio of Native boys leaning against the brick wall of the gas station eyed him like he had taken something of theirs. He returned his gaze from the slot between his open door and interior. They shared a forty-ounce wrapped in a wrinkled brown paper bag. He shut his door and approached them. Their attitude never left, and they weren't shy or afraid of the fact that they were drinking underage in front of an officer of the law.

"Off to save some more white folks," the boy in the middle, wearing a stocking cap, said while taking a swig.

"You boys got any ID on you?"

"You're Nation 39?" another boy asked.

"I'm glad you can read double-digits."

"My dad said it's funny that Natives die here every day, and no one does shit, but when a white girl dies, it's national news, and all the law agencies get involved."

Charlie scoffed and nodded. It was a ragtag group of boys in front of him, rambunctious and pissed off like he had been at one point. "Well, that's not the whole story, boys. But I agree with you. However, I believe I asked for some ID."

"Hell, I got ID," the third boy said while grabbing a handful of his nuts over his pants. "Identify those, Marshal."

"Shut up, Trip," the ringleader in the middle said, scolding his smaller friend. The third boy, quietly sipping on the adult beverage, stopped immediately. The leader's neck twisted, and his head darted to his friends, who kept their eyes on Charlie. "So, you think it's true then? Those government types don't care what happens to us?"

"I'll tell you this, boys, they're succeeding." Charlie stepped forward. "They don't care if you die. They don't care if you drink yourself into nothingness. They don't care. Make no mistake. There's a reckoning for all people. Ours happened a long time ago and never stopped. My priority in life, as should yours, is never to forget that. Our ancestors endured a great trial. The mission against us was one of extinction, but here we are. Here you are, sipping on a forty outside a gas station. They didn't have the freedom to fuck about and piss their lives away like you boys. No, theirs was taken. You remember that."

They all side-eyed each other.

"They tried so hard to kill us off. I would say go check your history books, but I doubt, even here, those are a reliable source of information." Charlie paused. His tone became serious, perhaps too serious for these boys. "Resilience. That's what flows through our blood, thanks to those before us. So, don't throw it away waiting for someone to save you. 'Cause it won't happen. Not here. Not anywhere. Because if they have it their way, the access to healthcare facilities, education, and housing will remain understated. However, they'll ensure we never run out of alcohol."

He stepped away.

"Drink up, boys," were his parting words.

As he drove away in his marshal-issued vehicle, those boys remained in place, contemplating their next sip.

CHAPTER 53

In the solace of his car, Charlie could roll his eyes as he passed beneath the sign of Thorpe Ranch. To him, it might have been the massive gates to Jurassic Park.

The vast expanse of lush green grass and trees that should provide tranquility triggered the opposite emotion. He was familiar with the area, like a home he once had but that was now occupied by someone else.

By the enemy.

A set of ranch hands meandered through the pasture and tipped their hats to the squad car, eyeing him the entire way on entry. Perhaps they believed him to be Nita, perhaps they were just giving him a friendly cowboy greeting, but then again, he didn't want to give them that much credit.

When he stepped out his car, a German Shepherd waited at its post on the elevated front porch. It was so still, unflinching that Charlie believed it to be a statue. The dog turned its head to watch his master emerge in a brown Carhart jacket from the front door, blowing into a steaming cup of coffee. The king of the cowboys leaned against the post at the top of the steps, his eyes peering from underneath his hat like a nocturnal predator. They were eyes that no matter how much Nita told him to trust them, he didn't.

"Marshal," Blake greeted.

"Cowboy."

Charlie remained at the bottom of the steps.

"Coffee?" Blake asked.

"I'm fine."

"You sure? Just put on a new pot." He took a sip and sighed, satisfied. "Good shit."

The dog stepped down and circled him, brushing against his legs. He was reluctant to pet the dog. He'd worked with K-9 officers enough to know that the breed could tend to be aggressive. He held his palm out over the dog but didn't pet it. The thought of a good lawsuit against Blake for getting bit by his dog did cross his mind, and those were happy thoughts.

"She won't bite. She's mellow unless you fuck about." The pitter-patter of feet rumbled closer to them from behind Blake. His daughter poked her head around him as she hugged Blake's waist.

"Daddy, can I ride Sunflower today?"

He patted her head, which led into a soft hold. "Yes, but Daddy's got some business to attend to, and I have to leave. You'll have to convince Little J or one of the others to ride with you." She ran to find Little J in the pasture, but Blake stopped her. "Don't go runnin' off till you greet our guest."

"It's fine," Charlie said.

The girl approached Charlie and extended her tiny hand. "Nice to meet you, sir."

Her wild nature reminded him of his niece. He returned the handshake. "Nice to meet you as well."

"My name is Lyla. What is yours?"

Charlie couldn't help but laugh. It pained him that this little blonde, white girl was too cute for her own good. On the other hand, it seemed to soften the grudge-filled exterior Charlie wore on this ranch. He convinced himself that something so cute and innocent couldn't be an Edwards.

"I'm Charlie. Charlie Soap."

"Soap? I like that name," she said with a smile and a chuckle.

Though it was a common Native last name and didn't raise any questions in Cherokee County, he received more laughs and teasing when he went to school less than fifty miles away in Coweta, directly east of here.

Blake squeezed Lyla's shoulders. "Charlie here is a marshal, like Aiden's mom."

"Woah, have you shot anyone before? My daddy has."

Charlie barely got out his, "Is that right?"

"All right, run along now," Blake said, waving her away like a pest.

Blake rested his mug on the flat railing of the wraparound porch. His boots clapped against the step on his descent. A horse neighed at his back. The ranch hands followed along the fence line. Their looks didn't appear malicious. However, a harsh curiosity was present. Lyla was there to greet them, and their harshness melted away as they welcomed her with broad smiles.

"I know Floyd, but the other ones?" Charlie said.

They were now on equal footing, as Blake watched his daughter trot around the ranch. "The rest of them are Marine buddies. Yeah, they do their part well around here."

Charlie nodded. "How long have they been doing their duties?"

"Near ten years."

He was genuinely surprised. "Fuck me... Time keeps going."

"Yep, time will fuck you. That's a fact. Do you ride?" Blake asked as his men escorted Lyla to the stables.

"Not anymore. I broke my leg in junior high, fell off a horse, and missed a full basketball season. I haven't been on one since, and I don't plan to get on one ever again."

"Interesting stance for an Indian man." An awkwardness built between them from things left unsaid as Blake reached back for his mug and took a sip. "I'm just fuckin' with you."

"Let's go," Charlie said.

"We're gonna have to take my truck. We pull up in your marshal wheels, and he'll press a sawed-off against the door and wait. That's even with me along for the ride."

———

They drove in silence.

Anguishing silence.

Wilkerson Farm was not even half an hour away, but each minute of listening to the air conditioning felt that times by ten.

"How's Nita been?" Blake asked.

Charlie didn't want to entertain this conversation. "How do you mean?"

"Well..." Blake sniffed, gripping the handle above the passenger side window. "I suppose I'm talking about Jackson's death and how she's managing."

Charlie's thumbs rubbed the steering wheel. He checked the rearview mirror, both side mirrors, and blind spots. He reckoned there was no reason for it, just a nervous tick. "She's been trying to work it out. Quite literally. She's been doing nothing but working ever since."

Blake curled his lip. "You've been right by her side the whole way. Good for you."

"What the hell is that supposed to mean?"

"It wasn't supposed to mean anything more than what I said."

"Well, everything you say is spoken through a condescending prism."

"Don't know what a prism even is, friend."

Charlie scoffed. "Don't bother with the 'friend' shit."

"Oh, the door shut on that possibility?"

"Locked with the key well out of sight."

Charlie breathed heavily through his nostrils. If he could flare them, he would. When it came to Blake Edwards, his fuse was relatively short.

The silence returned. They had attempted conversation, and it didn't turn out well. They went the rest of the ride that way and didn't make a sound until the handles of the car door clicked open.

Blake took the lead out of the truck and Charlie followed. "You might wanna hang back."

Charlie looked at the old farmhouse. It was as if it was frozen in time or leftover from the Dust Bowl.

Harsh times.

Charlie accidentally made eye contact with Blake, who flashed him wide-eyed, almost as if to agree with him about the state of this place.

"Yes," Blake said.

"What's that?" Charlie asked, examining the bare roof full of tarp-covered holes as he stepped over loose shingles.

"It's always looked like this. Ole Wilkerson ain't been shopping around for fixer-uppers. Guess they're locked down in Waco."

"Waco?" Charlie asked.

"You know, Chip and Joana Gaines. They got that show *Fixer Upper*. They're from Waco, Texas. You didn't know that?"

Charlie didn't want the conversation with Blake to go any further. He'd already had enough of the cowboy today. "Only thing I know about Waco is the cult."

Charlie followed Blake reasonably far, taking in the dead and overgrown surroundings.

"The Branch Davidians—David Koresh... crazy motherfucker," Blake said.

A loose screen door covered the main. The meshy interior was torn from the frame and only held in place in a few spots. Blake gave a few solid knocks on the door. Not too many, not too few.

Charlie leaned against a rotting post and had to catch himself from stumbling as the softwood gave way. He cursed as he righted himself.

Blake asked if he was all right.

Charlie didn't acknowledge his concern.

Blake knocked again. Harder this time. "George! George!" He tried the door, and the door opened. He kept calling out for Mr. Wilkerson but never got a response.

"He not home?" Charlie asked still testing the firmness of the post holding the awning above upright.

Blake looked at the pair of beat-down work trucks out front in the grass. "Maybe not."

Charlie glanced around the back of the house, believing that perhaps the old man was working in the shop held together by sheets of rusted tin.

But out the front door walked a white-haired, sunken-eyed, decrepit farmer who he assumed was George Wilkerson. Charlie's little hope in this mission deteriorated faster than Wilkerson's organ function. He doubted the old man could remember the knocks on the door that got him outside, let alone what happened so many years ago.

George looked Blake up and down. "James?" he asked in a soft but sure voice.

Blake placed his hand on George's shoulder and enunciated, "No, I'm James' son Blake. Do you remember me? You used to take me and your grandson Kyle noodling in the summer."

A smile of recognition came over his face, showing the remnants of teeth left behind. George slapped Blake's chest most endearingly. "If I recall, one of those flatheads took you for a ride on Lake Tenkiller."

They both shared a laugh. "They did! I can't believe you remember that."

"My mind's like a steel trap, young buck." George's hunched frame turned to notice Charlie standing next to his post. "Although, I don't remember having an Indian boy with us. Be careful leaning on that beam, young fella. This home here gotta lotta wear and tear on it, like its owner."

Charlie thanked him and stepped closer inward on the small deck.

"Oh, Charlie wasn't with us back then," Blake said, patting his palm on Charlie's shoulder. Charlie wiggled away. "But we were wondering if we could ask you some questions about a fire long ago, if you remember."

George stiffened. A cautious nature took over him as he looked back and forth between the pair of them. "Why would y'all wanna know about that?"

Charlie stayed back. He figured there were better courses than engaging.

"Well, I don't know if you heard, Mr. Wilkerson, but someone killed many people here recently because of a fire. All trails lead nowhere aside from a statement you retracted to the police."

George's head never stopped moving back and forth between the two of them. "Are y'all with the law?"

"Absolutely not," Blake assured him, shifting his stance on the rickety porch.

"So, you hear to cash in a favor from your old man?" George said.

Blake cocked his head. He shot a glance at Charlie. Both had no idea what the old man was on about.

"That ain't your reasoning?" George asked.

Blake cleared his throat. "I'm sorry. What exactly are you talking about, Mr. Wilkerson?"

"Bout the cow thieves in the early 2000s... Law didn't do shit about em' so I asked your dad to help me. Christ Almighty, he did. He said I didn't owe him anything, aside from a potential favor he'd be able to cash in at any time indefinitely."

Charlie observed the disdain flash across Blake's face.

"So, this ain't about that?"

"No, it ain't about that."

George gave a big toothy smile. "Boy, you should've seen the way your daddy strung those boys up that stole my cattle. Some good ole frontier justice."

Blake narrowed his gaze. "Then, you know what, George, I might just be cashing in that favor, and I didn't even realize. Do you think you could tell us about the fire? When did that take place? Before or after the cow thieves?"

The old farmer waddled over to the lone rocking chair with a few backboards missing and took a seat. "Oh, this would've been in the late nineties sometime, so before. Man, gas was under a dollar back then, but don't kid yourself. We were bitching about it still, as we should've. I tell you what, it's criminal what they're doing to us now."

"Right... and the fire?"

Recognition snapped George to attention. "Yes, the fire! Anyway, my grandson Kyle had one of his friends over once when he was probably thirteen to come to help me haul hay. I remember the kid appeared like many other thirteen-year-old boys out there, but his fascination with fire was something I ain't ever seen before. I guess Kyle introduced him to an old ferro rod I had that I used for starting campfires. Unfortunately, my grandson taught this little pyro head how to use it. The next thing I know, it went from two innocent boys startin' a campfire to Kyle trying to get this boy to stop setting the damn pasture ablaze."

"Did he succeed?" Charlie asked. "In setting the field on fire."

"Sure as shit did. He burnt up the whole hay field. Had to get the fire department out here to stop it. I was furious and initially told the police the truth about the kid and everything, but I didn't want to ruin his life based on what could've been innocent."

Judging by the potential of who this might be, George's decision might have been a severe miscalculation. Both Charlie and Blake knew it well as they shared another glance.

"I know this is going to be tough," Blake said, holding out his hands. "But is there anything you can give us to help us find out who that kid was and where he is now?"

Now, it was Mr. Wilkerson's turn to cock his head and look at Blake like he was the geriatric. "Shit, I know who he is. I see him around town all the time filling up his work van."

"Work van?"

"Yeah, I think he's got his own plumbing business, or maybe a relative does. I doubt he remembers me, but I remember him. Gil... Gil Burke."

CHAPTER 54

Accompanying Amos was a man by the name of Clarence Lee Fletcher. He was a tall, broad-shouldered behemoth who usually moved furniture without assistance. Hair emerged from every opening in his shirt, from his neck to his arms. Some around the compound referred to him as "Squatch," but they didn't dare utter that in his presence.

On this night, the pair of them wore all black with gloves. However, Clarence's inability to find any material to fit his hands forced him to wear surgical gloves.

"You start getting the stuff put up out back. I'll be right behind you with Gil," Amos instructed.

Clarence took Amos' command through his massive, Easter Island-sized head and drove forward and around Gil's house to the backyard. The house was on the edge of town, and a wooded area obscured his closest neighbor.

They were alone.

Amos walked to the house and knocked on the door.

Gil expected their visit and was there to answer in seconds. His curious head peeked out and darted in every direction.

"It's just me and Clarence. He's driving around back. Is the truck there?" Amos asked in reference to Arnold's stolen work vehicle.

Gil nodded. "Yeah, it's in the barn."

"Good, let's go inside then."

The interior of Gil's home was painstakingly average. It was a three-bedroom, two-bath American dream home, only with darker-skinned occupants and, ironically, no fireplace.

"So, Father sent you here to help eliminate anything that could incriminate me?" Gil asked.

"Yes, absolutely," Amos replied. "Starting with the truck. Are there any guns you have in the house?"

Gil's head darted back. "Yes, but I didn't kill anybody with a gun."

"It could still be used against you. We're just taking precautions."

Gil wore his skepticism.

"Go get whatever guns you own and bring them in here loaded with any additional ammunition you have."

With that, Gil escaped into his dark house into the master bedroom while Amos stayed in his spot. It didn't take long for Gil to return with a twenty-gauge, .38 special and an old deer rifle that hadn't been fired in years, judging by the obstruction inside the barrel.

"Good." Amos said. "Did you write that confession as Father insisted?"

Gil removed a piece of paper from his breast pocket. "We are gonna destroy it, right?"

"Yes, along with everything here. We got to destroy and leave it all behind you. Father will perform the ritual when we return to the compound."

Gil liked the sound and seemed to relax his tense shoulders. He handed over all his guns and placed them on the coffee table in the living room.

"Go ahead and have a seat, Gil. We're just waiting on Clarence now."

Gil groaned down into a withered recliner that sported tears and exposed cotton.

Amos continued looking at the guns and lifted the .38 snub nose, checking to see if it was loaded. "Nice piece," he said.

The front door opened, and Clarence had to duck to enter the house. As he walked over to the both of them, he asked, "Everything ready to go?"

"Almost." Amos handed Clarence the .38 special.

Clarence's gloved hand swallowed the gun. His index finger filled the entire space of the trigger guard as he put the gun to Gil's head and pulled the trigger.

CHAPTER 55

Law enforcement descended upon Gil Burke's residence. No fewer than thirty vehicles surrounded his home in the middle of the fall. The FBI tactical unit and the Cherokee Marshals tactical unit found their suspect DOA in his living room with a suicide note. The medical examiner informed Teller that Mr. Burke had died several days ago.

On the property, OSBI identified the stolen Arnold truck. The tires matched the tracks left behind at the church youth center, and some coordinating tools were littered throughout the property. The home itself was in such a state of ransacked smash that a hoarder would find it comforting.

In a guest bedroom, tucked away in the closet, was a locked chest with no key. The heftiness of the chest intrigued their curiosity. The FBI and OSBI placed friendly bets on the box's contents. FBI went with guns, while OSBI went with generalized memorabilia. Wanting to ensure no stone was left unturned properly, Teller pried the chest open.

"I think OSBI's going to take the W on this one," he said coldly and sarcastically.

The contents of the box contained memorabilia, which was true. Blood-stained clothes were folded neatly on the right side of the box. Human teeth filled the entirety of an empty tomato paste can. Articles of clothing stained with blood were glued in a book like a macabre scrapbook. He turned page after page. At the top right of each were dates that went back to 2008. Underneath the dates was an additional five-digit number. Marc gathered those were numbers that coincided with the zip codes of where the murders took place.

There was also a pouch with needles filled with a dark, near-black liquid.

Perhaps our meth and LSD concoction.

A stack of Bibles piled to the top in the back corner. Marc couldn't bear to look at them as they were smeared with blood and tended to exceed his limit for blasphemy. Some pages also had streaks of blood, and some had their owners' names on the cover. The name on top took a while to process, but when it did, Marc audibly spoke.

"Holy shit."

Pastor Rick Folk. The missing preacher from Kansas.

Marc spoke to an investigator for the OSBI and FBI and said, "Find out the status of all these people written on the covers."

"Fuckin hell, this guy was prolific," Agent Sampson said.

Teller exhaled. "Yes. Yes, he was." The flood of mixed emotions crashed into each other within Teller's gut.

We got our man, but perhaps too late. We got our man, but was it because of anything we had done? Will the public be satisfied with such a conclusion?

A feather poked upward out of the chest, crammed behind everything else. Marc reached for it himself. He removed a homemade owl mask that remained terrifying. The eyes were black, and the feathers flayed out all around the sides, aside from a fracture on the right that sent a crack streaming into the top center.

Nita nearly got you.

CHAPTER 56

Every time the basketball passed through the net cleanly was on par with any of the best music Nita had ever heard. It was a close second to powwow drums that beat energy into her veins. Regret for not attending the past several came over her as she spun the ball on her palm. This had been her routine for shooting free throws since she was ten, ever since her father painted this red line in the middle of the concrete fifteen feet away from the basket.

Spin, dribble, dribble, hand placement, drop hips, look at basket, rise and shoot, keeping everything in motion.

For her, a ball or a gun provided its form of therapy. One that didn't require speaking or vomiting any emotional scars to Dr. Whitekiller.

Teller informed her that everyone from the OSBI, FBI, US Marshals, and Cherokee Marshals raided Gil Burke's home last night and found him with a self-inflicted gunshot wound to the head. Accompanying his corpse was a mountain of evidence, placing him at the fire at the church and several other murders, including the murder of Collette and Wyatt.

Part of her was thankful the monster met an end, but part of her felt unfulfilled. She spent so much time working on this case, and she didn't get the opportunity to bring this man to justice. That was the job, unfortunately, but that didn't make it any less digestible.

Based on the report, Gil Burke wasn't that big of a man.

She pushed the thoughts out.

It's over.

The ball passed through the net once more, bounced on the concrete, and descended to the street. She looked down at that faded red line and stood motionless as if the paint had put her in a trance. The was an urge to stand by and not cross over it. Her muscles tightened, and her legs locked. A whoosh of wings sounded above her head, the wind whipped her hair behind her shoulders, and she stared in awe at the bald eagle perched upon the decaying basketball goal.

Behind the line, she remained.

The sacred bird's talons scraped the backboard, denting them. The yellow eyes pierced her, and its feathered brow lowered. All she could do was look at its mere prowess and grandeur. Then, the eagle's head darted up and away toward the house. Nita followed to see Aiden with his nose pressed to the glass, looking back at the both of them. His hands also touched the window from the inside. His touch turned into a wave directed at her, but her attention was drawn back to the bird as it unfurled its wings, ascended straight into the sky, and took flight to the northwest. The speed with which it flew out of sight, leaving her to contemplate behind that red line, forced her breathing to become heavy. She had the sensation of an anvil sitting on her chest.

With all the events in her life, she believed it irresponsible to deny this as a sign of action. Her eyes moved back again to her stepson, still staring and waving. The hint of a smile erected on one side of his mouth, but she averted her gaze back to the line at her feet and stepped across it.

Her direction was forward, following the eagle.

CHAPTER 57

Nita never let the eagle out of her sight as she followed its flight pattern from below. As she drove beneath, a feeling in her gut never left, telling her she was doing right by pursuing the bird to the town of Locust Grove. The destination never occurred to her until she grew closer to Cookie Road.

Here? This can't be right.

The backroad's silence was violent. Everything had been overgrown ever since the dark dealings over forty years ago. Camp Scott was the site of one of the most, if not *the* most, notorious murder case in Oklahoma, where an individual killed three young girl scouts in their tents in 1977. The case remained unsolved and was still active to this day. But, unless anyone came forward with new information after so many years gone, she knew that case would be open till the end of time.

There was a locked gate leading into the abandoned camp. A Master Lock was supposed to keep eyes from looking upon the murderous ruin, but all it took was a near effortless climb to find herself on the other side. The grounds were now private property, used for virtually nothing besides hunting. Nita didn't have to worry about the consequences, though. Her jurisdiction as a marshal gave her free rein, and her Native blood gave her more.

She followed the path sat before her by her instincts and the subtle smell of iron and rust. On her walk, she saw the abandoned camp begin to come to life. The ruined cabins, latrines, and the great hall all reformed anew before her eyes. Every building was apart from the next, and the thick foliage of the area shrouded this place in mystery or, worse, malice. And while the structure of the camp was revitalized, the eerie atmosphere remained. A tire swing swayed side to side. The creaking rope sounded more like a swaying noose.

Whispers emerged from the woods ahead of her. Her hyperactive and sensitive senses were on overload. Forty years later, this place harbored so much hate that it began to give her a migraine. Thunder blared overhead, yet the sunny and bright day remained. Giggling followed. She whipped her head around and saw three girls playing and chasing each other, paying her no mind. They all wore camp attire, and the one with blonde pigtails led her darker-haired friends the entire way. Nita wiped her damp brow and rubbed her eyes. Her mind was a haze like she had drank too much and was attempting to fight the alcohol.

A heavy thump and glass breaking emerged from the old staff house. Nita drew her service weapon, trained it on the door, and approached tactically as her training forced her. She peeked through the window, avoiding the broken glass on the elevated porch. A hooded figure lay flat, facing away from her, entirely concealed in heavy and worn clothes. She brought her pistol to her chest and tucked her elbows into her body. She gave the rotted and handle-less door a bump with her shoulder. It creaked open.

The hooded figure did not move. She crept forward. Trash littered the floor around this individual. There were droppings from God knew how many animals. The man couldn't be comfortable flat on his side. His slender frame crumpled atop himself as if his shoulders were touching.

A heavy shove sent her barreling into the short hallway as Nita went to nudge him with her boot. She pivoted like she was turning two on the softball field. Her sights found the center mass of another hooded individual standing there.

However, the young white man's interest in her vanished. His head and body swayed as he mumbled incoherently. A needle fell from his arm and another from his pocket. Soon after, he collapsed to his ass and sat in the middle of the dirty floor. The belt remained tightly fastened around his arm before he eventually drifted backward and away from reality. Nita holstered her gun. The tweakers were not a threat nor a concern.

She examined the needles and contents as they resembled the pictures of what Teller found in Gil Burke's chest.

Meth and LSD.

She went out the door, pulled the loop where the doorknob used to be, and was met with blackness. Camp Scott went dark. Storm clouds gathered over one another, and pulsating lightning flashes burst through them. Rain began to pelt the wooden porch.

She tried telling herself that this wasn't real but lacked conviction.

A dim light in the woods ahead of her fluttered across the trees. For a moment, it stopped, and so did her breathing.

Until it began moving once again.

What unfolded in front of her eyes mirrored the description of a camp counselor so long ago. That being June 13, 1977.

The light quickened its pace. Nita drew her weapon and hunted it down. She ran fast. No matter how fast, she never made up the ground. She passed a pair of canvased tents along the way. They flapped harshly against the strong winds and rain.

The light stopped.

Nita slowed, sliding and kicking mud in front of her. The source of the dim glow was a flashlight that outlined the silhouette of a tall, broad-shouldered man. He waited outside a lone tent, standing there like he had all the time in the world.

Tent number eight.

She raised her gun again, and simultaneously, the man entered. Knowing what followed this moment, Nita sprinted with her weapon ahead of her, near reckless. She came to the tent entry, threw open the flap, stepped onto the short platform, and met someone different than she expected.

Sitting cross-legged was a familiar face, one that had changed due to the passage of time. An elderly Native man wearing a weathered face was surrounded by four little fires. When he spoke, it seemed only second to the Creator.

"I've wandered through all the lands this hemisphere has to offer, only to return and sit here before you. Have a seat, please. I know your journey hasn't led you as far, but the short road traveled can be more perilous given the circumstances."

She remained at a loss. Had this not been a man she trusted, her gun wouldn't have holstered so readily.

"You remember me, child?" he asked. "Your road has been littered with many impediments looking to be your ruin, yet here you are."

"I see you in my dreams... along with others."

"They say we can't dream of people we haven't seen before. I doubt that the law of nature applies to Natives, though. Do you remember the origins of our introduction?"

Still shaken, Nita couldn't place any real memory of an interaction.

"Many years ago, a father was going around town seeking a willing medicine man of able power to help heal his daughter from horrible night terrors that plagued her after laying eyes on a monumental tragedy. One that should've bore no witnesses, let alone a child. An event that quite literally and figuratively shook her to her bones. His desperation to help his daughter made such an impression on my soul that I offered assistance. You were so frail." The medicine man pointed underneath his eyes. "You had dark, near-black circles underneath your eyes. However, in your weakened state, overwhelming strength persisted."

A hint of a smile rose on his wrinkled visage. "I worked right away on a ceremony I thought appropriate. As I began to work to remove such dark dealings, I informed your mother and father that to alleviate such a thing as this might have to call on the generosity from the Creator, and once in his hands, I was no longer in charge. Regardless, I went through with the ceremony and stayed around the area for a month or two to monitor your progress. To my and your parents' delight, the darkness that plagued your nights never returned."

His hands then went to his eagle feather in his lap, held at the shaft as he fanned his face. "I ask, what filled the void of such darkness?"

She had her answer. "It remained. It never left me. The only thing that changed was my ability to cope with it and recognize its presence."

For the life of her, she couldn't remember the medicine man's name. As she thought about it more, she wondered if she had ever heard his real name spoken.

"The serrated cut of the events surrounding this place leaves an unhealable scar," he said. "Three girls were murdered, but countless lives were changed forever. We all fear the darkness and those who prowl it with ill intentions. The Creator allows such darkness for the prevalence of light. Sometimes that reality exposes itself to an unparalleled result. Countless poor souls are brought up with beauty and potential but meet an unfortunate end in such darkness." He paused and used the feather to fan the back of his neck. "Everyone at attention will be blessed to receive the call to action to help others. Now, those who hear it can deny it all the same. Stories travel far and are sometimes inescapable. Imagine my surprise when I hear tales in the heart of the Great White North of one from Oklahoma who can bring ruin to those who hurt others. Another man of my station was convinced Deer Woman managed to pass her antlers onto you."

"That day I saw it," Nita said, nearly interrupting him. Sure, she was focused on what he said, but the talks of her abilities or hypersensitivities brought repressed memories. The tragedy of Camp Scott was a mark on their history, but that wasn't the most famous tragedy in the state's past. No, she witnessed the primary one firsthand on April 19, 1995. "I saw the man responsible caught between this world and another. His form shifted between the two as he walked away from that van. His monstrous counterpart dominated that day."

The fires radiated comforting heat around them, but they produced no smoke. "Imagine if you were older then. Imagine if you were at this very camp that night so long ago... the lives you could have saved." He stopped, took in the surroundings, atmosphere, and breathed in. "When people can do the things you or I can, and problems against our people continue to mount, they happen because of a lack of action. Yes, you are burdened with something most cannot understand, but your burden is your advantage, opportunity, and power to make change. If you don't wield it, that doesn't make you on equal footing as everyone else. It makes you worse. Up to this point, you have represented yourself with honor and pride. Others sense what I know. But your journey is not over."

"I don't know what you mean."

"In the White North, a dark place was erected by a man claiming to be a vessel for the Creator, who knew the verses well enough to speak the words through his prism as if they were the absolute truth. This man garnered a devoted following at a rapid pace. His ascension also coincided with occult murders and black rituals in the area. A great fire broke out when there proved to be a link between this man and his followers. The flame was so vast that some believed it would char the cold north."

The medicine man held out his hands with his palms up, the eagle feather now resting in his lap. He didn't say anything, but Nita instinctively reached out and grabbed them.

Again, she experienced a hallucinogenic phenomenon. She stood directly in front of a massive flame that stretched as far as her vision would allow in any direction. Wet snow melted beneath her boots. In the center of the fire, she saw an upright figure with the broad shoulders of a man. The face, however, had no resemblance to a man at all. The animalistic face that glared back at her with red eyes was that of a goat. Its horns curled into a sharp point towards the back. The eyes glowed brighter red before she snapped out of her vision and returned to the more familiar and warm medicine man grasping her hands.

He gave Nita no time to recover. "I have come all the way home on my journey to seek you out. Many would like to convince others that true evil doesn't exist. I'm here to tell you that is false. If true evil did not exist, then the Creator would not have given us such power to defeat it. You know who must be defeated, don't you?"

She shook her head. "No, I don't."

"You do. You have already met him, and he's seen you for what you are. Given the chance, he will rid himself of you."

"Are you positive?"

The medicine man wore a rawhide bag around his neck as a necklace. He clenched both sides of the string and said, "I am certain. In this bag is the medicinal power to protect you from evil and its instruments. The only stipulation is that when I place this around your neck, you must not remove it until the task is complete, or else it can no longer protect you."

She didn't know what to say, but she accepted the parameters.

"You must confront this evil." His low and guttural voice had an angelic and wise quality to it. "Or he will bring ruin to many like he has countless times before. His power is ancient and biblical. When you enter that vast thicket of engulfing black to face him, keep the pace."

A chill went down her spine as the medicine man spoke Jackson's words. Her eyes began to swell, but she pushed the emotion back down.

"You feel alone, I know," he said, sitting solid and still like a stone fountain. "Do not despair. I assure you that those that have suffered against such evil, those you have bonded with from faraway lives always ride with you. Those that are here now, and those that were here long ago."

A heaviness weighed on her shoulders. Not one of pressure but of endearing touch. The ancestors who came to her every night since the ride for removal were with her now.

"Go," he said. "It's time."

She nodded, turning away from the medicine man while clutching the rawhide bag hanging from her neck. The sunlight blasted the tent and blinded her as she stepped outside.

It was day.

The storm no longer raged, and the wind was at a hush. She put her forearm up to shield her from the unrelenting sunlight. Her eyes adjusted, and tent number eight was no longer there when she turned around. Only a rotted wooden platform remained, and the solemn quiet returned to the surrounding woods.

Chapter 58

Nita drove through the entrance of this newfound church. The privacy fence was nearly ten feet high and carried on into the woods on both sides. It was now more of a wall than a fence. The progress since the last time Nita was here was extraordinary. The gate was open and seemed welcoming to visitors until the stares of people across the property met her gaze through the car window.

She parked in front of the modern home, which acted as a secondary barrier to entry. The tinted glass teased the silhouette of all in the interior. Two large warehouses had been added on opposite ends of the tree line and flanked the main chapel by a hundred yards.

The number of workers had significantly decreased, but the opposite occurred for people seemingly living their lives as they smiled and walked about the grounds. If she took a random guess, a hundred-plus people enjoyed this place in the middle of the day and week. Some took walks in the extended field or played catch, while others tended to the gardens or picnics. Others seemed to be in the process of moving boxes from one of the warehouses to the church.

These people live here?

CHAPTER 59

Ezell, Amos, and Clarence oversaw his most trusted visionaries clear shelf space for the next shipment of incoming guns. Barrels lined the left side of the wall in rows. They contained Ezell's liquid concoction of altering drugs. He ensured his visionaries were careful with the goods because he didn't want his guys high and hallucinating off their asses on such an important day. The room was lit by a blue light that made everyone look like the moon was directly above their heads. That was until the sun burst through the main door.

Everyone stopped working and waited for Ezell's command.

One of their own, Wayman McDaniel, shut the door behind him. "Father, one of them marshals is here. The woman."

Ezell recalled the Cherokee woman he briefly interacted with not long ago. The aura that came with her left him trepidatious, with the barrier to her soul so impenetrable. Her unprompted return gave him a queasy sensation in his gut. "She's alone?"

"Yes, Father."

"Is she wearing marshal attire?"

"Looked like she was in regular clothes, Father."

He went to Amos. "Make sure this gets done. I'll get her out of here before the club arrives."

CHAPTER 60

Many eyes found her—countless eyes. Men, women, and children traveled to and fro, but all the heads turned at the outsider now in their midst. A man with a pale face, red facial hair, and tatted arms of every color made a beeline for one of the warehouses in the distance. His head snapped back in her direction with every other step.

"May I help you, Nita?" a feminine voice said.

Familiarity washed over her. Nita had known this woman since they were kids. However, no name came to her mind. "No," she replied. Not rudely, just short.

"Oh, well, are you lost? I wouldn't expect you here."

Nita had grown so used to wearing her uniform that she forgot when she sported civilian clothes as she wore a tribal fleece jacket and jeans. "I know where I am."

Finally, the woman's name came to her.

Kate Mills.

They had competed against each other countless times in both basketball and softball but never spoke to one another. The Sequoyah v. Tahlequah rivalry ran deep, and Kate was in opposition. Kate came from a long line of small-town athletes, but that was the only positive part of their family's reputation. Her father was a well-known alcoholic around town. If Kate's batting average dropped below .300, she often attended the next game wearing long sleeves to conceal the bruises, and long sleeves under the scorching summer sun in Oklahoma was a death sentence.

Kate's smile faded. "Perhaps if you truly did, you'd stick around."

"Is that so?"

"Of course, many lost people are found here."

Nita didn't want to entertain the conversation any further.

"Kate," a familiar voice said, "thank you. I'll take this one from here."

With that, Kate said, "Yes, Father," and took her broad-shouldered ass back to her blanket in the middle of the yard.

Ezell slicked his hair back, then shook it out, defeating the purpose. "You'll have to forgive Kate. She's very passionate about the mission of this place."

Nita nodded. "What mission is that?"

Ezell smiled. "Walk with me."

———

She didn't know how to address him: Pastor, Brother, Preacher, Father? She stuck with Ezell, and he never corrected her. He walked her around the entire grounds, very proud and inspired. With each new path he took her down, more feats presented themselves.

A long rock pathway extending over a mile in length first took them to the principal place of worship. It was a classic chapel structure on the outside. White walls led to an arched roof where a ten-foot cross towered over the compound. On the inside were about fifty rows of pews on both sides of a long aisle. The stage stood higher than an ordinary chapel's would. Instead of a couple of measly steps to a pulpit, it was about ten. Whoever commanded this stage was king for the time being. It appeared that the king was the one chauffeuring her around.

There was also a section for housing about a hundred yards from the chapel amongst the foliage that merged into seemingly endless woods. While it was still under construction, it appeared usable. Ezell informed her that once it was completed, it could house around twenty families if they were needed.

"This is only the beginning," he would tell her over and over again.

A small schoolhouse was in the middle, with an accompanying bell tower. She went to ask him about it, but he cut her off.

"You garden much, Marshal Ross?" he asked.

"I don't."

"That surprises me."

"Cause I'm Indian?" she said.

Ezell laughed. "No, 'cause you're so Zen."

"Zen?"

"Well, I have a way of seeing people. It helps me help them, you see? Most of the time, people wear their emotions on their sleeves or faces. Perhaps they're good at concealing them at first, but all it takes is a couple of questions, and suddenly, that rough exterior fades away."

"I didn't know Zen meant having a rough exterior. I thought Zen meant peaceful in the classical, Eastern sense."

"Forgive me... perhaps I'm completely wrong, but you aren't peaceful, are you?" The way he asked it didn't come across as insulting. No, it was almost pity for her.

Nita tilted her head. "No. I wouldn't say that."

"So much has been taken from you, hasn't it? Not just speaking of your people, but you as an individual, Nita Ross," Ezell said, taking a step forward.

A silence built between them. His social instincts were acute and well-informed.

"I suppose that could be a reason a place like this exists." He stretched his lanky arms out wide, basking in his glory. "This is why myself and all these people take solace here. Community. Shared experiences and losses. I'm sure you're curious. Am I right?"

Answering his questions directly was not her style. That would be playing into his hands. She didn't want him dictating her emotions or the conversation. So, she believed a tonal shift was necessary. "I appreciate you showing me around, but I came here to ask you a question."

"Oh, so you're not here for fellowship and to live your life to its highest capabilities?" The most sarcastic of smiles followed that question.

"How did you pay for all of this?"

Ezell laughed. "Well, Marshal, if you must know, all that money comes through grace, tithing, and the wonderful contribution of Mr. Dyer."

"Well, I guess that leads me to my next question. How is it that you and Amos came into contact? The Dyer family has been here for generations. You, however, have not."

"You get right to business when you want to know something, don't you, Marshal Ross?" He scanned her up and down. "I wonder, however, why you're here, Nita? Are you here in any capacity as a law enforcement officer? You don't seem to be. I wonder what it is you're attempting to accomplish."

Nita didn't respond, seeing the question as rhetorical.

"If you must know, Amos was looking for purpose after his time in the military concluded. I hope I'm not speaking for him too much. Nevertheless, he was reluctant to return to his home. He was lost. Adrift. Until he stumbled onto a little pop-up congregation I had in Nebraska. He resonated with my ministry and way of life, so he dove in headfirst. Then, he received news of his father's passing and the sizeable inheritance and substantial acreage. Suddenly, our migration led us here, back to his homeland. 'Where the wind comes sweeping down the plains.'"

She nodded, taking in every aspect of his retelling.

His smile never wavered.

"You amused by something?" she asked.

"Oh, yes. I find you very amusing. Of course, I can never tell what you're thinking, but it's undeniable that those gears in your mind are turning."

"Where was it you say you came from?" Nita asked.

Ezell smirked. "I'm from everywhere, dear. However, my origins have roots in the Great White North."

Then, thunderous roars sounded near the entrance. A dozen bikers made their way to the main house. From here, Nita noticed their patches and colors.

Skull Draggers.

Ezell remained contained. "Excuse me, Marshal. I have to attend to some big bad bikers for a charitable opportunity."

Nita saw right through his smile. These were no weekend warriors looking for a charitable cause. She was positive these men could be responsible for assaulting Thorpe Ranch. While he tended to the other matters at hand, she split. She meandered, looking as casual as possible to avoid arousing suspicion. She began by checking the chapel but found nothing. She then went to the housing area, where she was cornered from time to time by people cautious of her presence as a new face.

Everywhere was clean, and nothing even remotely incriminating. The only unchecked place was the warehouse, where men were in and out, side-eyeing her the whole way.

That was her destination.

She made her way into the trees that merged into thick woods. She stayed put for a while to observe if she had any followers.

Ezell continued to discuss with the bikers at the main house around two hundred yards away. She went deeper into the woods than perhaps she needed. It was vast and overrun with dead branches and leaves.

It took a while to navigate through the brush. Longer than she wanted. Eventually, she crept to the back of the warehouse, only around twenty feet from the tree line. A man acting as a guard smoked a cigarette and journaled. At that moment, she realized she had not seen a phone in anyone's hands since her arrival.

His chair leaned against the wall beside the door, oblivious to her presence.

God... damn it... I'm gonna have to take this guy out.

She readied herself, cracking her neck and taking a few deep breaths. She planned to walk up on him casually and aloof, then strike.

She took a half-step forward, but faint whimpers cried from behind her, deeper into the woods. She blocked it out. It was so hushed that she wondered if they were real at all. As her focus returned to her plan of attack, the cries resounded.

Her curiosity and instincts took her away from the guard. She had to investigate the origins of the whimpers. It didn't appear that anything dire was occurring, but she had been wrong before. And given the situation and warning of her environment, she wanted to leave no stone unturned.

She crept farther backward, disappearing into the surrounding woods that went on for hundreds of acres.

Nita walked up on a young girl sitting hunched over and alone atop a tree stump of dead red cedar. She continued to cry, unaware of Nita's presence.

"Are you okay, dear?" Nita asked.

The girl turned. She was just as young as Aiden and Lyla. She wiped the tears away. "Oh, I'm sorry. I was just–"

"You don't have to apologize. Is everything all right? Why are you out here alone?"

The poor girl's cheeks were so red they looked as if they'd been slapped. "I just... I just... I'm sorry, I don't know you."

Nita approached, sat next to her, and pressed her hand on the girl's back. "That's all right. I'm here to help if that's what you need."

"Are you a visionary?" the girl asked.

"Excuse me?"

"I'm sorry. Father wouldn't want me talking to outsiders without him. That's what he said." She sniffled as the snot hadn't run dry.

"Father Ezell?"

The girl's emotion returned at the mention of his name. "I'm sorry. I can't talk to you."

"That's okay. I understand. I'll leave you be, but I promise I can help if you need it. I've helped people before."

The girl went silent on Nita. She decided to wait a while longer after the girl turned from her. After nothing came of it, Nita began to back away.

"I hate it here," the girl whispered. "I want to go home. My real home, but my mom and dad say our place is here now."

It's a goddam cult.

"What's your name?" Nita asked as the girl picked bark off the tree stump, letting ants and other bugs crawl across her hands.

"Susan," she said. "I used to go by Suzie at my school."

"Well, it's nice to meet you, Suzie. My name is Nita."

"I like your name."

"Thank you." Nita approached her again, and Susan allowed her to share the stump. "I'll tell you what, I can help convince your parents to go home if you can tell me more about this place. Does that sound like a good idea?"

"Yeah, that sounds good," she said through more sniffles.

"Do you know what's inside this big warehouse outside the woods?"

"Well, the kids aren't allowed in there. But one night, my friend Ruger and I snuck in there to see what was inside... and it was filled with a lot of barrels and guns."

"Is that right? How many guns would you say?"

"I don't know... hundreds."

"That's a lot of guns," Nita said casually. She didn't want to make it appear like a big deal.

"All we ever do here is help build stuff and go to church and school."

"That doesn't sound like fun."

Suzie shook her head in agreeance.

"How often do those bikers come around?" she asked. "Have you seen them before?"

"They come more often now. A couple of times a month, maybe? They spend all their time at the warehouse, though. They don't attend church with us. My dad doesn't like me to go outside when they're around, but they've never done anything. I wish –"

She stopped.

"What, Suzie?"

"I-I was just gonna say I wish he wouldn't let me see Father."

"Father Ezell?"

She nodded.

"Why don't you want to be around him?"

"He... he takes me with him all over. He even takes me away from my mom and dad, and they let him, even when I tell them I don't want to go."

"And you don't like going with him because..." Nita cleared her throat. "Does Ezell touch you, Suzie?"

The tears returned, and she began ripping larger pieces of bark that cracked and broke upon removal. "Yes. He does other things and makes me promise not to tell my mom and dad. He says he likes me because I'm special, and he needs to be around me... He always says he wants to become closer to each other—closer than anyone."

The words struck Nita. She couldn't speak or even breathe.

Mariah... Those words... That's what her uncle said to her.

Nita took Suzie by the hand. She wouldn't allow her to suffer or meet the same fate as Mariah.

Just then, the bell tower began to ring.

CHAPTER 61

They emerged from the woods after the conclusion of the bell toll. The compound had gone silent as if the Rapture occurred along with the low ringing. The abandonment seemed to be a surprise to both. Suzie assured her she had yet to learn where everyone had gone.

All was quiet along the eastern hills of Oklahoma.

Hand in hand, they rounded the warehouse into the exposed open. The enemy waited outside the entrance to the same warehouse that Nita had been attempting to investigate not long ago.

The sun was blotted from the sky. The bikers' faces were silver skulls. Black smoke billowed from their hollow eyes. The cacophony of idling bikes paled in comparison to the high-pitched humming rattling her brain. She winced in pain, pressing hard against her temples. Then, she clutched the rawhide sack hanging from her neck, and the noises died.

The circumstance didn't change. She was alone, surrounded by armed one-percenters, a backwoods cult, and their undeniable leader. Her vehicle was around a hundred yards away as Suzie clutched her back leg. Nita clocked two followers behind Ezell as their right hands went to their appendixes. More "visionaries" filtered out from different crevices in the compound. The men seemed to all act the same. Ezell had trained them well to be wary of outsiders, for they all shared an aggressive posture when they began surrounding her.

One of the men holding his gun beneath his clothes circled away from Ezell, flanking her like a gangbanger with a strut.

"Why don't you come on inside, Marshal Ross? We can discuss some things, and Susan can return to her family," Ezell said, holding out his hand for her to reach for, even at this distance.

Nita stood still like a heavy stone. Her grip tightened on Suzie's small hand. The skeletal visage of the bikers never faltered. The black smoke billowing from their eyes obstructed the field. It gradually crept closer, creeping up behind Ezell and swirling around his frame as if the mixture of gasses and dust had also worshiped him. Embers flared into existence, and his eyes reflected the dark oranges.

The smoke stopped around ten feet from her and circled behind the flanking visionary. When the phenomenon prevailed, it was difficult to rationalize that others weren't seeing through her eyes.

"Marshal Ross," Ezell said once more. "Please step inside. I assure you I can make sense of all this for you."

A vision of hell began to take form. The smoke's intensity built. Flashes of fire burst through the blackness. Embers fluttered like lightning bugs. The white trash follower moving methodically was nearly in position for a successful flank.

Fire and brimstone raged. Ezell was now less of a man and more of a lord of hell. His voice shifted into an abyssal cadence.

"Marshal Ross," he said once more.

The lackey turned his shoulder, and as he got within about twenty feet of her, his hand went under his shirt behind his belt buckle. Nita ripped her Sig from her IWB holster, placed him in her crosshairs, and blasted him in the chest with three hollow point rounds.

Silence.

Hell dissipated.

All the hostiles against her inhaled simultaneously after their communal gasp. The flanking visionary fought for breath, but not for long. Nita dragged Suzie and made haste for cover behind the schoolhouse. All she could do was hope the necklace lived up to its promise.

"The world has come to destroy what is ours! What we have built! We cannot allow such evil to prosper!" Ezell declared for all his followers to hear.

In elementary school, Nita learned about the "shot heard 'round the world" that marked the beginning of the Revolutionary War. The burden of pulling the trigger to start an event logically evaded her until now.

A bullet whistled past her head and into the brush. The first shot against her broke the seal, and many bullets followed. As she turned, rounding the corner behind cover, men pursued her, both visionaries and bikers alike, with a shared cause.

They were all of one mind to kill her.

No bullets grazed them. Poor Suzie wept at the growing onslaught against them. The live fire drowned out her weeping and innocent cries. Nita feared ripping her arm out of the shoulder socket while dragging the child across the compound.

"We're all right," was all Nita could say to comfort her with not an ounce of confidence. They continued down the back of the schoolhouse and sighted her car in the driveway, "Go, go, run!"

Luckily for both of them, the building provided enough cover from the pursuers still rounding the corners. Nita held out her hand, and the girl gripped it for her life. She sprinted, yanking Suzie the entire way.

They got to the opposite side of the car, and Nita threw her in the back seat. "Get down!" she commanded.

Nita climbed into the vehicle, started it up, and slammed on the gas. She pulled her phone from her front pocket and struggled to scroll through her phone while she bounced from the rocky terrain. Her first instinct was to phone Lowwater. She placed the call and checked on Suzie in the mirror as tears ran down the little girl's face.

The call continued unanswered as Nita sped away. She decided to leave a voicemail before trying someone else. "Randall, Nation-37 under fire! Nation-37 under fire! Please send TAC unit to 1831—" was all she got off of the address as bullets littered her vehicle.

CHAPTER 62

Lowwater spent most of the day communicating about recent events with local and national media. Even when it was all over, the unrelenting news and its reporters never let up. Luckily, the sheer volume of reporters dwindled by the day. But, on top of that, he caught wind that Cherokee Nation was putting together some type of surprise celebration for the marshals' involvement with the case. It was still early for congratulations with so much loss of life in their wake.

He met Agent Teller in the hallway, who had been the hardest-working man in Tahlequah the past few months. Out of the corner of his mouth, Lowwater asked, "You do whiskey and cigars?"

"Religiously," Marc replied.

"Step into my office."

————

Lowwater shut the door behind them and rubbed his tear ducts. "Let's hope I have some time off until the next press conference."

"I don't know," Teller said, making his way to the desk. "They seem like a way of life now."

"God, I hope not." Two glasses clattered together as he proceeded to close the blinds. "Buffalo Trace, white man?"

Teller laughed and sat down. "Of course."

"Good man," Lowwater said as he poured Teller's glass first and slid it across the desk. They toasted and enjoyed the smooth burn. They basked in the flavors as men should in the quiet of reflection. "So, you're telling me that that crucifix necklace and Bible belonged to that Kansas preacher with the video?"

Lowwater couldn't help but feel a little guilty, for it seemed Teller had been enjoying the silence as he took another sip. "Prints matched, and his wife confirmed that it was the same one that went missing after he had passed."

Lowwater bypassed a sip and took a gulp. "Fuck me."

A vibration intensified in his breast pocket.

He pulled the phone out and held it away from his face to see a text from his son sending screenshots of his grandson's basketball schedule. While that brought a hint of excitement, his attention went to Nita's missed call that accompanied a voicemail and a text message sharing her location.

CHAPTER 63

Charlie refueled his marshal-issued vehicle. He was back on patrol, pulling over Cherokee speeders and letting them all off the hook with a warning. Swarms of media outlets continued to filter into the area as they sped down Highway 62. He was glad to be in the field before the next round of media arrived. He didn't envy Lowwater for holding press conference after press conference. Hopefully, they would be good and gone before long, and everything returned to normalcy.

As he leaned against his vehicle, some familiar boys left the Cherokee outpost. It was the same group of boys he had talked to at another gas station not long ago. The former trio of boys was down one. Perhaps they were down a member, or they went and got wise and ditched the one convincing them it was a good idea to partake in underage drinking outside a gas station. They caught eyes with Charlie and gave a subtle nod that said more than words. He couldn't help but smile. Perhaps he made a difference. Even in this occupation, that feeling didn't come often, but for now, he would allow himself to feel as if he did.

———

Charlie drove the backroads, headed to assist in traffic detail closer towards Fort Gibson. He assumed that church attendance would be affected due to recent tragedies, but it didn't seem to do so. From his casual eye, it appeared that people sought divine guidance more than ever. He used to volunteer at a church as a youth sponsor after college but gradually drifted away from it all. Easter Sunday and Christmas seemed to be his only brush with the Lord.

Service would begin soon, and Charlie took his post in the middle of the road to monitor oncoming churchgoers and help get in and out of the parking lot. Working traffic for the churches in the middle of the road wasn't the worst job. At least the people behind the wheel smiled and waved as they passed by and appreciated the officer's task of ensuring the roads didn't morph into a clustered nightmare.

He was stuck in a conversation with some of the Fort Gibson officers, and of course, all they wanted to discuss the entire time was what everyone in the state wanted to discuss: the fire and murders. It wasn't like Charlie was privy to any more information than the rest of them, but they liked having the same conversations about it and walking through the case as if they had never discussed it.

The static from his shoulder mic whispered outward. He reached down to his waist and turned up the volume dial. The static shriek became clear. "All units be advised: we have a marshal-involved shooting in progress."

He looked to his fellow officers, hearing the same call. They waved Charlie along. "Go, we got things here!"

His car was moving before he shut his door. The radio sounded: "Marshal-involved shooting in progress—Nation-37. Location: 1838 West Iron Hills Road."

He drove, not looking out the front window with any regard for his direction. He took notice as he merged into oncoming traffic and whipped his vehicle back before anything could further sour the day.

Nation-37...

Nita.

CHAPTER 64

Fall began merging with winter, and preparations for the livestock needed to take place. Blake and the boys threw down some wheat straw in the massive pen to act as warmer and more comfortable bedding for the cows to rest after they ate. Winter for a cowboy was hard, but it was far easier for a rich cowboy, so he didn't take that for granted.

All this work for minimal results.

Blake's way of life was the land and the cattle that grazed it all. His knowledge of oil and the business surrounding it was fleeting.

"Floyd, we good on hay?" Blake asked.

"Good, boss. Our stockpile graze is lookin' good and grown in the northern pasture."

Blake nodded, believing that to be the case. "Then, their asses will be nice and fat at winter's end. Right on. J, let's go ahead and—"

Sirens blared at their back. A marshal vehicle hurdled towards them at the beginning of the long stretch of gravel driveway as gravel dust billowed behind it. Charlie Soap slammed on the brakes and skidded another ten feet, almost kissing one of their work trucks. He nearly leaped from the car.

"I better be under arrest if you're gonna come in here like that!" Blake yelled at him.

Charlie wasted no time. "Nita's under fire near the old Dyer farm! I wouldn't be here if I hadn't seen what it is now. It's a whole fucking compound! It's gonna take our tac units longer to get there than local PD!" Charlie shook his head, and his hands never rested. They went out wide, to his waist, then up high. "I doubt they'll be able to help much..."

Blake was aware of the time passing as he contemplated further. His guys waited on him, and Charlie grew impatient as he panted in place.

"The Dyer residence?" Blake asked with a cocked brow.

Charlie nodded.

"That motherfu—"

Under no certainty did he believe a man like Amos could conjure such things, but he was perhaps dumb enough to go along with something of the kind.

Amos Dyer. You son of a bitch.

Blake turned to face his guys. They all stood at attention in their work clothes of wrangler jeans, flannel shirts with Carhart jackets, and cowshit-covered boots. Blake decided what he was about to do, but asking them if they would join him would be an insult, for they had also made up their minds.

———

Hooves thundered beneath him.

A straight shot though his land was only a couple miles to the Dyer farm. All his guys rode fully outfitted in attire that rivaled their time in Ramadi. Their tactical vest carried plates, magazines, and an American flag patch in the middle of their chest. Their patriotism wouldn't be lost on their graves if death came for them. Blake's ancestral Henry repeating rifle was strapped to one side of his horse, and an M27 rifle bounced up and down on his waist.

Nearing the tree line, they passed that godforsaken tree where their brother Wyatt met his horrid end. After cursing the tree's existence and vowing to cut it down, Blake pleaded to God, hoping his brother was safe wherever he might rest.

His attention shifted. The agonizing sensation of pre-combat returned to him as they entered the cover of the trees with the sun falling behind them, and the sounds of gunfire peppered their ear like light rainfall on a tin roof.

CHAPTER 65

Glass shattered all around her.

The windshield cracked and split across it, making it difficult to see. Nita's confidence in driving safely dwindled rapidly. She had to get away. Behind her, a mob of cultists and bikers fired and loaded up for more.

She made for the main gate, the only way in or out, she knew. Her foot pressed into the bottom of the floorboard as she tested the RPMs of her Mazda. Suzie continued to cry in the back seat.

"Keep your head down!" Nita commanded.

Motion caught her attention. The compound's high walls began to move and slide ahead of her. It was difficult to process something as simple as the main gate closing in a high-pressure situation, looking through a shattered windshield.

No, no, no.

The gate closed but was still quick enough to impede her judgment. She slammed on the brakes and skidded sideways.

She was right to avoid powering, though. If she had attempted, she would either be gravel-paste on the opposite side of the gate, or her car would have been damaged to the point of no return. However, she was now stuck behind enemy lines. This was the point of no return.

"We're gonna get out of here." Nita promised, but lacked conviction.

A small light pinged her peripheral. On top of the compound wall, in a makeshift lookout tower, a rifle reflected a glare from the sun. She rotated the steering wheel as hard as she could to the left and again slammed on the gas. The shot blasted through the back window.

She drove aimlessly across the compound. She was a large moving target in the open. Shots peppered her vehicle. Her front tire being shot out made the situation more dire. The wheel violently shook in her hands. Keeping the car straight was a fight with an object much more powerful.

If there was a positive in the situation, the cover of trees was directly ahead. The dense woods could buy them some time. She let up on the gas approaching the tree line and located a spot she could navigate the car through as far as she could until the woods got too thick.

Her heart rate pumped at a rabid pace. She began a breathing exercise as a coping mechanism, taking massive breaths in, holding, then exhaling. The time to focus on just her anxieties weren't allowed. She threw it in park. "All right, get ready to—"

Her hastened state froze. She never registered Suzie's cries stopping. That shot from the rifle atop the wall had missed its target but struck another. By a sheer stroke of poor timing and positioning, the shot pierced Suzie in the side directly through the lungs. Her silence post-shot made sense but didn't lessen the devastation in Nita's heart.

The bullets ceased for now. However, a battalion of backwood cultists and cut-wearing bikers began to stalk her position through the trees.

CHAPTER 66

The Cherokee woman, purposefully or accidentally, had begun the process of a meltdown of everything he had built. Ezell's only hope to quell such a catastrophe was to deal with it and clean up any evidence that it ever occurred as soon as possible.

His followers blanketed him.

"Be prepared for the Devil's ascension. He and his followers attempt to do work here today, and we must not allow it to prosper. If he succeeds, our way of life and our duty here will be destroyed. We are required as visionaries to see our world through!"

Their faces remained clear. The disarray and exhilaration of the moment placed a slight haze on them, but he reeled them all back. His most loyal men were in pursuit, and while he was worried about the nomadic Skull Draggers, their way of life was also on the line. While they weren't visionaries, they sought the same end to this scenario. And as a pack of nearly fifty strong pursued the marshal, there wasn't one amongst them whose skepticism he could not diminish or erase by a few carefully calculated anecdotes.

Gunfire grew around him. The fight didn't scare him. The exposure did. Marshal Ross' attempt to leave would not be easy or quiet, so he

hoped one of his visionaries had been properly practicing their
marksmanship skills.

———

Amos returned with an assault rifle and a pistol at his hip. Clarence
Fletcher's heavy frame thundered behind him, casting the pair in
shadow. The twelve-gauge shotgun looked like a toy in his giant hands.

"Father, she's trapped in the trees near the gate on the southeast
side. We have guns trained on her. Don't know if she's come out yet,"
Amos informed him.

"Let's find out." Ezell then turned his attention to his visionaries,
who were innocent bystanders of such devious schemes coming for
them. "Sons and daughters, I humbly ask for your faith during this test
of ours. Please seek shelter inside, and I assure you I can explain the
events here today once it is finished."

———

More guns followed him to the location of the standoff between his
people and the marshal. The ones beyond the tree line had their
weapons trained on the vehicle through trees and fading brush now that
fall was underway. The sea of followers parted as he walked through
their ranks.

Eric Honeycutt led the charge against her, looking down the scope
of his deer rifle at the car. After converting to their cause, he became a
loyal and honorable visionary, constantly itching for a fight. Eric took
notice of the father's presence. "She hadn't come out of the car yet,
Father. But she's still movin'. I seen it."

"Very well." Ezell stayed behind the veil of people already prepared
to take bullets for him. "Marshal Ross, I beg you to come on out and let
us talk through this situation!" he shouted into the woods that stretched
as far as the eye could see.

No response.

The depths of those woods went as deep as one's imagination. That was at least what Ezell told others. They were vast, sure. But the mind could conjure a vastness greater than the ocean. His voice lowered to a whisper for only Eric's ear. "Mr. Honeycutt, if she doesn't emerge from these woods, I want you and a couple of others to subdue her as painlessly as possible."

"Ain't we past that, Father?"

"Perhaps. We'll have to see."

The quiet built. His followers' nerves were shaken. That was obvious. The responsibility of the battalion at his disposal seemed embedded in his soul. The will to lead men to such things was not a gift given to many.

"Marshal Ross!" he shouted once more.

Again, no response.

"Mr. Honeycutt... proceed."

Eric nodded and grinned like that prospect of violence excited his soul. His nod extended to Todd "Toddy" Belmont and Stan Zimmer, who shared their friend's temperament. Eric brought them into the fold of Temple's Vision not long after he started attending. Everyone else present stood around and watched.

Amos approached from behind. "Father, if she gets a call off to other authorities, this place will be swarm—"

"I know, son. It's being handled."

Eric moved like a hunter stalking a buck during the rut. He was a pretender, though. Ezell was certain of that. It didn't take a man of his unique abilities to see that. Eric liked to tell tales that weren't his and remember himself in a higher classification that many would be quick to dispute—more than anything, he liked to play badass when he was a sheep.

A boom sounded, rivaling that of an oak tree cracking. Two more followed that seemed just as loud and impactful. The heads of Eric Honeycutt, Toddy Belmont, and Stan Zimmer snapped backward and fractured open. Their bodies hit the ground before the raw chunks of exposed brains did.

The marshal was prepared for a fight.

Their unified front of guns all rose and began firing upon the vehicle, piercing holes and shattering any remaining glass. It didn't take long for the car to resemble more a cheese grater than a motor vehicle.

The volley of fire halted. Ezell turned to Amos to take point from here on.

Emotionless, Ezell said, "Make her dead."

CHAPTER 67

Perhaps the silver lining to driving her car to the compound was that all of her tac gear and firearms were stored in the back of her Mazda. While Nita lacked the proper communication, she made up for it in preparedness. She slung her shooting rig around her waist, equipped with mag pouches that ran along the radius of the entire belt, providing her with her competitive Sig. She followed that by throwing on her plate carrier, her current best option in body armor. The vest only protected her front and backside, but at the moment, she'd gladly accept it.

The two things that would assist her the most in this inevitable fight were her M4 carbine and Benelli M4. Both were fully modified to her specifications to make them as personal to her as possible.

The overlord of this place had a mass of followers convinced of something beyond themselves. They hung on every word he spoke and enacted his demands. They wouldn't let her leave this place and let any part of her be found again. There would be no evidence she was even here.

Her location to Lowwater delivered successfully, but she doubted his tech savviness. It wasn't a matter of him figuring it out. It was the timing in which he put it all together that she doubted.

She doubled down on her offensive roll in this fight when three men advanced on her position. The one in the lead looked familiar, but the rifle in his hands didn't offer her peace of mind.

She sucked in a deep breath and fired three shots downrange at her targets and sent them to whatever afterlife they convinced themselves awaited them.

Another volley of shots came for her. Rifle fire. Machine gun fire. Shotgun fire, both slugs and buckshot, all destroyed and shattered the remains of her Mazda. She escaped into the trees, and the bullets followed, snapping limbs and breaking off chunks of trees, turning them into wood chips.

She ran.

Bullets whistled past her, but farther into the woods she went. The vast unknown ahead of her was the only direction that could provide her temporary safety. Using the trees as cover, she ducked and snaked between them to avoid any of those many shots zipping past her. The rawhide necklace bounced on her chest as she ran, putting its power to the test.

Her boots crunched the fallen leaves. Being silent and covert would prove difficult in this terrain. She also had to maintain a grip on her larger firearms so they weren't bouncing everywhere. She contemplated posting up soon to return fire and attempt to get another call off. However, her position could have been more advantageous. In her retreat, she descended the wooded hillside. Her adversaries had home-field advantage, but she benefited from being ahead. That might not mean much in a situation like this, but it was something.

Bullets still fired upon her, impacting the surrounding woods. Their frequency diminished with each stride she took. She cut an angle so she wasn't tracked in a straight line. Her descent leveled off in an area where a pool of water collected with large rocks forming a barrier on the opposite side. She rounded the stagnant pool and hid behind the rocks, giving her time to remove the silicone hair tie around her wrist and put her hair up. Her face was sweating, and the last thing she needed was her thick black hair impairing her vision and getting her killed.

She propped her semi-auto Benelli against the rocks and readied her rifle. She tucked her offhand into the angled foregrip and tapped the side of the trigger guard with her other. The bullets had stopped momentarily, for she had lost them.

Her safety didn't last. Shuffling from the opposite side of the rocks told her two, maybe three, attackers searched for her.

"Andy," one of them said. "You circle 'round that side and head down. Us two will keep going this way. We can flank her towards the bottom at the creek."

Nita popped up with her rifle ready, using the rock as a stabilizer. She fired two shots at the one angled at her, blasting him in his chest. Then, down the line, she repeated the exact shot count and placement to the remaining pair. She returned, giving each one more blast to be safe.

Their agonizing gasps for air wouldn't last long, but she wouldn't wait around to listen to their finality.

CHAPTER 68

Nita needed higher ground. Unfortunately, she had to go farther down before ascending on the opposite side of the creek. The rolling hills of thick, though dead foliage were already getting to her. She hadn't pushed her cardiovascular capabilities in recent months. Given the circumstances behind enemy lines, her disadvantage never overwhelmed her. The blood of her lineage flowed and spilled throughout these lands long before any visionaries arrived. Her bond with her ancestors was always strong, for they still came to her at night while she slept, bringing stories, good and bad. Fear did not grip her. Adrenaline, sure. Performance anxiety, but not fear. These lands were hers long before her adversaries'.

A branch snapped behind her at higher ground. She turned and found her target, another flannel-wearing cultist lined up, shot with a sawed-off shotgun. His weapon wouldn't be considered lethal at over fifty yards. He fired anyway, sending tiny pellets to disturb the terrain and leave her unscathed.

"Over here—" he started to yell before Nita permanently shut his mouth with shots through his neck and shoulder.

His alert seemed enough, along with the exchange of adrenaline that would have to take her upward.

Those shots surely gave away her position. She hoped her aggressors' sense of direction could be thrown off in the woods. Her thumb pressed the mag release, and she reloaded her rifle.

Two left. Elevation.

She started up the hill. Stopping momentarily made her realize how out of breath she was, and her marathon wouldn't end anytime soon. She tucked the rawhide necklace under her shirt before continuing up, but another thundering clap coincided with a small tree bursting into wood chips only a couple of feet away.

She instinctively dropped down, took cover behind some brush, and readied her rifle toward the shot. However, another volley followed, peppering her undersized fallen tree and stick collection.

Nita drove her rifle through the brush, squeezed down on the trigger, and provided her self-cover fire while looking for her shooter.

Got him.

Around fifty yards at a lower elevation, a man with a hunting rifle used a low-hanging branch to stabilize his shots that were each getting closer. His next shot was coming. She had to beat him to it. She began to focus through her scope, but a dark mass crossed her peripheral before zoning out the rest of her surroundings.

A visionary wielding a splitting axe rumbled towards her. His obese frame slowed him, giving her time to unholster her sidearm from her crouched position and put four fragmented holes in his chest.

As he fell, another took his place. The new visionary came upon her much quicker, almost manifesting himself from his fat companion's dying body as it rolled down the hill with leaves sticking to his damp clothes.

They exchanged pistol fire, a contest she'd go into confidently with any of these people. Her shot placement was nearly identical to the man he'd replaced. The only difference was that his momentum didn't take his body as far down the hill.

More fire occurred behind her. She returned to her rifle and noticed it had fallen on its side after laying it against the brush pile. By a fluke or sheer luck on their part, her carbine took a shot from that hunting rifle at the end of the barrel, rendering it useless.

Another shot zipped just above her head, dropping her back down. Yells sounded below her as they were homing in on her position.

"There! Up there!" the rifleman shouted at a distance.

She gripped her shotgun and retreated further up the hill and into the infinite unknown.

Then, something came over her. A warmth. In the presence of such cruel and near-unimaginable evil. Her late husband, Jackson's poem, came to her.

Into the void, I travel
A vast thicket of engulfing black
Keep the pace, I say
Keep the pace

CHAPTER 69

A herd of law enforcement agencies descended upon the compound like the once mighty buffalo that stormed nearby plains. Nearly every local agency was en route. After Lowwater called in the emergency and Agent Teller listed the number of additional concerns and threats the people of the compound might serve, as one of their own was under fire, everyone came running.

Maybe thirty cars slammed on their brakes as they skidded on the gravel entryway outside the high metal gate. It was heavily reinforced, and the only opening was a closed window that appeared to open only on one side.

Every command fell on deaf ears.

In the distance, beyond the gate, muffled shots could be heard, leaving the time for cooperation from those on the other side of the fence to be at an end.

A booming blast quaked the earth as a Fort Gibson squad car exploded. Flames burst from the car. All the law enforcement agents ducked and took cover. A thin line of smoke followed back toward the top of the gate, where a man wearing everyday attire loaded another rocket into the launcher.

Lowwater hadn't seen any weapon of the kind around here.

Weapons like that were for war, but as the smoke billowed around him, perhaps the weapon belonged.

The officers returned fire at the man atop the fence. Then, from the other side of the gate, single shots of efficient rifle fire found their targets. One ATF agent took a headshot, another center mass of his body armor, and a third struck the man in the side while attempting to help his fellow officer.

The Cherokee tactical vehicle, driven by Grant Kingfisher, barreled down the road. Its momentum never slowed as the heavy-duty military vehicle crashed into the main gate. It wasn't enough to pierce through the metal, but it did leave an opening between where the gate met the wall.

Another RPG round was loaded and ready to go.

"Get down!" Lowwater yelled to anyone who could hear. He shot at the man with his pistol, but he was far away, too far for him. The only one that could hit him with a sidearm from this distance was fighting on the other side of the wall.

As the visionary hoisted the RPG onto his shoulder, his leg buckled. Blood spewed backward before two more bullets found his chest.

Teller kept firing from his AR-15, peppering the man like a target at the state fair. If this was a competition, Teller was on his way to winning an oversized teddy bear.

The man fell backward with the RPG still on his shoulder, but he still managed to fire. Luckily for the law, the rocket went straight down into the wall and blew him and his partner to kingdom come.

Shouts of commands to storm the complex sounded all around. Around fifty officers and agents became foot soldiers as they filtered through the gate's opening.

Chapter 70

Chaos. The constant tolling of a bell transmitted through hidden speakers across the compound. The cacophony caused any attempt at order by law enforcement to die out. Though brave, those who stormed through the gate were met with fire from the main house.

The marshal tactical vehicle continued to ram until an opening was big enough to allow other cars to get through and provide cover. Charlie and a few other marshals jogged behind the armored vehicle that stopped around thirty yards from the house as shots pinged off of it the entire way.

Lowwater returned fire behind a squad car, firing wild. A firefight like this seemed beyond him. If he had to place a bet, it was beyond most of them.

Charlie never came close to firing his weapon in the field. He'd taken several people down and been in his fair share of fights on duty, but taking any lives evaded him.

A ricocheting bullet whistled off the truck and past his ear. The tac unit began to move forward on the house, leaving Charlie in the middle of the field. The number of bullets hitting the vehicle sounded like heavy rain on a tin roof. He cut and ran for cover, cursing and praying the entire way not to get stuck by bullets and hoping the tac vehicle got most of their attention. Pockets of dirt flew up in front and beside him. It seemed like he garnered some of the ire of those in the house.

The tolling bell and bullets were deafening. He couldn't hear Lowwater and Teller yelling for him to run faster. They waved him on like little league parents as their child rounded third for home.

Another sharp whistle flew by his head, shocking him. He dove behind the car. Lowwater grabbed him like a papa bear and rolled over on top of him for extra cover.

He was a good man. Not just a boss but like a father to all the marshals. He patted Charlie down. "You all right, Charlie!"

He didn't feel any pain anywhere, but his adrenaline was pumping so hard that he couldn't tell if he was shot. "I'm good! I'm good!"

The tac vehicle turned back into the glass entryway of the house, shattering it and destroying the foyer. From the balcony, canisters were thrown into the field before them as smoke filtered from them.

"Smoke!" an officer yelled, but the sentiment was redundant.

The battlefield was obscured from view as the smoke acted as a visual barrier between law enforcement and the heart of the compound. Their tac unit was now behind enemy lines, so to speak.

A helicopter roared overhead. More tactical units from other agencies began to make their presence known.

They needed some offense. Quickly.

Several women emerged through the smoke with their hands thrown in the air, and others carried limp children. Tears streamed down their faces. They cried for help from the officers, but stray bullets still found random targets.

Charlie's instincts to protect kicked in for better or worse, and he ran for them. They were frantic and could hardly form words in their speech. He ushered all of them away from the smoke and the action going on at their backs.

A mother with an apparent lower leg injury limped behind them, crying the entire way. Charlie wrapped his arm over her shoulder. Upon closer inspection, it was a miracle she got this far. Her calf was non-existent. All that remained was exposed meat as blood stained her white shoe. She was in shock as she limped. Charlie couldn't take any chances with bullets still flying past them. He hoisted her off her feet and carried her, sprinting until he returned behind the cover of the squad car that had received so many bullets it was no longer drivable. Luckily, a first aid kit underneath the back seat was still usable.

Charlie turned to Lowwater and Teller. "We're gonna need ambulances!"

"We're gonna need a lot of shit!" Lowwater said.

Charlie's attention shifted back toward the sweating, bug-eyed, and unresponsive woman. A pool of blood flowed beneath them. "Ma'am, I gotta stop the bleeding on your leg. This is gonna be painful, do you understand that?"

No response. She stared into the distance as her chest moved up and down normally. He began cleaning the wound, pouring water and rubbing alcohol which would have sent an ordinary person into a frenzy due to pain, but she did not react. He proceeded to wrap it with gauze, using the entire roll. The blood continued to seep through.

"Ma'am," he kept saying, trying to get her attention, "did you see a woman? An Indian woman?"

As he waited for a response, he witnessed the life leave the woman with tears falling parallel down her face. He tried to get her back, but she had gone so pale. The blood loss was too much for her to overcome.

"I saw her," a younger, feminine voice said from her crouched position, nearly clutching the tire.

"Get down!" Teller commanded to no avail.

"All this started after she arrived. Our men chased her into the woods. If all is right in the world, she'll suffer God's wrath at their hands!"

She should have listened to Teller's command, for untrained, friendly fire through the smoky haze blew the back of her head twenty yards behind them.

The gate was destroyed. Charlie would believe it if around a hundred law enforcement vehicles were filtering into the compound.

Those cars and trucks were also met with resistance from beyond the smoke. Random pockets of explosions began to occur. Blasts of pellets and shrapnel crippled officers and vehicles alike. Some of the grenades seemed military-grade, while others appeared hand-made. Dirt fell from the sky like rain. The officers spent most of their time aiding the wounded rather than pressing the house.

Charlie caught a glimpse of a familiar car inside the tree line from the house. A Mazda CX-5.

"Tac units are gonna have to engage the house!" Charlie yelled.

"No shit!" Teller yelled back.

"Our boys are already pretty well fucking engaged!" Lowwater added.

Charlie clenched down. "I'm going after Nita," he said, pointing his forehead toward her car.

Their eyes followed, and they caught sight of it too. They looked at each other and nodded before breaking off in that direction.

CHAPTER 71

Ezell and his most loyal visionaries, primarily Amos and Clarence Lee Fletcher, reacted differently to the current situation. Ezell was cerebral, already planning what would come while packing a leather briefcase. He only added one additional item: his Bible.

Amos squeezed the barrel of his AR-15 while Clarence reloaded his shotgun and ensured all his knives were where he wanted them to be. To an average person, his pocketknives would be considered too bulky and oversized for concealment, but his extensive and tall pockets could hold many large and even grotesque things.

"We are finished, Father," Amos said. The concern in his voice was evident.

"We aren't finished." Ezell replied. "We just have to start anew."

"*Start over?* You know how much work it took to build this place? How much *money?*"

"There's always a new place and new money. If you'd like to stand here and dwell on losses, you're more than welcome, but we will rebuild somewhere else. There will always be a place for our Eden."

"We can't just start over!"

Ezell slammed his hand down on Amos' shoulder and pressed him downward. "Of course, we can. I've done it before. If you believe in me, you know what I am capable of. Do you know, my son?"

Amos' unmistakable visage began to focus once again. "Yes, Father."

"Then it's time to leave this place behind." All of his attention shifted to his behemoth, Clarence. "Lee, you've done everything I've asked of you."

"Of course, Father."

"You've hunted down so many lost souls in this area, and I'd like to believe I've given you proper guidance. When you came to me after slaughtering and stringing up those two sinners, you were terrified of those who might judge you for what you did."

"Only you assured me I wasn't a monster."

Ezell smiled, reached up, and patted Clarence on the cheek. "Oh, you are a monster, my son, just the right kind of monster."

CHAPTER 72

She was lost. Enemies homed in on her position. Pop shots continued to whistle nearby. Twigs snapped and leaves broke under her aggressors' boots. She stayed far enough ahead of them and used the terrain to ensure they couldn't get off a decent shot. Lactic acid built in her thighs with each drive up the hill.

A sense of kinship to the land and her ancestors came over her at this hour, which appeared so dire. It was as if they were with her. The same ones that were on the Ride for Removal. The same ones that entered her dream space. Perhaps the same ones that warned her of dark deeds finding their way into her life.

They remained like watchful guards as if they were around every corner and at the edge of her sight line. Observing without judgment. Protection without intervention.

She came upon a faint trail leading east and west.

A man appeared behind a tree farther down the trail. Nita brought the Benelli to her shoulder and fired a buckshot into his body. He flew back, and his head slammed on a sharp rock that finished him off.

She sprinted along the trail that rounded up the high hill. However, as she rounded the corner, the landscape dropped significantly and fell steeply into a ravine below. Nita had to slow her pace and proceed cautiously around the bend to avoid falling.

Horrible squeals deafened her. A cross between wild pigs and demons from the pits of hell made the hair on her arms stiffen. She turned, and the broad shoulders of a woman drove into her abdomen. The surprise impact loosened her grip on her shotgun as she and her attacker tumbled down the hillside.

The fall felt like minutes. In reality, it might have only been seconds. It was a miracle she avoided the impact of any of the trees standing firm.

Leaves ruffled behind her. The woman who attacked rose to her feet, but she now sported a gash on her forehead. Her forearms were the size of a D-1 linebacker, and her rounded shoulders made it obvious she worked the land. Women didn't get that big unless they threw hay bales all over a pasture for years. Looking at her straight on, she looked bald with her tight ponytail.

Kate Mills

The tough bitch closed on her fast. Nita pulled her Sig from the holster and fired a shot but was off target. A colossal grip enveloped her wrist and threw her to the ground. Blood poured onto her flannel shirt and gray tank top beneath Kate's face. They fought for control of the pistol. Kate's strength rivaled the bulkiest men Nita rolled with in Brazilian jiujitsu.

Both of their hands fought for control. Nita shrimped on her back and wrapped her legs around Kate's waist for control, but she was still losing the fight.

Nita threw her right leg over Kate's head, trapping her massive arms in the beginning stages of an arm bar. However, Kate planted her feet on the ground and stood, keeping downward pressure on her so Nita couldn't get leverage.

Nita shifted her focus to the gun. She rotated the barrel toward Kate's head, but the country girl knew her way around a firearm. Kate pressed the mag release, dropping the magazine onto Nita's chest. And with her top hand, she drove the slide backward, ejecting the bullet in the chamber.

Nita held on as Kate hoisted her into the air and slammed her back into the earth. Something popped into her neck as the muscles from the back of her skull to her shoulders strained.

"You're destroying everything we built!" Kate grunted.

Kate lifted Nita again, but the Cherokee swam her arm under Kate's leg, locking her in place. Nita pulled Kate's trapped arms down, sweeping her off her feet, and drove her to her back.

Now, she had the dominant position with her legs pressing Kate's chest into the ground. Nita dropped back and thrust her hips into the air, where Kate's right elbow fought from hyperextending.

Crack.

A deep cry followed.

Kate's right arm was out of commission. Nita reached behind her, pulled her backup Glock 19 tucked in her belt, put the barrel to Kate's temple, and fired.

She rolled away from the limp body beneath her, gathered herself, and crept forward, grabbing her pistol and shotgun that had tumbled down into the ravine with them. The trail she fell from was around fifty feet up. She started in that direction, but her fight was not over.

She adjusted her quad loader along her hip and prepped her shotgun for what was coming for her. The rustling of the forest was overwhelming from the south along all elevations. She trained her shotgun ahead as she walked down the ravine. Adrenaline surged. Anyone who emerged in the open would meet their end. Nita was going to make it so.

Had they all appeared at once with guns aimed at her, they would've stood a chance, but coming into the open one or two at a time in a disorganized manner was a tragic misstep for their cause.

Shot after shot, she blasted into them, continuing to backstep the entire way. Nita painted these woods red with the blood of those who believed these hills were theirs, but they were learning in the worst ways. The caliber of their weapons didn't matter. The fire rate of their weapons didn't matter. The mods on their weapons didn't matter.

Nita put them down before they got a shot off.

All of them.

She loaded shell after shell, switching from buckshot to slug depending on the distance of her enemies coming into the fray.

Her vision narrowed, and her targets downrange came into view with a glow that set them apart from the natural world. Whether it was the strength of her skills, her abilities, or the rawhide pouch dangling from her neck, she didn't know.

On this day, she would be their ruin.

She littered the ground with smoldering shells until her loaders ran empty. When it was all said and done, around fifteen of Mr. Sunderland's followers saw his vision no longer.

CHAPTER 73

Charlie and Lowwater ran with Teller into the woods to track down Nita, hoping more than anything that she was okay. Charlie had more confidence in her abilities than anyone, but witnessing so much destruction in their wake, he had doubts.

Lowwater's whiskey habit showed in their cross-country pursuit, but he hid his struggle well. He was the only one among the three who carried a rifle. The newly issued Watchman LE was a competent AR and lethal in Lowwater's hands if his skills at the range translated.

The trail of bullet casings never ran cold, but it was difficult to pinpoint the brass in the fallen leaves. The gradual ascent, even with adrenaline, was proving brutal.

A small pond of stagnant water remained where the land leveled out. Bullet casings and shotgun shells were everywhere, even floating in the water. Close by were the remains of several pale bodies.

"She lit these fuckers up," Lowwater said.

Charlie continued trailing up the hill, where he stumbled upon a highly modified M4. However, it had compromised damage on the barrel. "Looks like she ditched her rifle."

Teller raised both of his eyebrows. "How did you spot that thing?" he asked, seeing the gun covered by thick brush.

"Native eyes, Teller," Lowwater said, waddling up the hill.

"Let's keep–" Teller was cut off by Lowwater being blown back and collapsing to his back.

A large-caliber bullet caught him directly in the center of his body armor. All his air was gone. Lowwater held his chest and fought for breath. They had no time to aid him in their position as more shots homed in on their position.

Charlie and Teller each grabbed a shoulder strap on Lowwater's vest and dragged him behind the cover of a tight collection of trees. Bullets turned the surrounding wood and bark into sharp chips raining down upon them. Downrange, a sea of country cultists and a couple bikers amongst them fired a diverse selection of weaponry.

Teller scooped Lowwater's rifle as the marshal director struggled to catch any air. Agent Teller managed to take out one or two of their aggressors, but more seemed to appear the longer the firefight continued.

Charlie conserved his ammo as long as he could until the enemy got close. He knew more than anyone the proficiency of his sidearm skills, and they weren't close to Nita's.

They were pinned down. Teller could take out a couple more, but the rate of fire directed at them never lifted in intensity. They remained as low as they could, taking cover behind the base of the trees.

"We need to move!" Teller yelled.

Lowwater was beginning to come around. The old Indian was a tough bastard. He rolled over onto his stomach and removed his sidearm.

"You good to go?" Charlie asked him.

"Ain't got much of a choice!"

A heavier volley of fire peppered them. At this point, Charlie had nearly buried himself in the ground as loose dirt and wood chips covered half his body.

Charlie couldn't look even if he wanted to. The opposite side of the tree was being torn to shreds. Still sending shots at the enemy, Teller shouted, "AK fire coming at us now. We really got to–"

A shot nailed Teller's side, pinging off the side plate. However, he kept his composure and somehow stayed upright.

"—backtrack out of here!"

They started back east, but a few shots came from that direction, effectively flanking them.

"Uphill!" Teller shouted.

"We'll be out in the open!" Charlie said.

"We can't stay here!"

As they started up the hill, a bullet sliced through the meat of Charlie's arm, grazing his shoulder. The sting was comparable to a cattle brand. Blood poured down his arm instantly, staining his shirt sleeve.

The cultists wouldn't let up, and their ammo never ran dry.

Then, their momentum was once again halted. Charlie noticed the sounds of gunfire, and sequential whistles began to soften and die out. A new sound snaked through the trees like mighty whispers aggressively forcing their way into a two-way conversation.

Against his better judgment, Charlie peeked into the battlefield from behind the tree. Five men at various flanking positions covertly emerged from the trees.

Blake Edwards and his Marine buddies made their presence known at the best of times. Charlie couldn't fight the hatred. The idea of that motherfucker saving his life made him sick, even in the heat of battle.

Their suppressed assault rifle fire shredded the people of the compound. Their numbers diminished at a rapid pace. Blake was a maverick, tactically weaving through the terrain into firing positions that never exposed him.

In a matter of seconds, the battlefield flipped. Teller and Lowwater recovered and prayed to God that the bullets didn't travel up or down a few more inches.

A few began to flee as things shifted. Blake wasn't allowing that to happen. One of the bikers carrying an empty Uzi was far out of his element. He kicked up dead leaves on his escape and took massive, wheezing breaths.

Blake trotted into the clearing and shot the biker's leg from behind, approaching with his rifle trained on the man the entire way. "Who was on my land, motherfucker!" he shouted.

The biker shouted and rotated over. Charlie had no clue what Blake was on about. The three of them were bystanders at this point. It seemed they were all in mutual agreement that Blake was allowed his moment.

Blake stomped on the biker's leg, and the cries rattled the man's vocal cords. "Who sicced the dogs on me!"

The cries continued with no answer.

Blake shot his other leg.

Somehow, the cries grew louder.

Charlie went to speak and try to end the madness to find Nita, but the biker said, "I-I wasn't there! I promise!"

That was enough said.

Blake ended the conversation and the biker's life.

CHAPTER 74

The dust settled.

Lowwater and Teller surveyed the situation, side-eyeing each other at Blake and his guys' involvement. Gunfire continued to sound in the distance in multiple directions.

Blake and Lowwater exchanged a glance. A *thank you* didn't seem appropriate for the moment, so a nod sufficed from the director.

"Anything on Nita?" Blake asked.

"Still MIA," Charlie said.

Quick and efficient decisions saved lives in his former line of work, so he made one. "Did y'all have her trail?"

"Seemed to be going back northeast."

"Gettin' elevation, it seems," Little J chimed in.

Blake nodded. "Let's track that way. We'll split into two groups. One will drive straight up the hill from here while the other will track along the base."

"Fuck them hills, boys. Regardless, we gotta get going," Lowwater insisted.

Blake sent Floyd, Cody, and Parker with Lowwater and Teller, who appeared to be sticking together as they recovered from nonlethal gunshot wounds. Charlie veered closer to Blake's group, which caught him by surprise. Perhaps he believed Blake's group would manage to find Nita first. Perhaps not.

It didn't matter. The groups were set, and Lowwater's was on its way with a bit of marine assistance.

It was evident that Charlie didn't want to waste time. He started up the hill with a grunt until Blake stopped him. "That all you got?" the cowboy said.

"Excuse me?"

"The Glock?"

Charlie nodded.

Blake walked towards him and offered him his rifle. Charlie had a reluctant glance the entire way. Blake turned around, and his horse trotted into the clearing like the well-trained companion he'd known for a long time, a close second to Nova. He gripped the butt of his family's repeating rifle and pulled it from its leather scabbard. It would be considered sacrilegious not to keep the firearm in pristine condition.

He walked back to Charlie with his rifle high, checking his ammo in the cartridge holders until foreign guilt traveled through him. A deep sadness and pain churned in the pit of his stomach. His right hand shook. He squeezed and rubbed his wrist to shake it, but his heart pumped fast.

"You all right?" Little J asked.

It took a moment for the question to process, so his answer was too late. "Yeah, I'm fine."

Little J didn't seem convinced, and by the look on Charlie's stoic face, he wasn't convinced either.

Blake tried to shake it out and put on a front. He started up the hill and said, "Let's go."

CHAPTER 75

Near the top of the hill, with her legs swollen from the climb, Nita came upon a fire tower. It was thin but still traveled high in the air. It bore a striking resemblance to the more well-known fire tower on Beaver Mountain in the Cookson Hills, not far away. From her knowledge, this tower was a bit shorter, and while she didn't believe the one in Cookson Hills had been abandoned for years, this looked to have been left alone for centuries. Everything had rusted, and consecutive steps leading to the cab were hard to come by. Making the climb up would not be in her best interest. The elevation she had would have to suffice.

For the moment, she had lost her pursuers or violently knocked them off her trail. She decided to take a moment to check her ammunition. All she had left was a couple of mags for her Sig as her shotgun had run dry.

The decaying beams holding up the tower began to vibrate and increase in intensity, merging into a rattle. A small engine chugged up the high hill towards her as it repeatedly revved, fighting against the terrain. She took cover behind some trees on the opposite side of the hill. The lower elevation concealed her as she could no longer see the tower's base.

A four-seat side-by-side crested the hill. The engine idled, and Nita held fast.

A trio of voices conversed. From this distance, it was difficult to determine what they were saying. However, their soft pitch hit her ears like malignant snakes. She did her best to settle at the tree's base and find calm, but a new sensation of dryness and an irritating itch ran from her exposed hands, arms, and face. The blood caked on her skin darkened and dried. She ran her fingers across her cheeks, and a layer of crusty blood had remained stuck to her face for God knew how long. She shared the texture of drywall.

Her hair was stiff. It reminded her of Colette's lifeless body on display not far from here.

She contorted her body to peek around the tree and to the top of the hill, but that was easier said than done, given the soreness taking hold of her and the added challenge of remaining quiet. Her pistol was pressed tight across her vest, and her body shuddered the entire way.

The identity of the trio was made known. Ezell stood amongst his two most trusted visionaries. The one whose size rivaled a professional offensive lineman cranked a pulley that lowered a wooden crate from the top of the tower. It was heavy as it met the earth with a thud.

She brought her pistol out in front of her and positioned herself to shoot. However, her range wasn't ideal, and Amos, who was former military, constantly scanned the perimeter with his rifle. This was not an exchange she could win from here.

A crowbar crunched open the crate and they removed guns... bigger guns. They rushed through their contents, piquing Nita's survivalist interest as much as she hated to admit it. She couldn't make out everything, but she got eyes on GPS systems, binoculars, flashlights, trail cams, radio equipment, MREs, additional sets of clothing, blocks of cash and cocaine, first-aid kits, plastic storage bags of medication, a stack of license plates, keys, journals, and smaller weapons like knives and hand-axes.

Nita's expertise taught her they had been prepared for a bug-out situation for the apocalypse or the exact scenario they were living out.

Ezell ran through the keys. "Which one of these is to the boat?"

"Smaller one is Clarence's Jon boat key on the creek about half a mile north. The other is to my old man's pontoon at the boathouse. We'll use that to get on the other side of the lake where a couple of trucks are waiting at that house I'm renting."

Their attention from underneath the tower shifted in the exact opposite of her direction. Their swiftness to turn told her they were caught off guard. Ezell stood solid. Unafraid.

As they were distracted, she decided to advance on them. She pushed herself from the ground and burst to her feet. However, she felt resistance around her neck, followed by a soft snap. Her rawhide necklace snagged on a curled branch.

She froze.

No more power. No more safety.

She never questioned the power of the medicine man, but she refused to believe it was the sole protector over her. She was not short on confidence. Anything that would conquer her would meet resistance, rawhide bag or not.

Her attention returned to Ezell and his men, who were now aware of her presence. Ezell smiled and said, "I will never forget you, Marshal."

She didn't have time. Amos' burst of fire traveled from her thigh up towards her opposite shoulder. Two bullets hit her vest, knocked her backward, and sent her tumbling down the hill.

Every attempt to stop herself failed due to the sharp, burning sensations flaring in her leg and right shoulder. She bounced off a tree that struck her in the spine. Her body hyperextended, and the heels of her boots slammed the back of her hands.

Her descent slowed, but she still had no strength to stop. She struggled to keep her eyes open. A thump in her brain pulsed like the bullet hole in her thigh. A shock of cold startled her.

The upper half of her body settled in the creek at the bottom of the hill. The water flowed past her head, going into her ears, wetting her hair, and splashing into her wounds and mouth. The coolness brought some comfort, but she had no strength to fight the shallow water attempting to drown her.

CHAPTER 76

Blake and his men stalked up the hill, following the sound of an ATV. Little J watched their six the entire way as Charlie remained between them. Like always, J took the role of protector. He made sure nothing would catch them off guard. They were lucky to have him at this moment, and Blake thanked God daily he had J to watch his back like he had been doing for years.

Whispers emerged.

Blake squeezed his rifle closer and nodded back to Little J and Charlie. They continued, trying to avoid dead leaves, but that task was impossible. Blake figured as long as the conversation above them continued without any fluctuation or interruption, they would be considered unnoticed.

A fire tower came into view. It had been out of commission for a long time. Since the 50s, if Blake remembered correctly. But then again, he also thought they tore it down. Fire towers and those who worked them were no longer needed. They were one of the many victims of the rise of technology. Their death and way of life became a thing of the past. Blake hoped his way wasn't following, but doubts amplified when he looked upon the decaying structure that once stood firm.

A branch snapped behind him, and his head twisted around to see Charlie scrunching his face at the broken stick under his boot.

The soft-spoken conversation just out of view stopped. They readied themselves and began sidestepping behind nearby trees for cover.

A moment later, Blake jumped at the sound of fire. However, none came their way. He looked at J and Charlie, and they nodded back, signaling they were okay.

Perhaps warning shots?

Little J was posted up behind cover. He held up a fist, ordering them both to hold as he would be the first of them to make the first move. In doing so, he was putting himself at higher risk.

He kept a low profile as his knees stayed just above the ground on his crouch upward. J aimed down the sights as he crested the top of the hill. By now, whoever was at the top would have come into his view.

A sudden and violent shot hissed through the woods.

No, no, no, no, no!

A bullet struck Little J in the head. His body dropped and slid ten feet down the hill as he drowned in a pile of leaves.

Blake quit breathing. Years of combat experience were lost to sheer emotion. No one could get used to seeing this. No one should. Having Little J as his best friend was one of the greatest accomplishments of his life. In those prayers of thanks to God, Blake often mentioned how lucky they were to make it out of that hell alive. He never could have imagined that he would lose his best friend in his home.

Shame. Guilt. Sadness. They coalesced into rage.

"Father, go!" he heard above him.

Blake ran. He didn't converse or wait for Charlie. The enemy made their presence known. If today was the day he died, he was fine, but he would make J's killer pay.

He fired downrange without a clear target, slamming that lever forward and backward with hatred as three adversaries came into view. Two were escaping on the opposite side as they carried bags over their shoulders, one of which was massive. He jogged out of sight like bigfoot in the Patterson footage.

A familiar face, who had a rifle trained back at him, came into view. A fellow Marine. A neighbor. Amos Dyer.

Thoughts on the circumstances surrounding Amos' arrival not long ago and the cultivation of this place were all pushed aside by the sheer rage boiling over in Blake's system. Everything was clear. Amos was the enemy.

His rounds thundered towards Amos, who took cover behind the tower beams. Blake had to reload, but he was exposed in the open, and Amos readied a shot toward him as he angled away from the tower.

CHAPTER 77

They flew down the hill with their arms out and minding their step the entire way. "Clarence," Ezell said, waving the giant away. "My son, go help Amos. We'll need him. I can get to the boat from here."

Clarence spent no time questioning his father's reasoning. "Can you carry both bags, Father?"

"No. I'm not as strong as you, son," he assured him with an exhausted smile. "You will have to leave it here and get it on the way back after those men up there are dealt with like the Cherokee woman."

Clarence hurled the oversized duffle off his back like a sleeping bag. He pulled a hand-axe from the pack and started back up the hill to accompany his massive Bowie knife dangling in a leather sheath on his belt.

Ezell didn't have to give him any assurance about killing. It was what he was proficient at and better at doing than anyone Ezell had run across in his many years.

CHAPTER 78

Charlie fired upon the Dyer man, but he used the cover well. Blake was in the process of reloading his lever action yet keeping his eyes on the target. Blake rolled out of the way behind the tree cover with no time.

Charlie continued to fire, but his bullets either bounced off the metal beams or went wide. He angled away to reload. He made sure to stay on his feet the entire way.

He hardly knew Little J on a personal level, but the loss weighed on him. Only inside his head would he express his pity for Blake.

Something landed at his feet that continued to slide farther into the dead leaves. Poking out from them was a gray cylinder. Unfortunately, in the time it took him to discern what the device was, it was too late.

He went partially blind. The shockwave sent his hearing into a constant ring. It was as if a fox was inches away from his face screaming in his ear. He dropped the rifle, covering his ears to reduce the ringing sensation, but it didn't help.

———

The stun grenade left a plume of smoke. Blake was far enough away to avoid the effects, but knowing from experience, it would take a bit.

He didn't waste any time. Blake had to make his move if Amos' attention was on Charlie. He emerged from behind cover with his rifle in front of him.

Move. Shoot. Angle. Positioning.

Amos poked his upper body out again. He made his body a small target and used his tactics well.

The Marine never left him.

Blake ensured his repeating rifle lived up to its name as he closed the distance. By the fourth shot in the exchange of fire, Blake caught Amos in the shoulder, winging him.

Blake slung his rifle over his shoulder and removed his M18. He fired three more shots, all finding purchase in nonlethal areas of Amos' body. That was by design. His enemy squealed in pain, and Blake breathed easy.

The tough bastard still went to his rifle, even with limited arm movement.

Blake shot his hand.

People in OKC probably heard Amos' scream.

"There's a dark corner in hell waiting for you." Blake said. "The place in hell reserved for Marines that kill other Marines."

With labored breath, full of bullet holes, Amos strung together a chuckle as tears ran down his face. "If you finish this, you'll be there alongside me."

"Maybe so."

Blake shot both legs three more times. The agony was what he was after.

Suddenly, pain bloomed in his side just above his hip and below his tac vest. From there, he was hoisted off the ground. His hands went to brace the back of the axe-head embedded in his side. Blood shot from his mouth and onto the massive man holding him in the air like a tomahawk steak.

Blake had played football since he could walk, but he had never been thrown to the ground as hard as this man did. The bedding of the woods might have well been concrete. His head was the last thing to hit. After that, his vision went black.

He drifted in and out of consciousness. A sense of nakedness came over him as his inherited rifle was ripped from his back, and his sidearm holster no longer had weight.

A new pain that was much harsher brought all feelings and awareness back into this world. The man stomped on his back, taking Blake's wind with him. He then ripped the hand-axe from Blake's side, and he couldn't help but yell in pain, just like Amos did.

Perhaps he was right about us being in hell together.

"Father allows me to remove sinners from this world." Clarence said. "He knows it is my calling. His knowledge of how the world should be is beyond the stars, cowboy."

Blake extended his right arm above his head while holding his breath until air shot out of him. He attempted to return oxygen to his lungs, but the small amount that came back was a brutal tease. He clenched a handful of dirt and dead grass and pulled himself along to escape his attacker, whose boot gently lifted from his back.

He could see the writing on the wall. If he couldn't get away, he was dead. If he did get away, he didn't have long with the blood leaking out of him like water through a fissure in a dam.

"You can't escape me, Mr. Edwards," Clarence said. "Many like you have tried. There's no point in fighting anymore."

Blake pulled himself one arm's length away from the giant and kept going.

"Your little ranch hand couldn't escape me."

Blake stopped. With a grunt, he planted his hand on the ground to rotate and look up at the man.

Wyatt?

Clarence smelled of sweat and body odor that rivaled the feral hogs. His hair grew in thick and all over. "He caught me when I finished my work with that beautiful young lady. I couldn't let him see anymore, so I pried his eyes from their sockets with this Bowie."

All his work to try to find Wyatt's killer meant very little. For the killer had found him. The fantasies of revenge and justice were empty thoughts and emotions. Hell was already upon him. Blake had failed his friends and was indirectly responsible for their deaths in his home.

His family was cursed.

They were a line of people with unlimited wealth but limited love.

Greed. Violence. Arrogance. Those were the things passed down from the beginning. Nothing more. Blake and his family disputed those rumors of what his kin had done so many generations ago to the Indian families in the area to begin their path of fortune. There wasn't a doubt in his mind now that all of that was true. Part of him always knew it had been, but pride ensured he'd never admit it.

His family was cursed.

All the men in his family before him died alone with very little to mourn their passing. They all entered the world as they left.

Rich. Broken. Cowboys.

"The state will know of your death but won't know me." Clarence said. "Oh, what pleasure I will take from being the one who erased your wretched soul from this world. I'll know. It was Clarence Len Fletcher that killed the richest man in Oklahoma."

The man he now knew as Clarence flipped the Bowie in his hand, dropped his weight onto Blake's chest, and straddled him.

His breathing turned into faint wheezing.

Clarence's smile was pure evil.

This evil had prospered under Blake's nose for a long time. His greatest fear was coming to fruition. He would die with shame, with no proof that showed without a doubt he was different from the ones before.

The broad blade reflected the setting sun. Blake closed his eyes. He was ready to meet the pain and the death to follow.

Then, shuffling as something rustled through the leaves at Clarence's back. Blake opened his eyes. Clarence turned and was met with the brunt force of a Cherokee man's shoulder that knocked him from his dominant position and onto his side.

Charlie readied himself and got to his feet much quicker than the giant shifting his weight to gain upward momentum. He had no weapons. He ran through that single magazine in the rifle Blake gave him.

Charlie soccer kicked Clarence's face, knocking him upright. The goliath stood faster than Blake thought he could, nearly defying gravity. However, he was human. Blood leaked from his shattered and crooked nose.

Blake held his side and started using his legs to push himself back and away from the fight. Every movement sent a shockwave through his body.

Clarence swung his hand-axe and Bowie knife at Charlie with reckless abandon, grunting like a grizzly with each heavy slash.

Charlie, by sheer Native agility, dodged every swing and even got off a punch of his own back into Clarence's nose. However, the strike seemed to anger him more as he barreled towards Charlie. But, with each attempt by the much larger opponent, Charlie could avoid damage and pepper away at Clarence with single strikes.

Blake continued to push away.

Then, the Bowie caught Charlie on the arm, leaving a good-sized gash in his forearm and effectively knocking him out of the trance allowing him to avoid danger thus far.

Clarence closed the distance and came down from the sky with the axe. Charlie used Clarence's heavy downward momentum against him by getting under his armpit and throwing him over his shoulder. His judo skills appeared subpar, so the move wasn't executed flawlessly, but it worked well enough for the moment to get him out of a disadvantageous position.

Charlie put his knee on Clarence's belly and somehow ripped the axe from his hand, but he had no time for offense. The Bowie knife thrusted towards his thigh and Charlie did his best to keep it at bay as much as he could, but the blade dug into the meat of his leg. The giant's strength seemed not of this world.

The giant's free hand reached around Charlie's back, and fish hooked his mouth with his dirty, scabbed hands.

Blood spewed between his fingers.

Clarence pulled Charlie over as they wrestled on the ground, side by side, fighting for the dominant position.

They fought for the knife, and Charlie was losing. Clarence rolled him over and won the position battle. All Charlie could do was hold him off as the knife inched closer to his eye.

Blake's head clanked against something hard. Something metal. He reached back.

And grabbed his lever action rifle, passed down from so many generations. Blake couldn't remember how far back it went. It had been modified so that whoever purchased it in his family long ago would probably no longer recognize it. However, contemplating his family's history, perhaps that was a good thing, and maybe, he had more in common with the gun than he ever imagined. A change had occurred, but the core remained.

Charlie saved his eye by angling away, but now, the blade tip quivered above his chest.

Blake grunted and spat blood through gritted teeth as chambering another round with the lever action had never been as challenging.

He was weak.

He remembered when he was a boy, and his older sister could pull back the twenty-pound draw weight on his compound bow before he could. He tucked the rifle close to his body and lined up the best shot possible. He wavered, and there was nothing he could do to stop the movement.

His target was small.

Both Charlie and Clarence continued to fight for position.

Clarence's squeeze grew tighter. The tip of the Bowie broke the skin on Charlie's chest above his vest. The marshal screamed in pain as the blade drove deeper.

Blake had two targets bobbing around in his sights. The tops of their heads wiggled around, and the added struggle to focus his aim made the shot much harder. They might as well have been two balloons tied to a post in the middle of a tornado. Any attempt to control his breathing would fail. He simplified the process. He took a deep breath, no matter how bad it hurt.

He held.

Held until a steadiness found him.

He squeezed.

The rifle fired.

It took all his remaining strength to hold his head up and look downrange.

Charlie rolled over, limp.

The Bowie remained lodged in his chest at the tip.

Fuck.

However, the tough Indian slapped the blade out of his body and rose to his knees. His eyes focused clearer on the giant lying flat on the ground, no longer moving. His basketball-sized head began to leak like a hole in a fully fractured barrel.

Clarence Len Fletcher was dead.

Wyatt's killer was dead.

Blake's vision went foggy as Charlie ran towards him and grabbed the back of his falling head.

CHAPTER 79

"Blake! Blake!" Charlie yelled as the cowboy went unconscious.

He was at a loss. He didn't know how to help, given the circumstances. He stood behind Blake's head and grabbed a fistful of his shoulder straps. Charlie dragged him about twenty feet, but Blake's agony and the idea of being so far away from anything halted his progress.

"Help!"

But no one arrived. Not even Lowwater and the cavalry. Gunshots continued, so their encounter would only be one alarm amongst thousands.

He gave himself a moment to think.

He didn't have the time for intense contemplation.

Blake was going to die.

He could call a helicopter, but he was in the middle of the woods. He tried the ATV the enemy arrived in, but it had been shot to shit, and the engine wouldn't turn over.

Then, something came to his attention. Something was idling at the bottom of the hill, but it would literally and metaphorically be an uphill battle.

"Shit," Charlie said while sprinting away, leaving Blake fighting for life in the dirt. "Hold on, cowboy, motherfucker!"

————

Long ago, Charlie made a personal vow that he would never ride a horse again. He still contemplated living up to that vow as he untied the horse's reins that held him in place.

He rubbed the palm of his hand along the horse's neck, feeling his fine coat and groomed mane.

The stallion was strong.

Even with Charlie's biased opinion of hating horses for over a decade, he couldn't help but admire this one.

Fear kept him from horses. The fear of breaking his back, sure. It wasn't like every Indian he knew rode horses all the time.

That wasn't what scared him.

What scared him was not being able to overcome the fear that held him hostage. That fear involved an ancestral bond with the animal he worried he'd never get over.

"It's all right, boy," he whispered, drawing him farther into the clearing. He put his head to the horse's head as they shared each other's eye line. "Please, don't buck me off. Please."

Charlie climbed, swung his leg over the horse's back, and started up the hill. The sensation and awareness came back to him. Charlie began to believe that riding a horse, like a bike, never left someone, especially a Native.

Part of him still questioned what he was doing. Given all that had transpired, the thing that helped him continue to help Edwards was that it was the right thing to do. Blake was still an asshole descended from a long line of greater assholes, but they deserved redemption too.

CHAPTER 80

Whispers in her native tongue danced from the surrounding woods as she found enough strength to rise from the creek.

Where the hell am I?

Her hair was soaked and stuck to her face. She had no sense of how long she had been lying there with cool water flowing past her. Her body was sore and beaten, but she did feel a bit refreshed. The sun was beginning to set, and darkness would soon be upon her. She had no bearings on her location or where to go.

Even if she was familiar with the topography, traversing it at night would be damn near impossible. She wasn't afraid, but there was an uneasiness to her situation, with presumably those still hunting her.

She had no bearing. There was nothing that cued her to Ezell's general direction or destination. She wanted to slam her fist into the nearest... anything. She shot harsh breaths through her nostrils.

The pain in her leg and shoulder increased as consciousness returned to her. She removed a tourniquet that ran down one of the straps of her tac vest. She applied the tourniquet high on her thigh to reduce further blood loss as the bullet was still lodged in the meat of her leg.

Another bullet hit between her shoulder and collarbone, luckily piercing all the way through her body. She applied some EMS gauze to that area, both on the entry and exit side of the wound and held the gauze in place by placing HyFin Vent seal over both holes.

She spent nearly half the contents of her trauma kit patching herself up, but there was no point in being conservative with any of it now. She clipped it back onto her vest, which was attached to her side beneath her jacket. Jackson always kept her well-stocked and ready as he had cultivated her obsession with survival gear. For Christmas a few years ago, he bought her a rolling workbench filled with various survival, tactical, and medical supplies. To this day, it was one of the best gifts anyone had bought for her.

It was never lost on her that his gifts still assisted her from beyond the grave.

The whispers grew in volume.

At first, she convinced herself it was all in her head, but as they progressed, they were as real as the creek flowing over rocks behind her. The voices began to alleviate the anxiety starting to overwhelm her. It had been a long time since she had spoken Cherokee, so the whispers took a lot of work to delineate meaning. However, even amongst this darkness, wise words of encouragement returned power to her body.

She stood and looked almost directly above her to see the top of the hill. Figures came into view. Their features were hard to make out with the sun at their backs. Their descent was slow and weary. Men, women, and children all occupied this vast party, and they hardly spoke a word.

Once proud Cherokees marched past her going west. They wore traditional Cherokee attire of linen shirts, deerskin moccasins, and multi-colored, beaded jewelry. However, their clothes were now ragged and fading. Their journey had been beyond brutal to get here. Blood from their feet soaked into the earth as their malnourished frames struggled to hold themselves upright.

They had all been with her for her whole life. She hoped they never left her despite the harsh reality of their existence.

The forced march had not killed their pride. The forced march had not killed their spirit. And as more continued to crest that hill, it was certain the forced march did not kill them at all.

They're strong.

They remain.

Tears fell from her eyes. Her ancestors walked past her. Her family walked past her. She dropped her head and wept. The pain was too much to bear as she covered her face with her dry, bloody hands and dropped to her knees.

The cycle will never end.

Then, a hand rested on her chest above her heart. She was met with a woman elder, wearing a slight and wrinkled smile. She was beautiful. She had gray and white hair with kind yet dark eyes.

She spoke nothing.

Her hand remained over Nita's heart, and she gently grabbed Nita's elbow. In return, Nita grabbed her, and they rose together.

She wiped the tears from Nita's face and continued marching west. More ancestors followed in her footsteps, approached her with smiles, and touched her chest. Children trotted towards her with no hatred in their hearts, overcoming their tired and weary souls with child-like wonder. They giggled together, hugged her waist, and grabbed her hands. And before they continued, they always placed their hands on her chest just like their elders did.

The children returned to assist their elders, and their whispers turned to singing. Nita stood there basking in the beautiful sound of gentle voices singing songs of old.

The line of Cherokees coming down from the hill seemed never-ending. She greeted hundreds that passed her as they continued to interact with her wave after wave, repeating the same gesture as those before them.

She loved them.

Lyrics came to her. The old Cherokee grew familiar once again. She cocked her head as her brain churned with thoughts as she put the words together, as the women and children continued to sing softly. Tears returned, but not ones of sadness or grief.

They sang:

Into the void, I travel
A vast thicket of engulfing black
Keep the pace, I say

Keep the pace

A boy came to her and stared up at her with big eyes. He smiled and held her hand as countless had before him. However, he waved her down to his level, and she followed. He placed her left hand over her heart and made her leave it there. His fingers went to her forehead. He slowly dragged his fingertips down her face, grazing over her eyebrows and pulling her eyelids down to shut them.

She knelt there with her eyes shut for a few more moments.

She was alone in the woods.

Lost.

The manifestations of her ancestors were gone, but she could still feel their presence. She always could.

Her hand rested above her heart over her jacket. A thick, folded piece of paper stiffened it. She reached in and removed it, not remembering what it was until she unfolded the laminated map Aiden had gifted her of Thorpe Ranch.

She smiled and appreciated the artistry in it that was beyond his years. She started to fold it up again to place it back inside her pocket until something in the upper left-hand corner caught her eye. Beyond the boundary lines of Thorpe Ranch, amongst the woods, was an elevated hill, and a tower was placed in the center of that hill.

"Holy shit."

A creek moved east to west and stopped upon entry into the river, which met the edge of the map. Where the stream and the river met was a small collection of metal squares. Nita brought the map closer to her face, still struggling to understand what those tiny squares represented. Then, her elementary map knowledge came back to her. Had she done more to be with her son and taken the valuable time to understand him and his passion more, she would've known immediately to check the map key he created at the bottom right corner. In Aiden's maps, tiny dark triangles equaled homes, and tiny dark squares represented boathouses.

She looked to the creek and then to her watch with a compass on its face. She followed the creek farther west, going as fast as possible with limited mobility as she fought her harsh limp. She took notice of the grin she subdued. With the coming darkness, she needed a way to navigate these woods more than ever. For Aiden had provided her with a key to regain the upper hand.

It was time to pursue.

Thank you, Aiden. Thank you, son.

CHAPTER 81

Ezell threw the bags in the johnboat. He nearly crashed into it with his downward momentum and the heftiness of the load. He climbed into the boat from the small, makeshift dock along the creek. The water was shallow, but the boat should have no problem traversing through the woods.

It took three pulls on the starter motor to get the engine rumbling. He kept his emotions close to his vest, but he could finally catch his breath after the first two pulls were unsuccessful.

He dropped down, untied the rope around one of the dock posts, and started down the creek.

He would take no chances waiting for Amos or Clarence. Their sacrifice would not be in vain.

The speed of the johnboat was not ideal. He rotated the throttle all the way and tried to push further, but to no avail. The max speed was equivalent to a brisk jog in the woods.

Ezell kept his head on a swivel.

A new beginning must occur. My revolution will not die this day.

CHAPTER 82

The gunfire around them never ceased. The bulk of them still sounded from the direction of the compound. Some shots were close. Very close. Worries about the fallout from the situation mounted. Everything had transpired so quickly amongst many different organizations, and Teller hoped the public would see things as they were. However, in a red state, in the heart of Indian country, distress for government organizations filtered through the water.

These woods were foreign to him. He kept his nerves about him, but a sizable portion of him was thankful Director Lowwater was with him and a couple of random cowboys who knew their way around a gun better than he did.

They hadn't had time to exchange formal introductions, but he listened when one of them, who wore a mustache like Val Kilmer in *Tombstone*, said, "Hold."

Teller stood still. Too still. His eyes moved about the terrain but didn't see any cause for concern. As they stood in silence, more pop shots occurred, but they were distant. The Marine-cowboy put his back to him and Lowwater and waved them to return to the creek. They were at a low elevation as the creek wasn't far away. The Marine kept his gaze towards the top of the slope.

Screw this place.

The sense of being hunted never came over Teller until today.

Then, men emerged behind cover, shooting down at them with hunting rifles. Teller clocked two men close to one another, about fifty feet up.

Until the cowboy shouted, "Get cover! Five up top!"

A new firefight began.

Teller was pinned down. Bullets impacted on the opposite side of his tree. He had no intention of moving. The cowboys didn't share that philosophy. They shot up the slope and moved, weaving between the terrain, refusing to get caught flanked.

"Shoot and move!" they shouted.

Then, something caught his eye as it chugged along the creek past them.

The man he held responsible for all this appeared alive and well. He single-handily manned a johnboat to flee the scene.

CHAPTER 83

Charlie rode hard through the vast hills. The constant change and elevation forced the stallion to work. He strapped Blake's fading body across the back of the horse as if he was already dead. He apologized for the brutal ride ahead, but there was no alternative.

He had cell service at the top of the hill underneath the old fire tower. He made an emergency call and requested a life-flight helicopter to their location. He intended to mark their location via Blake's flare in the pack saddle. If this all worked out, Edwards would be thankful for that gun.

As he rode, several helicopters thundered above the trees toward the compound. He couldn't determine whether they were law enforcement agencies, media outlets, or medical services. Judging by the volume of aerial vehicles, it could've been all of the above.

He kept checking on Blake as the blood leaked through the bandages and onto his horse. Charlie gripped the paracord that tethered the cowboy to his horse, making sure he didn't slip through the bindings.

"Blake!" he yelled.

There was no response. His head and legs continued to bounce on the horse's backside.

———

As the tree's tight formations ceased, the sun spread its orange glow across the open pasture. Everything came in flashes, like fading consciousnesses in a recliner after a hard day's work.

Charlie fought like hell to get Blake here. That much was true.

He was weak and had no strength to fall off the horse alone. Charlie disappeared from atop the stallion and transported behind his back, gripping the vest straps, and peeled him off his horse. He brought Blake down gently into the grass as the calm, nightly winds swept past. The air brought the first ounce of relief since that axe entered his side. That relief faded into nothing as quickly as it arrived.

"Where are the flares?" Charlie asked him.

"S-saddle bag. On the left. Bottom."

Every word hurt.

———

Charlie rifled through the saddle bag, removing a couple of red flares and tossed them into the field to mark their location.

"I called it in. We'll get you out of here."

Charlie knelt on one knee beside him, posting up on his hand as he caught his breath.

Blake coughed blood into the air, landing on his chin. Through his pain, he spoke, "I'm sorry."

He repeated it, along with more, but it was soft and incoherent, like whispers in the dark.

"S-sorry for what, Edwards?"

"For what..."

"What?"

"I'm sorry... for what my family did."

Charlie said nothing. There wasn't a doubt in his mind that the apology was genuine. Many a man admitted their offensives at death's door, so perhaps their consciousness could step through the afterlife's threshold weightless.

Blake stared up at him. Charlie had difficulty discerning whether the water around his eyes were tears or the result of physical pain coming to the surface. Perhaps both. Perhaps deep inside, the cowboy recognized and carried some emotional baggage that had never been unpacked.

Charlie nodded, hopefully assuring him that all was fine from him. Part of him struggled with what his ancestors might think, so he kept some reserve. It wasn't his place to forgive Blake's family responsible for those wretched things long ago. All he could do was forgive the dying man next to him.

And he did.

———

A Marine chopper was inbound above him. In his foggy state, Blake couldn't make out the model. It seemed to alternate between all the different ones he had flown in on his way to and from the battlefield.

Flares ushered its landing as it moved like everything else at the moment—in still frames. The blades whipped heavy downward wind on them as Charlie ducked his head, and the chopper landed on the grass.

Then, Marines filtered out, establishing a perimeter around the landing. Along with them was a quad of Marines holding each end of a gurney. Their pace was hurried, and the movement determined.

Voices emerged, assuring Blake that he was going to be okay. His eyes focused for a moment to see the man offering those encouraging words was none other than his best friend, Little J. If the words were coming from him, he knew them to be true.

The remainder of the three were all brothers he was forced to remember from when last he saw them in Ramadi.

His brothers carried him to that chopper as if nothing else but his survival mattered to them.

Blake's head dropped to the side. Standing at attention was a line of warriors in uniform saluting the end of the fight. He last saw these familiar faces around 2006 when they shared the battlefield in the Middle East.

It wasn't just Marines welcoming him home. Those of every branch that saw combat that day stood at uniformed attention. Their stoic and battle-weary faces had a softness to them. Their physical bodies were destroyed, but they were not killed. Their souls remained as beacons of proven sacrifice and unbreakable spirits, their legacies not remembered as failures but as victories.

Blake held Little J's hand as darkness took him. His fading hopes were that his memory would be viewed similarly to the brothers and sisters he served alongside. He hoped he instilled enough strength in his daughter so she could grow up strong and not be pressed down by the world's weight.

He hoped.

He faded.

CHAPTER 84

Teller sprinted along the creek as he made ground on the fleeing johnboat. Its speed was nothing spectacular, but it seemed fast enough to keep just out of Teller's reach as the terrain continued to fight against him.

He kept pushing. The gunfight behind him echoed. The Marine boys and Lowwater's scrappy, big ass had it covered.

The johnboat entered a narrow stone archway that doubled as a train bridge. The bridge was so overgrown and decrepit to time that Teller doubted a train had passed through in a century.

He rounded that archway with such speed that he surprised himself. Nothing shocked him more than meeting Ezell at full tilt as he passed through the short tunnel. Teller ducked his head, leaped, and made full contact with Ezell like a linebacker.

They landed on the opposite side of the creek as the boat rocked side to side downstream. Ezell held his palms open above his chest, meaning for no resistance. Teller wasn't positive, but he could swear the hint of amusement washed over the bastard's sick face. He grabbed an exposed wrist, rolled him over, and slapped cuffs on him as fast as possible. He took a moment to catch his breath as his knee dug into Ezell's back.

"Fair play," Ezell said. "Fair play."

"Shut up."
"Of course."

———

He lost.

However, this loss was in no way a precursor to abandoning his mandate. On the contrary, they had only delayed his progress.

Ezell Sunderland can die, but someone will arise from his grave and continue what he started, just as before. I am infinite.

As he lay bound in the dirt, presumably with all his followers either dead or sharing a similar outcome, he did not fret.

The agent sat him upright and looked through his phone for service in the bowels of these endless hills, and Ezell exhaled freely.

"Oklahoma State Bureau of Investigation," Ezell said, attempting to begin a dialogue.

The agent paid him no mind. "I told you to shut up."

"Very well. Very well. However, I want you to know that this could have been avoided. I am no more than a man of God. This was a beautiful and private community I built here. I assure you, I did not want this to occur."

"You were prepared for it, though. Hell broke loose, and you were ready."

The agent's out-of-focus visage had a streak of clarity along his cheek. A crack in the armor. "Well, sure. History has not been kind to outsiders seeking their own way of life. Those that can't accept change seek to tear it down. My flock were lost souls like we all are at one point or another. They were scared and distrusted the world. I was trying to show them that there was nothing to fear."

Agent Teller said nothing. He listened, and that crack grew, moving across his face like embers along a dead leaf.

"My visionaries were afraid of the agendas of those in high castles that cared very little about them. It's difficult for people to prosper in a world where they have no say." Ezell curled his nose and lips at the ones not present amongst them. "Those people dining in ivory buildings claim to have our best interest, but they don't. You know as much. We go along with what they do and say because they assure us they keep the monsters at bay. War. Nuclear Holocaust. Fascism. However, we don't dig deeper, do we? Perhaps because of fear."

Teller scoffed. "They hope it's fear."

Ezell's hooks embedded into the lawman standing above him. There was no expectation of this man letting him go. However, there was power in making people question their existence.

"It's funny. I'm sure if you gave me an honest response, you'd agree that corruption on the home front is alive and well. However, when they tell us they will send eighteen-year-olds to fight and die in a foreign land because it's for the greater good, the masses go along with it. We bomb a school in the Middle East. Greater good. We torture innocents in search of answers. Greater good. We kill via remote while staring at a screen a thousand miles away from those on the other end of the lens. Greater good. We can avert our gaze from these things so easily, can't we? But the moment towers and buildings explode on home soil, we never stop to ask the question: who caused this problem?"

"So, what, you can do bad things because more powerful people do bad things? Teller said, his hands shaking. "Two wrongs make a right in your eyes?"

"No."

The answer was stern. He allowed the agent to stew on his response.

"No, Agent Teller. No one is right."

A limb snapped from atop the archway. Its harsh break made Ezell jump. His eyes went up.

Fear gripped him. His jaw dropped, and his body locked.

The antlered creature left him in shadow. Its bipedal form stalked its way down to him. Its upper half was a broad-shouldered and exposed woman whose face and breasts were hidden underneath a thick layer of the blackest of hair and dried blood. Its lower half, from the navel down, were the legs of a deer. Her hooves clapped on the railroad ties and the rocks that followed. Shadows followed her and submitted the entirety of the wooded hills into hellish darkness. The Deer Woman looked down upon him through her hair as water and blood fell from her antlers. Her cold breath left her lungs thick as cigar smoke. Her rumbling breath was equivalent to that of an idling coal train.

Her lanky arms reached out, and her hands gripped his chin and the back of his head. She shoved her head forward, screaming as the souls of those killed directly or indirectly by him exclaimed their finality.

Ezell's body tremored uncontrollably as warm liquid poured from his ears, and the cacophony of cries assaulted his senses.

Fear overcame him, but he never sought God's forgiveness, only his mercy.

The Deer Woman's arms jolted in opposite directions.

A deep crack in Ezell's neck followed, and he felt no more.

———

When Nita crept down to them, she hardly made a noise. Scales of blood flaked off her skin.

He made a short plea to her in an attempt to take Ezell to justice via court, but the marshal had her own version of justice she wanted to see through.

She never stopped to talk with either Marc or the man in handcuffs. She met him eye to eye, pressed the end of her pistol into his forehead, and pulled the trigger before he could utter any words of reason.

Lowwater and the Marines shuffled into their location upon hearing the lone shot after their firefight ended.

Teller looked at Nita, and she stared back at him. They didn't need to exchange a dialogue on the morals of killing a captured man. He began to question his philosophy of justice.

"Nita..." he started. He took a moment and dropped any elaboration. He reached down and removed the cuffs from Ezell's wrist.

There was a collective understanding between all of them. Even the cowboy-Marines surely had little context on the situation.

Ezell's words struck a cord with Teller. The fact that the man was beginning to make sense made him question his worldview. The more he contemplated, the more he respected Nita's decision to end the man who wielded such charismatic power.

Chapter 85

Nita didn't bother sticking around for the media shitstorm to follow. She dreaded the days and weeks ahead of her at work. However, with all that had transpired, she figured now was as good a time as any to take that sabbatical.

Lowwater would be satisfied.

After such an event, there are many unanswered questions and protocols to be followed for damage control. So, her paid leave would have to be pushed aside for at least a moment. For now, she had one thing on her mind. Something that she should have been focused on for a long time now.

She cleaned herself off before Lowwater drove her back home, where her family waited on her in the driveway. She climbed out of the car before it came to a complete stop. She made haste for her family with a limp and a sling over her shoulder. Aiden's usually subdued temperament was nonexistent. She hobbled straight for him, his arms opened, and she scooped him off his feet.

"Hello!" he said.

She gave into the emotions she failed to express for so long as she began to weep into his ear, dampening his shirt around the collar. "Y-you saved my life, Aiden. You saved my life."

He smiled further. "Cool!"

He pushed away. His affection only went so far, but the arms of her mother and father wrapped around them, trapping them in a cocoon of love.

On the front porch, Greg Mercer rocked back and forth. A single tear ran down his cheek as he toasted his glass of water in her direction. He had quit drinking in 1995 but managed to take another puff of his cigar with a wink.

The overwhelming emotion coming to the surface was both elation and regret. Burying herself in her work was a disservice to the ones who bent over backward to provide her happiness. The sun disappeared for a moment in a flash. Nita glanced up to see a bald eagle making its way north.

There was nothing to be said. She offered her thanks to the medicine man soaring to spread its power to others that needed it.

CHAPTER 86

Charlie drove along that long patch of gravel he frequented more often nowadays. The expansive pasture fields blended into the rolling and wooded hills of Thorpe Ranch. The hazy day fought against the land's natural allure.

He pulled in front of the house to greet the morning chill. An involuntary shiver went down his back as he zipped up his vest. Floyd was putting out feed, and they shared a melancholy nod. Cody walked a horse into the barn, rubbing his neck the entire way. Charlie rode the same stallion not long ago, breaking his decade-long drought.

He went to his backseat and retrieved the thin paper bag. He continued to the house, and the front door creaked open.

A cowboy hobbled out the door.

"That an Indian walkin' up my porch?" Blake asked with a soft smile.

"Guilty."

"You better be bringin' whiskey then."

Charlie removed the Buffalo Trace from the bag. "I'm gonna need some glasses."

Blake grunted all the way down into the rocking chair. Even with his injuries and bandages, he still outfitted himself in cowboy attire. He removed his hat and rested it on his knee. In the aftermath of the siege, more gray streaks appeared in his hair. "Inside on the bar."

Charlie returned shortly after with two glasses of whiskey on the rocks. "There ya go, white boy."

"'Preciate it."

Charlie sat in the rocker next to him with a large stump between them that acted as a side table. Blake went to take a swig, but Charlie held up his glass for a toast. Blake smiled and obliged.

"How are you doing?" Charlie asked.

Blake gulped half the contents of the glass. "Better."

They sat in silence for a while, taking in the quiet and the natural beauty of Thorpe Ranch. The overcast was a sign of the coming winter, but still, the land's power remained. It was possibly the first time in Charlie's life he didn't look upon the land with disdain.

Blake spun the hat on his knee. "I used to think your family cursed mine so many years ago... before either of us were even thought about. I've seen the ways of the men in my family and concluded that if a curse was possible, it was by our own doing. A-and I don't know how to fix it." The cowboy seemed to grow emotional but kept it inward as best he could. However, his words became shorter, and he took in more breaths with a few sniffles in-between. "I just hope my baby girl doesn't reap such punishment."

Charlie took a swig as big as Blake's. "I used to hate you."

"I noticed."

"I heard the story of what your family did to mine over and over again. I've heard it so much that details in my mind feel more real than anything that most likely took place so long ago. I understood the hatred, and it made sense because rumor had it that my family wasn't the only one to fall victim to the Edwards family's greed. The hatred grew when you somehow managed to score Nita, and though we were no longer together, the fact that she chose you seemed like a slap in the face to me. I was in denial that she would choose such a man. You and I know her ability to see such evil, but she never saw it in you. I just couldn't fathom that. I guess... after all this time, I finally get it, though. Our past doesn't tell us fully who we are. That's certainly the case for you. You're a good man."

Blake cracked his neck as he sunk deeper into the rocker. They returned to the land as the minutes of peace continued. They sat, side by side admiring the rolling and wooded hills that went on for miles. The clouds were low, and a light mist moistened the diverse topography. The rocking chairs that once creaked at different tempos became synchronized after a few minutes.

"It ain't settled till it's settled," Blake murmured.

"What's that?"

"I sold it. Well, a sizable portion of it. Ten thousand."

Charlie cocked his head. "Sold what? The land?"

"To Cherokee Nation. To do with whatever they pleased. Of that, there's also a hundred acres allotted for you and your family."

Charlie stood still.

Time itself might have as well.

"Come on." Blake finished his drink and went to place it down but kept it in hand. "Fuck it, bring the bottle with us."

"Where we going?"

"We're gonna pick out a good spot to build on, neighbor. Don't worry. We'll take the side-by-side. My body couldn't make the ride on horseback."

Charlie sat with a cacophony of mixed emotions running through his mind. Pride kept him from enjoying the moment. He wasn't one for handouts.

What do I do? Have I been on a journey of redemption for our family this entire time? Why should I be the one to relish when none of you were allowed such charity? Is it an insult to accept or deny? Please, tell me.

"Come on. Life's good, Soap. You reclaimed your family's land."

CHAPTER 87

Distant and faint cheers and claps began on the edge of Water Street. The year's riders for the Remember the Removal Bike Ride were home. They had left this place weeks ago to return home to where it all began, only to come back changed.

Nita stood with her family as she welcomed others like her home. Her mother and father were at her side while her arms were draped over Aiden's shoulders as he held onto her forearms. Nothing made her happier than sharing this moment with her family. With her son.

The riders came into view with sun-battered skin and tears streaming down their faces. Nita understood their emotions well and was so proud of them, even though she didn't know them all well enough. However, she would have a bond with them that could never be broken or shaken. Their link to the past was more significant than anyone could imagine.

They were family before. They always would be.

On that journey, thoughts of oppression and first-world problems became fleeting. The clarity experienced through that difficult journey proved more eye-opening than anything she could imagine. It was only amplified by the contextual knowledge the ancestors gave freely on that path even after so many years gone. For they knew the struggle of the path well.

Tears ran down her cheeks, and Aiden looked up at her. "Why are you crying?"

"Cause I'm happy," she said, kissing his forehead.

He smiled and giggled. "Me too."

They've kept the pace.

About the Author

C.J. Caughman is an author from Tulsa, Oklahoma, who has been obsessed with storytelling since childhood. As an avid consumer of books, movies, and television, it took him a long time to realize crafting narratives was his passion. He began cultivating his enthusiasm for writing at the University of Central Oklahoma, where he graduated with a degree in English-Creative Writing. In college, he focused on writing short stories, screenplays, and eventually novels. Several of his short stories went on to receive publication in various literary magazines. C.J. was a quarterfinalist in the 2019 Final Draft Big Break Contest and is a proud member of the Cherokee Nation Tribe and their Cherokee Nation Film Office. Currently, he is an elementary English teacher in his hometown of Coweta, Oklahoma.

www.ingramcontent.com/pod-product-compliance
Lightning Source LLC
Chambersburg PA
CBHW021957130726
47903CB00014B/1506